'I'

T0159800

THE
SEAGULL
LIBRARY OF
GERMAN
LITERATURE

'I'

WOLFGANG HILBIG

Translated by Isabel Fargo Cole

LONDON NEW YORK CALCUTTA

This publication has been supported by a grant from
the Goethe-Institut India

Seagull Books, 2015

First published in German as »Ich« by Wolfgang Hilbig
© S. Fischer Verlag GmbH, Frankfurt am Main, 1993

First published in English translation by Seagull Books, 2015
English translation © Isabel Fargo Cole, 2015

ISBN 978 0 8574 2 715 1

British Library Cataloguing-in-Publication Data
A catalogue record for this book is available from the British Library.

Typeset by Seagull Books, Calcutta, India
Printed and bound by WordsWorth India, New Delhi, India

Contents

About '*I*'

(Wolfgang Hilbig's novel proposal as submitted to Fischer Verlag)

The prose piece entitled 'I ' (I envision a novel-length work
of 150–200 pages) is the attempt to find a literary form for
the 'inner biography' of a so-called IM (Inoffizieller
Mitarbeiter). An IM—the abbreviation has become almost
universally familiar, at least since the collapse of the GDR—
that is, an Unofficial Collaborator of the State Security Service
of the GDR, reflecting on his existence as such in the first
person, is the protagonist of the first part of the story.—Am I
playing a role? the author asks himself.

As the public debates, mainly journalistic, on the subject
of the 'Stasi' seem to have brought to light little of substance
about such figures, who must have existed by the hundreds of
thousands, it seems possible to me that what best suits the subject is a literary form—that is, a form that eschews the attempt
to 'clarify'. Indeed, so far we have had little illumination
regarding the nature of IMs: this seems to be explained by the
very so-called conspirative element surrounding such figures,
who, after all, conduct their 'clarification' in the dark.—
Reflecting on the conceptualization of such a protagonist, I
asked myself a rather disturbing question: To what extent can
the work of an informer be compared with the literary work
of a writer? Immediately I told myself that the results are different . . . but that posed the question of the extent to which

a secret service, too, is dealing 'only' with a fiction of reality; and is this not in fact its intent?—I asked myself to what degree reality, in an IM's reports for his superior, must be a fiction approaching a literary fiction. Isn't an IM report also supposed to contain the greatest possible authenticity? How does an informer cope with this demand for authenticity when, in the dark of his underground work, he must forget his subjective interpretations in order to maintain his credibility? Or are the IM's superiors—as a rule these superiors are able to psychologically assess the IM—not even interested in authenticity any more, only in reacting to their own image of reality? Couldn't a clever informer hit upon the notion of reaching a consensus with his case officer on a fiction of reality ... on a reading of reality?

After the fall of the Berlin Wall, when several writers were exposed as Unofficial Collaborators of the Stasi, I was surprised only for a moment; immediately I asked myself whether a writer, in particular, must not be especially well equipped to report for a secret service. And perhaps, I said to myself, the loss of the 'I' experienced by a collaborator, who works in secret on an image of reality, can be compared with that experienced by a writer, who in the course of his work is confronted more than once with the question: Who or what does the thinking within me?—I am aware that I am posing the question of 'vocation' here in a very provocative fashion. But probably, literature can be expected to 'clarify' only by continually posing questions. The second part of the story is a fictitious treatment of the IM's background; he finds himself no longer able to precisely reconstruct the circumstances that led to his collaboration with the secret service. Here the text shifts entirely to a retrospective narrative, and the protagonist describes himself in the third person; his life story seems to have taken on a completely fictional character. And yet it is not an unusual life; it is one of the many fatherless lives of the post-war generation. Growing up in impoverished circumstances, confronted with adults who seemed to lack an 'I', the young man was forced to invent the parameters of his life, apparently helped by his introspective tendencies. Early on he occupied himself with writing attempts, and the only people who seemed to take these attempts seriously were members of the secret service.

In the third part of the story, the narrative shifts back to the first person. The hero as subject seems to have reorganized himself. But from this moment on, the author finds it necessary to use the quotation marks that belong to the title of the narrative of 'I'.

Wolfgang Hilbig
Edenkoben, 12 August 1992

the framework of the public sphere is static.
within this framework for achieving
a dynamic of one's own,
the 'i' is purely provisional.

Statement from the Scene, Berlin, 1983

Oh, how I've lost my life in a dream!
said he to himself;
years have passed since I descended fromthis place ...

Ludwig Tieck

The Operation

I'm moving around my cold corners again. Back on my way, but I won't report on that. No brief movements of the lower face; at this point I'd have to say that being on my way is in my nature. Better leave nature on the sidelines, though: in our game, we're just here to pass the balls, and leave everything extraneous out of play, that's the kind of game it is.—On my way, up the streets, down the streets . . . up above and down below: take things a step at a time, as they say, that's my nature. Let me put it this way, I'm not the type to get ahead at all costs. I'm not exactly what you'd call scrupulous, but I weigh the steps I take—most of them, anyway, but more on that later.

Still, I have an unusual knack for running my head through walls. And on the whole, I've had things come easily to me. Early on, I was taught that seizing advantages from the powers-that-be goes quickest with their cooperation. That's the thing to understand: you don't coax forth their acquiescence, you force it from them. And they may feel cheated or robbed, but more than that they feel flattered, for with each advantage for yourself, you lay claim to what is theirs. Each modicum of privilege you extract from their control pays tribute to their property, an honour it would lack were there no one to ogle it. That's why the powerful are most comfortable believing themselves threatened. And lacking signs of a palace or street revolt, they invent them.

Let me go back to the beginning: when running my head through walls, I did use the appropriate apertures, that is, windows and doors, occasionally chimneys or skylights; but more and more often it's the basements that give me the access I seek. This option first presented itself in Berlin, though: I lived for some time on a street that was all bleak rows of soot-blackened tenements, probably dating from the turn of the century. Beneath these blocks, one continuous basement passage led from one cross-street to the next, often even beyond the cross-street to the next row of houses. No matter which house entrance you used, if you got into the basement you could always find your way underground into the house where you had some business, or where you lived, as long as you could keep track of the houses you passed under by counting the basement stairways.—For a time, whenever I entered a vestibule, I would first look for the basement door and unlock it if I could, aiming to minimize the element of chance in the city's usable entrances and exits—that was a time when I took my duties much too seriously. Such precautions—so often thwarted when the very next orderly coal-scuttle-lugger locked the door again—now strike me as overrating the so-called conspirative element inherent to my field of activity. Incidentally, a jaded view of such unnecessary and amateurish pedantries is the first sign of a certain advancement, which many of us who go for years believing ourselves beginners (a belief attended by a slender and very deceptive hope) are unable to see, or refuse to admit.

First, then, I would crane my head through the crack of the door, seeking to take in the vestibule's atmosphere as a whole with all my senses. I strained to pierce the darkness with my eyes by turning my face back and forth several times, almost a drilling motion: the vestibule was completely dark; even the window around the corner on the first landing admitted not a gleam of light, looking, I concluded, onto a dark courtyard. At the same time, listening with bated breath, I scented out the vestibule: I sniffed . . . there were the usual smouldering smells of coal, the cool nitrous exhalations of old walls creeping out from beneath peeling oil paint; I saw the vestibule in front of me even before turning on the light. Perhaps I also caught a whiff of unappetizing cooking smells from the flats that mingled down here as in a trough, and noted that there was no sign of cigarette smoke; no one had smoked on the stairs for at least half an hour, which meant that I was very late on the scene.—All this I had observed and registered with my body still outside up to the neck, both shoulders pressed to the door's wooden wings, my stooped back projecting over the pavement, legs slightly spread to keep my footing in the slush.—I monitored the vestibule this way for more than a minute . . . and once, I recalled, I'd been surprised in this position. Someone had tapped me hard on the spine with an index finger, like a Morse signal. I started; I hadn't heard footsteps. It was Feuerbach, who'd crept up behind me and said with a laugh: By Jove . . . what kind of a pose is that?—By Jove! I mimicked him—I knew he liked to flaunt things he'd picked up from books, especially stock expressions from translations of English and American literature—By Jove, you sure sneaked up quietly!—I didn't want to disturb you, he said, you're on the scent of the Muses again, no doubt?—Not waiting for my reply, he moved on with that walk of his which was supposed to be a casual saunter but was always a bit too fast, too hectic, as if, in his mind, he were constantly trying to shrug off something disagreeable.—He's just a military man after all, I thought, staring after him until he turned the corner. And I wondered if he'd glanced back at me as he vanished.—No, I said, that would have put him in the awkward position of having to wave again; he's an observant person, and he must have felt me staring at him from behind. And since he makes a practice of deriding Prussian style in every shape and form, and generally greets people by waving two studiedly casual fingers, he'd have to resist the urge to look back at a moment like this—for discretion's sake.

If I might digress this one last time: Feuerbach, of course, is a nom de plume, and it's said—surely I'm not divulging too much—that his real name was Wasserstein. He himself despised the name; in a club that does all sorts of things with names, it was often cause for ridicule. Out of sheer spite, he refused to change it, though now and then one of the chiefs would ask him: Wasserswine, how long do you intend to go on provoking your clan with this epithet? It's a bit much even for us philo-Semites. And if you ever have to go abroad, won't it crack up the West German border guards?—That was a definite request, an ultimatum almost, considering who it came from. But it seems Feuerbach didn't back down until a warning written in blue felt-tip was discovered in the lavatory: 'Do not take the AquaRocks orally'! Everyone knew this referred to the lumps of a white, waxy substance that were dropped into the urinals as a deodorizer; it was a truly hoary joke, repeated almost ver-batim on the walls of every public facility. But a long roar of laughter was heard echoing down the halls, and the stunt ful-filled its purpose. Feuerbach is said to have fumed: When I find out who that was, I'll have him cleaning toilets for a year!—But in the end the butt of the joke adopted his honourable pseudonym.

I pressed the light switch and saw that my senses had not deceived me. The walls, painted murky ochre, let through the dry rot everywhere; just above the filthy, chipped tile floor the paint had literally been washed away; broad, brownish tongues of moisture crept all the way to the once-white stucco ceiling; seeming to emerge straight from Berlin's swampy subsoil, they

welled up especially around the basement door.—I headed
slowly up the stairs, reading in passing all the nameplates on
the flat doors; I can claim to have memorized at least half of
them, which put me far above average; and there were two
flats on each floor. At the very top, on the sixth floor, there
was only one door, and here I'd reached my destination. On
my way up, the stairway light had gone out and I'd had to
switch it on again, first propping myself on the sill of a stairway
window in the dark to rest; the last thing I wanted was to
arrive at my hosts' out of breath. From the window I looked
out over the wide wild field of the roofs behind this row of
houses, where smoke rose from the chimneys and merged with
the haze of the sky. And I saw that the nights over the city
were not really dark, only a shadowy smudged grey, reddened
here and there by the light shining up from a few busy
streets.—As I caught my breath I recalled a short story by
Thomas Mann called 'At the Prophet's'. I thought of how the
author spends an entire paragraph climbing a flight of stairs—
but in what sentences, sentences that make the length and
labour of this climbing so wonderfully vivid and ironically significant.—What a story! I thought. Amazing, a gem of prose,
perhaps quite simply a work of genius. None of you will ever
pull off anything like that!

I thought this with a strange grim fury that seemed completely uncalled for just a few minutes later, when I'd rung at
the top of the stairs and been admitted. I was told to be quiet,
since the reading had already begun.—Inside I found myself
in a smallish room crowded with people lined up on long
benches and rows of chairs, listening in what seemed oblivious
concentration—hardly anyone looked around at me. Facing
this audience, a young, very slender man—I knew him
already—sat at a small table, quietly reading a text that poured
forth into the room a jumble of words and sentences, without

paragraphs and, I heard it at once, without punctuation. He didn't falter as I entered; immersed in the sequences of his words, he went on reading unperturbed, soft and quick, not once lifting his eyes behind the little round glasses. But I drew reproachful or irritated looks from several listeners as I gingerly squeezed past behind the audience and sat down at the far end of the last bench, where there was just enough room for my left thigh. I mumbled an apology to my neighbour, who vainly tried to shift an inch to the side, turning her pale face towards me and raising an imploring finger to her lips.—Now the reader behind his desk lamp was invisible to me, hidden by massed shoulders and the phalanx of heads, some bowed, some tilted back. But I knew who was reading up there, and the text he delivered was familiar to me too, at least in essence. It was an interminable succession of metaphors, linked metaphor sequences; most of them were clearly taken from literature, but even an expert in the field could have recognized only a fraction of them. Thus many of these quotations might have been fabricated, or at the very least garbled, transformed, rendered unrecognizable. Yet the writer of this text had evidently developed a method that made all his constructions sound like long-familiar passages lifted indiscriminately from a whole range of works—especially works of so-called modern literature. Or this was just the effect of his delivery, non-stop, rapid but not hurried, monotonous but always clear and precise.

What I had before me was part of 'Operation: Reader'; the operation I faced was one of the most interesting and vexing I've ever had to grapple with. At times—though perhaps only in my eyes—it took on the character of a wildfire, breaking out unexpectedly in the oddest parts of the city and keeping us in suspense . . . though perhaps it only kept me in suspense. And this over the course of a year or more: again and again the fire seemed contained, or it seemed consumed—it was a mystery to me who could have stopped it, or how—but then, somewhere, it would flare up again.—Of course I was using a bad comparison; the whole thing wasn't a wildfire, it was a well-organized affair, but still I'd occasionally succumb to the alarming impression that in the interim, in the weeks of its invisibility, it had worked its way onward underground, in the basements of the houses—I didn't know all of them, not by a long shot—in the profusely, bafflingly branching passages beneath the pavement of the city of Berlin: there the fire had smouldered on, slow but steady, glimmering lurid in the darkness and filling the subfloor of this sea of houses with the dangerous masses and clots of its smoke, while up above in the light ludicrous figures like Major Feuerbach went about their vain, naive routine.—And of course it was presumably he, the lover of American novels, who was responsible for the name of the operation now resting in my hands.

It was known that Reader, the author of this text—in his own words a text without closure—now enjoyed a steadily growing audience whose small congregations lurked in many quarters of the city; that Reader's reputation had in fact begun to spread beyond the city limits, but that he strictly declined to seek an audience above and beyond his readings, though his chances would have been excellent. Some radio station over in the West would occasionally feature one of his recitals, but as Reader apparently couldn't be moved to discuss himself and his objectives with the radio producers or the journalists, their interest soon faded; there were plenty of more willing figures in what might be called Eastern Berlin's unofficial cultural scene, and there were enough events that appeared more spectacular. Now, this very abstinence ought to have piqued the media's interest . . . that was not the case, though, and as usual our own interest reflected that of the media, persisting at a very lukewarm level. Just a year ago we'd been wide awake, and seemed poised to deploy the entire spectrum of activities that the Target Group Section generally lavished upon an emergent phenomenon—but nothing came of it, and soon I had the unpleasant suspicion that I and I alone was saddled with a sideline. No one seemed to think of mobilizing my competitive tendencies; a whole year passed without a soul far and wide whose findings I could envy . . . and then I seemed to notice Feuerbach hiding the files on 'Operation: Reader' from me. I'd always seen that the file was thin—it was weak in the chest and failing to thrive! When I rested in the office late in the afternoon—usually with darkness falling and the staff gone home (one of my last remaining privileges: permission to sit alone in Feuerbach's office!)—diagonally across from the desk of the first lieutenant . . . who sometimes went by 'Captain' as well . . . on the clients' stool, which I'd dragged over to the window ledge—I knew this annoyed the Major no end, but he merely vented his feelings with spiteful barbs: Don't get my future chair dirty, you catacomb swine! . . . or something of the sort—anyhow, when I sat there for an hour or two . . . and I sat there because I wanted to be disturbed; for undisturbed hours I had another place entirely . . . I stared, chain-smoking and drinking vast quantities of coffee, at the operation file that hung in the pale yellow pressboard cabinets behind the desk: they didn't even grant it one of the grey-black binders amid which it hid, childishly pink and nearly squashed; it was only a slip of a folder, it was consumptive, this file, a miscarriage.—Soon after the operation's launch I was already noting, astonished, how stubbornly it lingered in the verbal sphere. And I looked for signs of dissatisfaction with this state of affairs . . . once—perhaps even repeatedly—I had referred to Reader's readings in Feuerbach's presence as a phe-nomenon. Whether it was deliberate or merely a sudden inspi-ration, I no longer recall; the word was utterly unthinkable in our parlance, seeming as it does to describe a problem with no immediate solution, perhaps even a certain inherent impenetrability. In that moment it was my own word; Feuerbach tolerated it with that grin of his, a mixture of underhandedness and magnanimity, but from the adjoining office, whose door stood ajar, a furious bass rang out: Would you tell the man once and for all that we're dealing with intelligence here . . . and he should kindly leave his mystical mutterings down in his lodge where they hold their rites!

I thought about that in the nights when I had nothing to do, no duties but my desensitization.—All the same, there was something unfathomable about this Reader: he read and read; in front of a small but growing audience, at regular or irregular intervals, in flats all over the city, he read the same text over and over; there was no discernible system except that—and I found this rather arbitrary—he always began by rereading the sentences he'd finished with the last time, and then went on for about an hour, neither raising nor lowering his voice, so that even the individual sections had the character of something uninterrupted; he looked up only at the end, acknowledged the listeners' homage, always waiting patiently for the last of the applause to die away—as a rule several enthusiasts would go on clapping for several seconds after the ovation had ebbed—then announced that the date of his next evening would be made known in due course . . . less and less often did he know the time and place in advance; he was probably looking for new venues; he'd used all the available ones long ago, and the locations were beginning to repeat themselves . . . or I tried to see it as a sign that the first burst of his production had exhausted itself . . . and he gave a perfunctory bow, tucked away his papers in a black portfolio and promptly left the room.—Nothing could convince me otherwise: Reader was a phenomenon. He risked everything with this hermetic

11

behaviour, and he won every time. He withheld himself from the media with astonishing firmness, rejected the fame he could long since have achieved; evidently he was content to exercise his influence within the narrow bounds of his scene— whether this influence actually existed, and what it looked like, that, it seemed, was the aim of my investigation.— Incidentally, I was also astonished that our side was neither creating nor encouraging any of the usual media contacts for Reader. Since when, I asked myself, is it our policy to wait for the target person to take the incriminating step of his own accord? I could hardly think of a single case that had played out this way. For here too we had the most infallible means at hand; we could programme a so-called illegal contact with quasi dead certainty—how many authors helplessly adrift in the Scene owed their discovery to our unsung ministrations? Those authors who'd always had our blessing, with their print- ings in the West, the hard-currency hustlers, the semi- and three-quarter oppos, they were no skin off our nose, any- way!—Or had Reader's staunchness thwarted such measures?

I wondered whether to regard it as arrogance, and no everyday arrogance at that. Or he had something else in mind that I hadn't yet managed to grasp.—It's like he's waiting for things to explode! I thought. But I shook my head at the thought, not knowing what kind of explosion I meant. If he's waiting for an explosion, he can wait a long time, I said, but at the same time I felt my palms go damp and maybe even my forehead break out in sweat. It was ludicrous; I'd strayed into the fantasy realms of the chiefs. Though I felt more at home down here . . . we, Feuerbach and I, we felt more at home down here. And yet, when I thought about it, I'd even heard him drivelling on along those lines recently.—No, I was tired, that was all . . . it was three in the morning, and I hunkered exhausted on the stone steps in an unfamiliar stairwell. I was drained, and starting to see things—for a few moments when the light went out in the stairwell, I'd had no idea where I was, which neighbourhood, which street, which house. I hadn't been able to unlock the basement door outside which I sat ... for half an hour I'd fumbled with the lock, the light in the stairwell kept going out, the skeleton keys and wire hooks I had on me proved useless, and it was the third or fourth lock I'd failed to open that night ... I struggled, throwing all caution to the winds and filling the house with resounding scrapes and rattles. With an effort I'd suppressed a bellow of rage; then revulsion overcame me and I sank down trembling on the cold, damp cement of the stairs.

You're pale ... what's wrong, aren't you feeling well?—I started; it was the young woman at my side—very young, in fact, evidently a student—who had addressed me. I stared at her in bewilderment; I'd known her for some time, but she didn't seem to know me. The Reader had finished and left, the listeners came to life and shed their almost transfigured expressions of worship. Did he say where he's going to read next time? I asked the student, who gave me a worried look with what struck me as overlarge eyes. Her eyes were dark, and matching them her hair was dark as well, with a reddish shimmer at the ends, standing up straight in a short spiky cut. Her temples were bare and snow white above the cheekbones, where they formed shallow hollows which gave her face an exceedingly narrow shape. It's all right, I mumbled, I just felt a bit queasy. I think I need to get some fresh air.

Down on the street it had grown slippery; the slush had turned to ice, and a frosty glitter flew at me out of the fog. I walked slowly and gingerly, eyes lowered, and suddenly I was standing in front of a familiar-seeming house. The outside door was open; I went in and a moment later found myself outside the same basement door I'd been unable to unlock. I took the next best hook out of my pocket, and after a single concerted effort, the lock gave way as though its spring were made of paper.

The basement passages beneath Berlin's houses are generally clean, and most of them are well lit. And this winter they were warm; the frost barely penetrated to their foundations. There were places down there—I thought of one place in particular I often resorted to—where I'd sat for hours on a wooden crate, smoking cigarettes and listening to Berlin's vast mass asleep above my head. Of course it was quiet down here, you couldn't hear a thing; down here probably nothing but explosions could be heard. There was but a quiet hum in the stillness, perhaps only my imagination, or perhaps it was the air in the windings of my ear, compressed by the colossal weight above me. The city above my head was like an enormous generator, its ceaseless vibration barely perceptible in everything stone, echoing that faint faraway hum, inexplicably present in all the cement foundations surrounding me, and in the mind-boggling quantities of red and brown bricks assembled and reaching down and anchoring the city's sea of houses to the earth. A thousand years long—how long, I didn't know—the stones had been sunk into the bowels of the earth, and it was unclear how many more thousands of years the city could hold out, could endure, with the inconceivable weight of its foundations driven into Europe's heart. And all we could learn and grasp, all we could clarify and reveal, above and below and in Berlin's midst, was the realization that we must cease—but not the urban Moloch Berlin . . . that we must vanish like streetsweepings and sooner or later the stones of Berlin, grown into the earth, would tell nothing of our era.—That was what I had discovered in my years of operation, and I had a great desire to submit my findings to First Lieutenant Feuerbach.

I already knew his reply. It would consist of his grin—in which I increasingly felt I detected uncertainty—and a dictum such as: Arrival isn't the goal, the way is the goal!—The way! he stressed. You know that, and if you don't, you can look it up, probably word for word, in the great Le Fou you think so highly of. Or in one of his colleagues they're lapping up these days . . . there's much food for thought there about desire and its mysterious ways . . .

By Le Fou, as I now knew, he meant the philosopher Foucault, who along with his following had indeed come increasingly into vogue. The Major was enthused by all that was allusive, fond of circumlocutions, grammatical riddles and abbreviations; that is, he loved the accoutrements of his duty . . . besides, he seemed to have believed for a time that le fou was the French word for fire; it was a mistake I might have made myself.—I, on the other hand, knowing only the titles and a few of the first sentences of Foucault's books, probably didn't love him. It irked me that in certain enclaves of the so-called Scene, being an avid reader of Foucault provided your *raison d'être*, and that this then entailed the obligation to read Derrida or Paul de Man as well—I didn't like books printed in Gothic type. Next thing you knew, I'd have to read Heidegger . . . and then *Mein Kampf* to top it off.—Admittedly these were merely obsessive notions of mine, but my aversions were increasingly disqualifying me as a collaborator in such serpentine circles. Staying in context: my only chance would have been to see myself as the simulacrum of a collaborator. Thus attaining the ultimate goal of each one of us.—Reason enough for Feuerbach to repeat with a smile, by now slightly menacing: All you ever think of is the goal, Cambert, I do believe you're aiming high. But as I keep telling you, you'd do better to think of the way . . .

My way was still the sojourn in the substructure. And I hoped they'd need me there a while longer. No, I didn't want to move up, by no means: certain linguistic developments running rampant up there seemed to present themselves in quite concrete form here below, and examples were more important to me than theses. It always astonished me, for instance, to see here below how cavern led to cavern, in this I seemed to see something both imperative and static: the extended network of underground cells virtually forced me to follow it, and yet the whole thing was but one closed circuit.—And it made me think of a sheet of paper I'd once stumbled on up there. It was covered with peculiarly interlinked sentences whose meaning revealed itself only when I made the effort to follow them step by step.—I had little time; never mind who, intentionally or not, left the piece of writing on the desk and me alone in the room. I'd smelt it immediately: it was classified material, the sort of thing our ilk usually never set eyes on.—Get your nose out of Kesselstein's papers! came the permanently aggrieved bass from the adjoining office, a voice I knew, though I didn't think I'd ever seen its owner. I knew I was in the eye of the camera . . . and yet I had the audacity to jot down a few lines: . . . stipulation of the implementation of the disruption and neutralization measures on the basis of the precise appraisal of the achieved results of the processing of the respective Intelligence Operation . . .

One of these days, I thought, a document like this will get leaked . . . and once again everyone will plead ignorance— the minister wrote his classified material for his own eyes only. And every secret service in the world works with these devices, they'll say.—Quite right, all too true!

All that actually interested me was the monstrosity of the serial abstractions I had before me. I'll recognize this usage to all eternity, I thought, within myself as well . . . in future it will serve me as a signal. By their rampant genitives shall I know them. By their genitives sequenced until they obscure the starting point, by the excesses of the second case ... as though again and again disgorging itself as the first case, as the worst case. It was ultimately a usage that destroyed realism ... an unintentionally surrealistic method producing a psychotic automatism. Something the real surrealists might only have dreamt of ... they'd originated the famous image of the cube emerging from the cube, with another cube inside it, and another inside that and so on.—The machine of the genitives does this in earnest, I thought. It subverts reality with this phantasm ... thus it's the simulation of an infinite logic.

Such hysteresis of the genitives probably wasn't even possible in a language other than German. In this mental language you were reduced to taking one step at a time, only to realize that you still weren't at the goal and had to take another step: if at last you did arrive at the goal of the sentence, you already felt so entangled, and perfectly interpolated in a conspirative sequence, and possibly for ever, that you could only look back, obliterated, in infinite fatigue, to where you once had started—as though hoping for escape you'd kept chasing the end of the sentence, but this end had only revealed the full extent of the impasse.

When I thought of this piece of paper, fatigue followed me down into my basement passages. And at such moments I wondered whether the channels down which I dragged myself, with no thought yet of return, with the end speeding further and further ahead of me, were merely those of an ineluctable language.—Had I ever made a real effort to trace back the course of my thoughts step by step, with absolute precision, I told myself, I might have hit upon the source of my fatigue. And I would have stepped back into the space in which it had begun ... I was always too tired to take this path.—I remembered; it was a moment, a bare quarter of an hour, up in one of those offices of which multiple versions existed in the city, always with deceptively similar decor . . . or no, it was earlier, in an office in the town I came from, in a deceptively similar room in that town: the neutral, unadorned interior went dark, and for a quarter of an hour the town's brown, debilitating smoke seemed to have seeped inside . . . for half an hour I'd done all they asked of me; it wasn't much, just the absent dash of a signature on a paper lying in the gloom . . .

Since then this fatigue had been stronger than I . . . it wouldn't let me sit to think it through in peace, to wander through its shadow, to seek the crack in it, the crack in its wall, the fissure through which sometimes the light fell . . .

It was stronger; it was a caesura for which I found no comparison —only down in the basements were there moments which came close to describing the situation. I'd be standing outside the passages of an as-yet-unfamiliar house and ask myself whether I should enter here as well. And perhaps it was a door that suddenly barred my way . . . when I went to work on it, it was usually already open, probably I'd forced it myself half a year ago. And when I'd turned on the light for the musty chamber before me—it too, of course, was long familiar—and now had to walk back several yards to turn out the light for the section of corridor I'd just left . . . then, all at once, the fatigue would come.— I flipped the switch down, and this stretch I'd just covered was extinguished behind me as though it had never been a segment of my reality. And the memory of my steps through this reality was extinguished, the void sank down behind me in the passage . . . it sank down over that brief portion of my reporting period, which I could now forget. The sudden darkness made me forget my entire being, all I had spoken and reported, and all conceivable consequences of the words and statements of mine I'd compiled and passed on . . . and so that quarter of an hour that had filled an office with its darkness plunged the whole preceding reporting period into oblivion . . . the numbing fumes of extinguishment descended on my origins, on all my ties from the time before . . . and from the passage I'd left behind me and switched off, the I I'd served had fled, its reality fled like the result of a simulation.

And before me lay a new stretch in which I righted my 'I' again, seizing on the manifestations of the visible in the light I'd known so long. Slowly I regained myself as I brushed past the long-familiar walls through which strange liquids pearled in the yellow lamplight; the stone exuded acrid smells of faeces which seemed to change with the neighbourhood, and often enough I thought I could get my bearings by them. I spent most of my time in the lap of the underprivileged classes—or rather, below the lap—and here, in the depths beneath decrepit, densely massed housing blocks, beneath pillaged streets and courtyards, the foundation walls were porous and penetrable, more often and more persistently discharging the residues of human vital energy. The glittering flux from the walls told of brute nourishment; roughage, mixed with rancid fats and third-rate spirits, seemed to seep, searing and giving off dark emanations, from the joints of the bricks, and here harsh, acidic urine ate its way deeper and deeper into the ground.

I strayed more rarely into affluent areas, perhaps I only imagined I was there, and perhaps the basements of the middle cadres smelt of olive oil or vanilla . . . there was nothing there but impermeable walls, clean, closed-off rooms of considerable size, empty storerooms that were more like garages, now and then bicycles or prams, empty rat traps that never snapped shut because there were no rats here. And here you never got far, you had to keep crossing the street when you wanted to move between high-rises, and then, once again, there was nothing but these clean-swept chambers in bright neon light.—There was no life beneath the high-rise blocks of Friedrichsfelde Ost or Marzahn, and in fact whenever I found my way into these basements the faint whiff of urine wafting through the concrete chambers smelt to me like medicine.—I would have liked just once to penetrate further, on into the higher cadres' basement levels, for it was there, one increasingly heard, that the conspiracy's true loci could be found. Perhaps you'd actually stumble across the workshop where the whispered-about mini-submarine was being built, or the basement where someone was sewing a blimp . . . where the sons and daughters of the functionaries were preparing their timely getaway, familiar as they were with their fathers' secret bulletins . . . of course I wasn't responsible for that sector—my higher-ups justifiably mistrusted me, sensing that I wouldn't have betrayed the hiding place of such a workshop.

No, those parts of town weren't Reader's turf, the orbit of his readings didn't extend that far, and so they were none of my concern.— In any case, the main thing for me lately was my interest in his texts, my interest in the opinion of his texts in the mind of a listener, male, for instance, or female; perhaps it was these very verbal sequences without closure that held the paradigms of the real conspiracy, only I was failing to find them out.—Time and again I returned to the shafts better suited to me, wandering once again down the rows of basement cells, cells indeed, barred with wooden slats or chicken wire, filled with rotting coal or stuffed with junk . . . ultimately all these passages looked the same, though I had the impression that their desolation and decrepitude increased towards the city centre.—And here, too, in the same old new passage that now opened up before me, I saw expanses of standing water on the floor, dully iridescent in the dimming light, like petrol or oil. Sometimes lines seemed to snake towards me through the deep pools, like the weird trails of creatures fleeing the light I had lit. And the vapours rising from the wet floors wove darkly about my senses and obscured my view ahead. I saw that a row of bricks had been placed a step apart through the puddles . . . I had done that myself so that I could cross the water; the bricks had parted from the masonry almost without resistance; the walls were worn out, seemingly held up only by their own weight. Here and there rubble had slid into the passage as though, not too long ago, convulsions had taken place, upheavals of the earth, breaches as from major building activity . . . and behind the broken walls came a trickling like urine, stale-smelling, milky and quicksilver from the vault's greasy substrate, and more and more bricks worked loose as the swill soaked through: it couldn't be much longer before this path was blocked to me.—But of course the piles of rubble also shielded me . . . once I had passed them, I had a stretch of utter darkness before me, until after a sharp bend in the passage I came to another light switch; with the help of my lighter flame, burning faintly in the oxygen-poor air, I groped onward, seeming to hear the ticking trickle of excrement to my left and right . . . but the flow from the walls let up, the harsh smells seemed neutralized, and a strangely cleansed air gained the upper hand—clearly few people lived above me now, clearly most of the buildings in the streets above me were vacant. I stopped and listened: What a silence up there . . . I never heard anything in the basements, but this kind of silence was like extinction. Only rarely was the rush of liquid audible in the defective drainpipes, and when the sickly diarrhoeic fumes filtered down to me, I stopped short and pointed upward with my finger: What's that stuff he's drinking up there?

What's he guzzling up there? I asked myself. I believe he's guzzling dishwater! That's a fact, he's guzzling dishwater, he's feeding on the leftovers rinsed from the dirty plates . . . and what he spouts is mixed with solvents and twice- and thrice-used, chemically asepticized drippings. And his excretions are cleansed, and his bodily passages rinsed with ammonia and soap . . . just as lukewarm and used as everything he puts to paper, and passes on, and rinses from the paper again and administers, enema-like, to the open ears of his consumers.

It's right here, I said, pointing up at the vaulted ceiling, that I find myself under Reader's domicile! And what would he say if one fine day his papers should vanish? I could do it easily; I'd often thought of climbing those stairs . . . quietly past the lifeless flats, past those calcified mouldy honeycombs, and opening that inhabited den I knew so well, while he was off reading somewhere; I could easily learn the time of his next reading, break into his flat and grab his manuscripts. Take them down with me into the depths . . . for in some unclear way those texts belonged here. I pictured myself running through the basements to whisk my loot to safety . . . safety from whom? I could read them down here, in that place of mine where I felt safe, and no doubt find that these texts—read closely, line by line—fell short of the impression they'd made when read aloud.

No—maybe I shouldn't be maligning these texts! If anything I should fetch them down here to shore me up in my realm beneath the pavement, where I alone lit an occasional circuit of guttering light . . . no, I was lost to literature, I had no more business with it, nor it with me, my only business now was with security . . . I persevered in this place and thought about Reader, ensconced high above me in an attic flat, whom I might—I no longer quite knew myself—some time at the beginning of this story, have designated as my rival:

Oh! I knew all his texts, I was his best audience . . . at some point someone had to notice! . . . while he knew none of my work, he knew nothing of this competition! The nature of the competition was hidden, deep below him in the labyrinthine storerooms beneath the surface of the city of Berlin, where so many thousand tons of darkness were kept.

Then I lowered my finger and stumbled onward. In the darkness I clambered over piles of rubble, groped my way around twists and turns and crawled through holes in walls which emitted a rushing noise, and I came to grates in the ground through which the suffocating smell of the sewers welled . . . after squeezing through a bottleneck where the passages met askew, at last I'd regained the light of several faint bulbs which I myself had once screwed in. If I could trust my experience, I was now directly below the upper end of Normannenstrasse, which opened up here in a small square and led down to the district's wide, multilane artery where the floods of traffic rolled and the U-Bahn roared beneath the pavement.—Just a bit further west and I'd be at the end of my path: I could turn out the lights behind me, first, though, screwing tight one last light bulb—it belonged to a nearby power line I was unfamiliar with, hanging loosely in its ceramic socket—and letting it shine out.

At this point the concrete of a comparatively recent wall descended. It looked as though it had been riven into the ground in one piece and with prodigious force, abruptly severing all the passages and foundations that extended to this point. One sensed that it reached much deeper into the ground, and was long enough to interrupt the substructure of entire streets; in the light of my bulb I saw its bleak indestructible grey; it had to be reinforced concrete, immune to the dampness of the depths. Evidently it didn't even stain . . . this concrete wall had been poured for eternity.

It was here that the vast new building complexes had been erected at the city's margins, beginning directly above me in their labyrinthine legions; they were off-limits to almost everyone.[1]—Only once, for some reason I couldn't explain, had I found my way in there. And emerging from a huge, tunnel-like gateway I'd seen but a small part of those bewildering cobbled courtyards surrounded by boxy multistoreyed buildings. I spent just a few minutes waiting for Feuerbach, who had vanished into one of the angular stone blocks . . . evening was approaching, most of the countless windows were already dark, and yet I felt observed, and walked up and down at a leisurely pace in an effort to act as innocuously as possible amid these many-eyed walls, or rather as though I were here as a matter of routine . . . high above me the sky turned a dusky purple and flocks of crows wheeled screeching, but these cries sank down to me with a considerable lag; it was as though the birds sought to gather in the brighter oblongs of open sky above the courtyards, as though they shied away from the black brinks of the roofs whose long straight lines cut off the light . . . I was still staring up—demonstrating my total disinterest in the dark buildings for far too long already—when Feuerbach hurried up with a harried look on his face, grabbed me by the sleeve, steered me through the gateway and onto the street; I failed to notice whether a lightning-quick exchange, wordless and gesticulated, had taken place behind my back between him and a gatekeeper sitting in the dark behind the glass; my last step out onto the pavement almost felt pushed.—The moment you're in there, you'd ask yourself if you'd ever come out again, I said, if you got . . . I broke off, sensing from the quality of his silence that my loquacity annoyed him. A minute passed before he retorted: You're better off keeping your mouth shut.

I'll tell you a secret, he went on after we'd walked down the street a minute. Right now they're talking with a close lady acquaintance of yours in there. Do you know what that means?

A lady acquaintance? I can't imagine . . . what could it mean?

It means we have to spend a hell of a lot of time on things you should have reported to us long ago. And it's a pretty annoying business, am I right?

An annoying business! I remembered asking whether the matter had anything to do with 'Operation: Reader'; he gave only a vague reply, everything had to do with the operation, or something like that; I realized I was bothering him when he was trying hard to think, and felt mildly offended . . . down on the main thoroughfare he pointed his arm to the left—himself heading to the right—and said: In that little cafe there, you know the one I mean, you can wait for me there. Or did you leave the house without money again?—I could have had money enough for the whole night, and still it would have been pointless to await him; but I knew I could wait for him in the cafe perhaps three days from now. Whenever I stood where my basement passages ended, before the grey concrete wall—which I had crossed once before . . . one single time . . . up above, on the level of reality—I was reminded of this annoying business. And not just because the wall down here was adorned with an extremely primitive, larger-than-life graffito which the light of my forty-watt bulb had revealed to me just a few months before. An unknown hand, probably using a steel nail, had scratched the outline of a massive, upward-aiming phallus, and the lines had been painstakingly traced with black pen, evidently with indelible ink, for the seeping water failed to wash away the contours. Pictographic testicles, like outsized rimless spectacles, were slung over the base of the shaft; at the front was a sketchy, football-sized glans whose opening spewed a widening jet, like the muzzle of an antiquated firearm with a high scatter effect.—I had no idea what this graffito was doing down here; all that came to my mind was a term from Baudrillard: empty significance . . . but that no doubt referred to different matters.

What also reminded me of the so-called annoying business was my discovery that the graffito was signed with a big fat 'C' . . . the signature was so ostentatious that it seemed strange I hadn't noticed it first. This was no doubt due to a certain professional blindness . . . up in the offices, in such cases, they'd use the word suppression only towards a new recruit; a long-time practitioner like myself would be accused at the very least of a lapse in vigilance, that is, a sort of precursor to treason . . . I laughed at that audibly, and somewhat affectedly —of course the letter 'C' hadn't been added until later, and its appearance beneath the graffito indicated that my resting place down here at the end of the world had been paid more than a single chance visit; it was frequented, a term that had to be used after two or more visits.

Suddenly it hit me to interpret the character 'C' as my own initial, but I quickly dismissed this as nonsense . . . I wasn't called by a name with the letter 'C', not under normal circumstances!—A much more disturbing reason to assume that I was being visited down here—in my absence, that is; it wasn't I who was visited, but my shadow . . . and the appearance of the 'C' proved that these shadow contacts were increasing in frequency—was a fact less easy to forget: the removal of a seat that had been perfectly tailored to my needs, for which reason I had to spend much more time resting up in the offices. And I was forced to compensate this loss with a plain wooden crate which initially kept me awake much too long for my liking.

It was a largish, stable produce crate, perhaps a potato crate; I'd overturned it and placed it against the concrete wall so that it served as a tolerable seat.—Leaning against the wall, my aching feet stretched

out in front of me, I reflected in this pose on my dark paths through the city of Berlin; I struggled to collect my thoughts and think only of the paths still ahead of me, or the past few days' paths, above and below the street surface . . . and no further back, I was here, and here I wished to remain— with my ear to the scoured-smooth concrete, thus I rested.— Sometimes, though, I tried to make out the sounds on the opposite side of the wall. I heard nothing; over there, it seemed, there were no sounds. Only now and then did I imagine there'd been a very faint clinking jitter; it was always gone at once, and my ears merely seemed to echo it—it could have been a large refrigerator switching on; after that a fine hum came through the wall, and when it broke off, again with that barely perceptible jitter, I started out of my sleep. And in this sleep I'd seen the light behind the wall: a warm, bright light that shone behind my shut lids when I thought of the future in my sleep—over on the other side, where the interiors were pale and tiled and reflected the light back still more brightly; there was furniture there, and probably proper toilets and baths, and perhaps storerooms, shelves stocked with full bottles, and the little end tables in front of them, with clean glasses upturned on trays . . . it haunted my sleep, the thought of the tunnel beneath the wall, it haunted the sleep of the entire country, perhaps this was the thought I was supposed to bring to light . . . and maybe there were houseplants there, dark green large-leafed plants from southern climes, flourishing in the constant warmth and the radiant light, for over there, in the basements on the other side, it was always day, while here it was always night.

Oh, how he wished he was over there . . . I thought, as though speaking in my mind of a stranger from my past. No, not up in the offices, not one bit, down in the basement would have suited him just fine. Where the administrators of the supplies proceeded at their leisure, demonstrating diligence, repeatedly counting the still-sealed, neatly stacked cartons and the sacks lined up as though ready to march, and, bored and complacent, checking them against the quantities in their lists; here . . . he would have thought over there . . . the question of flour, the flour question posed to Lenin has been answered: Here comes the flour! Here you walk through the series of rooms where the endless rows of reserves repose, you can rest a cautious hand on the neat and well-filled produce crates, and think purely contemplatively about security: the supplies will last, and last a long while, when up above ground the explosion has come and the world has gone out of joint.

And over there perhaps he could have a small desk, somewhere with good light, not authorized, but tolerated, with his properly stacked papers upon it—and the content of these papers would long have been known to his superior Feuerbach, he'd have read them in secret, but that wouldn't matter . . . and at some point Feuerbach might even comment: Not so bad, the stuff you write . . . you'd cut an excellent figure back there, in the back-courtyard scene! You don't need to hide from them.

Oddly, such thoughts reassured me . . . they actually exerted a certain power upon me, they flowed over me, clouding my vision, and under their brunt I nodded my head until my eyes fell shut.—It was almost warm below ground, at least not downright cold, I didn't feel chilly when I drowsed here for an hour or two. I was hardy enough, I could rightfully claim, to serve in the underworld—though this thought harked back to a romanticism that had little to do with our reality, Feuerbach's and mine. Feuerbach was a pen-pusher, or at least that was the part he played, and he held all thought of practicalities at arm's length. He let nothing slip about his past, but I could have sworn from some of his remarks that he'd been familiar with certain forms of grassroots work . . . had he once walked the same paths as I?—It was hard to imagine his hypersensitive David Bowie face down here in the dark. Sometimes he'd hinted that he approved of what I did . . . that was at a time when any encouragement on his part annoyed me and made me suspicious. He'd commented then that my mobility in the city was likely to gain me the right to a coffee-making receptionist one day. Naturally he didn't have one himself . . . and a remark like that already seemed to deal the first jab from the opposite direction; of course he wasn't allowed to rein me in, but I wondered whether I'd suddenly become too active for his taste. He had no idea that I didn't want an office with a receptionist, at least not one that was imposed upon me . . . he couldn't understand where my inter-est lay, I thought, he saw the things I did out of this interest as a striving for advancement.—The gracious comments with which he received certain of my reports still rang in my ears: If I'm supposed to countersign your works of art, you'd better start leaving yourself out of them. He could understand, he said, that being of a poetic nature I had to have a penchant for the autobiographical, but I should keep in mind that official documents had to be drawn up somehow from my lyrical prose. For instance, he said: Personal details are very useful. But about the people you're trying to get the dirt on, of course. So just think of the words of a much more famous writer: The person is always at the centre . . . —Who was that again, Gorky? I asked.—Most good ideas come from the adversary. The point, however, is to change them . . .

For some time, then . . . quite a while now, and increasingly in the past year or so . . . I'd noticed signs of dissatisfaction on Feuerbach's part. But perhaps I was confusing things, and these signs were in myself, and arose from my own dissatisfaction with Feuerbach's behaviour . . . when I thought about it, it had started when Reader's first readings attracted our attention. I myself had discovered the 'phenomenon' and—albeit belatedly—brought the news of it to Feuerbach's desk. I had first heard Reader while trailing a young woman—a student, I guessed, who cropped up at most literary events in the so-called Scene, and had caught my eye because she was constantly writing down reading dates in a tiny notebook—of whom I'd then lost sight again.

Literature, literature! Feuerbach exclaimed after hearing my report to the end . . . I'd delivered it orally; realizing immediately that I'd caught him on one of his nervous days, I kept it as brief as possible, forgetting to mention the student . . . and he exclaimed it in such a tone as to say: Can't you think of anything better than to keep coming to me with literature! Then, a bit more calmly, he said: Literature's always got surprises in store, even here. And Beckett, you said . . . his texts are like Beckett's? I still maintain that that Irishman ruined the isle's literature. And probably French literature too. And the same thing's going to happen here. That was a bad idea, these texts à la Beckett! But what can we do? I for one don't like Beckett's stuff at all . . .

Again I'd thought I heard a tiny noise . . . directly behind the wall something must have gone out, something had silenced a machine, a complex of machines, a ticking, and in that silence I'd started from my sleep. And one of those rare moments came in which I perceived, with full awareness, where I was—I stared, revolted, into the dim desolation around me. How could I stand it down here? Before me a grimy passage vanished into the dark, the walls casing this tunnel seemed already to have run to rot, noxious liquids trickling down and draining off in unseen places; they seeped down into the city's cloacae whose bitter fumes sometimes swamped me. Those were the moments when I took flight, overcome by loathing, and swore never to descend again.—And as I fled towards the exit, I had to pass a partition that blocked off a side passage. It had been added later, you could tell . . . which was why it was even more rotten and crumbly than the rest of the masonry: a section of bricks was breached, and this hole in the wall—behind it was the densest, most noxious darkness —filled me with a special dread. I couldn't explain why, but I hardly dared to approach this stretch of wall; only now and then, when my curiosity got the better of me—taking cover below the hole, as I feared an instantaneous gas explosion— I'd tossed some burning newspapers through the opening. They didn't fall far; the air in the hole was so poor in oxygen that the flames couldn't catch. There was nothing in there but stench and putrefaction . . . The coal! I said to myself. Coal, when it reaches the stage of decay and disintegrates, gives off this veritably organic smell. Only far to the back did I seem to see a dull red gleam. This, I surmised, was the glimmer of the dilapidated red foam-rubber armchair I'd once placed by the concrete wall at the end of the passage. For comfort's sake I'd transported the prize through the basements in a gruelling effort; it was purloined just a short while later.—I was being frequented down here, from that day on I could doubt it no longer. Whoever was sniffing me out, they wanted to chase me away . . . everywhere I wasn't alone, I felt chased away. And down here was the last place I'd been alone with myself. There was one single character who had to reckon with surveillance down here: I myself . . . surveillanced by me myself. That was a thing of the past now.

When I'd passed this partition, I had to walk back quite a way to the first door that opened onto basement stairs leading up and out. Here I had always taken particular care that the door remained unlocked . . . only once, I recalled with dread, had it been closed, blocked from outside by junk dumped in front of it. I had an appointment, no time left, and I lost all sense of direction; I spent half the night blundering through the passages in a panic and swallowing sedatives . . . now the basement door was open. Standing on the street, I was astonished to see that it was already broad daylight. Like a blinded bat I peered into the winter morning light which dazzled me, though it was cloudy and a few snowflakes fluttered through the damp cold. Traffic noise surged around me, the stores were already open; as usual at this early hour, clusters of shoppers had formed in front of the bakeries. I had to pass them, bleary-eyed and pale, feeling filthy and foul; all I could do was walk down the street with head held high and ignore their gazes.

Down on the main thoroughfare I recalled the little cafe where I'd waited for Feuerbach many times before. It was more of a dive—and the first lieutenant was inconsiderate enough to call it that—tastelessly decorated and not always clean, but it was open early and thus one of the few places in the capital referred to as a boulevard cafe. The decor, later redone, consisted of bare plastic furniture in artificial, long-dingy trend colours, with a relentless proliferation of unsightly black marks from the cigarette butts stubbed out on the flesh-coloured curves of the chairs and tables. Once it had been a non-smoking cafe; the pictogram meant to convey this dictate had been hung in an awkward location and covered beyond recognition with cryptic dates and addresses. Now people smoked here all the more, using the saucers of the coffee cups as ashtrays; when there was a fastidious phase, or a fresh start—unlike the staff, the cafe manager was constantly changing—

these saucers were no longer served; now you went to the bar yourself and fetched a saucer from the leaning stack. The counter was screened off by an ornate iron grille, at its foot a growing pile of newspapers, several weeks' worth; the grille also provided a place to hang up coats, with the disadvantage that the barman was usually invisible, and the guests were invisible to him; if you didn't want to shout for the waiter, which was frowned on in the cafe, you had to make your way around the grille, where the waiter was almost always hiding, if he was in the cafe at all.

I'd stopped wondering whether to find it odd that you rarely saw two people at one table in this cafe, though this behaviour changed over the course of the evening . . . and so it was usually very quiet inside; it did happen that one of the waiters, if he was new, would slide a cassette into the recorder, the current hits would blare out, one of the guests would make his way to the front to complain about the noise, and the cassette would be ejected—it was clear that people were working in this cafe. Each of the exclusively male individuals at the tables—all were about the same age, in the indeterminate years between thirty and forty—seemed intensely self-absorbed, none seemed to know the others but all were on a first-name basis with the barman. And nearly all of them drank that peculiar beverage, far too expensive for me, which was known as a champagne shandy and was concocted from a beer . . . it was crucial to use a Czech pilsner, which had become a scarce commodity, or, better yet, one from Radeberg near Dresden; Berliner Pilsner came in for regular disparagement . . . and a mini-bottle of champagne. I stuck to coffee and schnapps, even in the summer, as multiple mini-champagnes in the morning hours still struck me as a luxury. Out of habit I took my place at the window . . . which the others seemed to avoid now that I'd occupied it several times . . . where I sat hidden from the outside world by the grey–yellow curtain—it held the nicotine of years, as curtains in a non-smoking bar didn't need changing —with a good view of the street, and the pedestrian traffic right before my eyes, since the window ledge was almost level with the pavement. And if two people stopped outside to talk, I could even hear what they were saying through the big window.

Not far from the cafe was a U-Bahn exit that I could easily see into if I tilted back slightly in my chair, leant my shoulder against the window and looked down the street to the left. It was a pose Feuerbach referred to as 'snoozing'; when he came in he'd greet me by rapping his knuckles much too hard on the plastic table, and I'd pretend to be startled. Usually I'd already seen him through the window; he stood out, the way his long strides put him at the forefront of a wave of humanity pouring from the gloom of the U-Bahn, or perhaps it was also his disbelieving face that struck me, in some uncalled-for fashion singling him out from the lethargic look of the crowd.

Floods of people mounted the stairs from the tunnel at several-minute intervals whenever a train arrived below. I seemed to hear the trains' distant rumble even up in the cafe, detecting it in the faint jitter of the coffee cup on the table, in the barely perceptible tremor of the windowpane beside me— and then the people came, always twice as many from the city centre as from the zoo in the suburbs . . . each afternoon the tunnel disgorged mindboggling throngs which dispersed as expected on the broad pavement.

What if they suddenly massed together, ceased to disband, took over the street? There were certainly enough of them, in their multitudes they could easily halt the capital's self-centred rotations . . . what if they suddenly grasped what they revolved around—life—in its progressive debasement, and chose to ignore it!

And ceased to disperse?—I lived in a world of the imagination . . . time and again my reality turned fantastic, anomalous, and from one moment to the next the only tranquillity left me consisted in a barely tenable simulation. No wonder; we lived under constant pressure to take into account behaviour which might not even exist. We lived in a dichotomy: we were perpetually conducting intelligence, investigations to clarify how far reality had already approximated our imaginings . . . but we couldn't let ourselves believe that our imaginings might actually come true. No, we disbelieved our own imaginings, for we conducted constant investigations clarifying—for ourselves!—that there was no reason to believe them. But it was difficult to investigate without imagining what this investigation was supposed to ascertain and if necessary prevent, if possible nip in the bud, as was our explicit aim. Thus it was necessary to simulate that the budding reality conformed with our imaginings . . . at what point, I asked myself, would we have outstripped our ability to decisively categorize the things we clarified: as still belonging in the realm of simulation, or already as budding reality? The words 'still' and 'already' conveyed the crux of it: Could the simulation become reality, and where was the transition? Could what was still a simulation already have made the transition to reality before we had clarified it and brought it to light? If simulation could become reality, reality could answer us with simulation. If we had to concede this, we were probably lost . . . and so we couldn't believe it.

So: we could believe nothing, for what we did not believe did not occur. It could not occur: from sheer disbelief . . . this we knew, with adamant certainty. It lay deep in the consciousness of each of us, there was no deeper layer of our consciousness than disbelief. With our scepticism we emerged in a straight, purposeful line from the Enlightenment . . . and now and then someone went so far as to call disbelief the tenet of our faith. Disbelief was deep-seated, it was the growling coffee grounds in our guts ... hah! Maybe we drank too much coffee as we pondered; we were Nestlé's best customers, someone had said. And when we transitioned to conviction we drank champagne with beer, which made us jovial and disbelieving.

So: there was no God, there were no phenomena, there was no subconscious, there was no turning back ... this, if we liked, was the creed behind the cant.—Nothing could happen that we didn't believe, because we didn't believe it ... and already we were indispensable. Before all the world we could have pointed at what didn't happen ... because we didn't believe it. Once again: all we believed in was our disbelief. All the intelligence we conducted, never flagging, tirelessly vigilant, consisted of conveying the belief that nothing could happen, nothing, to that end we couldn't be wordy enough. Even if everyone knew it already, in the course of our investigations we had to re-convey and reaffirm that the people out there on the pavement were doing no more than coming out of a U-Bahn tunnel, walking along and going back down into the next U-Bahn tunnel. We unbelievers believed firmly that nothing dubious could occur, that they weren't massing together on the pavement, even if they came in groups, in many groups, in crowds, in multitudes and cohorts.—That changed only in winter, the pavements emptied when darkness fell, there was nothing but the cars on the lanes of the street ...

We could have pointed right at the calm and cool-headedness that prevailed among us ... but sometimes the too-oft repeated phrases seemed to undergo a strange reversal, and the cafe was too close to the U-Bahn for my liking. It happened that I spent hours unfolding my thoughts, ceaselessly, far from drawing conclusions, staring through the curtain:

everything outside was grey, and I thought and thought about the people.—The people . . . I thought when the streetscape came into focus once again, there are more and more people out there.— With a sense of vertigo I saw them climb up from the tunnel, wave upon wave, and scatter on the pavement; now, in the afternoon, the intervals between arriving trains were quite brief, and the crowd poured forth with barely an interruption. What if they suddenly ceased to disperse . . . and all of them suddenly came into the cafe. What an idea, to see hundreds of people crowding in, the cafe bursting at the seams! To see the tables swept clear of us, us pushed to the back wall, already pushed behind the bar . . . soon still more would come, another train was arriving. We've done them no harm, really . . .

Once, I recalled, I'd joined the annual march to the Memorial to the Socialists.[2] That is, I wasn't in the midst of the demonstration, I was one of the escorts strolling casually along beside it, and it seemed to me that these escorts were observed still more keenly—by the closely spaced kerbside cordon of double sentries, who went unrecognized—than the demonstration itself as it surged sedately onward. Progress was slow on the main street, much too slow for me . . . I shivered; the January day was frigid, and I was growing increasingly nervous—I'd have liked to spur them on, this lame herd, I'd have liked to yell and swing a stick and set them trotting . . . by the time we reached the cafe I'd had enough, I pushed my way through the rubberneckers on the kerb and went into the packed cafe. Immediately I ran into Feuerbach, who like me had only found standing room.—Get out! he hissed at me. They're already skipping off to the U-Bahn out there and you come in here to sit on your hands!—What am I supposed to do? I said, Send them back?—I left the cafe again and saw that Feuerbach was staring after me, leaning in the doorway. Unable at first to get through the cordon to the street, I walked along on the pavement. A few hundred yards away, at the next U-Bahn entrance, I saw that he was right, droves of people really were vanishing into the underpass; they hurried down the stairs, giggling and looking triumphant as if they'd snuck out of a bar without paying. Of course no one cared about them, even our boys lounging against the tunnel wall yawned jadedly. But I was unnerved, sensing that this child's play could turn serious if only enough of them came together in one place. As a rule I dreaded crowds . . . when I pictured them swarming the platforms in the gloom down below, storming the arriving trains in their mushy sense of community, reinforced at each station by new masses all the way to Alexanderplatz . . . I was glad to be elevated from their midst, by a terse, unremarkable agreement. In crowds, amid the attraction they exerted, it was ultimately hard for me to maintain the distance I needed; my ability to accurately assess people vanished on a regular basis when there were more than ten of them in one place; I stopped registering the details and distinguishing their voices; it wasn't long before I heard them speak in chorus . . . in fact, they even thought in chorus, their gazes merged into one single gaze, soon they moved in one direction only . . . it was easy to be gripped by their excitement, and already you'd joined them, for better or worse, and that was somehow liberating. Perhaps it was because they were held together not by commands but by the melody of the chorus.

I wormed my way through the flood of people and continued along the pavement, forcing myself to walk slowly, to don the impassive expression I'd rehearsed; gradually it worked, the nervous flutter subsided. Where Frankfurter Allee ended I turned left onto Siegfriedstrasse and walked up to the next intersection, where Wagner's was located, a cheap beer bar that was packed with people as well. Here there was no one I knew; this was where the workers who'd absconded from the demonstration had settled. At the bar I drank a large glass of beer which ran ice cold down my gullet and calmed me still further. Then I moved on, in the opposite direction now, parallel to the main thoroughfare, past the open entrance gate of the Oskar Ziethen Hospital, where the ambulances stood on call in the courtyard; I put a few more cross-streets behind me, then walked back down to the boulevard. By now the marching formations had dissipated, the little cafe was empty again. At any rate I found my window seat unoccupied, and ordered my usual coffee and brandy. When the waiter brought my order he said to me: An acquaintance of yours told me to tell you to wait for him here!

In nearly all such instances I waited in vain. And I realized that I was supposed to wait in vain ... so that he could accuse me, when the time came, of not having waited for him. That too I put down to the universal practice of simulation which we extended to all realms and in which there was never a pause. It was one of the peculiarities of our function that we were unreliable in every respect ... which did not preclude us from standing everywhere as one man and always being utterly reliable. The simulation enabled us to make one mistake after another in moments of the keenest vigilance, but just when everything threatened to get out of hand—it was just like the movies—we were keen as hound dogs and got right on top of things. Our life was one long training session, and that wasn't a bad thing at all.—Keen as hound dogs! was one of Feuerbach's special phrases; I disliked it, but more and more often I used it myself. And I had the fantasy that our eyes were keenest when they were shut. With our eyes shut we really did see frighteningly far ahead. Don't ask me how that's possible.

When Feuerbach failed to show up for a rendezvous, I could count on his coming the next day, or in three days. It often happened that he had the waiter tell me a date, and then asked me a month later why I hadn't come on this day or that. I didn't even react to such questions, knowing he preferred it that way.—You didn't wait for me, and that snarled a whole series of meet-ups, he said to me. Because of you we'll have to start all over again from scratch, I've got to come visit you.—From scratch? I said. That's good for training.—You'll see, all right, he said, we're already fitter than fit can be!

I'll have to call quite late, he said, I'll come to your flat.— He knew I felt threatened by his home visits, and that was exactly why he kept starting up with them again. There too, of course, I usually waited in vain; I could concretely recall only two or three of his visits. One night he had appeared unannounced; it was a mystery to me how he'd got through the locked front door. I just couldn't picture Feuerbach wandering through the basements.—I could still see him standing at the desk where I had just been sitting, his left hand casually, absently—the way he moved seemed dismissive—leafing through my papers without actually reading them; in his other hand he daintily held a cigarette at chin height . . . though normally a non-smoker . . . when he took a cigarette from my pack without asking and nervously lit it, he was simulating growing interest . . . and he breathed out the smoke disdainfully. He was a good-looking man, this Feuerbach . . . unlike me, I thought . . . he was taller than I, with blond hair, streaked with grey, that looked sophisticatedly unkempt; usually he was badly shaven, underscoring the slightly raffish look of his pale, younger-seeming face, a perfect blend of naive and hard-boiled. Perhaps he sometimes seemed enigmatic . . . on me, looking back, he even made a rather demonic impression; my desk lamp lit his face from below, his dispassionate grey eyes invisible, as the shadow cast by the hand with the cigarette covered his nose and brow. As usual he had little to say to me, and I forgot about it . . . once, during one of these visits, he murmured something about a photo he needed.—Or he asked me: You didn't happen to notice, by any chance, the cigarettes that young lady smokes, the one who's running after Reader? They're West German cigarettes . . . —So? I said.— All right, he said. But you didn't notice the excise stamp on these West German cigarette packs, the excise stamp with the federal eagle! You're not noticing that those packs were bought over there. The young lady's from West Berlin . . . and you don't even notice!—He vanished again just as abruptly and silently as he had come.—He mixed up my papers on purpose, I thought angrily after he'd left.

Suddenly, in the crowd leaving the U-Bahn tunnel, I thought I saw her; it was the student who had caught my eye in the audience at the so-called Scene's kitchen and living-room readings. Or wasn't it her . . .? I'd paid her too little notice so far, she had a somewhat too-smooth, expressionless face, an open face, but at the same time remote and hard to reach; I still had no connection whatsoever to this generation, there was something androgynous about it. She was already past the cafe window when I thought I recalled exchanging a few words with her once: only trivial phrases, though . . . apparently she'd noticed that I didn't speak the Berlin dialect, she'd asked me about it . . . now it occurred to me that some-one who lived in East Berlin would hardly have asked me a thing like that, at least not in the Berlin Scene, where people came from all over the place: it was a typical West Berlin question!

I hit on the idea of running out and accosting her; she was walking slowly, I could still catch up with her. Before I'd entirely suppressed my reservations about the idea, I was already out on the street; I recognized her, some distance away, by the short sure steps with which she managed to cut straight through the hectic scrum of people. As though on a sudden intuition she turned half towards me, I waved at her, but she turned her head away and continued on her path, perhaps even quickening her pace. I hesitated; someone, a passer-by, slammed into my back, and set in motion again by the collision, I walked on and caught up with her; she didn't react when I touched her sleeve—it was barely a touch, but she must have noticed me—now I overtook her in an arc so as not to step too abruptly in front of her . . . and of course in that instant I thought once again I'd been mistaken. Evidently she really was a student, smoking with her left hand as she walked; she wore dark clothes, a knee-length skirt over dark, patterned tights, a light black leather jacket with a skinny red scarf under the collarless neckline with its knitted border . . . I couldn't have given Feuerbach such a meagre description, I'd have been guaranteed one of his most venomous looks. Her face was white, there was no other word for it, snow-white, and especially the gently incurved planes of her temples had a translucent pallor beneath which I could have seen the pulse of every sensation—now, as she saw me, these temples seemed filled with agitation, and the close-set arcs of her eyebrows drew together before I'd said a word.—Do you happen to know where the next reading will be held? I asked . . . my voice seemed to burst alien and overly loud from my throat; later my harmless question struck me as an interrogation.—No, I don't know about that, she said; it sounded as though she really had no idea what I meant.—The follow-up to last month's reading on S. Strasse, don't you remember?—I named the occupant of the flat on S. Strasse; again I seemed to be gazing at a completely unfamiliar, expressionless face. She shook her head and tried to keep walking.—We spoke briefly, you must remember that, I said.—No, I don't know, she said, I don't know that we know each other.—But the reading, you know about the reading! We saw each other there, you must remember . . . You don't want to remember!—Knock it off! she said, it only sounded gentle. Knock it off, you'll have to try that on some other girl . . .

I couldn't stop her . . . Don't you remember, my name is Cambert! I yelled after her . . . at least I dimly recalled having yelled this name after her; and I'd forgotten whether I'd given her that name or a different name at last month's reading!— That was a bad blunder, the name business, altogether I'd done everything wrong . . . I was about to go back and sit in the cafe again, but suddenly I changed my mind. I followed her at a proper distance, but she sensed it or guessed it, ducking into the next U-Bahn entrance, one which took her back to the station she'd just come from, only from the other side, meaning that she'd probably take the same U-Bahn line she'd arrived on fifteen minutes before. I boarded the U-Bahn too and took it to the last stop . . . I'd lost the Student, of course.

Though I'd lived in Berlin for some time—was it two years . . . I simply didn't know for sure any more—I was far from having a handle on the passages under Alexanderplatz Station; over and over they conducted me into the open by different exits, over and over by one opposite the one I sought, and above ground I always had to reorient myself. Usually I went back down to seek the right exit, which as a rule confused me still further. Absently I wandered the spacious, branching, overlapping passages which held the din of the trains, indeed the din of the entire city . . . I still couldn't get my mind off the name business; I kept asking myself whether it was really the student I had run into.—When I came out into the open, off in the middle of nowhere again, near Alexanderstrasse, I believed—I gazed over in astonishment at the mighty block of the emporium towering above the S-Bahn rail-bridge a few hundred yards away—it was already beginning to grow dark. A grey light swam above the box of the department store and the glass roof of the S-Bahn station; behind me the sky, broken by roofs, had black stormy patches. Spring was coming . . . I was still dressed for winter; the weather outstripped my lagging thoughts. This evening, though, promised to turn cool once more . . . I crossed part of the square to the bookshop to look at the window displays; it was hard to make them out in the dusk. Just then it occurred to me how imaginary was the life I led . . . outwardly, or perhaps even in the reality of my own that was hidden from the outside world? Again and again memory and present reality merged for me in a diffuse mix of times, and I wondered if this might start to pose a danger for me: When would this also befall the information I selected for my work?

Maybe it had happened long ago . . . at the mere thought I lost my bearings completely.—Indeed the light over the city was growing weaker and weaker . . . the time I lived in swam like the city itself, this backdrop vaguely reflected in the glass of the shop windows; it seemed to be going up in steam, this backdrop of grey-black cloudbanks scudding straight through the transparent images of the high-rise facades, occasional flares of lamps amid the images of the clouds, and behind all this shadow-work reposed the dark illegible titles of the books, jumbled like upheaved paving stones.

What a simulation this reality was! How long had I lost touch with its contingencies—how long ago had I'd lost precisely the things I hadn't reported on. And these included forays like today's: hunting trips above the street surface undertaken utterly without consciousness, and utterly in vain, perhaps only undertaken to breathe in the light of this city, a light that brought forth faces so pale and expressionless as to seem potentially responsive to the expression of my nature. And perhaps I undertook nothing now but quests in search of the

Student, or other female apparitions associated in my imagination with her light and unmarked figure . . . these were imaginings and figures of which Feuerbach learnt nothing. Or very little . . . my superiors knew nothing of these thoughts of mine! And the result seemed to be that I knew less and less of them myself.

Memory Underground

I'd been mistaken yet again—like a ghost that walks through walls, First Lieutenant Feuerbach suddenly strode forth from the overlapping reflections of the high-rise facades, his pale face looming vivid against the twilight of the clouds; too late to escape, he was already plucking my sleeve.—It was my turn now to be grabbed by the arm, much less gently than I had done just before . . . reality grabbed me by the sleeve, and in that instant the evening grew still darker; turning around, I anticipated Feuerbach's smile, in which his eyes had no share. But there was no grin this time; in a conciliatory tone he asked me: Why didn't you invite that young lady to the cafe just now? Don't tell me you didn't notice me coming in right behind you, didn't you see me sitting by the window? We'd arranged something of the sort, or am I mistaken? Did you forget about it again? I would have been delighted to meet the young lady.

She didn't want to come, I said with an effort. She didn't want to come because the cafe doesn't have any outdoor tables. Now that it's spring, she said, she's not going to go inside a smoky bar.

My quick reply took him off his guard; he said: There probably won't be any outdoor tables at all this summer, I heard they can't get the waitress back for the outdoor service . . . she doesn't want to go back to that dive either.

Oh, and by the way, I left without paying, I said. Can you cover that for me? You go there practically every day, right? Then why don't you pick up the tab? . . . There might be a couple of bills I haven't paid yet, nothing major, I don't think.

Okey dokey! said Feuerbach. For all I care . . . let's talk about something else . . .

Actually it only looks like I have lots of time, I demurred.

You're chasing her, Feuerbach retorted, go ahead and admit it. Do you really think you're going to run into her again this evening?

He was right, it really was too much to expect now; I'd come into town for nothing, at a completely pointless time of day, and running into him precipitated one of those embarrassing moments in which I felt like a person with no function whatsoever . . . which I wouldn't have felt on my own. Not much was going on in the Scene, I knew, and I stood like a Kaspar Hauser in the middle of the city . . . Feuerbach was still clutching my arm. I'd almost always felt this way on Berlin's big, busy plazas, and had avoided them whenever possible; but recently this very feeling appealed to me somehow.

I was spooked by places where I came up against the people, mindboggling throngs of milling idlers . . . throngs crossed in turn by hurried masses pouring from the packed S-Bahn trains; and when I saw how the latter ranks had to fight their way through the snarls of loiterers, how they were slowed by the lethargy of those who merely moved from one snack stand to the next, I got nervous. And finally the hurriers seemed to succumb to the rubberneckers and gadabouts and started dawdling as well . . . transformed seamlessly into tourists, into schmoozing chatterboxes who, seemingly oblivious to their duties, gazed at the facades, the monumental blocks of metropolitan architecture, the Television Tower and the City

Hall, gazed past the little churches buried between the concrete hulks, the first trees, now that spring had come, blooming amid the neat raked lawns . . . all this made me suspicious, and what was more, I felt I was being observed: at my side I sensed a constant distrustful gaze and the question whether I was always sufficiently suspicious of the bustle on the city squares. Again and again I felt the question from beside me, and half from behind, whether I'd spotted a person who didn't want to stay . . . there were moments when this eternal question really made me sick.—Unable to hide my annoyance, I left Feuerbach standing there and headed for the S-Bahn station; suddenly I didn't care if this offended him. On this evening, murky and cold, Alexanderplatz looked nearly deserted on both sides of the rail line, the nasty weather chasing off the last of the pedestrians; dark smoke fell back from the equally dark clouds and mingled with the foggy dusk, which withdrew from the centres of the squares and crept back up the buildings. Only there, in the semidarkness, were there still a few people . . . in the midst of the open spaces the first streaks of rain lashed down, slapping the pavement, full of smuts; the rain stopped again, it grew darker still, the Television Tower reared up into a dense dark fog. I seized the opportunity to make it across to the station entrance, but already it was raining again, big fat black drops pelting the concrete. Sensing the first lieutenant behind me, I refused to run, and filthy water was trickling down my forehead by the time I finally reached the station.

Why are you running away? I heard him pant as I mounted the stairs to the train platform . . . evidently I'd finally managed to insult him, but he didn't show it. He kept one step below me and hovered behind me as we stood on the platform. Watching the people waiting for the train—relatively few, it was evening already—I felt his breath on my ear: How come you're so hypersensitive, anyway . . . all I can tell you is, cut it out!

Were you trying to get wet, or what? I asked.

You know what, he started up again, you're just overly sensitive about certain things. And since there do happen to be people who are always thinking along with us . . . oh yes, we've got our experts for that . . . this could end up hurting you. Because they have a seventh sense for it, so to speak. Overly sensitive people—that tends to be the thinking—are unreliable people, because at some point they let their sensitivities guide them.

What sort of things, I asked, am I too sensitive about, in your opinion?

Not in my opinion, it's no skin off my nose! But to answer your question . . . I hinted at it once, I'm sure you'll recall. I said that you simply clam up about some things. And we have trouble keeping certain things straight, you know what I mean. Usually to do with the ladies, you're trying to put something over on us there. And it's all out of hypersensitivity . . . apparently it's a catastrophe for you whenever there's some dame you can't manage to lay . . . and you don't say a thing about it, no, you actually seem to believe it happened, you actually seem to believe it! And we're left hanging and have to fit the pieces together. For instance, at one point there was a rather daft paternity affair . . . remember?

Vaguely . . . I said, I have a murky memory, the whole story was pretty murky. I didn't even feel it was me they meant, it seemed like something I wasn't capable of. I thought it was altogether a bit too much . . .

That's just it, he said, once again you played the sensitive character. You couldn't claim nothing had happened . . . and you signed for the child . . .

No, I said, that's not what I signed for!

Maybe it was! And now we're having problems with your signature . . . which is pretty distinctive, by the way!

When I was sitting in the train at last, the only passenger in the entire car, Feuerbach's interfering murmur still rang in my ears. What was it he kept trying to remind me of? For months he'd been raising the subject, almost regularly, but always taking me by surprise, so that gradually I came to fear these moments. But he never went beyond innuendos, always leaving me with the unpleasant feeling that up there, on the so-called higher levels above us, they knew more about me than I did myself. But probably I was just being too sensitive, for of course that was one of their tactics, two-bit police routine; you come out of every interrogation with that feeling, I didn't have to go buying into it too . . . the troubling thing was that Feuerbach's insinuations had such a lasting effect on me.—And it was in the nights when I hunkered in the cellar on my seat by the yellow-grey concrete wall, when I was beyond his reach, it was then that his talk gnawed at my nerves . . . the ringing tone of the cooling unit behind me, purely imaginary, the clink of keys behind me, purely imaginary, sparked this anxiety within me. I went over his insinuations from start to finish . . . they made no sense to me; if anything, they slid in front of my flimsy memories like verbal barriers, their resolution lying in a snarl of disquieting emotions behind this barricade . . . It was impossible to unravel Feuerbach's words because the reason for them had to take me back to the time before my conversations with Feuerbach began. It was almost as though I had to think about things that dated back before my birth.

For me the time before Feuerbach lay fully in the dark of oblivion . . . it had slipped from my grasp entirely, so far beyond the pale that I hardly counted it as part of my real life; over it hung a grey, hectically woven web of language which in fact I could describe as an impregnable fabric of simulation. Or everything that lay beyond these grey layers was simulation . . . behind them was my mother, like something from Beckett, I hardly remembered how she'd looked . . . and I'd had a different name back then, that of course I remembered . . . but only because it had become a kind of code name for me now.

Feuerbach had spoken of that 'hypersensitive character' again today . . . that was supposed to mean me, it could only mean the character from the time before my 'contacts' began. And if I rightly recalled, he'd even called me by my former name . . . I could be mistaken, but I wouldn't put it past him: by calling me by my code name the rest of the time, he violated the rule of secrecy . . . he destroyed the conspirative consensus between us . . . and increased my dependency on him!—In some instances Feuerbach had even described my sensitivity as 'neurotic' . . . at which I had asked him whether he'd also describe someone like Thomas Mann as neurotic.— He grinned at me and said: Way to go! Just keep resorting to literature . . . we can be proud to have such people in our ranks . . .

The train had pulled into the Warschauer Strasse Station and hadn't budged since. Probably I'd failed to hear the instructions to transfer to another, waiting train, a frequent occurrence here . . . I was sitting way on the right, the far side of the car from the platform, torrents of rain lashing the pane beside me, the inside of the car filled by the rush of the storm on its roof, on the roofing of the platform and in the air, whose blackness was impenetrable, broken only by the glare of a few lanterns which the plunging water blurred. I had laid back my head, resting it on the back of the seat . . . I listened to the rain's monotonous noise, the way this noise grew fainter to my ears, finally resembling the hum behind the concrete wall in the basement, that machine noise that shifted gears with a slight jitter, spreading into regions beyond—that hum which went on all the same, which he could pick up only with the greatest of effort, which perhaps did not exist at all, which rushed only in his imagination when he nodded off on his wooden crate, his head leant back against the wall.

Earlier . . . that was an utterly unreal time, slipped from his grasp like a flimsy web of overwrought fancies and self-deceptions. Scrap for scrap it had vanished from his memory, an untime. The reality which had commenced one day, which by degrees had taken him in and overwhelmed him, was finally all that was left in him; and that other, finished time, obliterated bit by bit, now seemed like a fiction. It included a third of his life, much more than that, almost half . . . and he felt that he'd gambled this time away, and no longer knew what it held. Indeed, back then he had simulated—for himself!—that chunk of life; he no longer knew how he'd managed, it was a life in which each command . . . that was the word . . . that drove it had come from his own person; and yet he'd never been a per-sonage in that play! Now it was the other way around—all his commands came from without, and he was a personage . . . the proof being that he received commands clearly tailored to certain idiosyncrasies of his lifestyle.

Earlier, then, he had simulated his life . . . so he was expe-rienced in simulation, and now it had become a necessity!—When had he actually woken into this reality . . . when had he been awakened? Even this was unclear—and he thought of the long spell of sleep that had been prescribed for him . . . he'd never known it was prescribed, he had neither noticed its beginning, nor had he once foreseen its end. At any rate, it was a time he thought of with a touch of pride: he'd lived these years rather boisterously, at least he'd thought so, uncon-ventionally, a little bit, he said, he hadn't scorned the pleasures available to him, and all the while engaged in harsh, sometimes filthy work, shovelling coal, coal upon coal; none of this had placed serious demands on him, for during this time he was always occupied with literature, focused on it alone: in his free time—deducting that of his pleasures—he was constantly snarled in writing attempts ... snarled, he said ... in vast numbers of drafts which he was always starting again differently or modifying and with which he surrounded himself as with an invisible screen, cutting an absent and obdurately opaque figure behind it. He lived in a sort of mental cavern which he always dragged about with him. He thought of positioning himself in public as a writer one day, not knowing himself if he could believe in such a possibility. And yet he wrote almost without cease ... some of these attempts were the only possessions he'd salvaged from the time of his simulation.

A child has got to have a father! they'd said to him. This notion was not news to him, but of course they'd meant that this child ... a very particular child ... needed a father because none was available. Now this was a view he didn't share at all, he himself had been a fatherless child all his life, and clearly it had done him a world of good.—But he listened to the story ... it had begun with these words, and from then on he was embroiled in those conversations which he often called his conversations with reality. Starting with these words—it wasn't Feuerbach who had said them, nor any other person he ever set eyes on again—the conversations took their course ... by the time the problem those words raised had evaporated from the conversations, it already seemed impossible to escape. What was the sticking point that even in his long sleep phase had kept him from believing in escape? Even before truly grasping the fact that retreat was no longer possible, he'd stupidly suppressed all thoughts of his ensnarement: doubtless this had been their intention. They had left him alone until he simply ceased to ask himself whether, and how, he'd still be capable of leaving . . . he didn't have to leave, since they were really just conversations, and no one even minded that he conversed like a somnambulist.—And then suddenly they'd brought the term reality massively into play . . . this hadn't come from Feuerbach either; this too was a person he couldn't recall, he only heard a rather penetrating bass voice, he no longer knew whether this person had been in uniform, and he didn't know whether it had been in Berlin or back in A.

Nor could he recollect the exact words that had been said; their basic thrust was extremely simplistic, they were taken from the endless stock of generalities specially designed to relegate the mere attempt at a counterargument to the realm of evil, or at least belligerency.—Herr W., said the man behind the desk, someone has to tell you this loud and clear! At some point you have to stop living life as one big retreat from reality. No one can sneak away from his place in society. All of us have a responsibility towards reality, if you try to weasel out of it, it'll catch up with you one day . . . hopefully before it's too late. Because for you that could be a bitter pill—reality takes no prisoners!

Later W. knew that these words had signalled the end of his sleep phase. When he heard them he immediately felt overtaken by an attack of fatigue so severe that he began to teeter on the chair diagonally opposite the desk. He felt overpowered by the urge to rest . . . I can't take another word, was his only thought, not another word, however meaningless!—In that moment he would have done anything just for a gesture releasing him from his seat and allowing him to walk out of this office. The lids sank over his pupils as though he'd spent days here on this chair already—it had been little more than a quarter of an hour. And the room swam with whirling vapours, darkness from nowhere seemed to veil his interlocutor, his tongue and vocal cords were seized by incomprehensible paralysis, he no longer saw a thing . . . perhaps the gentleman behind the desk had stepped outside; shaking his head, he signed the paper on the desk in a barely legible scrawl. In that instant the gentleman was back in the room and began to talk soothingly to W. while quickly stashing away the piece of paper. Now, the man said, now everything was hunky-dory . . . It was an expression W. later thought back on with feelings of disgust . . . Nothing could go wrong now really, that had been the right step to take!—Later W. wondered for whom nothing could go wrong: the officer behind the desk or him, W., the undersigned. His signature on the paper had been completely illegible . . . and later he'd changed his name on his own; he invented a name which, in a pinch, could be discerned in the ballpoint hieroglyph under that declaration.

For some time after that he'd tried to work out the repercussions of this signature. Sitting on his basement seat he sought to recall what had preceded it, sought the reason for reality's abrupt departure from that room; he'd sat in barely breathable air, amid shadows that had materialized, that were no longer contained by the walls of the room . . . Without reality, there isn't the slightest reason to go on withholding my signature! he'd thought. Right after the signature, reality had returned; he couldn't have said in what way it was changed. The little gleam of triumph in the sharply appraising eyes of the man across from him—that didn't count as a change. And he might have been mistaken there; the man behind the desk had assumed the most serene of expressions, his words were reassuring, his gestures dismissive, as though through his own persuasive example to eliminate any hint of ill feeling, of irritation . . . W. couldn't have said whether this had had any effect on him.

Later he suppressed every inkling of the consequences such a signed paper might have, and this, evidently, was just what Feuerbach wanted.—When he'd mentioned his signature once, quite offhandedly, yet looking at the first lieutenant in suspense, Feuerbach said: Forget about it . . . in this business there's so much paper fluttering around that we need entire wastepaper collection points just for ourselves. Didn't you know we're the best source of raw material for toilet paper? Yes indeed, we're an essential factor of the national economy . . .

Gradually W. forgot about the signature . . . when more and more rarely it did cross his mind, he told himself that maybe he really had signed a paternity declaration . . . he was gradually catching on to the type of jokes that were daily fare at his new firm. Yet it was a paternity declaration with no consequences whatsoever: the amount of monthly child support, income-dependent, with which he was to provide for a child he didn't know—or barely knew, to be precise—was never stipulated. And then of course there was no income to serve as a yardstick, since W. hadn't had a regular job for years.—He lived as though on the flatline that was his bank balance: when he thought of this line he felt like a dead-tired long-distance swimmer; though he hadn't made progress in ages, he never sank below its surface—this was one of the peculiarities of his existence to which even Feuerbach referred as a phenomenon. By that he meant the life led by a whole slew of so-called independent writers in Berlin's unofficial culture industry. They lived in constant danger of having their true status called by name and declared an offence: it was the status of asocial elements, forced to live more honestly than any comfortably installed citizen because the least blunder could bring the whole force of the law down upon them; a blunder far short of shoplifting, an inadvertent overdraught would suffice. Feuerbach admired these balancing acts in his smirking fashion, behind which always lurked the knowledge that in most of these cases he himself could tip the scales.—He doesn't admire me, though, W. said to himself, grinning too; presumably the stability of my bank balance is tied to the paternity declaration. One of these days I'll get my driver's licence and buy a car! Then we'll see if the line still holds.—With his signature, then, he had acknowledged Someone as his father! Of course he didn't know whom . . . Feuerbach would have denied it categorically . . . I'm not your father, I'm an interchangeable go-between, something like an editorial secretary with sleeve protectors, completely dependent on your chronologies, my dear chap! That would have been his take on the matter.—It was beside the point; at any rate W. had a father who made sure that his bank account didn't go into free fall, however much money he withdrew.

Earlier he'd even had an armchair down here, but one day it had vanished on him. It was a red easy chair, already gleaming greasily in numerous places, but comfy and wide as though built for two people; it was the only piece of furniture he owned, from a small flat in the outskirts of the city which he had actually inhabited, had sometimes, or even still, inhabited exclusively . . . his habitations were a murky affair; sometimes he'd had several different addresses, but most of them only on paper. He had transported the armchair downtown via S-Bahn, in late spring, when Berliners were already getting ready for holiday, and he'd almost provoked a riot in the over-crowded train. The armchair was tailor-made for afternoon naps, but then he'd kept it in the basement because in the flat—in the main flat—it had become too great an uncertainty factor for him.—And so the armchair had served him as a resting place by the cool concrete wall, when he fled down early from the summer heat and savoured the silence in the turbid light. He would literally sprawl, stretching his arms out on the plump armrests, resting his feet on a produce crate; his back fit perfectly into the concave backrest, the top of which bore a blackish impression from the back of his head . . . and the back of the head that had rested there before him . . . this smudge of grime marked the point where the back of the mind worked, above the upright, fully relaxed neck so safely cushioned . . . he sat enthroned, the basement air flowing through and seeming to invigorate him, as though he were sitting at the oxygen's very source. And so he thought about oxygen . . . it seemed to him that he breathed what was in him, and what flowed out of him, he took in again, so that he was one with the atmosphere surrounding him . . . he fell asleep and woke up again and woke to fall asleep again, down here where time stagnated and circled him as though humming, and it was as though he exhaled this time from his lungs as well. For a time he was the patriarch of the underworld down here, autocrat of an unknown twilit realm, he rested unchallenged, and all thoughts were such remote, wearying premises of the life above that he could easily drop them the moment they touched him.—This lasted until one day the giant phallus appeared on the concrete wall . . . or was it the appearance of the mark 'C' beneath the giant drawing—these were turbulent times! Soon after that the armchair was slashed with knives and then stolen; he had to make do with the produce crate. Was it really only from that day on he'd felt observed and menaced down here? . . . Looking back, he had to deny it.—It was like the incursion of reality into an invented state . . . suddenly he was no longer alone there. He might have to place himself in relation to those who, like him, were present down here, per- haps he'd have to compare his I with others, who perhaps said I as well, down here. Perhaps then he would find that his own I was hollow and fantastic; at least no longer independent, at least no longer to be forgotten or summoned from forgetful- ness at a whim . . .

How it had happened remained a mystery to him; there was no real motive for the red armchair's theft, it could only be an act of terror. Who could even transport such a monstrosity? It was unlikely that anyone knew the complicated access route by which he'd carried the thing in, and he'd carefully closed up and blocked off this access route again. Who could cross his path down here, who was observing him, trailing him, who down here was contesting his place? Probably these questions were quite pointless.

Not knowing something, he said to himself, has always been highly repugnant to me! His aversion towards all sorts of incomprehension had always verged on neurosis. He tended towards paranoid reactions when faced with things he couldn't get a handle on . . . making his character perfectly suited to his task. This quality was virtually providential; in his case it could almost be called a talent. What would have been regarded as an odd tic, to put it kindly, in any other field, was in his case a tenacious and reliable gift, practically indispensable. More appreciation should have been shown for his inclination towards small but purposeful steps; after all, that was the only way to create a network of disclosures throughout the city, a network of disclosures . . . somehow only Feuerbach had had an inkling of it. But Feuerbach was only a kind of secretary, and something was increasingly blighting him . . . his aversion towards any kind of purposefulness doubtless told of some kind of blight . . .

Why had these shadowy characters suddenly been unleashed upon him?—W. could only conclude that the destruction and theft of the red armchair had to be chalked up to the shock troops they were deploying these days . . . and who had now invaded his refuge. In other words, the sort of characters who had nothing to do but create a primitive sense of insecurity. It was old news that such groups existed aplenty, drummed together in outlying bars or on the sidelines of foot-ball fields. And increasingly they seemed to be bought on short notice, for one-time jobs, leaving wreckage and confusion and vanishing again. These were fringe elements—leather-jacket types, members of motorcycle gangs—who filled their per-petual free time with drinking and rampaging, often recog-nizable by their shaven heads. You got hold of these goons and told them they could go on practising their hobby, but now the 'object' would be picked out for them. And they could earn a few marks in the process . . . otherwise you'd bust them up, and their combined force, which after all was valuable, would soon melt away behind iron bars—ultimately it was the same principle they used to catch everyone. Now the preva-lence of these shock troops was increasing; there were some that were permanent fixtures and some that were recruited for one-time jobs from the sandy deserts at the fringes of the housing projects. The unpleasant thing about the latter was that they weren't integrated, they lurked everywhere, on call . . . you never knew if they were acting on orders, you didn't know if you could get involved with them, you didn't know what side they were currently on.—Surely W. wasn't wrong to see this state of affairs as a symptom of fatigue, as an aban-donment of the more intelligent approaches in favour of destructive force . . . a force which had ultimately ceased to believe in a goal.—Disruption: to his mind the word featured more and more prominently in the parlance of the service units . . . in fact, if he wasn't mistaken, more and more often it was even superseded by the word destruction.

And so he saw anarchy looming—and asked himself whether this wouldn't inevitably bring the collapse of the entire system. Probably the answer was yes . . . and he knew that thoughts like that took him onto thin ice. With thoughts like that he was practically courting closer scrutiny. It didn't matter that no one knew of these thoughts but he; he thought them only down here in the basement, he'd never thought them up in the light . . . the sunlight, it seemed to him, would inevitably summon to his brow the agitation that came in their wake, the thoughts would take eloquent form in the deeply downturned corners of his mouth, or the film of sweat on the skin of his face would seem to permit but one conclusion: he had thought of the end . . . not the beginning, when blind as a mole he ventured up towards the light.

Or perhaps there was no significance to such a thought becoming known? Actually he had to admit that the service he was in quite naturally engendered reflections of this kind. And this led logically to the necessity . . . definitely even the primary necessity . . . of watching the collaborators in service: security was the adherence to an infinite logical consistency! To watch those in the service as they performed their function, to watch the watchers, to maintain watchfulness towards the watchers' inevitable thoughts of their own through the knowledge that they were being watched . . . to watch over sleep . . . to watch that in sleep all that drowsed was the I, while the watch went on following its logic.

The goal of the service was to make everyone . . . I said: Everyone! he thought. Everyone without exception . . . into collaborators of this service, insane though this notion might sound. So that all could be watched by all—that was a security worthy of its name.—No, the thought wasn't new . . . and it alone meant that the service wasn't merely there for the individual, but rather was a service for all. Wasn't that the unspoken goal of all great utopias, from Plato and Bacon to Marx and Lenin? Everyone in everyone's hands, perhaps this was the ultimate goal of utopian thinking . . . and hence the utopians' secret desire for anarchy, since anarchy brings the thought of collapse to the surface and necessitates the thought-watching service in the first place. Ultimately they'd have had to approve of their own surveillance, those utopians . . . and didn't they, in the end?

Feuerbach was quite right to say, as he often did: I can tell by looking that you're taking off again. Your mind is already set on the great goal. But that's not our business, we're the men with feet planted in daily routine, in the centre of the movement, we have to hold the path, there's no way we'll still be there when the goal's reached. We have to keep our feet on the ground.—These were big words, they confused him . . . though possibly he'd merely formulated them himself in an attempt to articulate Feuerbach's innuendoes. The Major engaged in virtually nothing but innuendo; he was said to have taken several years of philosophy, one of the reasons why W. always felt at something of a disadvantage with his case officer . . . every attempt to think Feuerbach's tossed-out phrases through to the end seemed to wind up as a mental short circuit, abruptly cutting off his own thoughts. But in this the terms of their relationship were preserved: Feuerbach was the superior . . . Strictly speaking, I think like my superior, W. said to himself; and thus it remained.

I can practically tell by looking. You've always got to think everything through and plot it out to the end, said Feuerbach. What is it with you? Do you refuse to believe that other people have done it much better before you? If all you ever do is draw conclusions, and conclusions from those conclusions, isn't there a point where you don't even know what the beginning was?

Feuerbach was right about this as well; here too W. thought the same, all too willing to be roused from his broodings and listen instead to his master's voice.—It really was smarter to sit down at last, to lean back, eyes shut, for all I care, shutting out reality, and find out how the whole story had begun. What had set him on this path whose goal was so remote that it would take generations upon generations to get there.—This was the most self-explanatory question, as superfluous as asking the reasons for his birth. And at this moment, every time, his fatigue gained the upper hand . . . and he heard Feuerbach's voice lecturing on even as he drifted down into the grey world of sleep in which he was freed from all interconnections.

Feuerbach said: You know what, we can't even let ourselves reach the goal, because we're never wrong. We can only act as though we want to reach the goal. You'll kick and scream, but I'm telling you anyway: We are in possession of the sole truth. And for that very reason we can only act as though we were in possession of the sole truth. You know, we can't even let ourselves think it. No, we can't, since every truth exists only through its opposite. If we were proved right, and the sole truth really were on our side alone, we'd be abolishing the proof of the truth. That's why we can only act as though we believed in it . . . otherwise we might end up abolishing truth itself. We'd instantly be nothing but a hollow bluff if we ever achieved the state of sole truth. Probably the classless society would be the most horrific carnage you could possibly imagine. Let's not even go there. Let's go on making the most of our measly talents . . . and jailing people who refuse to believe our bombastic blather. Because that's where they all belong . . .

In other words, on a fundamental level you disbelieve in human goodness?

The very idea! It'd mean we'd immediately have to believe in the accuracy of every statement that lands on our desk. We'd have to take all the selected works of yours you supply us with as the gospel truth, and the same for all the other selected reports. For instance, when we get the assessment that someone . . . let's say you for instance . . . that this Someone, that is,

someone like you, is supposedly less intelligent or less dangerous than the lady friend he associates with, then we know we
have to go by the opposite of this characterization. But that
doesn't preclude our also having to go by the exact wording
of the report.

I don't even have a lady friend, I'm telling you with no
hint of sensitivity.

We always have to go by the opposite of a statement like
that. And then again by the opposite of the opposite . . . we've
worked at this art for a long time, practically done drills in it.
You ought to take more of an interest in dialectics, that's the
science we need, as long as we're still on our way . . . and
unfortunately you don't show much sign of it . . .

Feuerbach's closing sequences were always especially
impressive. These and many other phrases from the lips of his
case officer had accumulated over time in W.'s memory, and
during his leisure hours in the basement they would unwind
almost of their own accord. The assessment was all too justified:
W. had long begun to think exactly like his superior.—But
this thought gave him no satisfaction.

His conversations with the Major sidestepped all hints as
to how his career had begun . . . by which W. meant his career
as an Unofficial Collaborator or UnCol of the 'Firm' (this was
the standard term, which the institution's members had evidently put into circulation themselves) . . . he had always wondered whether Feuerbach even knew anything about it. He
himself saw the memory lapse as a result of his overlong sleep
phase; that was evidently why the time was referred to this way,
serving as it did to obliterate all the reasons for your 'collaborator's' existence, so completely that it looked as though you'd
acquired the position in a dream . . . that is, according to Freud,
as the result of a wish fulfilment fantasy.—It was hard to say
how this happened; evidently each prospective collaborator had

moments in his past he found necessary to conceal, believing them to be irreparable lapses; it had to be a blunder capable of causing lasting remorse. And when the repercussions were out of proportion to their cause, and the patient saw his offence, or his transgression, as the kind of existential catastrophe he'd find it hard to live with, the ideal conditions were in place for a dependency on the Firm . . . if necessary they had to be achieved by first stoking the patient's sense of guilt. The patient's sleep now served to heal his crisis of conscience; he awoke with the happy feeling of being a blameless, worthwhile person . . . once this phase was over he was surrounded by a hermetic space of profound silence regarding his deed.—Was it even a deed, in W's case? This was exactly what the hermetic silence made it impossible to learn.

No wonder he got the idea that all such catastrophes in the former lives of the Firm's employees had been meticulously planned and carefully constructed. The Firm was the world's most moral institution, pedantically registering every transgression that could possibly be developed. And when W. gave it serious thought, it struck him that this was its one and only function: the collection of punishable factors, or what looked like punishable factors, for every subject it singled out. And as practically every subject came into question as a collaborator for the service, the never-ending task of the apparatus was to create conditions in which a reservoir of punishable factors stood at the ready for, in principle, everyone. And should the utopian state be achieved in which no more offences occurred, or hardly any, then the limit would have to be lowered and lowered until ultimately almost every action could be classified as an offence. When this system came to an end, what a seed of offence would shoot up from its soil . . . I didn't want to think about it: at any rate, we were essential for this reason alone.

Of course it couldn't be about punishing everyone, it was about pressing everyone into service. This was the only answer to the question of each operation's aim, this was the only reason they had been instituted . . . each operation aimed only to engender as long a series as possible (best of all an infinite series) of further operations—and each operation had to end with a recruitment to the service of the organization.

The reality of this apparatus is the attempt to create a state of collaborators, thought W.; he thought it in the lethargic, muddled moments in which he emerged from his half-sleep. And if you see the whole story in these terms, it doesn't sound very menacing at all.

What catastrophe began it for me?—Either he hadn't had one, or there had been little occasion yet for him to be reminded of it. For of course the hermetic silence was sinister; the deeper it grew, the more it seemed like a lull before the storm; if you didn't keep on track, the catastrophe could re-emerge at any moment . . . from that half-sleep, and by then it would surely have blown up into an irreparable catastrophe. They kept this surprise in store, at any rate.—So in his case that meant he'd stayed on track so far . . . that was a favourite expression at the Firm: he'd kept on track, he'd had a good track record, been a good tracking dog!—If he wanted to know his catastrophe, then in future he'd have to steer in a different direction, sniff a bit to the left and right of the track, not always bolt hot and blind towards the goal, they didn't want that anyway, with their constant chatter about vigilance . . .

On the other hand, too much vigilance also unnerved them . . . this vigilance had to stay on track. There was a joke they often told at the Firm: At a big Party congress, one member of the audience is suddenly arrested. Why him? Because as we've always said: The class enemy never sleeps!

Don't get distracted . . . most of what you learn, you learn from the adversary! These could have been Feuerbach's words.—For a while he was determined to ask the Major who he'd meant by the woman on whom he, W., had supposedly provided sloppy reports or none at all, forcing them to spend 'a hell of a lot of time' filling in the missing information.—W. had an idea who was meant, though; how long had they already been grilling her—W.'s 'very good lady acquaintance'—up there on the higher levels . . . did they also go into the things best described as his catastrophe?—He'd always told himself the catastrophe was that there'd been no catastrophe in his former life . . . his signature was nothing but a symptom of fatigue . . . a fatigue now encased by a further shell of weariness.—All the same, his vague memories weren't very pleasant: this very good acquaintance was a creature who answered to the exotic name of Cindy (that didn't mean it was her real name); at the time she was the ubiquitous appendage of a circle of young men in the town where W. lived. He couldn't have said what advantages he'd gained by his entrée into this circle . . . but this entrée itself, he now knew, was seen as an advantage and gained him a further entry: to a higher circle . . . and there in turn entries opened up all the way to Berlin, as now he thought he knew. It was quite a few years back . . . Feuerbach, W. said to himself, probably remembered better than he did, although surely the Major had never been in A. and before meeting W. hadn't even known that the town existed . . . that there existed towns in the Republic where the only hope of survival for citizens of the younger generation was alcohol . . . or the hope of defection. The only thing W. had in common with these young men was the penchant for alcohol and the frequent patronization of the same pubs, of which the town admittedly had few to choose from. Unlike the establishments frequented by W.'s work colleagues, these were the gathering places of the slightly shady circles whose routines consisted principally of avoidance strategies: the avoidance of orderly routine and the drift away from the thick of the socialist production front. In other words, people whose abstinence from steady employment had made them lose the worker's finely tuned instinct which would have flagged W. as a foreign body in their midst. More and more often he had the opposite experience with his work colleagues: they knew the pubs he went to, you didn't have to explain it to them, they smelt it . . . and in the wrinkling of their noses W. thought he detected an olfactory sense in no way inferior to that of noses lifted in more bourgeois fashion. They sensed an outsider immediately; he wouldn't have minded if they'd taken him for a would-be intellectual slumming from sheer snobbery in the dingy dives. That's how he would have explained it to himself; a writer must be able to distinguish local colour from cosmetics. And that didn't preclude his occasionally developing understanding and sympathy for those who had fallen out the bottom of society and surfaced again in a pool of alcohol; they simply showed what this society was floating on. As often and as long as he tagged along in that loose-knit group, in his mind there was always an escape route open, and his tendency towards cool observation prevented him from fully acclimatizing to this circle where all differences were blurred by a haze of beer . . . a cool observer is homeless everywhere, he consoled himself.— In this loose-knit group Cindy fluttered tirelessly back and forth; more precisely, she passed from hand to hand, or at least that was his impression. But he told himself there was no need to make a fuss about it never being his turn, even though Cindy had gone round the circle several times already . . . each time he thought his hour had come, a certain Harry slipped between them . . . and no wonder; this Harry was slender and slick as a fish . . . besides, it was a point which kept re-establishing his outsider role, and that was what he wanted to cement. For all that, his relationship to Cindy wasn't bad at all, on the contrary, this fostered a kind of trust between them, at least on Cindy's part: he confined himself more to the role of her patient listener. In this way W. quickly learnt almost everything about the male members of the pub fraternity, disreputable things as a rule; it was a mystery to him why Cindy, with any number of embarrassing and occasionally horrific things to report, didn't grow more attached to her confessor, who, given that he agreed with circle . . . incidentally, this Harry came off especially badly, even if her stories about him sounded a bit more cautious . . . as though she had a certain fear of him.—One evening she told W. that she'd have to report for a prison sentence. He was sitting by himself in the pub, the door opened and Cindy made a beeline for his table as though she'd been looking for him, a moment that always cost him a struggle; she was a flamboyant figure in this small town, tall and radiating vigour, on her lower arm a purse laden with metal ornaments jangled with her long strides, her head bristled with a red- or black-dyed mane of kinky artificial curls known as an Afro-look, her eyes were always heavily made up, and her full lips beamed . . . She's almost a gypsy, thought W.— This time her lips weren't beaming, her mouth was oddly shrunken. She sat down and tried to tug the very tight skirt towards her knees, then without beating about the bush began to discuss her immediate future; W. thought he detected a faint tremble in her voice. She would have to report by eleven the next morning to start serving her sentence; due to a series of negligible missteps that had come to light, she had been sentenced—a year ago already—to six or eight months in prison (a minor sentence whose exact length W. had forgotten; it could just as well have been seven or nine months) . . . and now her time had come!—She fell into the category of the self-reporters, people convicted of petty crimes who had to wait until a place opened up for them in the overfilled prisons, a stipulation which most experienced as an additional form of chicanery.

The same went for Cindy; face pale, close to tears but fighting them bravely, she said: They can only do that because no one can bail out over their borders.

W. agreed; he would have thought she'd be more jaded, though, since it was hardly her first time, and besides it was really a minimal sentence. His explanation was that she'd had to live with the unpleasant prospect for an entire year. Now he thought he understood the rather grim expression he'd noticed lately in her otherwise soft and girlish face. Her eyes had begun to flicker, too; with the smoke from her cigarette she sucked air audibly between her teeth, then bit her lips together, which gave her a severe, determined expression. She stared at W. with bloodshot eyes.

He avoided her gaze and asked as casually as possible: Is it your first time in there?

Of course, she said, what do you think? But even if it weren't, I know what it's like for Harry . . . for him it gets worse and worse every time.

It's not like you have to compete with him! said W.

He didn't believe her, incidentally; as far as he'd heard, it wasn't customary to keep debutants waiting to start their sentence, given the incalculable risks which the involuntary postponement entailed; as a rule, self-reporters were repeat offenders whose behaviour was familiar to the authorities.

Over the course of the evening they drank a great deal of alcohol, and W. was nervous when it came to paying the bill. To console Cindy he walked her home afterwards. She lived at the other end of town, her street was in the exact opposite direction from his; she accepted his companionship in the ice-cold night as indifferently as she'd watched the bill being paid, taciturn and preoccupied as they walked. W., not without ulterior motives in accompanying her, was disappointed once again.—She had things to pack and didn't have the time, she said at the door to her building, and even refused him the obligatory parting kiss. W., holding her by the hips, hesitated, feeling rebuffed.—You'd just regret it, she said; and the words that followed seemed odd to him, but he put them down to the tension of her situation: You'd think about it for ever, but you'd have gotten nothing out of it, you'd just regret it. It's better if you keep your hands off me . . . I've got other things on my mind. All you'll get is trouble, if I were you I'd have gotten out of here long ago.

He wasn't the type to assert himself against other people's will; he headed home.—Over the following months he lost almost all contact with the circle of pub-crawlers; he had to admit to himself that it was really only Cindy who'd still kept him coming; and last but not least, he'd plunged back into literature, reading a whole series of books, each halfway through, putting back the rest for later, and continued working on a conglomeration of texts with no idea what it was meant to become. He'd been working on this opus—more a collection of fragments—for years now, but usually he'd given up again after a week of trying. This time he kept at it from early spring to the beginning of autumn, albeit without achieving any satisfying results. The text or texts—it was really impossible to say—were an uneven mixture of hypertrophic self-stylization (of an invented self) and the sober description of everyday details from his real life. In his 'fictions' his I often fled so far into fantastic realms—remote times or thought-up landscapes—that he had to drag it back by inserting his boring reality: to keep from losing it entirely!—Usually these were descriptions of his evenings at the pub, the alcohol he consumed there serving as a pretext for detaching his I from reality.

All that summer he spent most of his time at the bars his colleagues went to after work—as though this too might help him keep his bearings at a time when he seemed to struggle to maintain his grip on reality. And he was made to feel the extent of the mistrust that had already built up against him. A distance had developed, one he sensed nowhere near as clearly during working hours in the factory: now he suddenly realized that they had become suspicious of him ... no doubt, he surmised, due to his dealings with people who in his colleagues' opinion disdained steady employment; in other words, his colleagues felt disdained by a bunch of barflies, and punished them for it with redoubled contempt! Earlier W. had mainly had to listen to his colleagues' jibes after he racked up absences due to his alcohol-sodden nights (meanwhile putting up with his drinking buddies' jokes when he left to make it to work early the next morning, which he didn't always manage, not by a long shot) ... now the accusations against him had become more concrete—the less justified they were, the more vexing they grew.—Once he was asked whether he only took notes on what went on at the factory, or also on what they, his colleagues, talked about here in the pub. Alarmed, he beat a retreat for that evening, shaking his head.—Then he recalled one time at the factory when he'd been seen noting down a few thoughts he wanted to remember to put in his literary opus. He was sitting in the empty staff room, a largish basement room next to the factory kitchen; above him, at head height, was a ground-level window, and suddenly its light had gone dark; looking up, he saw the awkwardly grinning faces of several onlookers who made off as soon as he spotted them.

And so it wasn't just the disrepute gained by association with a bunch of so-called shirkers. Suddenly W. faced the suspicions the workers felt towards a person who wrote down mysterious words he refused to divulge to them.

This person laboriously plotting formulations onto paper . . . and they must have seen how he squeezed the words that wouldn't fit, how he choked on them; you could almost hear him holding his breath and groaning . . . whom was this grim-faced person describing, whom had this notary denounced just now, gazing up with such a stricken look? Whom was he fooling with his oil-stained, sooty clothes, if not his colleagues . . . what was he putting himself above, what was he agitating against? You could smell how he got off on the imperfection of the collective he'd wormed his way into . . . even if he was still hunkering down in his hole, he had long since risen to a different estate. He himself need not have sensed it yet, but it was obvious to each of the colleagues he'd forsaken. Each one smelt it . . . it was the class sense of smell . . . the workers had immediately grasped the full import of his actions.—He who first set pen to paper was all too deserving of suspicion. Their wordless wisdom recognized the rupture at once: he had erected a wall of letters between them. . . and from then on he was a man of the Party. There was no other explanation! Possibly, too, he was the man of an opposing party . . . no matter; true to the letter of the law, as the saying went, he was now ascending into realms in which they, the workers, were nothing but cheap propaganda material. And that made this scribbler a still sleazier character—as they'd always suspected—than the drinkers he associated with for his decadent purposes: it made him one of the scoundrels who wrote for the apocalypse . . .

No doubt about it, here he was getting at what went on in the minds of the working class in this country . . . any some-what-more-benign supposition would have been a lazy evasion (incidentally, Feuerbach appreciated those who harboured no illusions about the relationship between intellectuals and workers in this country; he was convinced of the truth of a certain legend: at the Firm they often claimed to have good relations with the real men on the production front, better at least than with artists and writers . . .)

Never you mind about that.—One evening at the pub, late in September, W. heard from a colleague—the one who had once asked about the notes he was taking—that the 'dyed redhead with the Afrowig' would be back from the slammer any day now, if she wasn't back already, and now the Nook and the Fuse would be hopping again, two of the pubs W. had avoided that summer.—It was hard to picture how this colleague had found out the date of her release; a small town had no secrets. W. himself had hardly given Cindy another thought . . . he'd been preoccupied with his writing attempts: the only possibly strange thing was that all the female characters in his texts had red hair—and no faces; their faces were left as white sheets of paper on which any mark might be made.

Tired of his colleague's insinuations, W. left for the notorious Beer Nook several blocks away, one of the pubs patronized by the other faction of his acquaintances. There he ran into Harry, who was part of this group, though not, in W.'s view, the best of company, what with his rather tiresome quirks. First, he never paid for his drinks, and second, he'd fasten himself night after night to any listener willing or defenceless enough to be regaled with tireless accounts of the prison terms Harry had served. These were so dragged out with endless repetitions that W.—initially intrigued by this intimate knowledge of all conceivable institutions—now found them unendurable; besides, he'd begun to suspect that Harry, at his age, could really have seen just a fraction of it all. Harry had always struck W. as a particularly shady character, though he'd felt moments of pity, even empathy towards him; he was an extremely thin, almost see-through man of furtive, hasty demeanour who wore his white-blond hair down to his shoulders, though that was long out of fashion; his face was sallow and sweaty, and in the overheated bar he had removed his light blue faded denim jacket to expose upper arms covered with crude tattoos. When he saw W., a flush of joyful excitement spread from his face down his thin sinewy neck into these upper arms; now that W. had patiently lent him his ear a few times, Harry thought the world of him and vaunted his friendship just as tirelessly as his acquaintance with penal institutions. W., about to beat a retreat when he saw the white-blond figure, was collared and told—after a gush of enthusiasm about finally running into each other again after all this time—that he'd come at just the right moment, like he always did, because Harry was arranging a rendezvous that wouldn't even be possible without him, it was a rendezvous for four, and W. absolutely had to come along. So W. sat down, they drank beer, Harry wrapped himself in pregnant silence—there really had to be an event in store if he was acting like this—only now and then twitching his white, nearly non-existent lashes. Sometimes he'd disappear and actually seemed to be settling something at the bar. At closing time, W., who paid the bill, was put off until the next day: same place, at the Nook, don't forget!—The next day W. went out of sheer curiosity, but Harry seemed to have forgotten about the rendezvous. Shortly before closing time he suddenly appeared with a young, slightly feral girl and announced that they could now go to the flat as arranged. He introduced the kid as Herta; she was utterly nondescript, dressed much too thinly for the autumn night, and said not a word the whole time; her brown eyes had such a blank, absent look that W. began to think she was either deaf and dumb or feebleminded.—But we'll have to bring along a few bottles, said Harry, and W. went up to the bar and bought those bottles too.

Shortly after that Harry rang furiously at the door of Cindy's building; it took an incredibly long time—next to W. the girl froze wretchedly in the already biting-cold air—for the light to go on in the stairwell.—Cindy went up the stairs ahead of W.; he'd barely recognized her. She was wrapped tight in an enormous bathrobe that dragged on the steps, its original colour impossible to guess . . . her hair, too, was so ruined and discoloured that W., eying her as they climbed, was unable to suppress a shudder. It looked as though her head had recently been shaved, and now the hair had sprouted back in irregular tufts that stuck out every which way, bare patches still showing like marks of violence or the traces of a skin disease. A clearly inadequate attempt had been made to dye the individual strands, leaving a botched tangle of unsightly shades with white bald spots gleaming in-between. And Cindy showed other signs of disfigurement: her face was scabbed, swellings not yet subsided were suffused with dark blood. W. was just about to ask what had happened to her when he saw the appalling state of her flat. Wherever he looked, some indefinable mush, grey-white to yellowish in colour, had been spilt . . . or stashed away. The substance was like a strange discharge, already partly dried, the mush accreting like plaster in every corner; pails, pots, cardboard boxes were filled to overflowing; the kitchen was saturated with a cloying smell of spoilage that could come only from this pale mass covered with brown patches of fermentation . . . W. promptly learnt the erstwhile purpose of the substance: without missing a beat Harry vanished into the sole adjoining room with the nondescript girl . . . Cindy yanked a pram out of the cramped room, as though it needed rescuing from the couple. In the carriage was a baby: it began to cry, and Cindy lifted it and rocked it with listless resignation at her breast, hidden by the filthy bathrobe, and after a while the baby actually quieted down . . . From sheer weakness, W. thought, now realizing that the omnipresent whitish mush was uneaten baby food; it was so-called instant formula, the kind concocted from a granulated powder and water or milk to make a drink ready for the bottle; now he also noticed the empty paper packaging scattered around the kitchen. The baby had clearly rejected this food, and now the liquid, in various stages of putrefaction, indeed petrifaction, filled every available container, wallowing across the floor and mounting in the recesses of the kitchenette; on the stove, on three-quarters of the tabletop, on the unused chairs towered pots, pans, bottles and jars, all of them filled or half-filled with the mush which, as it fermented or solidified, sent up bubbles and turned everything into an insoluble sweetly stinking chaos before congealing. The sink and the drain pipe were full of mush wallowing mountains of dishes and paper bags, also filled with mush . . . but the grimmest sight was the stove, where the ash-bin jutted out brimful of mush; the rings of the top plate had been removed, in the heedlessness of desperation the weeks' worth of mush cooked in vain had been dumped into the stove, and now it oozed out the cracks in the fire door, seeped out again through all the leaks in the guard-plate and collected on the floor. There the viscous, spreading puddle had been dammed up with baby nappies; but the dike of nappies, partly used nappies, had failed to contain the flood, which seeped through the petrified nappies and beyond, discoloured by the soiled bulwarks of cloth and paper, and flowed in reeking brownish rills towards the centre of the kitchen.

It seemed that all attempts to feed the infant this mush had failed . . . and W. saw the tiny frail creature dangling motionless in Cindy's helpless hands, he heard it utter cries in what could barely be called a voice, so faint and strangled that it was impossible to tell whether they weren't merely the short quick breaths emerging from the withered bluish little face.

In that first moment W. fled to the toilet, but he found it too brimful of mush, stuffed with nappies which in turn were drowned in mush ... when he came back Harry emerged— not half an hour had passed—from the adjoining room, holding a pair of elastic-less underwear over his flat stomach, tattooed like his nearly consumptive pink chest with its covering of white down; he pointed through the open door into the unlit chamber: Go on over if you want ... I'm done, and you can go on over if you want.

W. shook his head, casting about for an opportunity to disappear.—Is there a bar still open? he asked.—You might be able to get in the Fuse the back way, said Harry. But how come you don't want to go on over first? You paid for the bottles of wine, after all.—But not with me! Cindy broke in.—No, said W., I'd better be going ...

He was already in the hall when Cindy gave the baby to Harry, who was sitting on the couch, and followed him. She grabbed W. by the shoulder and pushed him up against the banister until he was

pinned by her slender sinewy body with the railing at his back. He breathed the smell of the matted, scabby bathrobe and leant his head back; she wrapped her arms around his neck and stared him in the face, her eyes flashing inches away: Why don't you want to go on over, over on little Herta, maybe she's waiting for you?

When W. gave no reply, Cindy said: Because you only want to do it with me, right? You only came because of me, you don't want to do it with her, you only want me, am I right? Could be, said W.

All right ... but it's no good your trying it with me, it's no good, because Harry's here now.

How long have you had the baby? asked W., Did you have it in prison?

Sure, in the slammer, that gave me a few days peace and quiet. Why are you asking, you ought to know . . .

And who is the father? Is Harry the father?

It's possible, she said, you could be right about that. Anyway, he's here now, and so it's no good your trying tonight. Whether I like it or not . . . you'll have to wait, till later, because Harry's going back to the slammer soon. It won't be much longer . . .

Does Harry know he's the father, does he even want to know?

He's going back to the slammer soon, she said. What does the baby need with a father like that?

Is he a self-reporter, does he have to report again . . .? asked W.,

Isn't there any way out of this mess?

Yes, he has to report . . . and it can happen to me again too any time now. A way out . . . no, it's not like we can hide here . . .

Several weeks later W. received a letter from the Town Council, Department of Child and Youth Welfare; it was a summons to a hearing and requested a statement from his place of employment confirming the amount of his most recent annual income. It noted that the unexcused failure to comply with this request could have legal consequences. Unsuspecting, he went there at the appointed time, though without the requested wage statement. An official of indeterminate, eternal middle age—eerily absent, processing, as she was, one case among many, which always ran along the exact same lines and required only a fixed number of phrases, making her adopt a tone of impersonal admonition even when asking for W.'s personal data—advised him that he had been named as the father of a child, male, born on . . . (a date followed, this too in a half-indignant, half-resigned tone, carried on out of routine into the mumbling repetition of the syllables typed on the typewriter) by the mother of the child . . . now a name followed. W. hadn't caught the name of the child's mother. He was herewith called upon to fulfil his obligation to pay the mother a monthly allowance for the child until it came of age, contingent upon his present average annual income.—Now, said the woman, we must determine the legally stipulated sum, which you may voluntarily raise at your discretion for the good of your child.—W. denied everything he had heard, utterly at random, immediately realizing the futility of every word he could possibly say . . . I've been had, was his only thought, and it was probably written all over him.—You can contest it, said the woman. But if you have any luck, it'll be a first in my career.—She pulled the sheet of paper out of the typewriter and laid it in front of W.—he didn't recognize the name under the heading Mother of the Child, but he guessed at once that it was Cindy's real name he'd stumbled across.—That has to be a mistake! said W., but evidently his own voice was inaudible to him. He was warned that he'd have to face the consequences, that is, bear the costs of the forensic examination, if it should turn out that he was denying his paternity in order to evade his legal obligation to support . . . Unfortunately you're no exception, quite the contrary, said the woman. And you should save yourself the trouble.

Possibly this last remark had come during the second hearing to which he was summoned a short time later . . . after the shock of the first one he hadn't reacted at all, waiting for the mistake to clear itself up. After a brief exchange with the official he was asked into a different office. The room was surprisingly inviting; unlike the previous one, at least, there was no grille with a chest-level writing ledge immediately inside the door, barricading it against petitioners and the subpoenaed.

W. was urged to take an armchair diagonally opposite a desk that was bare but for an enormous potted plant and a used coffee cup. Behind it sat a man in a grey suit (W. asked himself whether suits even came in other colours in this country), again between forty and fifty, his temples streaked with grey; he didn't look like someone who worked for the low-level department in which child-support claims were processed. Breezy, thought W., that's a good word for this gentleman . . .

No, it wasn't Feuerbach—W. shook his head, lost in thought—the first lieutenant hadn't appeared until later . . . still, this other man embodied an equally ageless type . . . Feuerbach could well have appeared at this point, and the other could well have appeared in Berlin.—One time another man in a grey suit, about the same age, came into the room, said two or three words, and left again . . . W. wondered whether this was when he first heard the bass voice from the office next to Feuerbach's (from the back office, from the main office?).—All he could remember with any degree of clarity was the first remarks by the man at the desk: Well, finally I get to see you in person! Actually, you could congratulate me on my birthday, if you like, but I'm afraid the coffee's all gone . . . He waited a little to see the effect these collusively ironic words upon W. . . . Nonsense, he added then, you have yourself to congratulate!

W. had still harboured the hope that this might at least be a public prosecutor . . . though it was improbable that an authority with the final word in child-support cases should make an appearance now . . . Who are you? asked W.; he shouldn't have done that, he knew. What he was told he later found downright implausible: the discussion seemed to labour in a spasm of contradictions; it was a maddening unresolvable error in which bo-th sides persisted in different ways . . . later W. had the sense of a nightmare. This sense was heightened by the fact that the issue ostensibly at stake was promptly forgotten . . . after the breezy gentleman had summoned him two or three more times (within weeks even the number of these conversations faded from his memory), the whole affair seemed to break off inconclusively. W., with only a very conditional belief in the congruence of his perceptions with reality, came more and more to doubt the accuracy of his memories.

The man in the grey suit had put it to him that they were quite grateful for a few very important pieces of information he'd provided . . . such timely assistance had not been anticipated . . . W. didn't feel he was meant, thought he'd been mistaken for someone else . . . Who is 'we'? he asked.—The other didn't even respond to the question: Concerning that circle where that Harry Falbe kept trying to play his role, unfortunately they were groping in the dark; they were less and less able to keep tabs on these people . . . We never hit on the notion that you might provide a valuable link to this circle, said the breezy gentleman, we didn't even venture the thought. —You didn't even venture the thought . . . repeated W., who is 'we'?—Another thing . . . the gentleman appeared to change the subject. Regarding your child-support obligations for your little son . . . surely you've noticed that the State is footing the bill. Punctually and in full, every month . . . yes, really you can congratulate yourself on that as well. Have you visited the child lately?—There is no child I should have to pay for, said W.; that struck him as the first concrete statement of the conversation—which was evidently why it evaporated without a trace.—He hadn't even been prepared to state his annual income—well then, they'd found that out for him too. There was no great sum to be paid, not much . . . and so it wasn't much they had in mind by way of a quid pro quo!

With surprising calm W. replied: Never! There will be no quid pro quo from me, and the State needn't pay a pfennig on my behalf. There is no child . . . that's a fabrication!

There is no child . . . I see! Well then . . . if you say so! As the grey gentleman continued, W. searched his face for a flicker of emotion he could read somehow—there was no emotion.—You know, we can imagine that you don't earn much, especially now that you've gotten yourself moved out of the assembly hall and into the boiler room, that's a setback. It makes you vulnerable when you suddenly have to pay child support too, that's why we're concerned. And we also know you could achieve more as a writer than in the boiler room . . . (W. asked himself whether the man had said: Achieve more for society . . .)

More valuable things than down there in the boiler room, the gentleman went on after a pause. But of course you'd earn even less, at first, anyway. Naturally, as you will have noticed, the payments have already begun . . .

Once again, W. interrupted him, speaking as though in a soundproof chamber, once again, the State doesn't need to pay me a pfennig . . .

Of course not, said the gentleman, of course it doesn't need to, whatever are you thinking? Did you really imagine we hadn't thought of that? You don't get a pfennig, of course, the payments go de facto to the mother of the child. But, as you probably know, she's run up big debts with the State . . . and she doesn't have a clean slate, either! But she'll give us what we need sure enough! So practically no money changes hands, you understand, we've just got to keep the receipts going strong. And as far as your quid pro quo, the only thing would be . . .

There won't be any quid pro quo from me, none!

That's all we ask. Don't you understand, the only quid pro quo is that you keep mum about it. That you genuinely keep mum about the whole business . . . not a word to anyone about this baby! That you genuinely act as if you didn't have a child . . . then you'll be acting exactly in our interests.

W. hadn't thought himself still capable of anything like bafflement: Now what am I really supposed to do, in your opinion—should I acknowledge the child, or should I keep quiet about it?

The gentleman sighed, as if overtaxed by the difficulty of the explanation he was about to provide: The best thing is for you to act exactly as usual . . . really, that's the best thing!

No . . . said W.

Yes it is . . . said the gentleman, it's not that hard, just act as if we didn't even exist!

No, said W., for me you really don't exist!

Wonderful! said the gentleman.

You don't! It's not: as if you didn't exist, it's: that you don't exist! said W.

What a subtle distinction! Isn't it silly of us to take it all so seriously? I'll think about it, I'll let you know the upshot the next time we see each other, maybe here in Room 17, maybe somewhere else . . .

No, said W., don't expect me to get involved with you. As far as I'm concerned, the issue is closed!

That's perfectly all right, he said, it's high time we closed it then.

I'd much rather talk literature with you, that's my issue, properly speaking. The matter is closed, no more child issue, no more Harry Falbe . . .

I'll be going now . . . if you don't mind!

That's fine, he said, I didn't want to keep you, you're a busy man. With us, mind you, you'll sometimes have to act as if the things that don't exist were really there.

W. hoisted himself up out of the armchair and was on his way to the door when the man behind the desk called him back again: One more thing! I'm going to shout something down the stairs after you, please don't get me wrong. It's best you act as if you hadn't heard it at all.—W. left without a parting word; as he went down the staircase a door flew open upstairs; he quickened his steps but could not escape the voice shouting across the town hall lobby: Don't do a thing for us, it's all for your child! And don't forget to do something for yourself!

That wasn't the last of it for the day. On into the evening he'd tried to come to grips with that morning's conversation ... the whole thing was a nightmare! He hadn't gone back to work afterwards; until long after dark he'd sat at home, impervious to his mother's hesitant questions, trying to gain back some sense that he was living in reality ... Who was that person actually talking to this morning? Certainly not to me ... his only hope lay in questions like that. The whole story has nothing to do with me ... the matter is closed, no more child issue, no more Harry Falbe ... no more Room 17.—Only when it had grown dark outside the kitchen windows and the influx of street noise had ebbed did he feel like himself again. As twilight fell in the rising autumn mist, the trundle and screech of vehicles on the street had seemed oddly urgent and theatrical, like the clamour of already sleepy children who feel it necessary, from sheer exhaustion, to make an especially vivid display of high spirits ... what a strange simile. Now the noise faded off towards the centre of town; his mother had finally left him alone and gone to bed in the belief that he wanted to work on his writing; the sort of reason for which he'd withdrawn from her all summer long, his thoughts seemingly elsewhere.

This evening he'd had that same abstracted and unapproachable demeanour . . . now, as the doorbell rang, he knew at once that they were back.—The gangling young man outside had to be a novice; at first glance he hardly seemed to have much self-confidence. He leant his entire length upon the doorjamb, bending slightly over W., but seemed to face him only halfway, remaining in communication with another person evidently waiting on the landing below, invisible to W. Only the slight creak of the wooden steps made this person's presence felt . . . and the young man leaning on the doorjamb spoke louder than necessary—the person below had to be able to hear the words—so that W. was afraid his mother would hear. He was requested to appear at the town hall again two days from now, once again in Room 17, and in the morning again, if that suited him . . . Remember: Room 17! And if you forget, then just ask for the boss.

It doesn't suit me, said W., I'm not going to talk to you at all any more. This is the last time, I refuse . . . if you come in, I'll make you a coffee, then we can talk more quietly. And you can explain the whole thing to me . . . I'll tell you my position, you can have it in writing if you want. And that will be the end of our conversations.

Nonsense, said the young man, you haven't even talked to me yet!

Now the light went out in the stairwell; W. turned it on, reaching his hand past his lanky visitor's lower arm to grope for the switch; with the light back on he saw the lanky man smile as though to ask W.'s indulgence for the trouble he was forced to cause him—or as though sorry about the trouble W. was causing himself—and at the same time, as though unintentionally, place his foot between the threshold and the opened door.

That's nonsense, he said, if we want you to, you have to come.

Fine, said W., then force me if you want, but I'll never come of my own free will!

No, that's nonsense! called a voice from the landing below (W. attempted in vain to identify it as the voice of the breezy gentleman from that morning). Tell him there's no way we'll do it in his flat! He can't want his mother to find out about this paternity affair. Do we want her there when we have to ask him the last time he and this so-called Cindy . . . no!

Though actually we know that, said the young man next to W.

You'll never be able to prove it! said W. I never . . . He was interrupted by the rattle of a latch; upstairs, on the next floor, a door had opened, someone was about to go out into the hall; there was only an old woman living up there.—Go back inside immediately! a male voice commanded from the third floor; W. realized that a third sentry had been posted upstairs. Get back in! Don't leave your flat when we're here. And don't even think of eavesdropping at the door again!—The old woman's hasty shuffle was heard, the door closed.

What do you mean, never! the man on the lower landing said much too loudly. Do you really believe we can't pin the child on you?

Oh yes we can, even if you never laid a woman in your life.

Fine then, said W., see you in two days . . . I'll be there!

At that the lanky young man unstuck himself from the doorjamb, but remained standing where he was, staring wordlessly until W. realized that he was supposed to disappear. He did, but peered out through the letter slot; only when the stair light switched off did footsteps approach from upstairs; in the meantime a car had started up in front of the house, a door slammed, the engine revved, and the car screeched off down the street; in every respect the soundtrack of a B-movie.

Further summons had followed, the details exhaustingly repetitive, he could no longer tell the meet-ups apart (suddenly this term for his appearances at the town hall had crept in), though each time it was a different grey-suited gentleman he met . . . all about the same age . . . no, it might actually have been the same one each time. The meet-ups interwove and intertwined, the conversations held there became more and more banal and insignificant . . . Spare me the details!

Soon the washed-out fog of the grey autumn and winter days, sinking over his path to the town hall and back, had covered the town for good . . . and in this dusk it was lost to him. In the oppressive, vaporous light he soon saw nothing but shadows meeting, or barely crossing paths, nodding at one another over their shoulders, touching hands conspiratorially as they came out of the doors, as they went in the doors, exchanging furtive words amid poorly feigned coughing fits. He himself was one of these shadows, he had soon forgotten which one . . . which one had gone to the town hall for a chat, which one returned from the town hall, angry at statements they'd chatted about . . . and he was angry at his shadow that remained in the town hall, sitting there and chatting . . . Don't make me say any more!

Even on that first evening visit, of which he still had an approximate picture, they hadn't actually negotiated with him, but with an imaginary character, with a notion of him they'd concocted in their minds. The lanky fellow leaning on the doorjamb, hadn't he all too clearly spoken over his head . . . into empty space? Not into empty space; he'd addressed his words to a ghost which invisible to W. had risen from the wall behind . . . the lanky man had spoken with a figure that filled W.'s shadow in the background. This shadow was a projection . . . yet made entirely of his being: of thoughts he hadn't yet discovered in his mind, of nerves he hadn't yet needed, of sensations he hadn't yet experienced within . . . and perhaps this projection commanded a language which he hadn't yet spoken, but which had lingered in him at the ready. And he knew he'd be able to understand it, if only he yielded to it.

They had completely passed him over, then, with those words they spoke in his direction from different sides; what he'd been until that evening, they had disregarded, merely using him as an interposed medium for their thoughts on the one side and on the other side, and in so doing they had spoken to—and brought to life—a structure within him of whose existence they could have had but a purely theoretical notion . . . perhaps every person harboured this structure, or every person of a certain character profile to which W. belonged? All they'd had to do was complete him to accord with this structure . . . they'd filled his customary stock of signs with more complete contents . . . previously he had lived in the delusion that complete contents should suffice, but they had found the heightened form.

They needed him in different places at once, they needed him in different times at once; this was possible only when chronologies were imposed upon the circumstances in retrospect; life was thereby transformed into a theory; apparently there was a structure within him that coped quite well with that. They had spoken to him from different floors, and he had functioned.—Now they needed only to seal him off from the voices of his former life, so that he would hear them from a distance, while teaching him to speak in different voices, in feigned voices . . . he could recall the desire to speak in a feigned voice from his very early childhood. Could this be about rekindling certain influences from his early childhood? —W. vaguely recalled that as a child he'd always been fleeing from his mother . . . and thus, perhaps, unconsciously seeking his father?

As far as he recalled, just a few days later he'd thought he noticed changes in himself. He had a certain detachment from his affairs, in some unclear fashion taking them more lightly than usual. During his early shift at the factory one of the foremen confronted him because he'd vanished after lunch several times recently. Instead of the usual stammering search for an answer he'd come to expect from himself, he'd given the foreman the brush-off: he hadn't seen him hanging around the factory then either, not to mention a couple of other guys from division management; in fact, when he left the production hall he'd seen them back in the factory yard busy washing their private cars during working hours. That had demotivated him . . . incidentally, in the near future he had better prospects opening up. Better than killing time tearing up holes in this factory because elsewhere more conspicuous ones were being temporarily plugged.

He recalled uttering this in a voice that made the foreman flinch. The man was left speechless; W. had enough time to turn around calmly and walk out of reach, head held high, listening through the noise of the machinery for any sound from behind. And the foreman didn't come after him; later W. saw him sitting solemnly behind the window of the production hall office, his face drained of colour, or so it seemed to W. No more cars were washed in the factory yard that week . . . the foreman must have sensed that W.'s speech was more than a feint. W. was surprised at himself: he'd actually spoken as though he had some sort of backing no one knew about.

And then once again he'd sensed that his colleagues were avoiding him. Previously he'd put this impression down to various flukes; now he noticed that they fell silent when he entered the staff room where they sat drinking beer ... they were practically about to hide their beer bottles from him. But no, they didn't hide their beer bottles as they would have done if the foreman had come in; they fell silent and changed the subject ... they wouldn't have changed the subject if the foreman had come in. Probably he was starting to notice things that had always been the case ... in a strange way his awareness of things he'd never thought about before was heightened. Like it or not, his attention to details was growing ... like it or not, he behaved like a person with an ever-honed eye for others' idiosyncrasies, for the interplay of these idiosyncrasies within the factory collective. Suddenly he registered banalities, he'd developed a sensorium for minutiae ... it struck him that they nodded to one another when he approached them; when three or four of them stood chatting amid the factory noise and he came past, they communicated with their eyes ... no longer would he learn the latest football results they'd just shared; when he tried to ask, they dispersed without a word.— It occurred to him that several colleagues had once observed him making notes for one of the writing projects he'd meant to return to after work ... they'd tried, using the dirtiest of tricks they'd tried to sound him out about it ... at the time he'd sensed them observing him, he'd felt their eyes incessantly scanning him, he was the sole theme of their mistrust, they nosed about him ... from a distance, but with unflagging zeal (with heightened vigilance!); they grew eyes in the backs of their heads when they knew he was behind them. He'd wanted to confront them about it, at least one of them, the one he'd known the longest, but he hadn't managed it. Then he had tried to ignore the whole thing.—Now the tables had turned . . . now they had decided to ignore the matter.

Once, up in the dining hall, he realized he was left all alone at his table . . . and soon after that it dawned on him that for more than a week now he'd been sitting by himself at the dining hall table, rapidly gulping his soup and barely taking time for a cup of coffee. For a week he'd fed like a leper, wanting to go unseen. And yet it wasn't even that they saw him . . . they all seemed to pass his table without a thought, crowding at the other tables, playing cards with a clamour of voices; each latecomer found a chair and pulled it up to one of the already overcrowded tables, preferring to set down his soup bowl in the smallest of spaces, in a flurry of playing cards, between ashtrays fuming with unextinguished butts . . . it was on a day like this that W. decided to hand in his notice.

Can you give us one good reason why you don't want to come any more? one of the grey-suited men asked him in the town hall. We'd also rather we didn't have to drag you in here. We'd much prefer to visit you at a location of your choice. Can you suggest a location?

Because I walk around the factory as if I had an infectious disease, said W. No, there's no place in this town to meet unseen, all eyes are always on you here . . . no, it'd have to be somewhere underground.

You're right, these small towns are just awful, said the other. Do you want us to find you a new job? What do you mean by somewhere underground, anyway . . . do you know a place like that?

No, said W., no, actually I'm very happy with my job at the factory!

What do you want to do, then?

I won't come to you in the town hall any more . . . and I'll tell my colleagues about the whole thing!

The gentleman in the grey suit grinned: I wouldn't do that . . . I'm advising you from experience . . . deconspiration is no picnic, it takes a lot of tenacity. And you have to be prepared to give up everything . . . and then suddenly you've got the enemies you only thought you had before. And as a writer you can't give up everything . . . you need a typewriter, stamps, you need contacts . . .

His relationship with his mother was becoming increasingly fraught as well. At first he put it down to the close quarters they shared. There was too little space for his writing attempts, so he'd got into the habit of waiting until she went to bed, content to devote himself to his writing for an hour or two until fatigue overtook him as well. Now he suddenly felt hemmed in for some reason and began to extend his

sessions into the morning hours—which meant that on the early shift he was rarely able to get up in time and no longer arrived punctually at the factory. But he wrote more often in the afternoons as well,

obstructing the kitchen and reacting with increasing rudeness to his mother's presence or her mere appearance at the door. More and more often she found him asleep at the table before dinner; when she set down the plates he woke in a foul mood and lashed out at her. Usually their fights ended with him threatening to find himself another flat. His mother, a quiet, unassuming woman, was alarmed, but expressed with no trace of gratification her fear that he'd have trouble finding a suitable flat.—I'll get help finding a flat, he said. I have support!—They had never spoken about his writing attempts. With characteristic self-effacement, the old woman—who firmly believed that she would never understand a thing her son did—had transformed herself into a silent shadow whenever she found him in what had long become his typical pose, bent over his notebooks, which seemed to absorb him entirely

. . . and now he claimed it was her silent scurrying that bothered him the most, in fact it was practically orchestrated to bother him—her constant, cautious, reticent circling of his person was an unconscious orchestration and the expression of her doubts about the necessity of his writing. She stopped making dinner and disappeared into the next room; of course she hadn't understood a word of what he'd said. And a short while later he understood himself no better than she; all he knew was that he'd become capable of this kind of carping only in the past few weeks.

Perhaps there was something he saw as a threat to his writing lately . . . not a concrete threat, no one wanted to hinder him. Perhaps it was enough that since recently there were people in town who recognized him as a writer. Yes, they affirmed him in his capacity as a writer; it was a challenge he had yet to live up to.

They dealt him the death blow at the factory by coming to visit one day. He had the early shift that week, and on Friday he topped off his tardiness by arriving at the factory two hours late. The foreman came up to him pale in the face; W., prepared for a royal dressing-down, was surprised by his long-time boss' trembling voice; he'd never heard him talk that way before. The foreman mumbled, barely audible in the drone of machinery, that he shouldn't bother changing his clothes, he'd been expected up in the engineers' office for an hour already.

The management office's two adjoining rooms had been cleared of all staff; two engineers and three female typists huddled by the window at the end of the corridor, leaning silent and shamefaced on the sill, expelled from their power's abode; they ignored W.'s greeting as he came up the stairs. In the back office, the inner sanctum, sat the breezy gentleman in the distinctive grey suit, and the same gangling assistant who'd once towered over W.'s doorframe, dressed in a green ski anorak of a quilted, silkily gleaming fabric blend. There was no leather coat hanging on the manager's coat stand, just a medium-length beige suede jacket with a fur collar.—W. was horrendously sleep-deprived and barely capable of following the breezy gentleman's words—he kept asking himself: Just who am I looking at now . . . which member of that grey-clothed series, or is there just one of them with six different grey suits?—and besides he didn't feel like following the chatty conversation he started (meanwhile the younger man in the anorak confined himself to nodding his close-cropped head, either earnestly or smilingly, as required by his superior's casually reeled-off words). It wasn't exactly a mystery to W. why the conversation had to take place here in the factory, since it seemed to concern absolutely nothing new or urgent; besides, it wasn't a conversation, since W. barely responded . . . he was busy mulling over the consequences of the visit, which had to have been noticed down in the production hall—of course they'd all noticed it, and if he wasn't mistaken, that was the very purpose of the visit.

Indignant at this dirty trick, W. didn't absorb a thing until the end of the conversation . . . he feebly recalled it centring on the understandable woes of a factory like this one, all attributable to the labour shortage; in concrete terms, for the past several years, each winter people from the assembly department has been assigned to the boiler house, where there was a lack of stokers; for the past two winters W. had been one of these people, which he liked just fine, for one thing because in the boiler room he was largely left unsupervised . . . the gist of the conversation was as follows: with all due respect, in the long run it was hard to sympathize with such measures because they kept people from developing their potential. These words having prompted the underling's last earnest nod for a time, the senior visitor laid a slender booklet on the table, bound in glossy black pasteboard, and pointed the cigarette he'd just lit (smoking was strictly prohibited in the manager's sanctum) at the title: Full Steam into the Morn. It was a 'Workshop Anthology of the Railroad Workers' Literary Working Group', as the caption declared; the working group met in the district town of Z., where the brochure had been published.

Take a look at this! said the breezy gentleman.

Reluctantly W. leafed through a few pages in the middle, at arm's length and without picking up the booklet from the table; he made out sequences of words arranged in lines and stanzas; he snapped the booklet shut again.

Putting it bluntly, we think these publications . . . almost all of this type of thing . . . are crap, if you'll pardon my French! said the gentleman. Of course you do, too, and I'm sure you don't want to be published in there. Still, it would be a first step, and besides, you'd be an enormous asset for a book like that.

Then at least there'd be something readable in it! the younger man in the green anorak piped up for the first time. Now the older man nodded: And we wouldn't have to keep butting in! Or asking the people to at least change their completely ridiculous titles, like we did here.

The young man in the green anorak gave a short laugh and explained the last statement: they were stuck between two titles. One was Full Steam into the Morn, the other was Full Steam into the Light of Morn. So we said to them, if you can't even decide in favour of a diesel locomotive, that is, progress, then at least you have to take: into the Morning!

Well, anyway! said the older man. All that would be completely unnecessary if, for instance, you were the head of this working group. Still, we wouldn't want to talk you into heading a circle like that, as a rule you'd be dealing with a bunch of philistines. The only option would be to get you excused from work more often, you ought to be given the latitude to do cultural work. That would be something to think about, although—and I'll say it quite frankly—it's my view that you should focus entirely on writing. And this work here . . . every winter, in this boiler house . . . we've taking the liberty of having a look inside . . . your know-it-all colleagues can perfectly well do this work by themselves.

You've been doing it much too long already, you have enough experience to go on! the young man added.

But seriously, we've got better things in mind for you, the older man said; he slid the booklet back in W.'s direction and rose to his feet. You can take that if you want.

W. pushed away the anthology in disgust and said: No . . . I've already decided against it. I'm not going to stay on at the factory anyway. And I'm not going to stay in this town either.

Where are you planning to go? asked the breezy gentlemen; the two were already standing at the door, only W. was still sitting where he was. To the city, to Leipzig or Berlin? . . . Berlin would be the best place for you, of course. And you'd be rid of me there . . . and I of you, I'd be very sorry about that. But let us know in time about a flat in Leipzig or Berlin.

I think I could picture Leipzig, W. replied.

For the most part W. had liked working in his factory, though at times he could hardly take all the conflicts. But never to see his colleagues again . . . suddenly the prospect was unbearable. In truth he'd loved them all in some inexplicable way, with all their mulishness and sheep-like stupidity, their meekness and arrogance, with all their morose and paranoid thoughts. Now they made as though they didn't want to see him, now the grey began to show beneath his black sheep's coat; dogged as they were, they'd finally scratched it free.

Down in the production halls the atmosphere was glacial, and he went about like a somnambulist; the wall of hostility he faced had acquired a menacing aspect . . . all day the foreman was nowhere to be seen, everyone knew that endless deliberations were being held up at management . . . he could have bet that he was one topic of discussion there. The secretary from the foreman's office, well aware of the ugly mood, accosted him shortly before quitting time: Next week you're going back to the boiler house. Take the night shift for three weeks, then you'll be out of the firing line. That's how we're fixing it.—W. was relieved . . . Do you think I'm talking to them voluntarily? he asked.—No idea! Anyway, you're doing it, and that's what everyone thinks. I'd think about it, if I were you. By the way, I'm not supposed to tell you, but you can probably figure it out for yourself—the foreman would be happy to accept your notice any time!

After spending the next two weeks in the basement of the boiler house, quietly performing his duties as stoker and using this solitary time for writing, he still hadn't come to a decision. Perhaps he'd thought that down here in the boiler house he could ride out the resentment that had focused upon him, waiting until the whole thing passed him by and passed over . . . which incidentally, he thought, was a tried-and-true method in this country: emerging conflicts weren't solved, they were allowed to age until they died of decrepitude. Besides, the writing blocked out his thoughts; the work he had to accomplish in the boiler house was gruelling, but it didn't take much time, mainly a matter of shovelling into the boiler as much coal as possible in as short a time as possible . . . and so, hunched over his notebooks, he sometimes felt that the hours passed too quickly, and especially at the end of the shift he felt a new surge of anxiety when he looked up, when he heard the racket of the mopeds in the factory yard, the first machinists arriving at work . . . and all at once he was wide awake and asked himself what would happen when the three weeks were up. He asked himself how he would have acted in his colleagues' place.—In their place, he thought, I'd never forgive myself.—He was in luck, the temperatures plummeted, the last of the regular stokers signed off sick, and W. continued to be required in the boiler house . . . this stoker had always been sick, but he'd stuck it out; now it seemed likely that the foreman of the assembly department had urged him to finally see a doctor. So they didn't want him up in the assembly hall . . . but inevitably he was up there for half an hour or so each day; he was treated reservedly, even coldly, but he was left in peace . . . ultimately this state of affairs could pass as a slightly exacerbated form of the universal suspicion that prevails in large industrial plants everywhere . . .

That was one way of taking it!—Much, much later W. learnt by chance that they had visited the factory once more while he was in the boiler house, probably to assess the effect of their first visit. And then came something they'd probably never imagined: when they headed for the boiler house, a group of people from the assembly hall planted themselves in front of the entrance in what looked like a blockade; their faces were grim and resolute, at the fore the scrawny little bandy-legged foreman, hair on end, trembling with agitation— supposedly they'd had to prop him up from behind—losing quantities of saliva as usual when he spoke, yelling at them in a barely intelligible falsetto: No access to the boiler house for unauthorized p . . . persons!—And they'd turned and left the hall.

If he'd learnt of this early enough, maybe everything would have turned out differently.—He'd waited for them in perpetual fear, they hadn't come, gradually something like relief set in . . . he ignored a further summons to the town hall,

Room 17, and even after that they hadn't visited, either in the factory or at home. Incidentally, the summons hadn't been the usual ominous pre-printed form; this time it was just a slip of paper in an envelope, expressing the typewritten request that he agree to a casual conversation three days thence. The slip bore neither sender nor signature . . . he didn't know then that so innocuous a piece of paper marked the beginning of a new phase. He tore it up and tossed it into the heating stove . . . he'd never set eyes on it! The date came and went and nothing happened.

Perhaps that was the moment when his sleep phase began; he didn't know, and probably it was irrelevant, being the moment from which all notions of time became blurred. The beginning had come some time that winter; perhaps it was that the summons ceased to contain anything by way of a date, and that he met the breezy gentleman in the buff suede jacket—he knew by now that this gentleman was the boss— only on the streets of town now, apparently by accident.—In this time W. wrote with an intensity he'd never known before, poems and short, one- to two-page prose miniatures, particles that sprang from his pen when he was in a sort of half-sleep, or in moments of resistance, when some unknown thing within rebelled against the torpor that otherwise gripped him. It really was a thing unknown to him, he no longer had a word for it, the rebellion within him was a relic from the time when he'd lived without this sleep. And indeed all day long he barely sensed himself, his mother nearly always found him in a state of collapse, in a sitting position at the kitchen table, his forehead resting on his lower arms, before his closed eyes the scribbled pages on which the words were little more than runaway horizontal lines. She slipped past behind him, wringing her hands; sometimes he started up and scared her off with an alien, barking voice, with cries he himself no longer understood.

At work he was a pale, bleary-eyed figure, unpunctual, unreliable, not to be trusted with the simplest of tasks; and yet fractious, standoffish, full of a strained, hypersensitive aggression which called to mind a perpetually angered insect. The foreman avoided saying a single unnecessary word to him; a worker like this was clearly one the old man would rather be rid of, and he soon banished him to the boiler room for good. The sleep phase—as W. had decided to call these weeks and months; he recalled them with horror—was a time in which he didn't seem to sleep at all. All he remembered about that winter was the sense that his brain was being sucked empty, down to the last stale dregs, down to the most necessary functions which just barely enabled his survival; and it was a time in which a great coldness grew within him . . . and perhaps this had hardened him up for his nocturnal paths through Berlin's frost.

The winter that year—his last year in the town—was long, icy and dry, almost entirely snowless. Permanent, dense, piercingly cold fog filled the streets, saturated with the sulphurous fumes of poorly burning coal; this oppressive, inert atmosphere had the entire town in its stranglehold. The streets came to life for just a few hours late in the afternoon, after the factories shut down. Then, around the marketplace, the eerily lit town centre filled with bundled-up pedestrians hastily running the most vital shopping errands, and with a multitude of crawling, smoke-spewing cars whose criss-crossing headlights tore to pieces the hurried melee in which all were in solitary, senseless flight. At any rate the quantities of food in town seemed sufficient, albeit with no variety whatsoever in the offerings, so that at least there were no shopping queues. When W. returned from his errands, he had the town's taste upon his mucous membranes and its bitterness in his lungs; it was as though the air and the fog between the houses were filling irreversibly with toxins . . . but perhaps, he thought, it was partly due to the quality of the coal he was forced to burn at work. It more resembled an earthen sludge, once wet, now frozen hard, mingled with sand and clumps of grass, barely describable as fuel any more. No doubt the excavator claws were scraping the very last remnants from the deposits, coal that didn't burn, but stewed and smouldered. And the smell it emitted sank down into the streets, ochre and leaden, and even the daylight could barely penetrate this haze. Once the grocery stores closed at 6 p.m., the town went dead; in the space of half an hour silence fell amid the houses, which seemed all at once, all at the same time, to be bolted and barred, as though the town had been warned of a hostile invasion. For budgetary reasons, street lighting in the town centre had been reduced to a minimum; mute, huddled together, the buildings seemed to await a gigantic blow that would smash everything to pieces . . . and indeed it was a state of siege that kept it in suspense, winter's siege; some time in December the mercury columns had plummeted and remained alarmingly low, as though frozen in place. —When the town came to life again early in the morning, when the light blazed up behind the factory windows, W. saw the workers hurrying towards the factory, bundled up, arms wrapped around their bodies, heads ducked, . . . it was one of those moments he'd always found poetic.—He himself had stopped going to the factory, one day he'd just let it be . . . one morning he'd woken up at the kitchen table, already an hour late; his mother hadn't been able to wake him, or she'd thought he had a different shift . . . he'd gone to the window and gazed out at the crippled town; it was dark still, and suddenly the town had seemed subterranean, buried and choked. He'd had to jot that down, and as he did time passed imperceptibly . . . at the factory they'd been at work a long time now without him . . . he could see the workers coming into the barely heated production halls early in the morning and making their cynical remarks: Just five inches of snow, and we can put the country up for sale!—Sure, they said, but there won't be any takers.—And so they carried on ... and the snow didn't come; it looked as though the country would last out the winter ...

W. was happy not to meet anyone in town who wanted to talk to him. He had the impression that people had begun avoiding him in public as well; an industrial plant as large as the one that had employed him held a certain sway over the public, and the opinions that formed among the workers soon found their way into town as well. If someone did talk to him, he hastened to assert that he was planning to move to Leipzig ... and immediately afterwards he generally forgot whom he had just met: it was time to be careful what he said!—In the town's half-light he met the breezy gentleman in the suede jacket, the boss, who stopped and greeted him.—How can you go walking around in this toxic stuff? said W., pointing upward ... It's not much better in Leipzig, either! the retort came after him. Or he'd simply walk past as though he hadn't noticed him, the boss opened his mouth, but it was as though the frost wouldn't let his voice out ... all the same, soon afterwards W. was no longer sure whether they hadn't had a brief conversation.—At a grocery store, buying the last kilo of potatoes, he met the boss' assistant in the green anorak, leaning on the counter and drinking a bottle of beer. Impulsively W. asked for a bottle of beer too (perhaps hoping to learn from the green guy what they thought about his moving to Leipzig) ... Sorry, takeaway only! the green guy replied in the store clerk's stead. It's closing time already!—So he was pretending not to know W. at all; but W. recognized the same uncertain flicker of the eyes with which the lanky guy, it must have been months ago, had once leant on his doorjamb. It was, in fact, three before six; W. left without the beer and wandered with the bag of potatoes in his gloved fist through streets that were emptying of pedestrians, an exodus, it seemed to him.—That was it, then, the sleep phase, he walked around town like a ghost, people looked straight through him . . . there was one incident, as though not all forms of reality had yet faded from the life of this town: he ran into Cindy, stopped her and said that he wanted to give her the watch back.—The watch? Why give it back . . .? she said. No, he should go ahead and keep it, he'd be sure to need it. And if not, then for old time's sake.— Harry had given him the watch as a pledge when he couldn't pay up after a game of dice at the pub . . . It's Cindy's watch, he'd said, it's yours until I've got money again.—He last saw Cindy in the coldest, most unendurable phase of that winter, in the fuzzy, ferrous daylight, pushing an old-fashioned pram on softly squeaking wheels. She tried to hurry past him but he asked her how the baby was doing.—And you don't care how I'm doing? she retorted.—Their brief talk was almost a talk between strangers, but it seemed to him that her voice throbbed with suppressed hatred . . . How should he be doing, she said, maybe bad, . . . maybe he doesn't even notice any more!—And she nodded in the direction of the pram; beneath the plastic tarp, patched and stuck together with filthy bits of sticking plaster, it was eerily silent. W. had taken her words for one of the coarse jokes one had to reckon with in Cindy's circles.—Is your son sick? asked W., looking at the tiny bundle in the carriage, completely motionless beneath the recklessly thin blankets.—Sick or dead, as if it was yours, Cindy said spitefully. And after a while: It's a crying shame to make a baby for a country like this! Making a baby in this country . . . that's something you can never, ever put right.—She said it in a strangely clear voice; W. was relieved that her anger had found another target: Why don't you apply to emigrate?[3]—We have

104

a chance at getting a flat in Berlin. Then maybe we'll be a bit better off . . .—W. announced that he was also planning to move away . . . I'd rather go to Leipzig, though!

Subsequent to such chance meetings he could never swear to their actually having occurred . . . Why is that? he asked himself.—Because no one asks me who I meet any more! he replied.—In point of fact, the gentleman he called the boss hardly ever asked now what happened to him on a daily basis . . . Literature!—the only topic the gentleman cared about was literature.—And so for me all things in this life were mere figments of the imagination, he said to himself later. And they were imagined as vividly as though he'd had to furnish evidence of his existence for this time period . . . as though someday someone would come and ask: Do you have any evidence for this time?

One or two years later he'd conceived the notion that during his sleep phase an unconquerable distrust towards every reality had been instilled in him . . . or had he instilled it in himself? It was a profound distrust of all perceptions and at the same time of his memory which stored these perceptions; and all the things he later believed to be anchored in his memory were either ones that had withstood a thousand doubts as to their existence, or they were pure figments . . . and that, he thought later, was as it should be.

Soon after the shops closed, town life had already clustered in the few lit rooms behind windows not sealed off by blinds or heavy shutters. Mostly houses with front gardens; it was there alone (apart from the activity inside the pubs) that human life still stirred. The light that spilt out soon faded in the fog, the shadow of the bushes in the front yard left you utterly invisible, even if you ventured up close to the window. —Most of W.'s perceptions were acquired by looking from outside into the interior of lighted dwellings; what he saw was filtered through double panes and veiling curtains . . . while he, outside, was in a different atmosphere, the fog-swirled atmosphere of the dark where all movement within the living rooms' inward light seemed unreal to him, shoddy fictions. He didn't understand the words that were spoken in there; when not completely inaudible they assumed an utterly different meaning in the glow of the light bulbs, the violet phosphorescence of the television screens . . . no, of these utterances' meaning he knew nothing, he sought their probable sense in the gestures meant to underline the words, he sought to follow the movement of the speakers' lips and read off syllables, finally he began imitating the interplay of the lips' forms to get at the words, the phrases . . . without knowing, of course, how they were received, these sounds, by those who showed him only the backs of their heads. He almost played the role of a person trying to follow the conversation of deaf-mutes . . . no, his role was that of a deaf-mute, tracking down the secret of those adept at speech. Rarely did he succeed in deciphering a serviceable sentence, or at least a few intelligible words . . . only one single fact could be assumed with certainty: if more than one person was present behind the window, the capacity for speech was exercised at least once each evening.—It was a capacity from which he was cut off, now that he had taken his place in the darkness outside the windows.—He had no recourse but to replace the unheard words from inside the rooms with ones from inside his head.

Initially, of course, he'd tried to make out what was actually said . . . as he later found, one could very well agree that what was actually said didn't matter at all. What was actually said tended to be buried under one or more layers of banal drivel anyway. Didn't this suggest that the essential thing was to know the completely trivial statements people made? You had to follow the everyday, interchangeable conversations, the mindless gibberish, the offhanded routines, to be able to reflect on the mood of the people . . . in fact, maybe you had to practically ignore the so-called substantive statements, which might merely be repeating the word supply from TV broadcasts or printed paper, at best reversing its meaning; in other words, these statements were worthless!—The people's other speech supply, the banal, interchangeable talk, which could just as well be made up . . . if you had an expert to do it. Probably you'd have to check now and then whether it changed over the years . . . which was improbable: in his experience it stayed the same from the time people learnt to talk to the time of their death.

But the business retained an attraction for him, a strong attraction even; it lay in his voyeuristic behaviour . . . and in the non-gratification which a voyeur's behaviour yielded. The non-gratification kept his craving alive, it was the motor of his unrest, driving him out into the fog each evening. What those mouths formed in there was completely irrelevant—and had it been sheer conspiracy, had these rooms hatched demonstrations or terrorist attacks, it would have interested him only marginally (and he might even have kept it to himself!) . . . at some point the acoustic aspect of the conversations he observed ceased to matter to him; the organs of speech which he palpated with his eyes suddenly had the character of body parts in the so-called private area. And from that moment on he increasingly succumbed to the impression that these wonders, these lips, these tongues and teeth, these throats, these moistly gleaming, secretion-filled maws were forming unknown and inconceivable obscenities . . . the attraction lay for him in the attribute inconceivable.

He would have dearly liked some sort of device, a kind of hearing aid; a curved old-fashioned horn, an ear trumpet from a past century might have been just the thing for him. Of course the boss could have offered him a better tool . . .

but he told himself that an instrument would only lull back to sleep the senses which he felt had now reached an extraordinary degree of development. Besides, he feared the boss would immediately envisage some sort of practical benefit from his skills . . . even without an ear trumpet he had learnt over time to divine some of what was spoken or yelled behind the windowpanes (in the outlying houses there seemed to be more yelling than speaking . . . conclusions could have been drawn from that). Doggedly he had learnt to interpret gestures, facial shifts suddenly led him to extrapolate the state of the country's economy—the only reason this didn't bore him to death was that the economic situation affected him as well. More interesting for him was the progress he made reading lips, and still more in penetrating synergies one could describe as cybernetic . . . in several cases he had managed from the visible reactions of one interlocutor to extrapolate what had been said by the other (presumably female), of whom he saw only a bit of the back of the head. According to his interpretation, almost all these statements could be filed away as negative-hostile.

Next he tested his abilities in the pubs . . . at an outlying table, undisturbed, but faced with as many people as possible, he listened into the thick of the voices that flew every which way, the dense fog of the swelling and subsiding conversations, and probed their separate strands; he brought order to separate complex structures that consisted of speech and gesticulation, emotion pent up and released, flowing down whole rows of faces united in one opinion; he studied the oscillations of separate themes (usually mere subvarieties of one theme, subvarieties that could be traced on the basis of minor shared features); with all his senses he pursued a certain current of conversation which for some inexplicable reason had suddenly vanished into thin air between one person and the next, though their shoulders almost touched, then reappeared, perhaps an hour later, in a completely different quadrant of the room, and was discussed further (for instance, the quality of a local beer which had abruptly disappeared from the shops . . . it had been gone for ten years now, and for nine years its disappearance had tirelessly been bemoaned and its quality extolled . . . and he heard it again and again: Oettler . . . Oettler . . . Oettler!—he knew how the name of this beer was spelt), as though the topic's glowing core had leapt like an electric arc to a different conversational unit where it was picked up seamlessly, or as though the topic had been transmitted via wireless straight across the room . . . and there, just as abruptly, it transformed into the discussion of a player from the town football team who had vanished seven or eight years ago, into the glorification of this player who had bailed out to the West (Now it was getting interesting!) . . . he had the feeling that conversations spread in the manner of odours—and could only be distinguished in the manner of odours—they were produced somewhere, somewhere in the private parts of the face, and then leapt or sailed, perhaps lofted by excessive conversational gesticulation, from one row of pushed-together tables to the next, where for incomprehensible reasons they were not caught hold of, or were even waved away, drifting on until, over the tables of another group (seemingly a completely independent conversational unit), amid densely rising clouds of smoke and in the fusillade of beer (which obscenely formed lips sprayed into the air with the word 'Oettler'), or in the diminishing volume of a multitude of voices, they were able to take hold and reignite, and the new verbal scent seemed to be gratefully received, a new union of throats breathed it for a time, and coughed it and wiped it all around, and an hour later put the odorous cloud to flight again . . . and W. didn't let these odours near him, he needed a certain distance, he needed a partition between himself and what he perceived, a wall of glass, or shadow, or fog . . .

During this time he'd felt he was learning a completely new language . . . or at least relearning the existing language from the ground up. Since now he no longer took in phrases for the sake of their message, rather seeking a hidden meaning in a dark realm behind them, at the same time forced to consider the language of gestures which carried each phrase (probably only falsifying it still further!), for him all speech had gradually become a conspiracy. And the more he attempted to penetrate this conspiracy, the more urgent a suspicion rose within him: everyone made themselves understood by means of language, everyone but him . . . he didn't know these means, these means lay behind the message which itself emerged banal and pointless. Suddenly all phrases had turned impenetrable . . . precisely because the words in them clove together by such force of habit that they kept repeating the same trivia. More and more he lived with the sense of having to break through a wall to arrive at the same understanding that came easily to everyone sitting behind this wall (behind the wall understanding was interrupted only occasionally by the jitter of the refrigerators).—All his life he had talked just like them . . . he'd only written differently; he hadn't even noticed what he'd been doing there. Now he'd been declared a writer, and suddenly the language he had once co-inhabited had become a room from which he was shut out.

Perhaps he could penetrate the closed rooms of this language from below . . . from underground, through its basements, through its floor?

Of course he shared none of these thoughts with the boss, suspecting that he'd agree with him; for the boss, too, it could only stand to reason that people who talked to one another constituted a conspiracy . . . which could be countered only

with the same means. But the boss didn't take it all that seriously; whenever they ran into each other in the town's fog, he
had good advice to offer . . . You have to listen to the man on
the street, he said, don't let anyone tell you otherwise. There's
not a writer here who can deliver that like you can!—And
when we've heard enough we'll kick him to the kerb, said W.

The boss looked flustered, unsure whether to take these
words as a joke . . . W. didn't know himself. But the boss
noticed at once that W. had troubling thoughts on his mind,
and barraged him with more and more ostensibly comforting
phrases.—Do you think I'm not feeling OK, or what? W. asked
him one day. What is it you're constantly having to cheer me
up about?—You know, a writer . . . actually, any thinking person in this day and age can't always feel OK. Maybe only rarely,
even, but that's how it's got to be, and it's better that way, the
boss replied. And then he brought to bear one of his key
sayings which left little to be desired in terms of universality:
You know, you see best when you look from the dark into the
light! And not the other way around . . . The boss proffered
most of his comforting sayings with a sort of breezy irony,
relentlessly constructive, completely unperturbed when he met
with occasional resistance. He was one of those functionaries
who went unfazed by his underlings' obtuseness so long as
they still functioned . . . and it always seemed to take a while
before he grasped that someone didn't want to function.
Usually he made a show of superiority that was just another
form of incomprehension; he thought resistance so absurd that
anyone who displayed the least sign of it immediately got a
pitying clap on the shoulder . . . it was stupidity, and for someone absolutely convinced of the human capacity for change
(he was one of those rare bosses who'd read Brecht), stupidity
was a deplorable thing.—And so at all times he radiated a semblance of broad bonhomie which showed how accustomed he

was to reigning irreplaceably and unconditionally over the town and the surrounding communities.

You see best from the dark into the light! W. had come to Berlin with these words in his head, and it surprised him what a distinct image of that boss' being he had here . . . in contradiction to his otherwise foggy impressions. But he had escaped the sphere of the gentleman in the expensive suede jacket (so his thinking went); here he could forget him . . . the gentleman's sayings were things he could, if he liked, assimilate, the language was public property, even if some regional potentate had performed his variations on it.

Here he could forget the boss . . . yet at this remove from the small town it was futile to deny to himself that he and the boss had had conversations one would have to describe as fairly exhaustive . . . down there he'd been able to deny it, even with a degree of success. Now he had to admit to himself that requests had been made of him which, strictly speaking, could be called commands. True, he hadn't taken them as such . . . his encounters with the boss had always followed a similar pattern; for W. they lay hidden in impenetrable gloom, even when he'd been accosted during the midday break (while still working as a stoker) on his way into town to buy one of the several identical newspapers.—Come on up for a moment, I'll treat you to a coffee in my office, Room 17.—W. shook his head, indicating his work clothes . . . You know I've got nothing to offer, he replied.—Oh yes you do, said the boss, I can talk about literature with you, and that means quite a bit! There's no way I can do that with that longlegs, say—there's no one in this backwater to have a real conversation with.

He said these things with ironic melancholy; W. felt how susceptible he was to that sort of tone. The boss seemed to intuit this, redoubling his efforts and ambushing W. at dusk now too: Did you see that on TV just now? They've arrested two of those young authors in Berlin again! Well, if that ever happens to you, and it can happen any time, I practically see it coming, just ask for me . . . You know, Room 17! But don't say anything until it happens! Not a word! Take care, one way or the other it can happen soon.—Do you know anything specific? asked W.—I'll tell you soon enough, if I can . . .

And shortly after that he said: I think we ought to finally get back to our conversations, they started off so nicely . . . tomorrow afternoon in my office! And forget all the things I told you the other day, forget about it, it's better that way . . . —W. was unaware of any conversations that had started off; here too he must have been peering into a language chamber from which he was shut out.—Finally he was unable to shake the suspicion that they were shadowing him on his fog-shrouded nocturnal errands (this settled his move to Berlin) . . . the boss had even indirectly admitted it when yet again expressing his dissatisfaction with the lanky 'rookie' whom W. had first met at his front door: apparently he was excessively cautious and always kept a respectful distance from his target . . . it looked like he'd stay a rookie forever, the long-legged loser! I'm sorry, I can't do a thing with the tall guy, I'm sure he means well, but I need a replacement! Best of all, let's turn the tables, and from now on you follow him. Put him to the test. After all, they call rookies probationers . . . don't they?

In this town the target the boss had mentioned could of course refer only to W. . . . he had a bad case of respectful distance as well, another thing he realized only in Berlin.

Now he'd put a real remove between himself and the boss . . . in Berlin it was like waking up for real (as opposed to that rude awakening at the kitchen table down there in the town, his head immersed again immediately in the fog, in the smoke); here in Berlin most of the phrases he thought he'd forgotten seemed to reach his brain belatedly . . . suddenly he realized he'd let himself be confused. And it still seemed possible to find his way back to the state before this confusion; perhaps first he'd have to stop regarding himself as this weird writer?

First he'd had to travel back and forth several times between Berlin and the town of A., the fog still seeming to swathe his brow, the frosts of the night streets still gripping his limbs and the smoke still stinging his eyes . . . when at last he walked down the Berlin street where he meant to live, the first pale green bloom was on the lindens. They lined the pavement of a tiny side branch of a larger thoroughfare, the main artery of an outlying southern neighbourhood, already in Berlin's periphery. When all hope had seemed lost, he'd found a rental room here: he refused to see it as more than a lucky coincidence. And it was in this neighbourhood that the city showed him its bright and spacious side . . . the first confirmation of the words in his head: he thought he was looking from the dark into the light.

He'd spent more than a week looking in vain for a place to stay . . . albeit in the clumsiest possible fashion: at a loss for ideas, he'd gone knocking at the doors of total strangers . . . each time he'd seen himself leaning rebuffed on the doorframe, just a bit shorter than the lanky 'probationer'—as the boss denoted the mode of existence W. had now escaped . . . each evening, frazzled and filled with feelings of futility, he'd returned to the town, almost sick with fear of running into the boss again, and the next morning he'd set out for Berlin once more; it was nearly four hours by train. Once he'd had to take a day's break, meaning to use it to finally hand in his notice at the factory; he'd failed, sleeping all day. And then, in the ghastliest exhaustion, he recalled an address he'd forgotten because from the start he'd thought it was a fiction. One of his shady pub companions had given it to him once ('Just for a weekend in Berlin!'), and he'd been carrying it around with him for a year now. Searching his papers, he actually found it—apparently Harry, Cindy's boyfriend, had lodged there when he wound up in Berlin in the brief interims between prison terms; the woman who rented out the room seemed to be a relative of his.—And this room was in fact still free; it was on the ground floor, poorly furnished (a cot, a chair, an armchair, an inadequate washbasin . . . the only table was a bulky desk), and as it couldn't be heated, it would be virtually uninhabitable in winter.—W. had told the woman, who seemed mistrustful, something he'd meant not to tell, but he felt he owed her an explanation: I work as a writer, I need the room on the side, so I can have some peace and quiet.—That's more or less what the previous tenant

claimed, she replied.—Could he have the room for longer than a weekend, too?—If necessary, she said, still mistrustful. But then he'd have to go and fill out his registration, within ten days at the latest, otherwise she'd get into trouble.—W. paid the rent for the next three months (a comparatively laughable sum) and explained to the astonished woman that he probably couldn't be there all the time, but she'd have to keep the room free for him.—The woman tucked away the money as quickly as though he might reconsider the deal that very moment. If he didn't want to take his turn cleaning the stairwell, she said, he'd have to add nine marks for the three months.—He gave her another ten-mark note, told her to keep the change, and withdrew with the key. That evening he took the train home again to fetch the absolute necessities and a small stockpile of books. The whole time the situation felt utterly familiar . . . it couldn't be, since he'd never left his town for long: but often, in his short narrative pieces, he'd tried to describe characters in a similar position. He'd contrived figures who arrived with a sense of liberation in some new setting, at long last, after unduly long attempts to free themselves from their habitual circumstances . . . and he'd always meticulously described the changes, indeed the transformations, that took place in such a character at that moment.

When he was back in Berlin two days later—after long arguments with his mother, who had realized he was serious about the move, and watched pale-faced as he packed his bags . . . After all Leipzig wasn't far, just an hour by bus, he'd told her, but his attempts at reassurance were fruitless—when, laden with the two heavy bags, he finally reached the little street again, he saw in the gathering darkness that the light was on in his ground-floor room. Probably that was why he'd walked past it several times already . . . for a long time, almost all afternoon, he'd searched the neighbourhood's short, identical-looking side streets, scanning all the facades behind the bare front gardens; he hadn't found his building . . . and he couldn't find the piece of paper with the address in his bags. Of course he remembered the name of the street, but every time he was about to ask a passer-by, the person suddenly seemed suspicious . . . afterwards he looked back on this afternoon as on an episode of madness. He'd told himself that from now on he'd have to find his way in the capital alone, he'd have to, and better than anyone else, as quickly as possible he had to become an expert at urban orientation (a resolution he couldn't even have fulfilled in his home town) . . . and so he'd failed in every way on this first day in Berlin; it was a bad omen for his fresh beginning. He'd worked up a sweat in the spring breeze which blew about the not very urban-looking houses (and which wasn't exactly warm); soon he was completely sodden and at the point of seeking the train station again . . . and there he was, standing in front of his room's lit window, standing for what had clearly been quite some time, staring into the stop-gap interior of which he had a full view from the pavement

... had he seen a human form in the room just now? Now he recognized it by the gigantic, bright red plush armchair which, completely incongruous, took up the middle of the room, flooded by the light of the burning bulb ... he'd forgotten to turn out the light when he left two days ago!—Towards noon the next day he woke up in the plush armchair, and darkness filled the room.

His torso produced a sharp crunching noise when he moved against the back of the chair; his shoulders, hair and upturned face were covered with the shards of the light bulb, which at some point that night, unable to cope with the unbroken supply of electricity, had burst. He recalled that on returning to the room he'd let down the blind, then collapsed into the armchair and immediately fallen asleep. And the crack of the bursting bulb had entered his sleep once, deep though that sleep had been; dimly he thought he recalled the explosion, breaking through faintly as though from a remote terrain ... the aerial mines exploding in the streets must have sounded like that, when in the war's final years he sheltered with his mother in the cellar ... probably he couldn't really recall this time; it was in the first three years after his birth ... but he vividly recalled the target of those air raids, the bombed-out industrial plants outside town, the playground and exploration zone of his childhood.

The memory of the sound of the bombs hitting is probably the idea of a memory, he thought ... often the idea of a dream's content is more vivid than the dream itself ... and it occurred to him that he must have dreamt of his acquaintance Cindy that night: in this dream he was somehow embroiled in the fairly hair-raising story of how Cindy had had her baby. Suddenly the waters had broken from her body, in a muffled explosion like a fountain, and the walls of the room were sprayed with the slick, shimmering liquid, and the room was a closed cavern, a cramped cellar, a cell . . . no one believed what was going on, her distress was ignored—and in the dream W. was among the few who wanted to get help . . . but only partly; partly he was on the side of those who saw Cindy's cries for help as a cheap trick. The dream's clearest manifestation was the breaking of the waters . . . in his thoughts a clinking spray had fallen: the light bulb!

He rose from the armchair, shook off the shards like drops of rain and raised the window blind. Light flooded in, for a moment so strong and glaring that he staggered back, blinded.—If everything had gone as planned, at the moment no one could know where he was. If anyone looked for him, at most it would be in Leipzig, presumably he hadn't even told his mother about Berlin, all he'd ever mentioned was Leipzig. And he'd bought the tickets in Leipzig, Leipzig to Berlin and back; he'd always paid for the last stretch from Leipzig to A. separately—perhaps he'd managed to cover his tracks now.

The boss was not to be underestimated, of course, nor even the lanky guy . . . but W. was prepared to claim—perhaps the dream had done this—that he was a different person since arriving in Berlin. If the boss cropped up, he'd calmly explain to him that he was set on living as a real writer now . . . in fact, he was even grateful to him, the boss, for the salutary impulse, for the inspiration. All right, earlier he'd given a different impression . . . since coming to Berlin he felt newborn.— The anticipated reply was utterly indifferent: Newborn? What mystical rubbish!

(But when he thought about it, that sort of reply wasn't typical of the boss. It was much more like a later, younger arrival—little older than W.—who banked on objectivity. This arrival had introduced himself in the stairwell: Sorry . . . I'm Feuerbach!)

He was grateful to the boss for a very literary idea: one of his characters had hit on the notion of determining the time of his own birth. This character had unexpectedly landed in a big city, where he suddenly experienced himself as a synthesis —after the first spring shower which came in the night, after a downpour which cleared the air of the character's memories of his former life in far remote territories inexorably falling to ruin. So as not to be guilty of drawing utterly transparent analogies to his terminated reality, W. had rendered his fictional figure's memories as a kind of troglodyte existence. His character had vegetated in the rooms of a bunker complex, a legacy of the last war which no one else knew about. This complex was situated beneath an expanse of ruins that lay in a depression between the outskirts of town and large swathes of forest that rose uphill towards the east . . . of course this setting was also taken from reality, but at least it was improbable, W. said to himself, and it seemed sufficiently abstruse that his character would visit the city only at night, when he crept out from his caves. And hour after hour this monster listened to a language which he couldn't understand, which was nothing but gibberish for him, beneath the illuminated windows of the houses, where he stared from the dark into the light . . . and stared anxiously at the gestures that aimed towards the outside, seemingly at him. Those inside had no patience with the outcasts who stood eavesdropping in the cold, no compassion for the phantoms whose heads loomed from the fog into the beams of light, for the shadows out there sniffing at the cracks of the doors . . .

At this point he stopped and asked himself whether anyone who knew anything about his past wouldn't immediately identify him as the ghost he was describing. But who could possibly know anything? He himself knew virtually nothing. And hadn't this phantom always lived solely in his papers, even back in the town? . . . This was the thought that had to be saved: his earlier life was a paper fantasy and had to stay that way; all other thoughts had to be silenced one by one. It couldn't be said too often: that I from back then was a literary character . . . and according to a not-unfounded hypothesis, the boss concurred with this point of view!—W.'s memories were sufficiently telling: 'I', raising his head again and again from the tabletop . . . and when the light of the kitchen lamp begins to seep into his brain and reality regains its foothold in his thoughts, the question looms inescapably: Where was I just now?—What is the place from which I've just returned . . . which streets had he roamed, in the light of which window had he crept up to hold his ear to the private parts of strangers' voices . . . ah, they'd all remained equally blurry, these private voices in the fog.—The question was nonsensical, his skull had merely slept amid a dense fog of letters (Was that so? Yes, the boss would have replied) . . . forehead bedded in a thick layer of papers, buried by a whirl of words and phrases, delivered up one winter long to the voices of his imagination . . .

The question was nonsensical . . . it was only in his stories that he'd eavesdropped on them all! And he'd never eavesdropped on himself! Now it was time . . . now he could eavesdrop on this spy, this product of his text fragments, now he could pursue this draft of himself that had seized his essence, this sleeper roaming the fog at the outskirts of town in his sleep, betrayed by sleep all winter long, the phony panting of the papers in his ears . . .

Now and then the doorbell rang . . . and each time he was too feeble to get up and see who'd rung. Just once he'd gotten up, gathered the interrupted manuscript from the desktop, folded it several times to form a slim, longish bundle, and stuffed it into the crack between the cushions of the red armchair, the narrow, deep hiding place between the back and the seat . . . after all that, the ringing had already stopped; he'd lurked to see if it would return, but nothing came . . . in the evening he fell asleep and woke with a start—the ringing had returned . . . he was just hearing things.—The room's bed was a so-called daybed, red plush, just as greasy as the red armchair; it cost him an effort to ignore the dark, slightly sticky streaks which marred the daybed's edges (of course this sleeping fixture had constantly been used without a sheet), so he slept in the armchair whenever possible, his feet stuck out over the seat of the wooden chair he placed in front of it, usually fully dressed, which wasn't a problem for him (he'd slept that way often enough during his night shifts in the boiler room) as he'd acquired the habit of consuming large quantities of alcohol in the first half of the night while trying to write. And he slept in a similar position on the daybed: on his side, stabilized by the seated pose, his head tilted back on a pillow, his lower arms crossed over his chest or clamped between his thighs, his legs bent and sometimes drawn up nearly to his stomach; this, he fancied, was almost the shape of a foetus about to slip from the womb (it was no wonder, he said to himself, that he was plagued by dreams of childbirth) . . . and each time the ringing signal at the door sent him back into this irresolute posture, or he doubled up still further; his first thought was always that the lanky guy was leaning on the doorjamb outside . . . it was as though his earlier life were ringing at his door.—Regularly it was a single ring, not repeated, and thus typical of the 'probationer', the gutless wonder (or so his boss had characterized him) . . . at the start of his time in Berlin W. hadn't been able to shake the strange sense that the lanky guy would crop up one day; it would be a miracle if he didn't, he said to himself.—For some reason the longlegs was the bogeyman of the game, precisely because he looked so harmless at first glance . . . he was the bringer of bad news . . . this clearly gave even

121

his boss the willies. Fear was a vital factor in this show, it always had to be available in sufficient quantities—and it could change hands very quickly.—W. had thought about making the 'probationer' a background character in his story, one who could crop up unexpectedly at any time . . . in his mind's eye he saw the lanky guy looming over a dense congregation of people, for instance, on a bridge over the S-Bahn rail tracks, and the sun transformed the tall, thin figure into a smoke-coloured silhouette, for the interim . . . till the time had come for this overlong shadow to stick to the narrator's heels . . .

But one time W. did open the door, and a different person stood outside in the stairwell, rather lost, hovering indecisively near the switch for the timed light.—Sorry, the person said, using the English word, I don't think you're the person I wanted . . . or are you?—The last part of the question was spoken into the darkness, since the light in the corridor had just gone out; there was no way the visitor could have had another look at him, W. thought, and behind him was nothing but the weak glow of his desk lamp . . . Who are you looking for? he asked.—At short intervals a cigarette could be seen flaring up in the darkness, pulled at hastily and audibly; he smelt the smoke, it had to be a very odd, foul-smelling brand, or a cheap cigar exuding acrid, almost sulphurous fumes . . . the embers fell to the ground and were trodden out with a crunching sound.—Maybe you have some idea, the other said, whether a certain Harry Falbe lives here?

The visitor made no move to press the button for the light, remaining instead in the dark.—No, said W., he doesn't live here. And I'm certainly not him.—Do you know him? the person said.—I said no, W. returned, I don't know him. And who are you, are you from the registration office?—At that he finally turned on the stairwell light; the other man squinted, seemed surprised by the brightness . . . From the registration office? He gave a short laugh. No, not that, but maybe we're something along those lines. Why do you ask, do you need a new flat?

Of course W. knew the man meant his old friend Harry from A., but the last name had thrown him off; the woman who'd rented the room to him had the same name . . . and it wasn't the first time he'd seen the man standing in front of him; once before . . . or even several times he'd run into him in the stairwell; he had looked just as helpless, as though he'd mixed up the address (a behaviour that struck him as familiar); and W. thought he'd even seen him coming down the stairs one time.—No, said W., Harry Falbe . . . is that what you said? I've never heard the name before.—That's right, you don't hear it very often! the person said—by now he'd lost his hesitancy, taking two or three long strides forward and glancing at the spot on W's front door where a name plate is usually mounted; there was no plate on W's door; then he peered— just as coolly and brazenly, W. felt—past the doorframe into the room . . . How can anyone stand living in a dump like that! he said.

W. hadn't even thought of disclosing to the gentleman that a few steps up, on the first floor, there lived a woman who also answered to the name of Falbe . . . of course that was completely immaterial, because he knew it anyway. Soon he was running into this person more frequently, repeatedly in the stairwell (and soon he'd introduced himself: Sorry . . . Feuerbach!), and more and more often the man dragged him into conversations about flat-related issues; he regarded W's room as absolutely uninhabitable, which he kept saying until W. asked: Do you have something else to offer, and what's the price?

It seemed there was an accommodation in reserve for him, much closer to the city centre, which he could move into immediately . . . that place wasn't anything special either, but still (and it was much closer to the city's real centre). Two and a half rooms, and at least there was an indoor toilet, he wouldn't have to go piss between the ashcans in the yard. And if necessary he could even have the rooms rent-free . . .

A company flat, then . . . it irked W. that he hadn't asked this question. This exquisitely casual civilian (only later did W. learn the military title in front of his name) had given a barely noticeable shudder as he glanced about W.'s four walls, tarred with the sticky residue of countless cigarettes . . . And if you accept my proposal, we'll have to find a solution for the renovation costs here, he'd added.—He goes around acting like a landlord, thought W.; and then he recalled the small-town boss: he'd also tended to regard his entire surroundings with the appraising gaze of a property owner.

So far W. had dodged the question of a possible move . . . in his own mind he postponed it to the following winter, but he didn't tell that to the gentleman yet. Also, his relationship with the landlady, previously rather tense, had sorted itself out—when he'd handed over the second rent payment (again for a quarter of a year, plus the cleaning costs for the stairwell), she complained that he still hadn't gone to the registration office. He kept putting off his registration, and avoided her . . . one day, when he failed to react to her ring, she unlocked the door (of course she had the spare key), stuck her head in and called: Are you still alive in there? You don't need to hide from me any more now that the registration is taken care of! And you've absolutely got to ventilate more!

W. seemed subjected now to a certain solicitude, especially when shortly thereafter he found pots of leftovers by his threshold; something, he didn't know what, had aroused the nurturing instinct in this woman . . . who couldn't be all that old, incidentally!—W. waited till night, then dumped the food into the garbage bin and tossed newspapers over it; he washed the pots and set them back out on the stairs. The very next day he found them filled again . . . it occurred to W. that she was competing with this Feuerbach, but how could she have learnt that he'd offered W. a flat?—You don't need to wash the dishes, she called to him through the door. Just put them back out!—And a little later she caught him as he was coming in from the street and held out a frying pan with a breaded cutlet sizzling in butter . . . Feel free to tell me what to cook . . . Harry, the guy who lived here first, he always ate with me . . . aren't you from that same town down south? Go ahead, take it, you always pay me much too much rent.—Very kind of you, Frau Falbe, said W., and took the opportunity to tell her that unfortunately he'd have to move out soon.—Yeah, yeah, she replied, I know, you're just like Harry, he was always moving out again too. Besides, it's really no room for a grown man!

Hardly had he taken the cutlet into the flat when she rang and brought a plate brimful of fried potatoes; W. thanked her and asked whether Harry, his predecessor, was perhaps a relative of hers.—A relative, no, said the woman. Didn't you know Harry doesn't have any relatives? He's an orphan . . . from a home. He doesn't even know his real last name, and he put my name on the registration.—W. was astonished at how lax the formalities were at Berlin's registration offices, if the woman wasn't misinformed . . . but the whole thing was neither here nor there.—After consuming the cutlet and the fried potatoes he felt the scarcely unpleasant, swiftly subsiding nausea with which his atrophied stomach reacted to the shock of an unaccustomed, copious warm meal; then a sense of long-lacking well-being set in—from that day on he devoured Frau Falbe's rations; delighted, she began cooking with redoubled zeal.—One day she stuck her head in again and announced that she'd set aside money for him . . . You've always paid me too much rent. Just let me know when you need it, I always gave Harry a bit of money too.—I'd rather buy your armchair, he said. I'd like to take it with me when I move, I've gotten used to it. But at that she shook her head: I don't think I can do that, actually that's my husband's armchair.

Why shouldn't he stay as long as possible, why shouldn't he keep letting his landlady feed him? For over a month, for nearly two months he'd eaten nothing but cold, rancidly shimmering tinned goods, the contents of cans, brownish jelly and stale, ivory-coloured fat hiding an over-salted kernel of meat, minced to the point of greatest possible undefinability . . . fearing he'd end up completely emaciated, propped in the armchair like a toothpick (like his old friend Harry), he'd made up for it with huge quantities of beer. Suddenly he'd won Frau Falbe's increasingly forthright affections, he was being fed, almost overfed, he was even being offered financial assistance . . . so why shouldn't he wait until winter expelled him from the room the natural way, as it were? Wasn't this the sort of life people pictured as a quasi-artistic existence . . . the ineradicable common wisdom being naive enough to regard this as disreputable, but at the same time indulge it in the literati?

Frau Falbe said: If you're really planning to move out again, then Harry can come back, and I can look after him a bit, my boy . . . It happened more and more that she'd turn communicative, and sometimes she stopped him in the stairwell and began talking to him in a strange tone of voice, switching between loud laments (loud enough to be heard from behind all the closed flat doors) and whispered interjections meant for him alone. For the latter she seized him by the sleeve and drew him closer: If only you knew all the things the people here say about me!—Right after that she exclaimed: But he's really not a bad boy! I'm telling you, he'll be starting at the university when his time's up!—She drew

126

him closer: Parole . . . I think he'll get parole again, she whispered.—And then, louder once more: You have to take people the way they are! If only you knew how they treated someone like my husband, if only you knew!—She dragged him up a few steps to the first floor and whispered: I'll have to tell you all about it some day! And about Harry too, how stupid is he anyway, what on earth am I doing? The whole time he's been wanting to go West, what does he want there anyway? He's been put away twice already, locked up for trying to defect, but he can't let it be, I'll have to tell you about it sometime . . . And she yelled: You've got to be able to talk to someone once in a while!

But you shouldn't go telling that to people you don't know very well, whispered W.

Oh . . . I know who I'm talking to! Frau Falbe shouted. I know who I'm dealing with here!

Unfortunately he had to do some shopping now, W. excused himself.—Go ahead, she said, and if you don't find what you're looking for, come to me . . . And once more she raised her voice: It's just about the rent . . . the people here'll be thinking God knows what!—And whispering again: But you'll have to come up and visit me soon, and I'll tell you the whole story . . .

When Feuerbach showed up again, he asked if W. couldn't find out when this Harry Falbe was planning his next escape attempt.—It was one of those fits of directness with which W. would grow familiar.

W. wasn't the least bit nonplussed (it surprised him that he wasn't nonplussed).—No, I can't, he responded coolly, because it doesn't interest me in the slightest . . . so is that what I need a company flat for?

Sure you can find it out! You could do it, you've got an excellent relationship with his aunt, but of course you think a case like that is way below your level. Maybe life really is better the way you live it . . . you with your bohemian existence. You know what, if you keep that up for long, one of these days they'll have you by the short hairs, and then you'll need someone to save your skin. Do you think anyone still remembers you down in your backwater . . . they all think you've drowned in Bohemia already. You know what we've got here . . . a few tattered pieces of paper with a big fat line through your name. See, the guys down there, they don't have any more truck with you, none of them is going to get you off the hook . . .

Another time (W.'s memories blurred more and more; the details of this running battle with Feuerbach, who courted him, who kept trying to induce him to move to the other flat, the separate fragmentary conversations with this person could no longer be forced into orderly sequences; they were scattered throughout the entire summer, in which at times he seemed to have escaped the first lieutenant . . . who was somehow always near, though; Feuerbach's meddling voice was in his sleep, and in his sleeplessness in the summer heat) . . . perhaps just two or three days later, his pursuer was in a more conciliatory mood, and said: Stay as you are, you're just right that way. Over in the West you'd probably run into trouble with this attitude, but that's exactly why you'd be believable . . . You live for literature, you lead a literary life. Or that's what you intend . . . honestly, I have much more sympathy for that than you can imagine. But you should ask yourself how you're planning to write in that icebox in the winter . . .

Suddenly it occurred to W. that the boss—down in the small town—had harped on this subject as well: the exodus of the literati, the fact that more and more writers were leaving the country, establishing themselves across the border, often in West Berlin; the boss had mentioned increasing reports to this effect in the Western media, while the media here ignored these things entirely.

And why should there be a public discussion? he'd said with a rather sheepish expression, as though hoping W. would object (of course he didn't). We're already in a position where all we can do is react to the West . . . we can't keep letting them put us on the spot . . . He thought for a while: I don't understand what people find so enticing about life over there. Of course some of them had their problems here, some of their books were published over there and not over here . . . so? The problems would have passed, and the authors would have risen like phoenixes from the ashes. And on top of it they'd have kept their bonus points from over there . . . of course some of them were smarter and just went over temporarily, with a visa from us!

Maybe some of them just don't believe the system has a future any more? W. had interrupted him.

That's a perfectly fine thing to think about . . . the way you can think about lots of things. But why don't these people think about it here? Do you suppose I'm not constantly thinking about it myself? I'm telling you, sometimes I don't believe in this future either, when I really think it over. But one thing's for sure, I couldn't care less whether this system has a future or not, because that doesn't change my function at all, not in the slightest. And a writer's function wouldn't change one bit either, believe me, it's exactly the same. You could ask yourself: since when is it even necessary for a writer to be sitting in a system with a future . . . just the opposite would be necessary, wouldn't it? What's a serious writer supposed to write about in a country that has the future on its side? That's got to be practically fatal for that writer's coming to grips with his world. Do we need the kind of author who preaches people better morals . . . no, we don't, I say, I say the police should see to that. Of course at the Ministry of Culture they have to go on claiming we need writers who grapple with the contradictions of socialism. But I say . . . we say, no, the police should take care of that, the judiciary. I don't know what we need, but we don't need the kind of authors who think we're a safe bet. Maybe we need a writer who goes down along with us, with flying colours. That would be true class . . .

Would you go down with flying colours, along with the writer, really?

Me . . . why me . . . OK, we'd have to wait and see. But after all, our sort needs role models!

W. asked himself whether this sort of speech could just as well have come from Feuerbach . . . probably not! At any rate, it all wouldn't have been set forth with the same vehemence (Feuerbach was less authentic than the boss! W. said to himself) . . . he, Feuerbach, had made only scattered pronouncements along those lines, and they didn't touch on the philosophical level, only on probabilities; perhaps that was why they contradicted each other from one day to the next.—What kind of a writer would you be over in the West, anyway, the first lieutenant had flung out one time at the end of a conversation. You'd get to play the token victim of oppression for a while, and then the next person would come along, and that'd be it with your popularity.

And so there were repeated pronouncements (W. mixed them up, his powers of recall were poor) essentially advising him against relocating his existence, his literary existence, to the West . . . and yet these pronouncements kept the issue alive . . . and they seemed to presuppose that he harboured such intentions, although he'd never spoken of them.—In this republic, evidently, these things were the be-all and end-all:

did someone intend to leave the country or not? Evidently this had become the main criterion for evaluating a person's existence. The question of this intent—to stay or not to stay—utterly dominated the collective consciousness (and had long since become a paraphrase of Hamlet's monologue); the contemplation of this question had become the sole shared trait of an entire people. The question haunted all levels of society, from the lavatory attendant's cubicle to the People's Parliament, and this state of affairs bore strange fruit: if anyone had so far failed to announce this intent, this was seen as a provocation. If someone professed the will to stay, he made himself highly suspect . . . if someone had nothing at all to say, heaven and earth had to be set into motion to elicit his thoughts on the matter. The organs occupied with investigating the thought processes in their citizens' brains seemed to know but one central problem: Is it true that those who persist in silence on this issue are planning their imminent defection? Why are they so adamantly silent if they don't have this plan? How can you be silent about things you aren't in fact thinking?

And so banners were carried through the capital at the mass demonstrations on national holidays, past the tribunes of the rulers, bearing the sober words: We Love Our Republic!

In this connection W. recalled having confided in Feuerbach that he'd had a long conversation with his landlady . . . That had been when autumn was approaching, but the weather was still hot; in his room all summer long W. had felt he was in an incubator; he was completely knackered as he walked up to Feuerbach, a fired-up nervous wreck who slept as he walked and at night, in his sleep, sweated, seethed and conducted crazed dialogues with his lost shadow; they met at the tables outside a small cafe at the eastern end of Frankfurter Allee.

Really? Feuerbach said, astonished (his face brightened despite the blinding afternoon light; he played his astonishment perfectly). You really went up to see her? Then it's too bad you'll be moving out . . . what was she like, your landlady?

Harry Falbe, as he'd been able to conclude beyond a shadow of doubt from his conversations with her, had completely abandoned the intent to go West a long time ago . . .

Impossible! said Feuerbach.

He's always been open towards his aunt . . . I'd say you can depend on it!

Feuerbach's face had darkened again: That's a completely false assessment, that's information we can't possibly submit. We could never pass it on like that, certainly not when you say aunt . . . that's not his aunt! When the time comes with this Falbe, we'll have to look sharp. And you're gullible, you fall for things. What we're doing here is proving our suspicions against him . . . and you're steering in the opposite direction, you're making him out to be a saint. As if he weren't thinking day and night of how to put one over on us!

Why are you so hell-bent on proving something against this pathetic character?

Whether I like it or not, when a guy's been mixed up in this as long as Falbe has, he simply has to have an intention of some kind. Understand? No, you don't understand, you don't want to, you're playing the sentimental type again. And you think too much about the great scheme of things, about the consequences of what needs to be done. It would be much simpler just to take things one step at a time and leave the rest to take its course, leave it to the people who understand a bit about these things . . .

Leave the rest to fate, said W. And we're fate, is that it?

Fate is old-fashioned. Fate will be getting a new name soon, I daresay! he said darkly.

Still later (or still earlier) he seemed to expand on his ideas . . . or seemed to set forth a preliminary stage thereof: You know, you're like most people, you're like a reader who has the frightening sense that he doesn't understand a certain book. This person keeps flipping back and forth through the pages, looking something up again, reading on ahead, starting over and over again . . . instead of trusting that the whole thing will gradually reveal itself on its own.

I'll make a note of that, said W., in other words we should kindly leave all thoughts about our future to the State authorities, yessir, I'll make a note of that. No one would ask himself if he wouldn't rather leave the country, everyone would just wait for the step-by-step results to come in . . .

Feuerbach laughed and said: But you are the State authorities, young man!

Feuerbach's thoughts often seemed to correspond to the small-town boss', or their mindsets seemed embroiled in conflict (incidentally, the two probably would have loathed each other, thought W.); once again, almost automatically, Feuerbach's speeches had called the boss to mind. Undaunted —all the more when W. tried to escape—the boss had barraged him with his literary views: Of course you could think about going West (he put this forth as though W. had just been thinking out loud on the subject). There were lots of things you could have in your head, especially as a writer. In fact, he'd go even further and say that a writer had to think everything, with thoughts there could be no holding back, or rather, with thoughts there could be no going back. Putting those thoughts into action might be a different thing . . . but thinking itself? You'd be amazed at the thoughts we think possible . . . and maybe you really will be amazed some day. What would you say . . . you'd probably look horrified if I told you a writer has to go so far in his thinking that he can be held criminally liable if that's deemed necessary . . . yes indeed, he has to be willing to go that far! What sort of pathetic literature would we have if the thinking in it were restricted or channelled? Ah well, you know, honestly we have to admit that this is the pathetic literature we've got, and exactly for the reasons I said. When what we urgently need in this country is a literature that runs the risk of being condemned lock, stock and barrel by the Party . . . and I'm saying this even though I myself am in that Party. You can believe me, you've heard it for yourself, I've had these thoughts myself for quite some time, I know it's better not to think them these days. Not out loud, at any rate . . . but I'm not a loud thinker anyway, I'm not a literary type. I'm just thinking to myself. But bit by bit literature could start thinking these thoughts louder . . . and literature, that's you! Now I want to tell you something, if you weren't a writer there's no way you could come to me in my function with thoughts like that . . . but you see, I've just exposed myself to you—I think the same way myself!

You say a writer ought to express thoughts for which he could be taken to court. What exactly would this achieve, in your opinion?

What this would achieve? The boss shook his head and looked genuinely baffled. You don't have a very high opinion of literature! Can you imagine all the things we could achieve with literature? You'd be amazed if you knew . . .

Strangely, W. felt utterly eviscerated each time he submitted to one of these sermons (and once again when he recalled the speeches in idle hours). The words had flooded him, seeming to infiltrate through every orifice and fill him like sand . . . but once inside him it was immediately clear how used up these thoughts were, how far they had departed from all language sprung from life; they were platitudes, bromides, run thousands of times through the mental mills, at best the wording was original. And here lay a resemblance between Feuerbach's speechifying and the boss', even if their messages contradicted each other: ultimately both said the same thing with insultingly dreary contortions.—After letting the memory of one of these lectures run through his mind, W. felt an intense need for simple, even primitive phrases, nothing but sheer human conversation, serving—without a trace of outraged rhetoric—only concrete, artless understanding; he stood once again outside the lamp-bright ground-floor windows of he old days and thirsted for banal utterances, and once again he recalled the boss' key phrase: You see best from the dark into the light!—But suddenly he had the opportunity to ring Frau Falbe's doorbell and chat with her.—That April he'd already taken her up on her offer: he'd had to borrow money from her (as he put it), he'd overreached by paying her three month's rent in advance. She returned him the money and then some; initially he'd thought she was greedy, but that didn't seem to be the case. However, she immediately offered to ask about a job for him, which gave him a scare.—The next day she reminded him that the husband of a friend of hers was the personnel manager at a nearby service company and could surely recommend some appealing jobs.—This happened a few more times; Frau Falbe seemed to have no other topic of conversation, and she began to get on his nerves.—He couldn't work until the 1st of May, or June, he told her, because he had to finish up his writing project by then. But after that, he promised for the sake of peace and quiet, he'd take a job.—In secret, though, that was when he planned to move (though it pained him to leave Frau Falbe before winter!); he decided to ask Feuerbach whether the two-and-a-half-room flat was still free. But now of all times the first lieutenant was nowhere to be found (and at that time

W. didn't yet know where he was fairly sure to find him . . . at that time: it must have been towards the end of April in his first year in Berlin, a time, that is, which was developing more and more gaps in his recollection).

No matter how often W. thought about these gaps, nothing came to fill them . . . finally he told himself he'd have to re-enact in his mind the end of his relationship with his boss . . . he'd have to kick the boss out of his head—then he'd see more clearly, even at the cost of getting completely stuck on Feuerbach.—He asked himself whether he'd ever told the first lieutenant anything about the boss . . . he'd passed nothing on, he'd acted properly . . . or whether Feuerbach had ever sounded him out along these lines: here too the answer was no. It was strange; Feuerbach had never asked about his life in the town of A. . . . who his associates were there, how he had ended up in this situation in the first place. No, the back story didn't interest the first lieutenant in the slightest (surprisingly enough, given that they had at least one mutual acquaintance, Harry Falbe, who'd dropped off the radar); no, Feuerbach asked no questions about the past . . . They're trivialists! thought W. Because how can there be a proper text that doesn't constantly refer to its back story?

The obvious suspicion was that Feuerbach already knew it all . . . and the source of this knowledge could hardly be any-one but the boss. Or the lanky guy . . . the lanky ruminant, running reports back and forth between Feuerbach and the boss and pocketing a tip on top of it, probably without either one knowing about the other?—How often W. had seen crowds crowned by one lone small-headed shadow, Berlin's petty bourgeoisie surging down the boulevards, towards the sun that blazed in the West, and in its midst a looming form: the bearer of the news, waving from afar.

The thought of the boss caused W. some chagrin; the boss had been, at least in A., something of an authority for him. Many of the boss' remarks had sounded quite convincing to W . . . now they made him shake his head.—The W. he had been at the time must have succumbed to a certain fascination; he could see how he had followed the boss defensively at first, then with increasing suspense: how the boss spoke, first in a murmur, mouth downturned, as though soliloquizing, then glancing more frequently at his listener and speaking with greater intensity, but never losing a certain elegant, breezy casualness, as though merely airing thoughts . . . mere thoughts. And as his voice assumed a provocative tone, he occasionally dispensed with the canon of set terms, which must have had a liberating effect on the W. of that time. And the boss was the only one who showed interest in this W.'s 'work as a writer'.

One time the boss had practically woken him up. Pull yourself together, old boy. You've got to show your face at work again tomorrow! Otherwise you'll lose the ground beneath your feet, you'll develop more and more dependencies. With us you can't totally go to the dogs, don't even try. You can't live from collecting empty beer bottles in parked S-Bahn trains . . . certainly not at the small-town station here. It's not even enough for the last few shots of booze you need for the day. And by the way, you ought to be in a position to drink better stuff, not this rotgut; if you've got to ruin your liver, at least do it with the good brands . . .

W. was barely capable of reacting to ambushes of this kind; it seemed he had indeed been startled from a kind of half-sleep . . . he'd been trying to write poems the night before (he could barely remember how many, or what they were like); after that he'd fallen into a deep depression, skipping work, staggering into town that afternoon and through a series of pubs; in the station restaurant—his back to the dining room, staring out the window at the rail yard that sank into the fog, where hollowly rumbling freight cars were being shunted amid the workers' muffled yells—he'd been picked up by the boss, already with a row of empty glasses in front of him, which no one cleared away in this dive; and the boss said: Are you thinking about Leipzig? It's not far . . . or have your thoughts already flown further?

By the way, if I were you I wouldn't think of living as a freelancer, said the boss, accompanying him through town unasked . . . W. had tried to shake him off but the alcohol lamed his limbs, and finally he'd even had to endure the boss thrusting a hand under his upper arm and leading him with theatrical courtesy through the pedestrian traffic.—If you do your job, the boss lectured on next to his ear, if you keep an eye out for a proper job, you'll have plenty of time still for your work as a writer. And then you'll be spared harassment from official quarters . . . which includes me—as you know!—and you wouldn't be completely at the mercy of these quarters . . . He gave a charming grin: So watch out for us! Think of your literature . . . And without missing a beat he turned earnest again: And keep behaving as usual towards any kind of recruitment attempts . . . coming from our quarters. Act indifferent. Act opaque—if you give a clear yes, you're in on the story, and if you give a clear no you're in on it too. And really, no one needs to know the things I'm telling you, no one from our quarters either.

We've never let anyone starve to death . . . just saying, in case you ever need support. If anything goes wrong at your factory, if they keep assigning you to the boiler room . . . assuming you don't want that any more . . . or I'm just thinking of those perpetual housing issues . . . or if people don't leave you in peace, I'm thinking of these dimwits with their eternal special work details in the factories, they ought to get a grip on their factory management themselves, or send the slow-pokes from the office into the production halls on Sundays ...just say the word! Or if you need a new rain gutter, or some pickets for your fence, a permit for a garage, or if you notice that you're slowly turning impotent, we've got Western meds, or gold fillings, gold fillings! Just a little trip over the Oberbaumbrücke to West Berlin and you can get gold for fillings; if you have any problems, let us know. As long as you can do without support, don't let us spoil things for you. Have a rest, and when you've got your strength back, keep on writing!

(Behind him the barely audible jitter of a refrigerator seemed to trickle through the concrete; the boss' voice was slowly putting him to sleep ...)

You'll be wondering, how come the guy's so well informed? Where does he get his insights ... it's all because we're so patient. With patience you can learn everything, we've got time. We keep telling ourselves: One of these days a harsh winter will come, and him with his broken-down heating stove! I wouldn't even call it insight, I'd call it my faith in literature. I've taken the liberty, from the stock of liberty we have, of permitting myself to read the submissions you've posted to publishers every now and then. I thought, I want to know who I'm dealing with here. In the long run I don't want to be stuck dealing with a dud again, I've had that far too often already ... and the last attempt was the long-legged loser, where you can see it a mile off. And I didn't even need to breach the sanctity of the post ... dear God, that sanctity of the post that doesn't exist anywhere in the world these days. And why should it, that relic of early bourgeois sentimentality ... maybe in benighted dictatorships like South Korea they still talk about the sanctity of the post ... because the intelligence services in those countries can't read and write anyway. No, all I needed to do was call up a few friends of mine. I've got some pretty good friends at a couple of publishers, and there's a lot of things they could do for you.

In a nutshell, your case is far from hopeless, on the contrary! So there's just one more thing I want to tell you: Don't sign anything! Better not to, better to stay independent. Independent people are better, there are no practical constraints, they're more reliable. Talk to me voluntarily, it's better that way! There's nothing I want to know from you! Not what that guy, or that lady, or your grandma, or that guy's great-grandma thinks about that other guy ... I know all that already. They think I'm a son of a bitch, and they'll soon think the same of you ... if you sign anything. So, I don't think much of what the little überfatso put in front of you with his chubby paws ... did he do that yet? If I were you I'd say, I'm not going to sign that, I'm staying independent.

(Enough! he thought. Enough, no more now ... He'd started up, frightened by a noise, by a ticking, dripping echo somewhere, lasting barely a second. He listened, but all was still; only everywhere, without beginning or end, was the barely audible hum of the stones. And yet there seemed to have been a step, several quick steps ... he'd thought for quite some time that he was being frequented down here.—But that was really enough now ... He stood up and started on his way. What made him spend hours thinking the boss' thoughts ... adding his own thoughts, completing the boss' speeches with his own words?—Evidently he barely had any choice left, evidently his mind could only choose between the boss and Feuerbach.

Painstakingly extinguishing the light behind him in each section of the basement, he made his way towards the exit, up towards the light of day, where perhaps now it was night again.)

As he walked he recalled what else the boss had said. After advising W. not to move to Leipzig . . . Preferably not, or rather, definitely not, down there you'll just be lost in the crowd . . . he'd explained his words as follows: Here we have a certain allotment of options that doesn't get used at all . . . true, it's much smaller than the one in Leipzig, but in Leipzig . . . and in Berlin . . . it gets exploited to the full, simply because there are enough people who can use it. There seem to be enough, I say to you, because opinions on these people can differ. Whereas with us there's just no one, however much I look around. I mean the question of travelling to NonSoc States— you know what I mean! Here things have to get crazy before we get permits, we'd have to have people dying over there. But one or two numbers . . . they say to themselves, numbers for passports, those we have. And I don't have a proper writer here, for instance, I can't keep requesting the visa for myself. I need an artist or a writer here in the district who I could con- science supporting over there for a year or more, sometimes a bit less.

Am I supposed to send the long-legged loser? I'd never see him again. You see, he's also trying his hand at writing . . . I could show you something he published, but let's not get into that. With you we'd be sure that you'd be quick to grasp what you're in for over there: publicity, publicity till you've got it coming out both ends, you'll be oh so grateful to me. All joking aside, with you we wouldn't be worried that you wouldn't get enough invitations, that's how the industry works over there, you'd just have to become a bit better known first . . .

Better known? No one knows me at all, W. lamented.

I do . . . and I'm not no one!—But moving right along, for these purposes a major publication over here wouldn't even be that advantageous . . . besides, it would take too long. Of course we could breathe down the printers' necks and get you run off in three months, but it would come out in the end . . . just imagine, because of you the, say, 111th edition of Kurella's[4] speeches gets postponed, that would draw attention. We'd have to place work of yours in magazines . . . by no means your best work, and then we'd have to kick out the editor . . . purge the whole editorial board, they'd probably be relieved. And all that because of your work, can you picture the press we'd get over there . . .

At this point the boss laughed like the young-at-heart protagonist of a well-intentioned novel.

Or we take you together with a whole group, we do a whole bunch, we do an anthology . . .

I've thought through all the variants, it would all take much too long. The drastic methods would be best, the press is more likely to fall for those, of course . . . those work, by the 1st of May, June of next year we'd have you on location. So we arrest the man in question, a month later the whole world finds out about it, two weeks after that the media circus is at its height, and before things get critical for the reputation of the fatherland, we let you out again . . . if necessary straight to West Berlin. Only the man in question would have to have a certain degree of stamina . . . probably not a problem with you . . . because of course things aren't very cosy in there. I know what I'm talking about, I know our rest homes from the inside, you have to know what you're doing, there are so-called imponderabilities, risk factors, if that means anything to you.

But even for that it would be better to make you known in the so-called Scene first, in a city, a larger one . . . Leipzig, Magdeburg, maybe it doesn't have to be Berlin right off the bat, the Scene knows no boundaries. You'd have to hang around there for a while and check things out. We'd ask you what form you'd like that to take . . . if you want an easy job that earns you your pocket money, or if you want to be completely ... they've got quite a social consciousness there! ... in a vacuum, quasi with a burnt-out background and a penchant for expensive liquor ... that's good, but better still: always after cheap booze, watch out for your liver, though! And after those Western women they've always got running around ... but you'd find that a bit more complicated. At any rate, you'd have to belong for a while, but not belong entirely ...

Of course you'd just be acting snoozy. In reality you'd have to be extremely alert. Even though nothing dramatic will be happening; you'll probably get bored pretty quickly. That's how I picture it being when you're writing a story and you have to fill in all the everyday odds and ends that have to go in there to give the characters a real setting ... that's what I'd keep in mind if I were you. That is, how to depict the day-to-day trivia ... that's when writing is the hardest, I'd imagine. How does this character live, what from, where did he get the watch he's wearing. And what do the people do when they're not sitting around in the Scene's bars and hangouts. How are the marriages holding up, if applicable, and always keep an eye on the kids, if applicable. Are there homosexual proclivities, that's important. And what does the character eat ... because he is what he eats. And does he use the toilet ... and when; you've got to keep that in mind too. You can fill in the time later, though. These are all questions that arise when you're writing, too ... the cigarette brand! Or are they cigars, reeking of sulphur and phosphorus. And of course you must never give clear answers yourself, you always have to be a bit mysterious. Then people will notice you, and you'll get drawn in. So it's best to keep mum about what you do, where you come from, act a bit confused, it's perfectly fine to be ashamed of your background ... all you've got to do is think of the boss. Give the wrong destinations, Berlin instead of Leipzig, and later say you just misspoke. This ought to make your job infinitely interesting, and when you think about it, it'll keep you on the ball ...

But W. couldn't recall ever having read a spy novel or mystery in which one of the characters used the toilet, unless it was crucial to the plot. And such 'day-to-day trivia' was always left out as well if it didn't bear on the reasoning in the case under investigation.—This was about the prose of everyday life, then, about realistic stories, about the realism of the stories he was to examine. It wasn't about the realism of his own story ... which was thus left outside in the dark.—And this, W. said to himself, was the main feature of the non-existent socialist realism of which the boss had had such a poor opinion.

Enough of that now; the boss had accompanied W., suede-soft arm in the bend of his elbow, two-thirds of the way through town; the boss' spiel had accompanied him, torn him from his late-afternoon doze, put him on edge and then exhausted him again ... to this day the boss' spiel had left him no time to reply.—Already near home, W. had turned around and walked into town again; the boss accompanied him; W. stopped in front of a pub.—What, said the boss, you mean we're supposed to go in there?

They found a free table, and soon there were two full glasses in front of them; the boss was about to speak, but W. had to use the toilet. He knew the way there led across a stairwell with a door to the courtyard; escape was possible through the door and across the yard.—And at the table in the taproom the boss sat talking, almost whispering, for the other guests' bovine eyes were fixed on him; he talked softly, smiling, constantly sipping his beer and clearing his throat in the smoke, at the shadow on the chair beside him, who didn't touch his beer.

There was no such back way in the little cafe on Frankfurter Allee where Feuerbach had invited him one day. He had found himself a window seat there and turned away everyone who asked to share the table . . . they accepted this, though the cafe began to fill up in the evening. He waited for the first lieutenant, several times seeming to see him appear amid the pedestrians who moved along the pavement in the light of the street lamps coming on; it was almost bright still . . . Feuerbach didn't come. Little by little the darkness falling outside began to impair visibility . . . he had time to stare out at the broad traffic artery and think his thoughts. Behind him, in the taproom, the murmur of voices swelled . . . gradually it displaced the torrent of his memories which lectured on unheeded somewhere near him, the taproom's babel of voices surging over them like rising waters . . . it was an unintelligible murmur; no one in the cafe spoke loudly enough for anyone else to listen in, that was the typical way of speaking here in the cafe, audible thanks only to the growing number of young men, who kept on coming, no longer sitting alone now, and floated their sotto voce conversations into the smoke-filled air . . . and when the medley of voices had reached a level that drowned the noises he produced himself (the clink of the coffee cup), when it had become an even muttering swell, the memories regained their foothold in his mind. They were called up by the gathering haze in the lamplight on the street, where the motor traffic still showed no signs of letting up . . . this fog reminded him that the winter wasn't over yet . . . his first real winter here in Berlin. Clouds of frost still swirled over the multilane boulevard . . . mixing with the blue-black clouds of exhaust spewed into the air by all the trucks still on the road now. Especially in the lanes on this side of the boulevard, close by the cafe's big window—on the right side, where the cars drove towards the city centre, that is, towards the West—

the traffic was increasing even now . . . the cars shot forward like bullets when the traffic light near the pedestrian underpass turned green, a dense squadron of vehicles, welded in an array whose inner structure never changed, seeming to form a fanned-out frayed jagged monster, luridly aflicker in a cascade of flashing, mutually obstructive lights, and trailing its glowing red tail lights, while over the racing agglomeration a bank of smoke washed, turbulent at first, but soon flowing more sluggishly and uniformly, and now rising into the red-yellow light of the streetlamps . . . and already a new convoy of cars had pulled up and released a new cloud of smoke beneath it; a moment before, down the street to the right, you'd heard the polyphonic shriek of brakes with which the previous automobile force had stopped at the next traffic light . . . And already they were driving on, you could hear it, and the next horde of cars abreast of the window accelerated, revving up even harder to finally outstrip and outdo the red light phases . . . and so cohort after cohort raced towards the West, and the drone of their horsepower rolled across the entire city: Westward, Westward, whither all motion seemed to strive unstopping.

There in the West all these forces seemed to gather . . . there in the West somewhere, beneath this sky shot with light, West Berlin droned and lived and creaked at the seams . . . there, somewhere, this country's real heart panted and pumped, locked in a choking iron ring.

Why do they still bother writing books in the industry over there, do you have any clue?—That launched Feuerbach's spiel, a variation on a theme familiar to W. Unlike the boss, Feuerbach took a less optimistic view of it all: Isn't a writer over there, if you can even find one any more, reduced to being a tool of the bourgeois consciousness . . . busy rearranging the clichés of consumerism? If he's lucky, no one notices, and everyone keeps on using the old clichés; if he's out of luck, they'll make a new cliché out of his last hard-won stroke of inspiration. Or how do you picture the outfit over there?

Due to the boss' lectures, W. did have a picture, leaning towards a negative reply in the question of whether you'd be able to find him over there.—Wouldn't it be tempting, he thought, to vanish without a trace in West Berlin?

Of course literature in Western society didn't necessarily have a utility value, he had to be clear about that. You didn't need to read the structuralists, who relished it, to figure that out. The way he saw it, in the worst-case scenario he had only two options: either you conformed to fashion, constantly chasing trends . . . what a low-down sort of spying, always having to identify and record the latest trends, and that without any clear, Classified Guidelines to stick to! . . . or you became a lone wolf who hewed to his literary imperatives. In the second case you could easily vanish on the margins of the metropolises, leading a shadowy existence in dark side streets. And you'd have to reckon that once there you'd have no opportunity to emerge into the light again.

As it was, he didn't need to worry much about it, since at the moment there was little prospect that such a suggestion on his part would be accommodated. Once he had tried, with due care, to talk about it with Feuerbach. First Feuerbach had refused to understand a thing, and then asked: Who put that idea into your head?

After some hesitation he said: There you are charging on ahead, way to go . . . So you're not happy with us any more? When you've only just left your podunk town behind . . . is it even a year that you've been up here with us?—'Up here with us' referred to the privilege of living in the capital.—Isn't there a bit more you need to do? Just what accomplishments do you feel you've chalked up?

So what's simply forbidden for most people, what everyone's supposed to see as treason, has the virtue, just as a side note, of functioning as a reward for good performance! W. thought with derision. Could it come as a surprise, then, if a people that was performing non-stop at its creative peak (you could read that by the yard in the newspapers) had now come in its entirety to crave exactly this reward . . . and long found it highly objectionable that this honour went only to the functionaries in the people's place?

I'm sure you've heard, Feuerbach said a few days later, that for some time there've been so-called embassy occupations going on? Yes, it's true . . . a couple of people have been hanging out at the Permanent Mission on Hannoversche Strasse for a while now . . . and I think there are a few crazies in the American Embassy too.[5] And we're having trouble keeping this from getting too much publicity. It's a rather tricky situation, you see . . . He seemed to cast about for the briefest and most plausible way to put it, staring intently at W.'s averted face: It's not the first time, up until now we've always managed to cope. Because it didn't get too much publicity . . . otherwise things like that can escalate. You know, if they start to catch on! Until now we've always given these nutcases the silent treatment . . . but if we keep it up, we give the Permanent Mission all kinds of options. In practical terms, this is the situation; they're demanding that we let the people leave the country as quickly as possible, or they'll renege on the agreement to keep mum about the situation, get my drift?

Of course W. had heard; there had been isolated incidents for the past year now, and he'd always heard the news with a certain sense of triumph. Now he had to put on an ingenuous look.

Have you ever been inside the Permanent Mission? asked Feuerbach.

W. said he had; it would have been pointless to deny it, since it was dead certain that lists existed of all the people who'd ever seen an art exhibition or gone to one of the poetry readings on Hannoversche Strasse; in the Berlin art scene where W. occasionally moved, attendance at these events was taken for granted.

The first lieutenant said: You know, we were thinking of sending you in there again. Not to see an exhibition . . . we might be planning to position you in there, yes, you ought to get into the Permanent Mission too. Is that an idea you could take to?

You mean I should infiltrate the embassy refugees?

Yes . . . but don't put it that way, you're worse than the Western press! Feuerbach made a pained grimace, then changed the subject: Do you remember working as a stoker on Chausseestrasse, in the branch of REWATEX cattycorner from the Brecht Bookshop? Back then you were still asleep for us, the last few months; at least you were half asleep, you were drunk the whole time! So I guess that's why you can't remember?

Yes I do, I remember, it's not that long ago!

And then when you got off work in the afternoon you went to the Brecht Bookshop to buy books . . . they always have a few more copies of the books that sell out right away everywhere else . . . remember? And then you took this packet of books to the pub on Hannoversche, right across from the Permanent Mission. Where there was a very good view of who went in and out of the Mission . . .

It was unnecessary to remind him of that time (the only thing he'd been reminded of was that you were under constant surveillance here in Berlin); the summer months in the Chausseestrasse branch of REWATEX were quite present in his mind. He had let Frau Falbe persuade him to get a job after all; undaunted, she'd kept coming with offers from that personnel manager, the husband of her acquaintance; finally, worn down, he'd accepted the last offer, perhaps the worst of the choices; he accepted the position due to the promise of good pay.

This time lingered in his memory as a singular concentration of scorching days (now, as Feuerbach reminded him of it, the next summer was not far off . . .).—Back then the summer had brought everything to a grinding halt, only the REWATEX branch went on laundering unperturbed and required vigorous stoking. The city clamour flagged and lay fallow, steaming away with smouldering, putrid smells over pavements that glimmered bluish in the sun's glare. The days were broken only by gruellingly short nights, when a fire-red moon raced at high speed over the urban desert; by day all the windows on the streets were closed and curtained, the heat crept through the city like a sickness with no cure. The cars ceased to move, and the empty streetcars trundled through the maze of houses like obscure iron machines whose function consisted in producing lethal noise, but in the end even it remained strangely muffled between the extinct facades. But on Chausseestrasse, and further down on Friedrichstrasse, the tourists marched along, swathed in gaudy, skimpy bits of fabric, clothing whose fantastical cut immediately betrayed that they came from the West, where the weather had to be still more excruciating. As he was still living at Frau Falbe's, he had an obscenely long way to work; just a month after starting at the Municipal Laundries he had been transferred to the small unit on Chausseestrasse, where the work was easy, but the hours unconscionably long. The branch consisted mainly of a self-service laundry accessed from the boulevard, but in the back building there was a section for so-called household linen which was dropped off at the front and processed ready-to-use in the back, employing steam-powered wringers and driers. Before these machines could be put to work at six in the morning, the coal-fired boiler had to be pressurized, meaning that W. had to start stoking no later than five. But before that he had more than an hour's journey with the day's first buses and S-Bahn trains. And then his work day lasted until four in the afternoon, sometimes longer, depending on the amount of laundry . . . with only the minor mitigation of a two-hour lunch break. Due to the long hours, he had abandoned his job at the REWATEX laundry combine that same autumn. And to avoid justifying himself in front of Frau Falbe, in the end he moved to a different neighbourhood.

And on these two-hour lunch breaks you sat in the pub and spent the whole time staring at the gate of the Permanent Mission, said Feuerbach. And what else could you have stared at, there's only the one window. It was a pleasure to watch the beer flow down your gullet . . . what might you have been thinking the whole time? You sat by the window, staring out . . . always the same things to see . . . is the beer better in West Berlin, you may have asked yourself. Or you asked yourself why there were more and more green-uniformed policemen out in front of the building. What would you say if I told you we really were planning to have you go along into the mission? It would have looked great if you'd showed up right on your lunch break, still in your work clothes, with that packet of books under your arm. That's the poor poet who never got to publish a thing in his own country and has to work as a stoker for REWATEX. That would have been a terrific legend for you, quite convincing, I think . . . Feuerbach waited for his words to have an effect; seeing none, he went on: Of course we left you alone on purpose until you'd acquired that image . . . you'll always have that, anyway, it'll be a great entrée to the local scene, for instance. But still, I think it's too bad . . . oh, what am I saying! . . . that my wonderful plan fell through. I'd almost sold the chiefs on it already . . . but then someone came and let the cat out of the bag! I'd had it all figured out. Of course you weren't really going to go to West Berlin. Just the opposite, you were supposed to cave in at the Permanent Mission. Yeah, you were supposed to go to pieces, what with the long wait and the uncertainty. That would have been understandable in your case, with someone who's got his decent job and good pay. So you were going to be the first to crumble in the negotiations, and you were going to be the proof that nothing would happen to the people who came back voluntarily. You see, for me you were our chance to take the offensive there. And what would have happened—the other people in there would have peeled off one by one, that would've been it for their solidarity.

And when the ones who peeled off came, you could have picked them up one by one and arrested them! said W.

I'll leave that part open! said Feuerbach. That wouldn't be our affair any more. But don't you want to know who came and screwed up my wonderful story?

W. gave no reply, and the first lieutenant said: You know the guy. He plays the big boss in the Podunk town you came from. You know the guy, a namby-pamby type with a salt-and-pepper fur collar, no clue about literature. He went and tipped us off, he let the cat out of the bag, or rather, he had it delivered by some lanky monster from his department. Hands off, he really does want to go West! That was the message . . . he really wants to defect, we've found him out: source-that-must-go-unnamed, that's it, period. And of course the chiefs threw up their hands: What, he really wants to go West . . . impossible, that's it, case closed!

Who knows, maybe they're right, mused Feuerbach after a while, who knows. You really ought to go on the record about that! What were you thinking about the whole time at the window of the pub on Hannoversche Strasse? The chiefs will have been wondering that too. But still, my dear man, I haven't quite written off this plan yet . . .

He'd had completely different things on his mind when he sat at the window of this pub staring out at Hannoversche Strasse, where there was almost no traffic any more. And where he gazed across between the People's Policemen and civilians practicing their changings of the guard on the yard outside the Mission. One arm resting on the packet of books at the edge of the table, in the other hand the beer glass, between his fingertips a cigarette he forgot to light until the waiter came by and held out a burning lighter. He couldn't help thinking how he was simply too tired to write, how all his recent writing attempts had failed in fairly pathetic fashion . . . the job in the laundry ate up his time, he barely slept any more, the summer's unbroken blaze did the rest. He was considering giving up the job and moving out on Frau Falbe . . . but this very idea of moving out on Frau Falbe had become a problem for him . . . and this summer his thoughts liked to dwell on her. He kept asking himself how old she could be . . . ultimately she could only be six or seven years older than he, ten at most, Frau Falbe was a chatterbox, always chattering the same things, she no longer placed much value on her appearance, going around in her bathrobe until noon, but you couldn't say she was bad-looking. Evidently she hadn't had children; most of the time she looked somewhat disappointed and let herself go a bit, but she had the energetic figure of a sturdy woman, not to be called fat. And she had intelligent eyes, when she wasn't wiped out by the dog days, as she put it.

Lately Frau Falbe had actually taken on the task of waking him early in the morning (he was incredulous at first; she herself had offered to do it after he'd badly overslept several times: How will I be able to face my friend if her husband the personnel manager finds out!) . . . and day after day he had the feeling that she used the informal 'you' in the morning when she came into his room . . . once he was fully conscious she used the formal 'you' again and kept it up all day long.—Just let me have my way, it's fine, I've got the other key, and I can't sleep in this heat anyway. You just toss and turn in bed all night thinking God knows what. It's impossible to stand it in bed . . . yeah, yeah, I remember from Harry what it's like getting up then. And you, you've got to get up just past three when it's still dark, where will it all end. You ought to lie down instead of sleeping sitting up in the armchair all the time . . .

You just brood too much, she said. And then you can't fall asleep, and when you have to get up, you fall asleep in the armchair. What are you constantly brooding about, that's no state for a young man like you.

Young? I'll be young again in my next life, said W.

Yeah, yeah, she said, that's what you're thinking about! You're constantly thinking about your next life, that's no state for a young man to be in. You'd be better off thinking about the here and now . . .

He woke up one morning at a time which struck him each day anew as profoundly ungodly, and saw light in his room (the blind was pulled down) . . . his pyjamas were drenched with sweat, he'd covered himself only with a sheet, and as usual even it was tossed off, lying bunched up at his feet. As his initial rebellion against this forced awakening died down, he smelt coffee in the room and knew that Frau Falbe was somewhere in the immediate vicinity. The next moment he felt an urgent, almost painful pressure in his bladder (from the beer he'd drunk that evening to put himself to sleep), and became aware of a conspicuous object on his lower body, straining the fabric of his pants and no doubt visible at a glance; he attempted a weary smile and turned away from the room to the wall; he heard a woman's low voice, his eyes fell shut again at once, and in the darkness that returned to his skull he tried to suppress a spasmodic twinge beneath the cranium. But Frau Falbe wouldn't let him go back to sleep, she seized him by the shoulder and hip and with gentle force— murmuring to herself ceaselessly—turned him onto his back again so he had to open his eyes; once again the aching organ on his lower body loomed into the light. Frau Falbe murmured something about her previous tenant Harry, in cases like this he'd been sensible enough to sleep upstairs at her place from the outset—otherwise there would have been even more of a drama on the days when he had to report . . . Finally W. put his feet on the floor. With the pain in his abdomen he had to sit doubled over; he stayed that way until the woman turned away for a few seconds to pour a cup of coffee, then went to the toilet outside in the stairwell.—The following mornings the coffee was already poured, and instead of turning away, Frau Falbe leant on the edge of the desk waiting for him to cross the room, and was still studying him unabashedly when he returned, relieved, from the toilet; then she sat sideways in her ankle-long bathrobe on the chair behind the desk, with the armchair pulled up for him to sit on. She'd poured two cups of coffee and set out a little jug of milk . . . Really I can't take coffee this early, she said, especially not in this heat! But on your own you might not drink any coffee at all . . .

You've got to wash your pyjamas, she said (of course he'd noticed her critical gaze fixed on the increasingly discoloured front of his pyjama pants). If you can't do it in the laundry, give me the pyjamas, I'll have them dry again by this evening.—

Probably I can have them washed at the laundry, and dried there, too. If you like, I can take the bedclothes as well, we've got permission to do that.—The next few days she didn't miss a chance to remind him to wash the pyjamas.—Take them off, she said, I've got to wash them!—Finally one day he packed a bag full of bedding, underclothes and the pyjamas and took it with him to the laundry, where they told him he couldn't have the things back until the next day. The next morning, a Friday, as he lay in his shorts on the unmade cot, Frau Falbe said disapprovingly: I told you you should give them to me . . . besides, just one set of bedclothes isn't enough. You can take some home from the laundry, they've got enough bedding there that people don't pick up again. But let me give you something more for the weekend.—She'd already lent him the first set of bedclothes that was now at the laundry: I used to let Harry use it, it was exactly the same with him, he didn't even have a sheet to call his own!

So why don't you want to move out on the old girl any more? asked Feuerbach, seeming to turn the question capriciously in his mind. I can imagine—you suddenly feel real cosy with the old girl.—By now it was autumn, the heat had died down, meaning that he slept better and was even harder to wake in the morning.

Well, soon you'll have to move out, it'll be quite an icebox in there when it gets cold. But that you never talked to her about Harry Falbe, that's practically unthinkable. Unthinkable. And she never said anything about me either, that Frau Falbe of yours?

So where is this Harry Falbe you're so interested in? W. asked back. Because I'm not interested in him at all, to be perfectly honest I'm glad not to see him any more.

Why don't you ask the old girl if there's a photo of this Harry Falbe? said Feuerbach.

Frau Falbe talked a great deal about Harry, the previous tenant (and it was long since getting on his nerves), but in all her talk barely a single solid statement emerged . . . she'd never wasted a word on Feuerbach. And now it occurred to him that the first lieutenant had come down the stairs one time, quite a while ago; it seemed he had been up on the first floor . . . in which case of course it was quite possible, indeed probable, that he had forbidden her to mention his visit.

The point of such prohibitions was to create an initial conspirative relationship, on a trial basis, as it were: if the other person complied with the vow of silence, he was already ensnared (and compromised); if he didn't comply with it, he had deconspired and was useless. It was a very simple concept: it took a negligible amount of courage to ignore the vow of silence . . . you could even have disregarded it out of naivety or simply forgotten it . . . all you needed was a little faith in life, and already you were free (retaliation against deconspirees seemed to be the exception, W. believed) . . . so it was completely logical that they were always looking for characters whose faith in community was shattered . . . and that included, among other things, writers . . . and that includes me, W. thought.

And now he felt that Feuerbach's question had ultimately been: Did you notice whether Frau Falbe has deconspired?— Right after moving out of her room that autumn, he realized that he'd developed some vague interest in his landlady; there was something incomplete, unsatisfying about his story with her . . .

In W.'s assessment, she was a woman—a good bit over fifty—who had resigned herself to a life as a housewife with no family. She had no relationships with men and probably barely entertained the thought any more (though she wouldn't have been too old for it); she played the role of a woman for whom such matters were a thing of the past, and probably this past itself was meagre and disappointing enough. Now her whole appearance sent the message that those years were behind her . . . and this itself made W. suspect that she still harboured desires. And there were even signs of that, but she didn't seem conscious of them, or at any rate she compensated by venting her nurturing instinct upon her lodgers. And she did it so uninhibitedly, once you had acquiesced, that it exhausted her libidinous energy. Only now and then—at moments when there had been some expression of gratitude on W.'s part—had something flared up in her ever-insecure features, and her body tautened beneath the eternal bathrobe, which changed in colour once a week, her movements became quicker and more youthful, her gestures took on a look of unpractised grace and always went a touch too far, she thrust out her bosom, and a barely noticeable blush glimmered in her face.—W. had often wondered what she lived on, as it seemed impossible that she was already drawing a pension. She couldn't be especially well-off; when W. slipped the envelope with the rent through the letter slot, he rounded up the numbers. Once W. asked her about the husband she occasionally mentioned, but he had addressed the subject too directly, and she shied away. Evidently she didn't know herself whether her husband (they weren't divorced) was still alive. He had worked 'for the State', then he'd been on business in West Germany, where he hadn't been heard from to this day, over ten years later.—Hadn't she ever tried to have him traced, W. wanted to know.—He'd forbidden her . . . she said; as though she'd already revealed too much, she shook her head and started talking about the bedclothes again.

He recalled that one day he actually had brought a plastic bag full of bedclothes—for Frau Falbe and for himself—home from REWATEX. This was prohibited, but common practice; each of the forgotten pieces of linen was marked as rags with a triangular cut which could easily be patched. W. had gone to the container in the yard, which the rag collectors emptied very irregularly, picked out a number of the best pieces, duvet covers and pillowcases and sheets, had them washed and ironed and took them with him. As he left the pub on Hannoversche Strasse (across from the Permanent Mission of the BRD) with the plastic bag, a policeman stopped him and checked his papers. This proceeded in the usual fashion: the man in uniform demanded his ID, opened it and stared at it.—Tell me your name, citizen . . . address . . . birthdate, birthplace!—W. reeled off the information, a tape recorder now storing his voice for the police records department. Then the officer examined his plastic bag, pulled the folded bedclothes halfway out and slid his hand between them: What have you got here?—Washing . . . picked it up from the laundry.—And why don't you use the laundry in your neighbourhood?—Because I work in the laundry here.—OK . . . move it along now.

Normally that sort of thing happened only when you came directly from the Permanent Mission; on this particular day it looked as though something unusual were going on in a swathe around the building; the mission's gate opened, big dark limousines lurched out, drove towards Friedrichstrasse and disappeared.—W. told Frau Falbe about the incident; she said: Maybe they let out the people in the embassy who were waiting to leave the country.—So Frau Falbe knew about it too; Feuerbach was wrong in claiming that these things were hardly public knowledge yet.

Later on the first lieutenant had made his usual remarks, just to show how well informed he was, as he kept deeming necessary, with a suitable delay to heighten the effect: Had W. taken along any of the ripped-off bedclothes to the new flat?—It was autumn, and W. had already moved. And this didn't surprise him; ever since moving to the flat he'd lived in the perpetual sense that all his things were swathed in an unbroken web of alien knowledge, and he himself was woven into a system of complementary bits of information, even if he formed but a tiny segment of it . . . and on the surface, as far as he could survey it, there was no possibility of escape from this web.

He'd told Feuerbach more than once that he was thinking of taking a trip out to see his former landlady; maybe he could learn more about Harry Falbe after all if he made a more concerted effort.—In that moment Feuerbach seemed uninterested, his reply blasé: Why not trek out there, it can't hurt to cultivate old acquaintances. Do whatever you like.—It was the first time W. had heard a phrase like that from the first lieutenant . . . what was that tone behind the casually spoken words?—I imagine a lady of that calibre is more your line, Feuerbach had added later, more than all the other women running around in the Scene.—W. could swallow insults like that, but those nonchalant words—Do whatever you like!— had given him pause, and it was another ten days before he visited Frau Falbe. She hardly seemed pleased; in fact, he thought she acted strangely. They had afternoon coffee in her kitchen, but the conversation was so dry that he stayed no more than an hour.

The very next day Feuerbach came up to him and asked: Well, what's the story . . . was he there?—Was he there . . . You mean Harry Falbe?—What are you doing trekking out there, then? So you still don't have a clue what we're racking our brains over . . . or what we're even supposed to be doing here?—What we're racking our brains over, that's exactly what I don't know, said W., and I can't even make it out. I'm just not as well informed as you are, Comrade Major.

And once again Feuerbach had asked about a photo of Harry: Mightn't the 'old girl' have a photo of him after all?

. . . finally it dawned on him that Feuerbach had asked that before.—He'd forgotten the occasion—he'd forgotten so many things he'd been asked and what he'd replied to so many questions he'd forgotten. And between the questions and the answers lay periods of time about which he no longer knew a thing. All that was clear was that this web had spread over his life, woven of questions and answers, a web of information that often enough was concealed in questions alone. And many of these questions had already received their answers in the past . . . but in that past no one had asked these questions. In the firm in which Feuerbach was employed (as W. put it), the chronology of events played only a subordinate role, serving merely to place a message—which might be contained in the question or in the answer—in a workable sequence. (Here by this window he had first realized how he was losing his sense of time . . . here by the window of the cafe on Frankfurter Allee, as the cohorts of cars raced down the concrete lanes in the chromatically lit night air . . . in one sudden opening of his eyes out into the fog iridescent with lights he had no longer known where he was . . . or if it was summer out there, if he was staring out onto Hannoversche Strasse, at the barren yard across the way with the Permanent Mission on its right, at the yellow metal sign with the federal eagle by the gate, outside which paced a policeman in green . . . if he was sitting by the window in this pub where sometimes in his imagination he gazed out upon a West Berlin street, the ceaseless paint-bright cohorts of cars outside . . . here, was it here, he'd forgotten if he'd been expecting Feuerbach for a day, two days, three days now, and as he waited without knowing since when, he'd sometimes thought he was staring into the bustle of a small-town pub and listening to the babble of voices, unintelligible and underlined by unintelligible gestures which refused to fit the incessant opening and closing of the mouths, while he sat waiting at a table on the margin, not knowing where he was . . .)

Quite right, he no longer knew when he had begun to accumulate in his mind vast quantities of the most minor everyday details that might have stemmed from any arbitrary time. There was a crazy jumble of details in his mind, but the relationships of these details to each given point in time eluded him . . . Little things, any normal person would have forgotten them, but he'd stored them away, he'd reeled them off into telephones, recited them on tape, recited them on tape over the telephone, from telephone receivers he'd heard his voice reeling things off on tape, redolent with a certain professional fear, repeating details . . . he'd made as few notes as possible.— Forget it, Feuerbach usually said, toss it out of your urn, whatever you've given us is all taken care of, don't think about things you've already delivered, make room for more. Don't bother with commentaries, classification, connections, that's what we've got experts for.

His organizing mind was not called for, in this chaos it became an irrelevancy, perhaps close to atrophying; his mind had become a machine that took in details and passed them on—the overall picture that emerged from the facts was a matter for the experts.—And thus the life that coalesced from all these details had practically become an irrelevancy . . . when he sat in the cafe listening to the chaos of voices repeating their irrelevancies next to him, and apart from him, depression came over him, slow and mysterious.—It was pointless to try conveying this feeling to Feuerbach; he knew what his answer would be. Or at some point Feuerbach had already given the answer: So you're worn out, run down, done in, at sea? The times are no better than they're made out to be, my dear man, we mustn't get smoke in our eyes. You're in just the mood we need. It attunes you to life's nasty little details . . .

And once again W. was reminded of the boss from A., who had expressed himself on quite similar lines.—Conversations of this nature regularly seemed to correlate with some other subject entirely: W. was waiting for Feuerbach's response to his question as to whether it would be expedient to apply for a travel permit . . . Whether it was a convenient point in time, or perhaps too early, he'd asked to defuse the question from the outset.—What do you mean . . . now? the first lieutenant flung out and went on his way.—When such 'difficult questions' came up, Feuerbach generally gave the impression that he wasn't really listening, his replies came weeks later, and always as a surprise; in the meantime, presumably, he obtained (in higher places) his information guidelines.—It'd be possible in six months, he said, walking up one evening to the table in the cafe, where W. had been brooding for hours. W. looked uncertainly at his superior, who leant on one armrest (playing the role of a man pressed for time), bent down to W. and yelled: Now, listen, you asked me about it yourself . . . besides, that's all you ever think about, you've got it written all over you.—He'd delivered the second half of the speech more calmly, but it was too late—the waiter came up and reminded him that they weren't the only people in the cafe . . . Feuerbach waited until he'd gone away again, then he said: You arsehole!—W., familiar with such tantrums, held his tongue; Feuerbach continued his speech, still standing: Probably both of us are more than ready for it . . . I'm authorized to say that headquarters don't think half-badly of you . . . of course, they don't see you snoozing away at this table here. All joking aside, well, their view is that naturally it's no go unless there's a compelling reason. That means, for instance, that you'd have to have a contact in West Berlin. Now my question is, do you have a contact there?—Feuerbach fell silent and glanced around the taproom; if any interest had arisen at the other tables, it had died down again.——Of course you don't have a contact! Feuerbach went on. But without one it's no go, you'd have to find a contact, start thinking about that. All I can tell you is, the Scene offers the perfect opportunities. But are you the type for that? In a pinch I can find a contact person for you, but you'll have to do the contacting yourself. You have six months' time, I think you'll pull it off by the summer . . .

(If he wasn't mistaken, the conversation had taken place around Christmas or New Year's; the six months Feuerbach had spoken of had not yet elapsed. It was proving difficult, if not impossible, for W. to establish the necessary contact, as he could well imagine which 'contact person' his case officer had in mind. He'd already mentioned her on occasion . . . for W. she was the student; Feuerbach had once characterized her as 'that kid who's running after Reader', but that was later on, once the author's rapid—and ephemeral—rise had begun.—— But, as Feuerbach insisted, even before that she had been a frequent presence in the so-called Scene in the Eastern part of Berlin, and for W. she was an extremely unapproachable being. And the role he himself played was that of a reticent, rather nondescript regular at the events in which the Firm was so very interested.——Thus, in W.'s view, she was the most inauspicious conceivable connection . . . for a while this seemed to be the very appeal of it for Feuerbach. W. felt overwhelmed—though not immune to the aforementioned appeal—and sometimes he was almost resolved to go to the first lieutenant with the question: How does one establish human contact with this woman . . .?)

Gradually it was fading again, the thought of an excursion to West Berlin . . . a S-Bahn journey of one stop, lasting about five minutes, for which the word travel had established itself. It wasn't just that by all indications the time was unfavourable for such a request; it was impossible to determine in a rational manner why it was favourable at certain moments and then unfavourable again; in the summer following the relevant conversation, travel issues even seemed to be a kind of red flag for the chiefs.—Feuerbach hadn't mentioned the matter again, and W. had increasingly frequent 'contact' with circles in which such issues were off the table.

Here the emptiness he carried around with him—he used the word exhaustion—made it easy for him to quickly adapt to the style that prevailed. The issue of leaving the country was not discussed at all here, or as a matter one was only remotely involved with, and this was not for reasons of caution but from the conviction that one's place was in this country . . . At least W. soon felt that this was how best to understand it. That conviction, however, did not come from an acceptance of the state in which the country persisted . . . and W. spent a long time wondering what else might explain it. He'd discussed this with Feuerbach, who also seemed to be thinking about it and failing to come to any real conclusion . . . this time W. didn't have the sense that the first lieutenant was holding back his thoughts only to deploy them as aggressively as possible at a suitable opportunity . . . no, even Feuerbach made a baffled impression. The higher-ups, in the regions above Feuerbach to which W. had no entrée, had to believe that most people in the groups that comprised the Scene were willing to stay in the country lately because they intended to offer resistance—they must have hit on the crazy notion of changing the Republic from within!—This meant that the Scene was converging disturbingly with the other groups known as coalition movements; these were groups occupied only marginally with art and literature, much more with ecology or conscientious objection, which got support from the Church and probably little response otherwise.—Feuerbach shook his head over this notion of convergence . . . We know the Scene much too well for that, he said to W., people feel that the grassroots groups are just using them. And if they don't yet, they will soon. And besides, the people in the Scene are much too intelligent for these night vigils on the street clutching candles.—In Feuerbach's view, it was impossible to find anyone in the Scene with a strategy to give resistance a manageable organization or even a unified line. On the one hand they simply lack a mastermind, that is, some guru who has the cheek to keep them on their toes, on the other hand none of them are dumb enough to fall for a charlatan like that . . . and that's what I love about them!—Feuerbach grinned and said they were considering the possibility of providing just this mastermind . . . Wouldn't you like to do it? he asked. You'd have to dye your hair green or white, change your parka for a yellow leather jacket and paint a Chinese pictograph on the back. Or you'd have to go about all in black, pitch black all the time, that'd do the trick. And after a suitable gestation we'd nab this mastermind and use him to bust the gang . . .

What struck W. most about these circles, or this 'milieu'— and what made both words seem righter to him than the expression 'Scene', though he used it constantly, it being the word that both the Scene and the State Security used in common (just as the term 'Firm' was used in common by the State Security and the Scene)—and what had also occupied Feuerbach for a time: the milieu had emerged unplanned, without preamble, as it were, and it continued its existence unplanned and divergent without anyone giving it a thought. Suddenly this Scene was there, in many places at once, in the urban neighbourhoods where renovation costs couldn't be covered, sprouting like weeds from the rubble whenever you'd looked away for a moment, characterized by the persistence of disorganization, in the equal credence given to opposing views, in the indifference towards all ideas; indeed, the sole common denominator of all the Scenes was their disinterest in any form of ideology. That made them appear, at first glance, completely unassailable.—If you could put them away just like that, said Feuerbach, they'd bore me to tears.

Unexpectedly W. had received an invitation from someone in the inner sphere of this milieu . . . before going he didn't even know the reason for the invitation; presumably it had to do with some poems of his that had appeared in a West German magazine. Feuerbach knew about the invitation the very next day; he came into the cafe with the friendliest face W. had ever seen on him: Well, how was it yesterday? By the way, we almost ran into each other . . . —Since you know everything already anyway . . . I was asked to read soon in a back courtyard downtown. I just have the funny feeling that right now I don't have enough pieces to fill half an hour.— Yes, said Feuerbach, that's bad. But you'll manage all right, put off the reading for two or three weeks, then you'll have enough. And so you're not just left to your own devices—you can take that as an order. But I meant the time around four in the afternoon, I was sitting in the liquor joint here and you came charging past the window. I thought you'd come in, I would've had a tip to give you. And you weren't heading home, either, you went down into the U-Bahn . . .

(W. peered through the big glass pane, covered in a fine film of dust bonded by the greasy precipitate of the exhaust smoke, catching the sunlight that slanted down onto the window from the upper right . . . now, too, it had to be between four and five in the afternoon . . . it was March, but it could have been October, even November, on bright autumn days the sun on the greyed pane had the same dazzling effect . . . shrinking the pedestrians outside to silhouettes. He tried to picture how the first lieutenant had seen him then: emerging blurred from the sun, heading east with long strides, towards Frankfurter Allee's barely perceptible rise . . .)

And then you went down into the U–Bahn . . . you could perfectly well have walked home! Instead you got on the train to Alexanderplatz, but you only rode as far as Frankfurter . . . there you went upstairs and changed to the S–Bahn. And I'll bet you weren't heading towards Pankow, you were heading south, is there a Scene there too already? Where is it you're always heading off to . . .?

I thought you'd come into the liquor joint and I could congratulate you . . . not on your birthday, on your success in the Scene, it's not everyone who gets invitations, after all. And it's not everyone who can come to listen, me, for instance. And of course in your innate modesty you won't tell me a word about your triumph . . .

You'll have to work more concertedly, with more purpose. It's about time a few new things fluttered from your desk again, poems, for instance. Or just write down the sorts of things you hear and see in the Scene . . . but poems take precedence at the moment. You shouldn't be cruising around the city so much, though of course that's your field. I ask myself what you're up to the whole time on the south end of town, you've got to have some sort of hideout there. Do you have a dead drop, is that it? You've got to have some kind of crack, a slit, a chink you're always gaping through. What kind of a world have you got your eye on?

He couldn't remember what he'd replied: You can't write poems every day.—Or: Do you think there's always so much news in the Scene worth reporting?—He had to admit that Feuerbach was right, though; his thoughts barely dwelt at his desk, this desk in the downtown flat, divided into two halves—on one side of the desk, the left, lay the crazily scribbled notes for his poems, and on the other side the neat stack of typewriter paper for his reports. And he knew that the left-hand section was by far the least interesting, for readers, for experts, for himself . . . and for future readers.—And likewise his brain was divided into two halves, and from the one Feuerbach's verbiage sloshed into the other.—Yes, Feuerbach had turned talkative now that W. was hobnobbing in the Scene; he was constantly talking about changes one could see in these circles, usually concluding his views with a question: Are the people there really that callous and indifferent, or are they just acting that way? And what do they hope to achieve by acting that way? What are they trying to hide from us?

Of course W. hadn't known the Scene as well and as long as Feuerbach; ultimately he was a newcomer there . . . though he doubted that the first lieutenant had ever seen the milieu from the inside . . . but the effect of Feuerbach's perpetual theories was that he mulled these things over himself. First it occurred to him that Feuerbach had clearly been wrong about something he'd claimed, what must have been a good year ago. The issue at hand had been deconspiration—it was a really tough thing to do, it took quite a bit of staying power, a massive degree of tenacity, even!—Tenacity, he'd said; it was striking that Feuerbach once again jibed word for word with the boss from A.; they must have met at some point after all . . .

You see, W.'s new boss lectured on in the manner of the old one, most people in the Scene, and not just there, don't take deconspiration as a pure proof of friendship, on the contrary: first of all you've exposed yourself as an enemy . . . Can you imagine the loneliness that entails at first, and possibly for quite some time? he'd asked.—It looked as though the Scene no longer had this sort of bogeyman, or at least the notion had faded or lost its edge . . . it had actually given way to a bored indifference.—And this, Feuerbach went so far as to claim, practically borders on tolerance . . . They tolerate us by ignoring us, he declared. Does that mean they're letting us have our way, or are they pulling the rug out from under our feet?

W. asked himself whether the ignorance Feuerbach detected wasn't, by this point, mutual: ignorant thinking in the literary underground—and thus, perhaps, products which ignored the antagonistic relationship between art and the State —could result in the ignorance of those who watched over the underground. Didn't that make it possible for more and more products from the underground to reach the surface?

(He'd finally managed to pay his tab; the waiter, who performed his duties in a trance-like state, hadn't responded to his flapping gestures—when there was a waiter in the cafe, which was far from the rule, the service was even worse, for then the barman too was seized by a state that precluded sight and hearing; the two cast a pall over the bar, where they leant against each other as though frozen in place; for the summer waitress who served the pavement tables, their relationship was perpetual grounds for threatening to quit.—Out on the pavement W. had wanted to take a look through the window into the cafe, where the lights were already on . . . but the waiter, suddenly coming to life, came to pull the dark curtains over the window. First W. had scanned the tables in the middle of the bar, filled with young men, young men only; in the upper third of the room a cloud cover of smoke hung beneath the ceiling, and in it, seemingly unmoored, the dim spheres of the lamps hung like grey-pink moons suddenly looming from a veil of clouds . . . and sometimes the smoke—diligently fed by the non-smoking tables—hung so low that people seemed to walk headless about the room.

W. had wanted to ascertain how well his table could be seen from the pavement: the empty table stood off to the side, the tabletop, already cleared, now bore a plastic sign that said Reserved . . . and the waiter came and yanked the opaque curtain to the middle of the window; the table vanished. But W. had seen himself still sitting on his chair right next to the windowpane, not very clear, lost in thought as usual, holding the teaspoon motionless in the cup, staring out at the street, at an indistinct patch of fog somewhere on Frankfurter Allee, looking straight through his likeness on the pavement . . . and the person at the table didn't notice that he'd been scrutinized for half a second from outside: W. remained invisible to the other man within . . .)

As for the new things that were supposed to flutter from his desk, there really wasn't much to speak of . . . there was simply nothing going on in the Scene, even if more and more often someone would act as though an entirely new light had been shed on the situation. In the manner of the ironist who stands above it all, Feuerbach played down the uneasy feeling that must have occasionally come over him. There were any number of roaring lions afoot in the worlds west and east of the so-called Iron Curtain, he said, and each believed himself personally responsible for a certain rethinking which was suddenly writ large . . . But have you heard a thing about us here getting any instructions to rethink? he asked.—One reason for this mood, at least one of the discernible reasons, seemed to lie in the emergence of an array of new poets who previously had become known only in the West, through their illegal publications, whereby illegal was a flattering term people liked to use. Mostly these were magazine publications, but there had been standalone books with West German publishers as well—also illegal, if not more than illegal—and what they all had in common was the note in the obligatory author biography, worded almost exactly the same way each time, that they belonged to a young generation of poets that had to be termed oppositional because so far they had been unable to publish in their own country. But now, more or less surprisingly, domestic publishers and magazines began printing these poets' work as well. Suddenly anthologies appeared in the bookshops —completely unannounced, and clearly put together in hectic haste, chapbooks that sold out in no time and immediately acquired a certain scarcity value—anthologies or slender books bringing together two or three new authors, and they created the impression that all these incriminated poets were a perfectly natural presence in their country . . . this, one learnt, had been preceded by protracted disputes within the highest cultural department.—And W.'s name had also appeared amid these writers' ranks.

Feuerbach's reaction was practically euphoric; for several weeks that autumn, whenever he ran into W. he produced the centrespread of a newspaper from his pocket—the culture section, which included book reviews—and unfolded it on the cafe table. In each of these spreads W. was included in the list of names to note when reappraising contemporary poetry. And inevitably the West German media followed suit: here too his name was rarely lacking, which the first lieutenant found especially remarkable.—At first his excitement infected W. as well, until he began to feel that his case officer was acting as though he'd written the pieces himself . . . and from then on W. reacted guardedly, sometimes almost dismissing the whole thing: Were the pieces really by him? Even if it was true that his hand had put them to paper, they had been authorized by someone other than him. And then it struck him that all the reviews he was shown were almost identical in content; here the term was truer still: they had been authorized! And in the end even Western newspapers used the same set phrases, the same interpretations, often enough the same sentences . . . What a brilliantly functional national culture! Clearly it wasn't even necessary for one person to whisper in the other's ear, no one had to crib a thing from the fellow before him, this sort of thing happened so completely spontaneously, you had to admire it. Little by little W. was finding this to be a crushing process . . . and he realized that by now he didn't even know how these pieces had gotten published. Whenever he'd submitted work, he'd always got all of it sent back. After that he'd made fewer and fewer efforts . . . before what he declared to himself to be his last attempt—his very last attempt before the point at which he'd ask Feuerbach for assistance—in exasperation he had cut three of his pieces down the middle and put them back together the other way around; he'd resubmitted them, and suddenly they were accepted. And right after that more of his work had been published in two so-called unofficial magazines, albeit with what W. regarded as the correct line sequence.

Feuerbach had heard about all the publications quickly, almost immediately, and he delighted unabashedly in all of them. He made one of his extremely rare pronouncements: I've got to admire you!

You had just the right instincts! he went on. We disapprove of it, but it's the right word here: instincts! You appeared officially and unofficially at the same time, and that's acting like an old pro. I can see that pretty soon I'll have to go and fetch myself some kudos for you. By the way, your poems were distributed just right, too. Keep it up, definitely just send the official organs your second-rate things, keep the better ones for the underground magazines. That's the order that makes more sense for us.

W. could recall having heard something of the kind before . . . the same proposal had been made—it was so long ago you could hardly call it real any more—by the boss in A. When W. mentioned that to Feuerbach, the reply was: What, him? Then he can only have got it from us.

At about the same time W. notched up an additional triumph. Feuerbach informed him that his code name had been accepted.—Did you even remember it, he asked, didn't you pick it out yourself way back when? And be careful with this name, no one knows this name besides you. If it ever crops up somewhere, the only person to blame will be you. Remember, many things can be guessed, but not known. And there will never be any proof if you don't expose yourself. Even so-called evidence needn't be proof, because . . . we might have just faked it all, you see!—We might well have, at least in our little part of the world . . . Names, poems, reviews, even unofficial magazines, W. commented, and Feuerbach pulled a sour face.

I meant the written part of the world, the first lieutenant continued his thoughts the next day (as he often did, strengthening W.'s conviction that time was immaterial for people in the Firm). At least in the so-called world of signs. And for the poet that's the real world, isn't it? And for him reality's but a demented dream, isn't that so?

Not just for the poet, of course, but for us too, more often than you'd think, he said (once again with several days' delay). There you've got the commonality you keep mulling over. Especially when we have to fulfil other people's dreams. With Biermann[6] and his buddies gone, the world's become a demented dream even for us. We are the perpetuators of the system, and what kind of system is it if it no longer has an opposition? What to wield all the power on, I ask you. It ends up finishing us off, I tell you. Do you think it's any fun having to build up a new opposition over and over again? New so-called hostile-negative forces, just to perpetuate the system? Sometimes I don't see any hostile-negative forces left at all, at least not in our bailiwick, but the fossils up at the top want to keep seeing them, otherwise their world view goes down the tubes. For ages all we've had is an empty phrase: Hostile-negative! But in reality . . . where, I ask you, where. We're living in a world of signs, my friend, is that a commonality or isn't it?

Maybe, he continued his musings (a weekend had intervened), we ought to get ourselves transferred to the skinhead gang. Supposed there's lots to do still in the department that does the skins and the punks. But then we'd have to run around in beat-up leather things, and we'd even have to duke it out now and then. I can't stand bike chains, for Chrissake. So me, I'd rather stay in the world of signs and ask myself three times a day who we can do a favour for this time. Don't you know anyone in the Scene who still wants to defect? One of these days we'll be the only two hostile-negative forces left . . . which isn't so far off with you, you're a poet after all.

Can't we finally, Feuerbach was far from finished, get this son-of-a-bitch Harry Falbe to start writing poetry? I mean, he is someone who wants to get out of here still, right? I don't understand why no one in your Scene wants to go West any more, when they all feel oh-so opted out. How can you want to live in a country you can't work up the slightest interest in? Isn't there anyone who wants to keep playing the same old game, out there in the world of signs? You've got to have heard something!

Everything I've heard, you know already, said W. If that's so, you'll have to go in yourself and say you want to go West. Say you're starting to get fed up. You'll let that slip at some point, to someone the group trusts the most. Then we'll see how the group reacts. Maybe you can get a few of them to go along with you, at any rate it'll make them nervous. I'd give you completely free rein, say something about occupying an embassy for all I care . . . say you have to put the authorities on the spot because here in this country you're worried about your kid's future. You do have a kid down there in A., don't you?

A kid? said W., alarmed; Feuerbach's poorly concealed edginess infected him. What's the idea with the kid, most of them have kids themselves. They might nod sympathetically, but then they'd just say, that's not our problem . . . That's no good, said Feuerbach. They must have lost all sense of respect. Either you break the laws, or you back them. But you can't act as if the State authorities . . . or, as if we didn't even exist any more.

Soon after these conversations the first lieutenant had vanished from the radar for some time; to be exact, first for about ten days, and then, after another seven days, for a whole month.—W. had listened to his case officer with malicious glee at first, but in the end with mounting concern. Then, left alone in the city, Feuerbach's behaviour struck him as peculiar; never had he seen him in such suppressed agitation. For all his witty talk (which, incidentally, was starting to seem a bit stale), his testiness had been noticeable . . . he'd given the impression of an imminent outburst . . . or a breakdown?

Three times in the four weeks Feuerbach went missing (the entire month of April), W. had received a summons to a so-called meet-up to which the first lieutenant failed to appear; that was nothing unusual. Three times W. had found a sealed envelope with no address or sender, two in close succession in his postbox, the third slipped under his front door. Each time the envelope contained the same slip of paper with one solitary sentence: 'You'll meet me tomorrow 19.00 in the cafe on Frankfurter Allee'; there was no signature, the date was noted in pen on the upper right-hand edge, so miniscule that it could hardly be in Feuerbach's lavish hand. The message on the slips of paper had been typed, but only once, and then duplicated on a photocopier . . . W. pictured the machine spitting out thirty such copies in barely a minute—perhaps he could expect still more of these notes, until such time as he finally ignored them . . . and then there'd be hell to pay. Feuerbach's typewriter was the same model W. used . . . and sometimes he'd suspected that Feuerbach had been in his flat and typed there at his machine; W. had found nothing to confirm his suspicion. When he received the third note, W. didn't even go to the cafe; a few days before, he'd tried to see his case officer in the office but hadn't been admitted; an unfamiliar middle-aged woman had turned him away: Feuerbach . . . she didn't know a gentleman of that name!

On the day of the third meet-up he'd had other plans, he'd gone out to visit Frau Falbe, for the second time that spring. He'd asked his former landlady whether she would rent him the room again—for the entire summer, perhaps the autumn as well, in addition to his flat, he could afford that now. He needed a crash pad for writing again, where he could be by himself once or twice a week.—Frau Falbe was dismissive, seeming mistrustful of him; he had to come by a few more times, and finally, towards the end of April, she consented.— Harry never paid me anything, she said, but I can use the bit of extra money. You'll have to pay full, even if you're not here every day . . . and one more thing, I can'tmake you coffee every day.—So the next time he came he brought her a pack of coffee he'd bought at an Intershop; since several of his poems had been printed in West German magazines, he'd acquired a number of Forum cheques which allowed him to make such privileged purchases.[7] Frau Falbe accepted the present without a word, apparently still mistrustful; as she went, W. thought that she suddenly displayed a frailty far from befitting her. W. felt a sense of disappointment; he'd recalled her as a woman still full of resilience, and asked himself how the past year and a half could have made such a difference.

That evening he'd moved his books and manuscripts to Frau Falbe's room. Feuerbach's temporary disappearance gave him the opportunity to set up a hideout . . . Frau Falbe as the holder of the duplicate key was much more palatable to him than Feuerbach . . . who might well think that W. saw the downtown flat solely as an office now . . . and these were his exact first words when he was back in town (incidentally seeming a totally different person, in the best of moods, at least at first, and radiant over his promotion . . .).

W. had taken only those manuscripts which he felt were current (which he'd written most recently . . . which he'd failed at most recently—in other words, only literary manuscripts!); he left the older ones on the desk as camouflage . . . and he left all his other notes as well: this way the down-town desk was like a silent reproach! Feuerbach would see them if he came, the notes scattered all around the typewriter: started and scrapped again, started afresh and scrapped anew, the reports that had been written in a void ever since the first lieutenant had abandoned his reporter without notice. And in between, time and again, the remnants of his poetic efforts, completely buried by the dry verbal chaff of laborious logs.

Returning to the tiny street in the south of the city with his bag full of papers, he automatically watched for the light in his window . . . he missed the window, since the light was out, the blind down. He realized this but kept walking almost to the end of the street, for he suddenly felt as he had that early spring day two years ago when he'd first come upon this street . . . perhaps because of the stirring of mild air this evening?—Then, too, he'd felt 'newly born', and not just because he already sensed the spring. This year it was several weeks later, more than a month into spring, and yet the light of the evening seemed darker . . . Had two years really passed since then? he asked himself suddenly.—No, these years had departed his mind, they were lost, and it could just as well have been three or four—they'd passed as though in a dream, flitted away, in a wink, as they say . . . they seemed not to have existed for him. And all he knew was that in this time he'd failed at everything he'd tried to write . . . absolutely everything? It was depressing, but that would change now . . .

He stepped into the room; it had been cleaned, the cloying smell of floor polish stung his nostrils, at the foot of the cot was a stack of folded bedclothes, seeming to shine faintly in the darkness. He recognized

them, the legacy of negligent REWATEX laundry customers. Suddenly it seemed too much to expect him to wander down Frankfurter Allee, to stop at a stinking cafe there, to head for the flat that was not his own, since Feuerbach could come in at any moment, in most cases without ringing . . . he decided to spend the next few days here in Frau Falbe's room. He sat in the red armchair, staring into the darkness of the tiny, still quite cold room . . . over the coming weeks it could only get warmer.

On one of the following days he woke up late in the afternoon, which hadn't happened to him for a long time . . . the previous evening had almost completely vanished from his memory; it was a long time, too, since he'd treated himself to a pub session as protracted as yesterday's . . . the eternal sitting around in the cafe on Frankfurter couldn't be described as such.—Frau Falbe was in the room, and embarrassed about it, as he thought he could tell when he peered through lids he opened with an effort. He had been woken by the rattle of the blind as she raised it; outside was bright daylight, though at this time of day his window was on the dark side of the house. Yet the street was filled with the reflection of a powerful glare blindingly intensified by the windows of the houses across the way. For a moment he thought he'd overslept his shift at the laundry . . . with Frau Falbe's help this had practically never happened. He turned towards her under the blanket, she pointed to the pot of coffee on the desk . . . You must have had an awful lot to drink last night, she said.—He stood up, walked past her to the toilet without a word, when he came back the coffee was already poured . . . it was just as always.

All this conspired to make him forget the whole last stretch of time . . . the last weeks, months, the last year, the last two years—if it was that many already. Here every last detail was unchanged, all at once it cost him a vast effort to think of the past year and a half (or the past two and a half years?), it was as though this time had passed in his imagination only, as though all his memories of it could be extracted only from a fairly bizarre, not to say perverted realm of his imagination . . . and it seemed to him that he'd come here to immediately tackle this task. Nothing in the past two or three years admitted the conclusion that he'd lived his own life . . . he had done nothing on his own initiative! And all the possible explanations for what he'd done with the time of his last two or three years came not from his reason . . . they were not products of any reasoning by W.—they had been devised by experts.

Only gradually did he feel a certain amazement that it had all turned out as it had; he didn't know how he could have articulated it . . . Frau Falbe seemed to waste no thoughts on the time that had passed, not at the moment, anyway; she seamlessly resumed the days spent with her lodger, and poured coffee. As always, as though it had been this way only yesterday, he sat across from her in his pyjamas—she didn't seem to notice—audibly slurping the scalding beverage, as always with slightly trembling hands, not producing a word until he'd taken a few drags on his first cigarette. This detail seemed as habitual to her as the gesture with which she took herself a cigarette from his pack, lying open on the table, and lit it.—Just to keep you company! was her formulaic excuse, recycled daily. She smoked two or three a day, only with W., who a year and a half ago had told her to help herself whenever she liked from the opened packs he had lying around everywhere. After finishing her cup of coffee she asked if she should go . . . all one summer and all one autumn she had asked him that almost every day, in the same tone of voice, when she finished her cigarette at three-thirty in the morning, and every day the question had startled him, as it did now, and there was regret in his eyes, which she took as confirmation, though he remained mute.

At the door she turned around again: You know, that really spooked me recently when you showed up here again. Because Harry told me you sometimes go around with that guy who was here and questioned me. And now that he's seen you with this guy he never stays in Berlin for long. You know the one I mean, the slick one who's always acting so polite, Wasserstein's his name . . . You know him pretty darn well!—And now you're not suspicious any more? asked W.—He's a snitch, you can tell that a mile away . . . she said, shaking her head. But now I saw right off how tired you are. I saw the way you were sleeping, I thought you'd never wake up again. He must be totally done for, I thought, what on earth have they done to him, I asked myself.—W. gave a startled nod, and Frau Falbe went on: First off, you've really got to get a good night's sleep. And then come and see me. Or I'll come down to you, I have to tell you something about that guy. Just so you know who you're dealing with . . .

He had plenty of time, and he was rested, he'd replied; if she liked, he'd come up and see her that evening.—Then, avid and urgent, he downed the entire pot of coffee to finally wake himself up, and left the house to shop for the bare necessities.

It was quite a warm April day; suddenly his nervousness was shed, he walked through the provincial-seeming neighbourhood, which had no hint of the cramped big city, and had no trouble whatsoever recognizing the whole environment in which two years ago he had still moved as though on call—pestered by Feuerbach to move away again . . . and clearly, in his heart of hearts, eagerly awaiting the Firm's commands—only now, it seemed, had he truly arrived here, the next winter still far off, and he couldn't let himself think it.—He'd meant to buy a bottle of wine for the evening at Frau Falbe's, but hadn't found anything drinkable, only some insultingly sweet purplish stuff. Back in his room he'd begun reading his manuscripts, and lost himself in them . . . starting up now and then because he thought he heard the doorbell. The manuscripts struck him as incoherent, and yet unpleasantly transparent. In each text, amid the elusive, sometimes cryptic strings of words, he seemed to detect extremely tell-tale formulae—precisely because they were exquisitely encrypted: for a reader with even the slightest clue about his double life, it would have been virtually impossible to misinterpret these passages. And then, it seemed to him, these constructions had to immediately become the centre of gravity for all his poems . . . yes, you could have pulled out these phrases and listed them one after the other, and suddenly they would have become intelligible of themselves: they were a jumble of accusations against an anonymous, secret power, and, that was the worst of it, they were supposed to arouse pity . . . yes, these were pitiful testimonies to a profound resignation . . . whoever had written them was too gutless to express himself openly, and had already reconciled himself to his gutlessness.—He'd have to start rewriting this very minute, expunging the tell-tale words! he thought, pale and streaming with a sudden sweat; at that moment a knock came at his window from outside. He

looked up, the room blurring in the nausea that overcame him
... he recalled his old quirk of never opening the door right
away when it rang, but waiting first instead: reading his old
work—some of it written two years ago, here in this very
room—had immediately reactivated this mechanism.—Frau
Falbe waved at him from the window; he was sitting in the
light, the blind still raised.

You've got the key, you can come in, he said as he admitted her. He didn't like going to the door when the bell rang,
he said, since the room was supposed to be a hideout.—I can
imagine who you're hiding out from, she said. I'd like to hide
from him myself. But can't he find out where you are?—I
hope not, said W., you're the only person who knows about
my hideout!—Good! she said, and that's how it'll stay, no one'll
learn anything from me, that's for sure. It's a good thing I know
... and you're not registered here any more either. I was going
to tell you a few things about Harry, but I can tell it's not a
good time for you ...

Sensing that W. was struggling with a feeling of dejection,
she lingered outside the door.—No, he said, it's a very good
time. Maybe I'm really not quite rested up yet. And I don't
know what I can offer you to drink, should I make you a tea?

He knew she didn't like it when he messed around with
immersion heaters in his room; regarding him as forgetful, she
feared he'd set the flat on fire, but she turned down the suggestion to make the tea upstairs in her kitchen, and sat down
in the armchair.—I wanted to tell you something about Harry,
she repeated, and about the guy you're hiding out from.

OK, said W., tell me ... What a windfall, she was talking
on her own about Harry Falbe, who was of such interest to
his case officer. Maybe he wouldn't even have to worry about
subtly sounding her out ... but suddenly the whole story left
him cold, all that caught his attention was a peculiar tone in

the woman's voice. She washed two cups at the little side table next to the water faucet, while he kept an eye on the filled pot with the immersion heater. She had left him the seat behind his paper-strewn desk; he set the teacups down heedlessly on the scribbled sheets and pushed an opened packet of sugar cubes over towards her; still hanging back, she tried to fish the tea bag out of the hot liquid with her fingertips. Then, haltingly, often repeating herself, she told a crude story about Harry, who had been chased around the city for weeks, even months, by a person who had to have been Feuerbach.—She gave W. a description of his superior which he couldn't have topped himself.—You know, that wiry guy, the tall lean one, she said; at that the agitation in her voice died down again, and her tone was disdainful. He was always wearing that plaid suit, you don't get those here, grey and yellow plaid, I don't know if people are still wearing those. And a scarf tucked in, probably it's supposed to look American, or maybe English, at any rate it's supposed to get attention. And to go with the dyed hair, he had some grey highlights put in, am I right? Everything's fake about the guy, even his eternal smirking is fake. Anyway, this guy, with those lips of his, like a man in the movies, so pale . . . yellow, I thought first off, that's the colour of his skin . . . and his eyes like fish eyes . . . maybe they were green, no, they were grey, he stuck his aristocratic nose in here . . .

Without missing a beat she went on with the story about Harry: they were constantly coming after 'the boy', that had happened even back in A., where he came from. When he was still living there . . . And here in Berlin it just went on like that, can you imagine?

Of course, said W.; he lifted the two teabags out of the cups with the spoon and tossed them into the ashtray.

And you know why? said Frau Falbe. They kept trying to prove that he wants to go West—when so many people want to do that! That's what it was always about, mostly, as far as I know. That's why they dragged him out of bed at night. This guy, this snitch, he'd ring my doorbell at six in the morning, for example, and say, Come on, go down there and unlock the door for me, right now . . .

Excuse me, W. interrupted, wasn't that what he really wanted? I mean, you already told me he really wanted to go West.

Of course they all want to at that age . . . and why shouldn't they? But he's over that now, he doesn't want to any more, and he's always told the truth to me.

Why doesn't he want to any more . . .? Maybe he has a girlfriend somewhere, a kid . . .?

A kid? Not that I know.

Do you have any idea where he is now?

She shrugged her shoulders: No idea where he is now. He was back recently, for two days, but not in your room. And now he's disappeared again, he's always disappearing.

How can a person disappear here . . .?

Ignoring his question, she went on with her story: Nuh-uh, I'm not doing that, I said. He's sleeping now, you can't go in there. Oh yes I can, the guy said, and can I ever. Unlock that door immediately, he's not sleeping, he just spends all night thinking about . . . you know! You know he does it to himself with his hand . . . yes, that's what the guy said, he'll just be lying there spending all night . . . jerking off! Yep, he said, you don't have to come in with me.—It must have cost her an effort to quote Feuerbach verbatim; W. felt slightly awkward, she had uttered the words 'jerk off' in a hollow, guttural voice, leaning her head way over the table; W. flinched as they hit him in the face.

And then he took Harry away, it was still dark, practically the middle of the night. And it wasn't the last time, once he even came at 11.30 p.m., I was still watching TV. And they had Harry there all night, they were trying to prove he wants to go West again. And you know what happened then? Harry told me when he came back at ten in the morning . . .

W. said he didn't, though he had an inkling of the revolting turn such interrogations could take; his discomfort increased.

They wanted to prove something else against him, they never talked about the business with the West for long, Harry said. They claimed he was that way, that was what he was supposed to confess there!

Homosexual? asked W.

Yes, that he's a homo, that he's gay, that's what they said to him, but I know better, Harry never lies to me. And you know the next thing that happened that night, the guy stuck the gun up inside him.

That can't be! said W.

Oh yes it can, he stuck it up inside him, Harry told me everything. Harry didn't have anything on, you see, just his coat over his pyjamas, that's how they put him in the car and took him with them. And in his office he stuck the gun up his butt and said, should I pull the trigger? That's just what you need, you son-of-a bitch faggot, he said, admit you're a faggot, or I'll pull the trigger . . .

Unbelievable! said W.—he tried to visualize this scene . . . was it possible to picture Feuerbach in such a tableau, Feuerbach the elegant cynic with his gingerly fingers? W. shook his head and said: That's an absolutely hair-raising story!

You can believe me, she insisted, Harry told it to me right afterwards. He'd never tell it to anyone but me. And you could even still see it, he still had a wound from the gun, I'm telling you. And after that he vanished from Berlin for four whole weeks. And where did he vanish to?

He said he couldn't tell me. Because they were sure to come back and question me. And then it was better if I didn't know. It was true, they did come . . . of course I didn't say a word. I don't know, I told them, I never know where he is, and then they went away again. And I tell that to everyone, no one gets anything out of me. And then Harry came back and said, I'll show them. I'll make a baby, yeah . . . he said to me, I'll make you a baby. He actually said that to me. Or I'll make a baby with another girl down there in A. Harry, I said, I believe you that you're normal, it's no reason to go making a baby. You'll never be able to pay for it, and the young lady's stuck with the kid. No good will ever come of that . . .

W. would have regarded this story as sheer fantasy if it hadn't come from Frau Falbe . . . Maybe Harry had made it up? You couldn't put it past him, he must have heard about plenty of crazy things in prison.—Still, there would have been no pressing reason to make up a thing like that; Harry could have concocted better stories to elicit his landlady's sympathy, and he wouldn't even have had to concoct them. Had he told the truth after all? In the end it didn't matter . . . but W. felt a certain pleasure at the thought that his case officer had suddenly acquired this sort of reputation . . . he didn't begrudge it to him! It would almost be a pity if the story were just made up, he thought gleefully . . . and besides he was personally familiar with certain of Feuerbach's moods when drunk.— The story was irrelevant, really . . . much more interesting was the tone in which Frau Falbe had told it to him.

Actually she hadn't so much told it as she'd hoarsely gasped it out, paying no heed to the questions he interposed; turning halfway out of the armchair she'd leant her upper body on the desk, one hand at the triangular neckline of her blouse, as if she lacked air to breathe, and while speaking she'd gone through two cigarettes.—He had to admit that the woman's agitation had infected him . . . and yet he had reacted too matter-of-factly, barely showing that he was on her side (why was it that even in this situation he refused to relinquish his solidarity with Feuerbach?); in his eyes the man was a criminal, that's what he should have said!—He resolved to go back upstairs to her—he had to hear that story again, in even more detail, he hadn't been able to get a handle on it, he'd only ever heard stories like that about some perverted Nazis. The next day, when he rang her doorbell around noon, there ended up being no time to talk. She'd opened the door in her robe, looking more uncertain than surprised.—She had to make her bed, it would only take a minute . . . she said; he glanced into the bedroom, where a double bed stood; the side where her husband must have slept was untouched, the bedclothes neatly covered with a curtain-like material. She hadn't lost the hoarse tone to her voice; she asked him in, and both of them headed towards the bedroom as though they had to finish making the bed together. Suddenly Frau Falbe leant against him; the next moment they were sitting on the edge of the bed.—Come back this evening, I'm busy now, said Frau Falbe; another moment later they were already sprawled across the double bed.

This evening I can't . . . he'd whispered into her ear in a strained voice . . . I'm a woman, too, she murmured in reply, stay here, don't come this evening.—And several times she said apologetically: I know, I know things aren't easy for you either . . .

The strangest thing about it all was that she kept using the formal 'you' the whole time . . . after barely an hour he was back in his room, overwhelmed and slightly giddy. With the blind down he sat in the armchair in the dark and tried to get his bearings; outside he heard Frau Falbe putter about cleaning the stairs, and so he didn't dare to leave the room; gradually exhaustion overcame him. The night before he had barely managed to sleep, despite several glasses of beer he'd drunk at a pub after Frau Falbe's visit; he'd constantly been woken up again by some harmless noise or other, only around five had he stopped hearing things. Shortly before noon he'd been wide awake again, it struck him that he had no more coffee left, and he recalled his landlady's invitation.

That had been in the morning, and now, as he woke up late in the armchair, there was of course still no coffee ... only tea, which he often drank, but never right after waking up.— It was too late to buy coffee, he'd have to go back up to Frau Falbe ... only now, still half-asleep in his armchair, did he form a clearer picture of that noon's events, for even in the bright daylight that fell through the two windows of Frau Falbe's bedroom, he'd sensed things rather than seen them. He recalled that she had torn open the buttoned-up robe, hands flying, and shed the rest of her clothing just as hastily, even as she buried him beneath her. She'd uttered a flood of unintelligible words as she ran her lips ceaselessly over his face and neck (and even at this moment, presumably without thinking, she had kept to the formal 'you') . . . amid continuous murmuring adjurations—a mixture of apologies, assurances and childish scolding—she had tried with one hand, then the other, to give him an erection, while he clutched her upper body as though to calm her down; at last her yanking, inexpert, tireless hand motions transformed his pain into pleasure; she noticed it immediately and spread her lower body astraddle his loins, making him feel his ejaculation a moment later. And she'd remained crouched over him a little longer, covering his face and closing his eyes with both her hands; her two thumbs lay just below his nose, and he breathed the scent they gave off . . . it had to be his own smell, quickly dissipating to nothingness, transformed to the neutral smell of her heavy, faintly trembling hands.

Then he heard his landlady in the stairwell again (it was as though she kept finding things to do there because she sensed he was evading her); he went out and said—avoiding both the informal and the formal 'you'—that he hadn't managed to go shopping, and a proper coffee would be nothing to sneeze at right now; she gave him a rather shy smile and said she'd come right down . . . He must have overslept?—He went back to his room, put on his pyjamas and waited.—As they'd embraced on the double bed he'd kept wanting to ask again about the scene with Harry . . . Maybe he hadn't understood right, could she explain how that was with the gun again?—He pictured the possible consequences of the question: You couldn't explain that, you could only show it . . . He hadn't even got a chance to speak, but maybe he had been too timid anyway.—This sort of rebuke had a tendency to ambush him but could usually be dispelled again quickly with reasonable words such as: ultimately he was after objective truths . . . yes, he was used to dealing objectively with heated emotions, something he ascribed in large part to the attacks by Feuerbach, who had badmouthed him often enough as hypersensitive. And the enthusiasm with which others spoke of their capabilities in the sexual realm had always struck him as exaggerated . . . still, he couldn't deny that he was prone to a sometimes irksome restraint.

And he'd wanted to protect Feuerbach, of course; he hadn't been able to face hearing that crude story a second time . . . which showed his dependency on his case officer. Still more irksome was the fact that Feuerbach had to intrude now, when his thoughts were focused on Frau Falbe. Whatever he thought about, everything had to do with the first lieutenant . . . wasn't he out here in his hideout because he wanted to change that? At any rate, in a certain sense he had Feuerbach to thank for the experience of that noon . . .

How long had he been waiting for Feuerbach, anyway?—No, how long had he been waiting for Frau Falbe; she had promised to come right away with the coffee. Too long not to start thinking about other things entirely . . . He'd have to come up with some very shrewd questions indeed if he wanted Feuerbach to tell him the real truth about the gun story . . . Whenever he was bored for a moment in this tiny room, his thoughts wandered, suddenly he saw himself strolling up Frankfurter Allee on a fine day, his face in the backwash of evening sun as it trembled and flashed in the exhaust fumes. Or he sat in downtown Berlin in one of the Scene's jam-packed living rooms, running his eyes from one female form to the next until they rested on the translucent figure of a little West Berliner he referred to as the student . . .

He put on his pyjamas in the darkness, with the door of his room open; across the tiny corridor, barely larger than the inside of a wardrobe, came a barely perceptible glimmer, the light from the stairwell glowing in the translucent pressed glass pane at eye level in the outside door.—Mightn't Frau Falbe have thought he wasn't there . . . or that he wanted to be with her in the dark, and that had frightened her . . . That would be foolish, he said, and turned the light on. At that moment the street door opened, and he heard steps in the stairwell . . . it couldn't be her, someone was climbing the stairs, just a few steps, then silence. Quickly he turned out the light again . . . on the first floor there was a noise at the door, then silence again; he listened, an uncanny feeling: Who could have gone up to Frau Falbe at this hour?

He waited for someone to come back down, in vain, and Frau Falbe didn't show up again that evening.—The entire time he pictured how she'd show up . . . and how he would act: nervous, of course, incapable of producing the trivial phrases which would remove the tension in the room . . . while she chattered, vacuous things, but things which in their very noncommittal nature created the lukewarm atmosphere in which you could swim together . . . He never would have pulled that off!

(Don't you remember my name . . . You asked me my name . . . You must have thought I'd forgotten it myself . . . Allow me to introduce myself: Cambert! . . . thus various attempts at conversation with the Student had ended.)

He had always been after unambiguity, after unequivocal behaviour, after unambiguous statements . . . in stark contrast to the texts that lay before him on the desk in the dark.—W. had so far been certain of Feuerbach's appreciation.—The things you write, he'd said, sound cryptic the first time you hear them, but your work is very obviously an attempt to gain clarity about something. And so ultimately we have something in common which you shouldn't underestimate . . .

Incidentally, there's another thing in common, he said after a while. You have pieces there where there's much more clarity. Those are the pieces you're supposed to hold back for now. In our metier, too, we always know more than we let on. One might say that we practically have to compel the object of our interest to make a move, that is, we must be able to wait until things reveal themselves in their nakedness. Doesn't that mean we work along exactly the same lines?

At some point you said we don't wait, we practically force people's fates. But that is our way of waiting, we never said we won't take the offensive. For instance, what would have happened if no one had fiddled with your literary progress . . .?

To this day you'd probably still be huddling in your garret over your unpublished works . . . you'd never have been in these two anthologies, what were they called again: Theatre of Sparrows or Circus of Mice . . . good Lord, the titles the intelligentsia comes up with! Or would you rather just be published in the samizdats, and under a pseudonym at that . . .?

(It's not your words that are inscrutable, it's the things you're trying to assimilate, or at least they seem that way, said Feuerbach . . . it was one of those conversations which W. saw coming to a bad end from the outset. Evidently Feuerbach realized himself how contradictory his words were, and his voice was testy: You're right, that's a problem, but it has a solution. Can we help it, for instance, if everyone speaks in riddles these days? What can we find out despite that, about the way people think in this city, for instance? You'll concede that this knowledge is significant for the State authorities . . . or at least interesting, am I right? I'd say it's crucial. Understandably, the figures who regard themselves as the authorities don't have the option of talking to the so-called man on the street every day. Besides, the man on the street would have far too many inhibitions to speak his mind to state officials . . . I, for one, sometimes feel like that nice sultan who dresses in rags and joins the camel drivers at their campfire to listen to his subjects' complaints . . . or I feel like the sultan's right hand, at least. No, let's stick to the issue we're faced with, we who've always got our ear to the masses—W. had the impression that he meant these sorts of clichés seriously, that his irony was a mere convention—or what we've heard with this ear is just the people's usual blabbing, the completely meaningless chatter. And our task is to take that and filter out a picture of the underlying thoughts for ourselves.

For ourselves? W. broke in. I thought the picture was supposed to be for the authorities.

It's supposed to be. But even if we know the people's thinking, that doesn't mean we have a picture we can convey to the State, not by a long shot. First we have to take the people's thinking and construct statements of fact, as it were. And of course we have to supply the implications of the statements at the same time.

And if that doesn't work out, the facts have to be filled in . . . W. presumably didn't say these words out loud, perhaps because he would only have been repeating himself, for the umpteenth time, and not getting anywhere.

And Feuerbach, too, was more and more apt to repeat himself, but still had the nerve to declare this a sign of stagnation . . . And one day this stagnation will bring us crashing down, it might not be much longer now!—At that moment he was on his way to the bar to bring back drinks he'd ordered a long time ago; the waiter seemed sunk in a profound reverie, and the two filled beer glasses stood orphaned under the tap. Observing the first lieutenant's slender figure from behind, W. thought he saw him reel a bit. Lately he seemed to notice more and more often that his superior was losing certain nuances of his well-rehearsed elegance . . . Something about Feuerbach is flaking off, he thought. Or was it a universal dissonance that was spreading through the city?—And one result was that Feuerbach had little use now for the reports that reached him from the so-called Scene . . . because the people in the Scene were acting just plain indifferent, as the first lieutenant put it.

As if they were learning from us! he said. W. remembered this so vividly because the words seemed so astute to him.— As if they'd suddenly started seeing things the way we do, he said. Now all we need is for them to think we're indifferent.

I could confirm that, said W.

There you go, ultimately we are, aren't we . . . they must have once had a completely false, falsified image of us, who taught them that? The cliques that are in the West now, or what? And in the Scene they're suddenly seeing the light! Because aren't we actually extremely indifferent . . . that's our strength, you see. Or did anyone ever demand conviction from you?

Returning to the table, Feuerbach set down the two glasses; suddenly he had a grim expression on his face.—Maybe he was annoyed at the waiter? thought W.; that couldn't be, since otherwise he found the waiter's absentmindedness perfectly OK.—Cheers! Feuerbach's voice had a hard edge. Do you have the faintest notion what I think sometimes?

W., his head tipped back to drink, gave him a questioning look.

Or what I actually think almost all the time? I think the reports you give me are all faked! Don't say anything, let me finish . . . at least they've been faked for quite a while. You know what you're doing, my dear man, you're writing poetry! Yes, you're writing poetry even in your dossiers. But you're doing it badly, if only you'd do it right. You're doing the same thing you do with your poetry, you only hand in the second-rate stuff. Lately your reports are second rate too, edited and watered down . . .)

How could he claim to know that? At what point in the reports could this suspicion have dawned on him . . . an absurd suspicion, in W.'s view.—And perhaps it was only a blanket suspicion: since everyone was suspicious, at irregular intervals everyone was placed under suspicion. At any rate, infinite grounds for suspicion were always available: the most idiotic conjectures, the most unforeseeable, it was part of the routine that they came like bolts from the blue . . . for instance, it had come to light that the lists of coup d'etat suspects put together by the Soviet state security service included, among others, the name Walter Ulbricht.[8]—When you needed security, you also needed suspicion; that was logical.

W. could no longer recall whether he had denied the accusation ... apparently he had simply said nothing. The matter was far from cleared up ... but it was like Feuerbach to leave him saddled with accusations. He was a trained security man, and he knew the devastating effects of deferment.—And finally it wasn't clear either whether the suspicion Feuerbach voiced might not give cause for hope—to the effect that he was no use any more because he was unreliable!—Maybe they wouldn't even come and get him ... maybe the best thing was to hold out here at Frau Falbe's and see what happened.

Frau Falbe came the next evening; he gave a start as the door was suddenly unlocked.—You're sitting in the dark? she said in surprise, and switched the light on. Are you sitting in the dark on purpose?—He felt foolish; since the evening before he'd neither bathed nor dressed, his discarded clothes still lay in a pile on the floor behind the rumpled cot, he was still wearing the badly fitting, not very clean pyjamas whose fly wouldn't stay closed due to the frayed buttonholes, so that his hand always hovered warily nearby. But that wasn't the worst of it; he'd spent a depressive night, too lazy even to go to the pub, sleeping just a few hours at intervals in the armchair, and every time he woke up he'd sensed vividly that the intangible beast still lingered in the room. Feuerbach had reached for him from afar and dragged him back inexorably. He recalled that if he'd any reason to think the first lieutenant was in the city, he would have set out in search of him!

The evening with Frau Falbe turned into a debacle; from a certain moment onward he'd positively dreaded having to get his sexual energies flowing for her ... he was glad that all she seemed to want to do was chat, but even then he wasn't really listening.—At one point he had the idea of suddenly telling her everything (deconspiring, that would have been the technical term) . . . he scrapped the idea at once, otherwise Frau Falbe would immediately have seen him as one of the people who had gone at her protégé Harry with the gun . . . when what he really wanted to do was share her disgust at the story, and at some point, he hadn't yet abandoned the thought, have her play the game of the fantasy of the thing with the gun . . . Today you keep looking at me like you've seen a ghost, she said at one point, I think I have come at a bad time . . . After a while she'd suggested that he come and watch a movie on TV. It's a James Bond movie, she said, Harry always liked those.—A movie . . . he said, I don't think that whole espionage thing is much fun in real life. Incidentally, he'd liked that thing yesterday noon much better, unfortunately it had gone a bit quickly . . .—She didn't give the impression of concurring with his words, it seemed more that the memory embarrassed her. But she did leave him with a glimmer of hope; already at the door, she turned around again and said: Yes, me too of course . . .

And then she stuck her head back in: By the way, I had a visitor last night . . . You can guess who it was . . . —He'd almost asked if it had been Feuerbach.—He asked for Harry. There's someone in the room again, he said, so Harry Falbe must be back. Falbe, he said . . . didn't you also think Harry has the same name as me?—What did you tell him? asked W.—I said, Harry Falbe, I don't know the man, I don't have any relatives. All I've got is my husband, and he's somewhere in the West, and he works for the State!—Was it the same guy again, you know, the one with the gun?—No, she said, a different one, I never saw him before. And then he asked about you. In a roundabout way, who's living downstairs now, he asked ∴. . I said, that's none of your business, you're not getting any information from me.—What did he look like? Didn't he say who sent him?—It was a tall guy, more than tall, I thought, good Lord, the guy's over six foot. And you could tell from his voice that he's not from Berlin, he talked the way you do.

About the name, W. explained, that just slipped out. I really thought Harry was a relative of yours. Maybe we're not even talking about the same . . . maybe you have a photo of him somewhere?

She shrugged her shoulders; W. said he wasn't feeling so well today, he'd have to take a walk now . . . And maybe we'll see each other tomorrow . . .

OK, she said, but not noon again already!—And it sounded as though she had felt flattered by W.'s obdurate desire.

His only option for the rest of the evening was to have a bite to eat in one of the neighbourhood restaurants. He knew of a tiny pub that served fried herring with fried potatoes, an exclusive rarity that constituted one of the advantages of the capital, and there he headed. He even managed to find a seat. First, with his back to the door, he sat across from a mirror that hung at a tilt on the upper part of the wall. He barely recognized himself in it; he had to hunt for himself among all the people at the table, strangely anonymous in their volubility . . . and the mirror reflected only the lower part of the door, which kept opening and admitting new guests; it was impossible to identify who came in, and he had the growing fear that at any moment he would feel the tap of a very familiar finger on his shoulder . . . or at any moment see a tall figure in the mirror, so tall that it lacked head and legs. At last a chair freed up across from him; he changed places, and now had time to think.

Before leaving the room he had cleared off the desk, stowing his papers in the empty drawers and leaving only a few white, clean sheets on the desktop. Intolerable, to return and have the first thing he saw be scribbled scraps of paper, phrases typed through a faded ribbon that were summonses to meet-ups, on their backs barely legible notes along the lines of the game of the fantasy of the thing with the gun . . . the fantasy of the woman's game with the thing of the gun . . . the story of the woman's fantasy of the game of the thing with the gun . . . and so on . . . the structure of the genitive of the genitives—that ought well to seem familiar!

He was sick of his work, it was second rate, Feuerbach was absolutely right about that. The work was mediocre . . . if only it had been bad, the media would have lapped it up. But the media . . . especially the Western media! . . . loved mediocrity . . . the measure of mediocrity was the medium of the press of oppression . . .

His work was some second persona's occupational therapy, or the products of a neurotic who with an enormous effort transformed himself for a few minutes a day into a writer . . . or transformed himself back, perhaps, it being possible that in this person's second, already half-forgotten persona there had once been the makings of a writer. Now nothing but a sentimental hope made him cling to these makings . . . some drivel about artistic gifts bore the blame for this hope, and that drivel came from his case officer. It had ultimately gotten to the point at which recalling his so-called talent cost him a nervous strain alleviable only by immediate sleep . . . and each time he woke up he was relieved to find that he was still the same old person: Feuerbach's best man . . . Go ahead, pat yourself on the back! said his superior.—And then, once again, he was that guy who gadded about bored but secretly attentive, who answered to a code name. Or didn't answer, depending, or answered to this other name which he had to use to sign things and which appeared above his published poems . . . above his first poem to be published, illegally in the Western press half a year ago, a year ago or a year and a half ago, and then above the next poem too, and he'd kept this name ever since then (and ever since then a character of this name appeared regularly in his reports . . .)

And often enough he didn't even react when he heard the name that stemmed from the so-called author bios of scattered poetry publications, garlanded by completely incoherent and legendary data about a person who was a pure fiction. And he could never say offhand whether or not this data was correct . . . once, he recalled, he had been turned away from one of the offices in the city because he wasn't clear on his current data. It was one of those identical, completely anonymous offices (the door sported a private, random name, furnished, as so often, with a spillage of consonants, the more consonants, the more expensive the flat behind the door: Pr Dr Dr h.c. E. Schulze-Lehmann, or perhaps something even more original); and there was actually—he didn't know when she'd come in—a receptionist; when asked for some year from his legend . . . either a birth or a death date . . . he'd replied: Ask the boss and have him check the filing card.

In the kitchens of the Scene, where people planned and debated round the clock, he was viewed as the most taciturn one, never contributing anything to the controversies . . . and perhaps he was the perpetually abstracted one, whose thoughts never dwelt in the same place as his person; but this very behaviour had garnered him the reputation of the imperturbable, reliable one, always on the spot . . . and sometimes in several spots at once.—He was absolutely everywhere, he always put in at least one appearance wherever people were holding readings or theatre performances, wherever they were exhibiting paintings that hadn't been reviewed by the authorities (abstract paintings?); his name was on every list (he just had to make sure it wasn't the name Cambert!), his face blurred in the background of every commemorative snapshot, he was the Scene's mute but never-tiring reinforcement, and sometimes he was the Scene all by himself. He was the eternal extra, then; his abiding spellbound attention emboldened the most inexperienced writer of prose or proclamations, and almost by habit all proposals and protests were given first to him to sign (he just had to watch out that he didn't sign as 'Cambert'). And when somewhere or other a van filled with detainees rolled off: he was there (he just couldn't identify himself to the police as Cambert!); and waiting for the interrogation he, the staunch silent block amid the others' flutter, was the first to catch the eye of the officer on duty, the first to be grabbed roughly by the lapel and dragged into the office (he just had to remind them not to throw him out with the words: Don't come back any time soon, Herr Cambert!).

The most convenient role for him to play was the taciturn type . . . Feuerbach carped about it, though: really he had nothing to offer (once W. had made this very threat to the boss in A., now Feuerbach repeated the words at every opportunity), every report had his name in it, but he never took any initiative . . . How was he going to find out anything more than the usual if he didn't take charge of the conversation himself? How was he ever going to penetrate to the heart of certain intimate connections if he couldn't even make up his mind on a little flirt with the West Berliner?

One day he had produced a profile of the person who bore his real name (a poet in the so-called unofficial literary scene, who, with others, had been the topic of conversation for nearly a year now). This job was a trial of patience; he'd had to provide a whole series of these descriptions, and after repeated, urgent requests from his superior he had completed the majority of them in the nights during and after a three-day workshop with the slogan Ecology and Perestroika, at which art was also shown and readings took place. As many participants as possible had to be recorded; identifying descriptions had to be supplied, along with brief summaries of their behaviour. On the list's many pages, he himself occupied a place about a third of the way through:

Participant No. 29

(unquestionably the operationally known M. W.)

Gender: male; age: 44–8; height: 165–70 cm.; stature: stocky, corpulent; shape of head: round; carriage of head: generally tilted, but variable; complexion: pale (unshaven); forehead: broad, furrow over the nose; chin: receding, tendency to double chin; hair colour: dark blond, grey temples; haircut: medium length, ears covered; eye colour: grey; eyebrows: bushy, short, separate; clothing: light brown jacket, unlined (so-called parka, People's Production), always worn open, faded blue riveted trousers (jeans, Lee brand), poor fit (too small in the waist), secured by black plastic belt, shirt (short-sleeved) with blue–green pattern; accessories: white plastic bag with the imprint RBI (Radio Berlin International), contents: 1 book (title and author not ascertained), 2 unopened packs of cigarettes (brand not ascertained).

Description in brief: No. 29 behaves as though he were not expected at the workshop. Shakes hands with approx. 10 persons. Displays little interest in the artwork on display, but when asked about it responds with exaggerated praise. Rarely takes part in discussions, rapidly switches interlocutor, exchanging trivial phrases such as: How're you doing. Fine and you. I'm doing just fine and you. No I'm not doing bad and you. Me too. Yeah, since yesterday I'm doing fine and you. Also fine since yesterday and you. All the time his gaze remains restless, usually directed away from the interlocutor and roaming the garden. He seems interested only in the female attendees, but does not speak with them, only with the male attendees. Once he quotes a passage from Roland Barthes near a group of female attendees (incorrectly). Smokes heavily, cigarettes, Juwel brand (old), drinks beer from the bottle without always contributing to the collecting-box. Displays no initiative, gives the impression of a hanger-on.

Striking traits: scratches a spot on the back of his head to the right at least 50x over the course of the evening (endogenous eczema?). Bored, perspiring, complains about the heat (temperature around 19.00 only +16° C), one of the last to leave the event.

This was followed by the date 27 April of the year in question.

W. was glad to move out of the mirror, as he'd been forced—the broad mirror tilted out from the wall and captured the entire table— to endlessly identify himself among the other guests: the furrow over his nose, intersecting his brows and giving him a bifurcated gaze. The film of sweat on his brow, the hair which had grown over his ears and absorbed all the filth of the streets, gleaming greasily in the lamplight . . . he decided to ask Frau Falbe tomorrow if he could use her bath.

As a matter of fact, he remembered the event, held in the spring (last spring?) on the grounds of a church in Berlin's Rummelsburg district. Long after darkness fell, throngs of young people kept arriving to stroll about the church's yard and gardens, children chasing one another in their midst; there were snack stands and tables where second-hand things were sold, the proceeds going to some good cause he'd forgotten; somewhere guitar music struck up, paper lanterns scattered coloured light. And outside the entrance several patrol cars had driven up in staggered formation; the loitering officers had long since abandoned the attempt to demand each new arrival's identification. When W. had arrived in the afternoon things were different, even from a distance he'd seen the uniformed officers, stressed out by the exhaustive spot checks . . . but with bored expressions they'd seemed about to let him pass. And he'd gone up to one of the policemen and provocatively whipped out his ID to the guy, who took it wearily and thumbed quickly through the pages . . . You're holding the ID upside down, Sergeant! W. said.

(C. took an S-Bahn train from Rummelsburg Depot to Ostkreuz, and one from there to Lichtenberg, where he changed for the U-Bahn to travel one stop in the direction of Alexanderplatz. In the dim underpass at Lichtenberg he already felt he was alone; from the platform he'd drifted slowly down the overlong, low, bare concrete shaft, past the long-distance rail platforms, all the way up front to the exit, avoiding the stairs in the middle, descending into the U-Bahn only at the front. There were only a few figures skulking about the underground platform: he was unlikely now to meet an acquaintance who might have seen him at the church in Rummelsburg. Now he took the U-Bahn to the next stop, at the Magdalenenstrasse Station he'd reached his destination; he took the eastern stairs—leading back in the direction of Lichtenberg—and up on Frankfurter Allee he went back the opposite way, heading for the cafe.—If Feuerbach had been sitting in his place by the window now, with his cheek to the glass, he would have seen him coming.

But to his surprise there was activity outside the cafe, tables and chairs stood out on the light-flooded pavement, almost all of them still occupied, beneath colourful folding sunshades held to the ground by heavy cast-iron bases. The cafe had started its outdoor service! Every year it went from the eve of 1 May to 31 August. A wiry little waitress was hired for the four months; C. recognized her from afar, a colourless creature of indeterminate age—between thirty and forty, thought C., his intuition failing him here—who served promptly and precisely, still more remote than her indoors colleague who wandered lost in thought between the rows of tables. C. had never seen any of the jovial evening guests elicit even the semblance of a smile from the waitress' pinched lips; her blonde hair was combed back tightly, adorned at the hairline by a tiny white cap which she didn't seem to wear for decoration; on her, for some reason, it looked like part of a uniform illustrating her function. And she fulfilled this function stony faced, moving from table to table with an even tread and pedantically noting even the simplest order on a tear-off pad . . . The manager's UnCol, Feuerbach had said after only a minute the first time they'd sat at one of the outside tables. Let's go inside, we're being watched out here.—And C. had never managed to get service from her, because she had been severely insulted by his superior. On their second attempt to take advantage of the outdoor service, she came up to their table and punctiliously uttered the mandatory three words: Your order please . . . And Feuerbach had requested: Two beers, three double brandies!—She gave a look of cool surprise and asked: Are you expecting another guest?—Feuerbach started to explain that the third brandy was for her, but shut his mouth again and screwed up his eyes. Then he said: Oh, by the way, miss, it works both ways . . . why don't you stick your cockade on that idiotic hat of yours!—With that they'd forfeited the chance of ever being served at the pavement tables again; they moved into the taproom.—She understood me! said Feuerbach, and explained to C. that in the Firm cockade was a very common code word for the human arsehole.

This evening—actually it was already night—the first lieutenant was not in the cafe; this knowledge was enough for C., and though his window seat in the taproom was still free, he headed for his flat. He had a bundle of papers in the inside pocket of his parka, the second part of the profiles for which he had taken notes during the Ecology and Perestroika workshop. The event didn't really fall under Feuerbach's purview, but it had been clear that a large portion of the Scene would show up there . . . It's about connections with the grassroots groups and so on, Feuerbach had said, not much fun for us, but work is work, and you don't have to be too particular about it.

And, no doubt unconsciously, C. had done just that: twice he had dated the documents wrong. At the end of the first third, which he had delivered the day before, stood the date 27 April; the sheaf in his pocket, beginning with Person No. 30, was marked 28 April . . . if it had gone on like that, the next day he would have written 29/04 under the rest.—But as a matter of principle the cafe tables weren't set up outside until the eve of 1 May . . . he had back-dated all his notes by one day. How was that possible? A little square daily tear-off calendar hung in his flat, and he never neglected to tear off the old sheet. At night he had typed up the list, because his handwritten notes were barely legible: you started sweating when you had to find five minutes at a public event to take notes unobserved, for instance, in much-frequented toilets which didn't really lock . . . the final straw would have been to get asked if he had diarrhoea—and he'd worked on it until five in the morning or later . . . after all, it was twenty people he had to process, had to plausibly alter if necessary . . . the second part of the list—Criminal profiles! he said—ought to have been delivered now, with the date 28 April beneath it . . . but on that day the event in Rummelsburg had only just begun.—The only explanation was that two days ago he'd forgotten to tear off the calendar sheet from 27 April . . .

The night before, he had slipped the first part of the list into Feuerbach's hand under the cafe table; Feuerbach had tucked away the pages without looking at them and said: And tomorrow you'll bring me the second day!—The whole thing was no big deal, of course, but it was a sign of nerves . . .

All that had happened almost exactly a year ago; he no longer knew how he'd revised the false dates back then, or if they'd ever been corrected at all . . . maybe he had gone on living with this faulty time ever since.—For perhaps the last year, he thought, we've gotten in the habit of arriving a little too late.)

Around noon he woke up in Frau Falbe's double bed. Blazing sunlight flooded in through the big window on the left side of the room . . . he had slept with his back to Frau Falbe's half of the bed, lying on his side—as always with his knees drawn up and his fists in his lap—full of unrest and as though in a paroxysm, but the dreamless void had drawn him down all the deeper. As soon as he woke he felt the dull pain in the back of his head like a distant drilling, the after-effect, all too familiar, of an overdose of inferior alcohol . . . of course he had sat in the pub for far too long, and in the end the drinking had become a sheer test of his endurance. Now he had that familiar taste of bile in his parched oral cavity, in his throat the uvula was sore and so tangibly swollen that it made him nauseous—he must have battered it with unbridled snores. Mucous had solidified rock-hard in his nostrils, and at rhythmic intervals a faint whistling noise escaped his lungs . . . it wasn't the bracing, cleansed awakening one marvelled at in James Bond movies . . . the alcohol was famously better on the other side of the Iron Curtain.

And as another consequence of drinking inferior alcohol in an East Berlin dive, he had rung Frau Falbe's doorbell again on his way back. Now he lay here in the bed of her long-vanished husband and had to extract his thoughts with an effort from amid the painful convolutions of his brain.

He hadn't been able to get the date 27 April off his mind, and he didn't know why. It wasn't necessarily connected with the fact that he had once set it down beneath a list of profiles despite it being the wrong date . . . no, it was connected with Feuerbach's disappearance and reappearance. At the time he had mulled fruitlessly over the first lieutenant's absence . . . and yesterday in the pub his mind kept wandering and he'd recalled the start of the summer season, which the cafe on Frankfurter Allee marked by setting tables and chairs out on the pavement on the eve of 1 May . . . for some reason he knew that in the year he was thinking of, this had happened for the last time: since then the cafe no longer had outdoor service.

And then he'd gone to the flat and got back to work on his dossiers (Criminal profiles! he vividly recalled the thought). Feuerbach hadn't showed the next day either . . . perhaps he could easily have found him . . . on the holiday, with Frankfurter Allee bustling . . . Had so-called counterdemonstrations on the national holiday been anticipated even that year?

Yesterday in the pub he'd glanced at the calendar behind the bar and happened to notice that it was 27 April . . . he could count on Feuerbach being back again on 1 May, or even the evening before, or even now, sitting in the cafe as though nothing had happened . . . except that the tables and chairs were no longer outside, one less bit of metropolitan flair in the city . . . Feuerbach had said: Just like in Amsterdam! Twelve at night, and everything's still full.—Now he'd be forced to agree, like it or not, if W. remarked again that in the past year bad vibes had moved into the city . . . Indeed, he'd replied back then, quite reliable, your seventh sense! And hopefully you've also guessed that it's because of our presence . . .

The problem for W. was that he couldn't remember exactly—that possibly he'd been lagging behind the times a year longer than he'd thought . . . how else could he know there was no more outdoor service on Frankfurter Allee?— Ultimately it didn't matter, the bad vibes hadn't let up, over the past year or the past two years . . . and now, this spring, in Feuerbach's absence, they were even worse. You couldn't put your finger on it (and the Western journalists, who came more and more often to check that all was well in the Scene, didn't notice it at all, on the contrary, they seemed electrified by an ongoing exhilaration, tossing Russian words about and beaming like Indian wise men on the threshold of nirvana) . . . the bad vibes were really only something you could feel, assuming that you wanted to. They were like an additive to the air people breathed, making them gloomy and depressive; W. had thought he sensed them even in the still-grey early spring, late February, early March, though the window of the cafe. But perhaps they—Feuerbach and he—were still feeling the shock of 17 January, when the grassroots groups had disrupted the Liebknecht–Luxemburg Demonstration and caused 'riots and provocations' (the official statement!) on Frankfurter Allee . . . At the time between one and two hundred people had been nabbed; by now they were all at large again . . . and since early April everyone had been claiming that a new production of the drama was planned for 1 May . . . and so it was a safe bet that Feuerbach would be back in the city on 30 April at the latest.

No, the bad vibes weren't visible: it was business as usual, the crowds emerging from the U-Bahn tunnels or vanishing into them had lost none of their haste and bustle, everyone wore their usual faces and greeted one another as emphatically as ever . . . on Frankfurter Allee the distances were large, and this was inimical to the typical Berlin understatement . . . and people talked just as much or as little, and, on Frankfurter Allee, in all sorts of dialects.

Frankfurter Allee was not the Scene, and it was not Alexanderplatz, dominated by the average folks and the tourists; by the time you found out anything on Frankfurter's eastern end, things were probably already going up in flames all over the place. And yet it seemed to him that the floods of humanity coming from the underpasses had suddenly thinned out . . . it wasn't noticeable yet, but their squadrons were less compact, fewer of them were spat out from the U-Bahns in the Magdalenenstrasse Station; even during the afternoon rush hour, when the trains came more frequently, there were fewer pedestrians walking down the boulevard and past the gigantic complex of the Ministry.—Even then W. had started taking long trips with public transportation in an effort to fathom this feeling for which feeling might not even be the word . . . and which possibly was nothing but a mood of his own. He almost always came late when there was a reading somewhere in the Scene, a stand-around party (five hours long, not good for legs you had to earn a living with), a costume affair (theatre with gender-swapped roles—very interesting!) or a scattering of shredded paper (described as a performance—with literary pretensions) . . . he arrived too late—missing the male protagonist's bare breasts once again!— because he'd ridden a few stations too far so as to wander along several streets which were still unfamiliar to him(often, later, through the sombre neighbourhoods near the Storkower Strasse Station) . . . and as lifeless as always; it was hard to believe how lifeless some parts of Berlin were on inclement evenings. And when he did he sensed, again and again, that a vague odour of futility had crept over the city . . . And the only interesting things in this city, he thought, are playing out behind the doors of the flats: the Western TV and radio channels were playing. And they were playing because people were looking for the country they lived in . . . but this country was hardly mentioned in the news and the commentaries . . . As if we'd already been gobbled up! said Feuerbach.—Things in Poland and Hungary, and especially the Soviet Union, played a far greater role . . . Finally our people are taking an interest in the Russians! said Feuerbach.—Even China had suddenly gained importance . . . W. had the impression that the country he lived in had been forgotten, and quite probably this impression was rampant among the citizens of the Republic in general. The Republic had sunk into an animated sort of deathly silence, against which any Eurasian earthquake was more stirring; there was no earthquake here. Suddenly the whole country's state was best described by a strange word: absence . . . it was as though no one had had to invent the term; all at once what it described was omnipresent. —Meanwhile the buzzwords of the day were of foreign origin, hailing from Moscow: glasnost or perestroika. For the first time the little German republic seemed to turn a deaf ear to Moscow; here it was the same old, same old, or no, it got older by the day—and the old men in the government seemed never to have heard those words before.

He would have liked then to ask Feuerbach about the two Russian words; they had never discussed them, apart from a few vague allusions. For half the month of May the first lieutenant complained about the profiles which W. was withholding from him . . . W. couldn't imagine what the superfluous stuff was needed for.—Much later he recalled that Feuerbach had mentioned a different division, evidently another section was putting him under pressure.—W. had kept putting him off, claiming he had to touch up the drafts, fill in the gaps, and Feuerbach reacted aggressively, threatening after several days of this to come to W.'s flat and tear the scraps from his typewriter.

On one of those aggressive days he waited for the first lieutenant in his flat until eight in the evening, windows wide open (it was mid-May, and chilly) in the hope of hearing the sound of the front door from up on the fifth floor . . . and then he really did hear the door's cumbersome leaf scraping across the tiles and falling to. Actually he'd finished the dossiers, apart from a few insignificant things, and he didn't quite understand himself what he was doing.—He kept thinking about the description of a young woman which had turned out somewhat oddly . . . which perhaps hadn't ended up being entirely objective. The page was in the second bundle which he had been carrying around in his pocket back on the eve of 1 May. He'd been relieved when the handoff miscarried; after that he had tried to rewrite the passages about the young woman . . . they were a failure yet again, now they seemed lustreless, lacking esprit . . . they were missing something, he didn't know what . . . Feuerbach would have sniffed it out at once!—Then he'd reread the first version, which had turned out . . . he hated to use the word . . . too poetic. Yes, the woman was portrayed too sympathetically, without expertise, Feuerbach would have said, now the word intimate occurred to him. A certain something . . . no, an uncertain something about this woman was a phenomenon (at least in his dossier), and discord always brewed in unexpected quarters whenever the word phenomenon cropped up.—W. slipped the relevant page from the stack of paper, rolled it up, put a rubber band around it, placed it in his desk drawer and pushed everything else in the drawer up against it and in front of it: pencils, rolls of adhesive tape, packs of cigarettes, cutlery, wadded-up coffee filters; then he went to a pub.—On his return he immediately suspected someone had been in the flat . . . the light was burning when he came in, no, he'd already seen it burning from the street. The dossiers on the desk looked very jumbled, and possibly some were missing . . . he removed the thin roll of paper from the desk drawer and took it down to the cellar.

As he stood down in front of his basement storage space—which wasn't even padlocked, just shut with a wobbly latch—it too seemed unsuitable: How could someone not hit on the idea of a basement hiding place? His basement had almost nothing in it, just a scanty heap of coal briquettes, left over from last winter. W. gazed further down the basement passage, irresolute . . . he had been left with the last storage space, the farthest away from the door . . . and then he lived on the very top floor, the fourth or fifth, he'd never really counted—and so the other residents had reckoned the longest possible distance for him to lug his coal . . . and the shortest one for the people on the ground floor, who of course had claimed the first storage spaces near the entrance.—Feuerbach had told him that the previous tenant was an old woman with no family, the great aunt of an officer who'd absconded to the West before the Wall was built. And one day the old lady had been found in her flat . . . frozen to death! In the meantime it had gotten warmer again, and she was already semi-liquefied . . . it was a story W. couldn't let himself think about alone in the flat at night . . . but of course it also reminded him of Frau Falbe's story, of her husband who had vanished to the West.

A few steps onward the passage turned a corner, where a door had been removed, and there was another light switch. He turned the switch and saw another long, lit passage in front of him: he was under the next building . . . he lived in No. 35, and here someone had chalked the number 33 on the wall, no doubt to guide the coal carriers. And the slatted doors of the basement cubicles bore the names of each tenant, but there were empty spaces too, ones left open, or ones in which every conceivable kind of junk had been stowed and hoarded . . . he walked onward as though through an utterly different, unexpectedly fantastic world . . . another bend, another passage, also lit, cubicles, gates, a little card with the tenant's name tacked to each, already No. 31, he guessed . . . and then onward, No. 29, more passages. At some point the way was cut off by a wall; he tried to picture the area: the grounds of a factory had to begin behind the wall. Turning back, he discovered a cross passage . . . by the time he was past he had already forgotten whether he had taken it or kept going straight. Once, possibly having already passed his building again, he climbed up a set of basement stairs, went through several open doors and found himself in a completely unfamiliar courtyard, a narrow rectangular shaft, dizzyingly high, dark, with a tiny square of starry sky above it, four doors leading through the four sky-high walls, and he took the nearest one, over which a tiny lamp glowed, and immediately discovered another basement, another basement passage, perhaps parallel to the one he had come from, or heading at a right angle towards it, or at a right angle away from it, or past his house in no particular direction, or towards a cross passage that crossed a never-before-seen cross passage, which crossed another one, or paralleled it, or met it at an angle . . . perhaps down here escape was possible? Who did he want to escape from, except his superior Feuerbach from time to time? And he resolved to get to the bottom of all this . . . if he couldn't find his way aboveground in Berlin, perhaps he could do so in this system down below. Was it a system congruent to the network of streets and rows of houses above him? That would have to be explored . . . this could be his task for the next few days, at least until Feuerbach had calmed down.

He found himself here—or so it might seem with a bit of imagination—in the very bowels of the city. It was like crawling under the skirts of Berlin, that monstrous old hag, and suddenly seeing all that she hid from the world in shame. Down

here the hag had concealed everything that embarrassed her
. . . and betrayed her true nature. Down here was all that
remained of her whoredom with the changing systems . . .
here she'd hidden her cast-off fetishes, here the languages of
her past were buried, in the bundles of old banned newspapers,
for instance, Wilhelmine, nationalist, democratic, fascist,
Stalinist, post-Stalinist . . . down here in the dark the corrupt
old paper phosphoresced like unwashed undergarments . . .
and down here the dead and the undead walked, amusing
themselves with the remnants of their erstwhile obsessions.
And here lay the city's unhatched eggs; no one knew what
might yet crawl out of them. And here the city's excrement
rotted.—After a week spent searching the passages beneath
the city for a place to hide his little roll of paper, he happened
upon a space that opened out in a cone shape, ending at a visibly new concrete wall. Up in the wall he discovered a still-
usable light-bulb socket, and a stable wooden crate lay nearby
. . . This, so he thought, is a safe place to think things over . . .

(Once C. had had a bad dream, he'd forgotten when and
where he had dreamt it: he had lost his body . . . at least it had
been transformed into some sort of mass which at that
moment seemed completely unacceptable. Something slimy,
slickly gleaming, brown, excrementous, and he'd kept casting
about for an apt expression. He hadn't detected any smells, but
they were in the words he used, the whole dream was filled
with the bitter taste of foul words he felt forced to repeat and
repeat, not only because he forgot them again immediately
but because he had to bury all public and conformist language
regimes beneath them. He had crawled down passages, or perhaps it was just one straight passage, very low, and yet he'd
moved forward unimpeded . . . or rather he had been moved,
it was a ploughing forward, slipping, sliding along an inclined
shaft—a mining term, as he recalled from earlier days—on the

slope of a passage that ran deeper and deeper into the earth, a square channel about a yard or a yard and a half on each side. There was light, glittering, and the walls were slurried and indistinct, seeming to consist of a loose, slimy substance that kept sliding along with him, he was a part of this substance, brown to black, and like a chameleon he blended in with each shift in the colour of the walls, all the while gliding or being propelled along.——At first he'd been appalled by the words in his throat, then they came to seem normal to him, until finally he was intoning them rhythmically, and soon they sounded like someone pounding at a typewriter: ex-cre-ment-ex-cre-ment-ex-cre-ment . . . Words such as shit, crap, crud struck him as innocuous and inapt, it was only the two old-fashioned terms excrement and faeces that expressed the full import. And in his dream he carried on with his rant and kept on moving these words even after waking: Faeces all around me . . . I am excre-ment . . . Code Name Faeces . . . Code Name Excrement . . .—— The words slid out of him without resistance, as though they consisted of the stuff they named.——And suddenly Feuerbach had woken him with the words: It can't be all that bad . . .

It must be a dream from a complete different time, C. told himself, a completely different region, maybe a dream from around the town where I was born . . . He had fallen asleep on his chair in the cafe on Frankfurter Allee, the right half of his face resting on the windowpane, fogged to the point of opacity by his fitful breath.——When you look out at the street, all's right with the world, said Feuerbach, striking up his long-familiar recitative. And that's all we should be doing, looking out, nothing but that, and not asking where the whole show's headed. Just so you know!——C. followed his impulse to remain silent.——And the first lieutenant added: And where the show's headed, that's for us to know, and no one else. You don't have to know, because you're the one who keeps it running . . .

C. looked out at the show, the usual picture: amid the fog of the exhaust fumes the automobile cohorts roared down the lanes and whirled their lights' trailing reflexes through the blue-grey dusk, the big glass pane jittered, and the motors howled; and by degrees the vast multitude of these racing vehicles let fall in the city a mighty thunder which people had already ceased to hear, and the years of uninterrupted thunder were slowly demolishing the world. And when C. looked out the window long enough, everything seemed to stand still outside, while the cafe interior fled nightwards in ever-greater surges of speed . . .)

When he opened his eyes for the second time, his headache was gone. The scent of coffee came from Frau Falbe's kitchen, across the hall and into the bedroom, both doors were ajar, he heard the clink of dishes and the clatter of silverware. W. had meant to sneak out down the hall, but it was impossible now that he'd smelt the coffee; perhaps the very smell had banished his headache. And he recalled a thought he'd sometimes had: Why shouldn't he act the artist and embrace the advantages that entailed . . . life was comfortless enough as it was, many writers he knew from the Scene scraped by with the bare minimum and still let no one spoil their fun. Soon enough he'd have to realize, yet again, that something in him was unsuited for this existence . . . or he'd have it proven to him. So why should he sneak away from a table set for coffee just because of a harmless attack of impotence . . . Frau Falbe was a woman of experience.—And she didn't even mention the incident when at last, having taken a cold shower in the bathroom, he perched in his underwear on the edge of a chair in her kitchen attempting to dispatch the Turkish-style beverage (Frau Falbe had experience in these things as well) down his swollen gullet in the largest possible swigs.—He was sitting here in his underwear . . . that meant the rest of his clothes were down in his room, where, back from the pub, he had first undressed before hitting on the idea of going upstairs and ringing the doorbell again. And now it occurred to him that his ringing had been prolonged, he'd had to turn on the stairwell light at least five times and ring unremittingly before there was any sign of life behind her door. And then he'd collapsed into bed next to her and at the first attempt to embrace her he'd fallen asleep. And he'd kept babbling uncontrollably about the gun, about Harry and Feuerbach, about the story he had to hear again . . . He turned uneasy, nearly flinching: Had he really blurted out the name Feuerbach? He was sure he hadn't talked; before Frau Falbe could even start in on the story he'd already been snoring . . . if necessary the name Feuerbach could be explained as the preliminary stage of a snore.

Your eyes are blazing red, she said once, when he glanced up because she'd spoken.—She'd been saying that Harry had also been like that a lot when he got up . . . she guessed he hadn't heard that. But probably it's getting on your nerves already, the way I'm always talking about him?—No, he said, go on talking.—He didn't even notice any more that she steadfastly maintained the formal 'you', completely ignoring what had been going on between them for several nights now . . . and in fact it wasn't disagreeable, it simplified the situation for him when all he could think of was disappearing.—But last night you wanted to know exactly how it was when they came for Harry, she said. I'll tell you sure enough.—You already told me, said W.—Yes . . . . I can see it's time for you to go again . . . W. thought he heard a touch of regret in her voice; she was drying the hair on the back of his head with a towel. I know, you have to go into town again. Just don't get caught by that guy who's looking for you . . . you know. And don't get caught by the longlegs who was here the other day!

W. ran down the stairs in his underwear; he found that he had left the key in the lock, fortunately on the outside . . . but first he listened a minute for someone in the room . . . and inside, from the door, he peered about for anything that might have changed.—All the while he had the feeling that Feuerbach would come in at any moment . . .

In his room he sat in the red armchair and let time pass by . . . he was actually rested and felt good, the second three or four hours of sleep up at his landlady's had dispelled the paralytic after-effects of his bender. A newspaper lay on the desk, which he recalled buying two days ago; the day before yesterday exactly four weeks had passed since Feuerbach had vanished from the city! He didn't know why he assumed Feuerbach's absence would be limited to a month . . . that was just how it usually was, and if someone wasn't away for four weeks, he was away for three months; one could say those were the established timeframes for official business. And so it wasn't unreasonable to think that for the past two days his boss had been waiting for him.—It was now twenty past four in the afternoon (judging by the alarm clock on the floor by the cot . . . his watch was anything but reliable); even if he set out this moment, he'd never reach the cafe on Frankfurter Allee by five. Five p.m. was one of the times Feuerbach tended to set for their meet-ups . . . another time was 7 p.m.; he could easily make it by then. There was no need to hurry; he could tidy up the desk first, where scribbled paper, illegibly scribbled paper, had proliferated once again. He folded up the papers one by one into the smallest possible packets and stuffed them into the crack between the seat and back of his red armchair.

And he still had time to brace himself for Feuerbach: he could expect their first meeting after the break to take a nasty turn.—W. didn't have the least little report ready! It was awkward enough when a week passed with nothing to show. Then

Feuerbach would clearly indicate that he was under pressure, but leave it at a few snide comments. Only once had he held out on the first lieutenant for longer than two weeks; that had been the affair with the profiles (the workshop at the Protestant church in Rummelsburg . . . The matter seemed to have blown over, yet probably hadn't been forgotten) . . . but there were a few cases in which W. hadn't delivered for ten days or so—and Feuerbach started acting like an idiot. He stuck his hand up W.'s shirt or way below his waistband, or he patted down all his pockets, in the middle of the cafe he pulled up W.'s trousers and hunted around in his socks.—Go on, tell me, where've you got the paperwork? he asked so loudly that you could hear it at all the surrounding tables. It looked like horseplay, but if W. still had nothing to show the next day, the first lieutenant's face darkened, and there was a jitter or hiss in his voice.—Once, W. recalled, Feuerbach had nearly taken his joking too far. They were leaving a pub, slightly drunk, there had been a scene about missing reports, but now they were friends again; in a dark, out-of-the-way street W. suddenly felt a blow between the shoulder blades, so rough it hurled him against a wall . . . and his case officer had actually drawn his gun.—Hands on the wall, spread your legs! Feuerbach growled. Cough it up, where'd you hide the goddamn paper!—And a moment later they both succumbed to a prodigious burst of laughter, gurgling and screeching until it echoed up the walls . . . but for W. there was a very queasy feeling about it: it was the first time in his life he'd looked down the barrel of a gun.

And now he'd gone four whole weeks without getting anything done! It was a safe bet that Feuerbach knew he'd been in the Scene quite a bit; this month there'd been one or two weeks in which he'd actually gone more often than usual . . . most of his visits had been short, though (too short, another thing the first lieutenant wasn't happy about)—as if he'd just been looking for someone.

Not a single report . . . nothing, in a good month's time? When he pictured his boss' voice, it didn't sound good at all; if he wasn't mistaken, there was even a kind of rabidity in it, something so rare that it had to be valuable. When Feuerbach turned rabid, and W. could count these instances on the fingers of one hand, he didn't raise his voice; it shifted from a jitter to a hiss (when things had calmed down, W. described it as frothing at the mouth), and he hissed faster and faster, as though to eerily accelerate the words linked by his hissing. Get outta here, man . . . nothing, nothing, nothing, nothing-andnothingagain, isitmeoristhisfuggingnuts . . . he shot off random outraged noises, and gradually calming down again: Man oh man . . . how the hell are we going to explain this? You haven't got a clue! We've got to have something to show four weeks from now! I praised you to the skies up there, despite the problems we had, and now this. Is this your annual spring blackout, or what?

And then, for the first time, Feuerbach might put his cards on the table: Of course all you've been working on is your special op again . . . and probably you've even got a report on it. You think there isn't a single problem in all Berlin except this so-called writer S. R. You tried to tell me once it's like a wildfire . . . well, where is it? Gradually I'm starting to think you're just envious of the guy's success . . . what passes for success in those circles. Don't you think it's getting a bit old? Leave the guy alone, for Chrissake, whatever the real story is with him, you'll never find it out . . . because you just don't want to find it out. How long has this been going on now, how long has this so-called author been peddling his wares around the Scene, since March, since February your report on Operation: Reader arrives punctually every week, since

January already, every time I forget it's Monday, there's your report on Operation: Reader to remind me. Since December, you say, or even since November . . . you don't say! But what's in your report, always the same old thing. And to this day we don't even know who the guy goes to bed with, for instance. Or if he even does, or if he does it from behind or from the front, or standing on his head, that'd be just like him. Or if he just fuggs Mary Fist. Nothing about that in your memoranda on fine literature. How long do you think it's been since I stopped even passing them on . . . solely for your protection. Three months ago the higher-ups were already saying to me, What do we want with lit crit . . . Beckett, they said to me, half of it's taken from Beckett, what do we care about Beckett, wasn't that some English monk from the Middle Ages? But thinner than Beckett, just Beckett's bathwater . . . do you really think I can pass that on?

W. had been waiting a long time for the first lieutenant to shake these cards from his sleeve; so far they'd stayed stuck up there, apparently for his protection. But in his imagination the chiefs had been asking for ages: What are we supposed to do with the lit crit that UnCol writes? Is he trying to teach us some literary taste? What good are these punctual, pedantic essays supposed to do us, is this UnCol down on the street a moralist or something?

That UnCol knew it couldn't go on like this for ever . . . and he heard the jitter swell in Feuerbach's throat, though for now it was just in his mind.—Yesterday he'd started hearing it again (and in the pub he'd been seized by the fear that at any moment Feuerbach could come through the door he saw in the mirror) . . . the rant's verbose unreeling, the mixture of remonstrance and monologue, which, empty as it ultimately was, infected him at some point, perpetuating itself in some receptive language centre of his brain . . . so that he could carry on the 'discourse' without ever having heard it. This UnCol down on the street could read his case officer's thoughts . . . because they were his own thoughts . . . because it was the Firm's faculty of speech.

Of course he'd long been trying to change this (trying to work out new perspectives on this case!) . . . sitting for days on a report about the young woman in the writer S. R.'s entourage. But everything in these reports just revolved around Reader again, and now they expressed envy not only of his popular success (he could have relaxed; it was dwindling) but of his success with the young lady whom W. called the student.

Two or three times he'd almost gotten into a conversation with her, but Feuerbach had learnt nothing about that . . . there would have had to be at least another three UnCols at the readings to give such fleeting verbal exchanges the chance to appear in a report . . . it was understandable that they hadn't shown up in W.'s dossiers either; aware of his occasional awkwardness when faced with female target persons, Feuerbach might well have taken the relevant passages for fiction.—Once, for instance, they'd greeted each other! Her handshake had been very tentative, and she'd said, 'Grüß Gott,'[9] which W. had heard only in archival films; in real life it sounded oddly ironical, she'd said it in precise standard German without a trace of a Berlin accent. Another time she asked him where his curious dialect came from . . . If I were the perfect UnCol, he'd thought, I'd be simulating a blush for her. It was on the third (or fourth) occasion that he recklessly let slip his code name . . . and for that he'd spent hours in the pub on Frankfurter Allee beforehand, giving himself some liquid courage.

And it was amid the ongoing lack of opportunity that he'd drawn up the dossier he hadn't delivered . . . because of the portrait of the young woman who darted across his field of view. And then she had lingered a while in his field of view, at least he'd managed to fix it that way. And he had regretted that there was no one around to introduce him to the Student . . . a poet with something of a name, first two poems published—illegally!—in a West German journal, six months later three poems in three unofficial and two official domestic publications!

Towards the end of last April she'd showed up unexpectedly in the park-like garden of the church in Rummelsburg, and because he hadn't passed on her portrait, along with a whole bunch of similar documents (withheld as camouflage), he was at loggerheads with his case officer nearly all summer long.—In fact, he had hidden the portrait . . . hidden it so well that one would have marvelled at his distrust of life. He thought: Distrust of life's probing rationality, which gives no weight to non-weighty things. He had folded the two pages comprising the portrait into a weighty packet and stuffed it into the gap of his chair, sinking it so deep that the fingertips no longer felt it in the tight crack.

And so he had failed to give Feuerbach a whole stack of portraits, rather than simply removing No. 30 (the student) . . . he would have had to type it all up again, Feuerbach simply wouldn't believe it was possible to miscount . . . It was Feuerbach who consistently encouraged him not to take meaningless things as meaningless . . . —After quite a while the first lieutenant had stopped mentioning the missing reports, as silent on the matter as though it were meaningless . . . but there was nothing the first lieutenant was less capable of than letting go, W. was sure of that.

He recalled sinking into depressions which confounded all attempts to finish his profiles, not only the Student's; it merely seemed to be the catalyst, and after that depression ran rampant. Perhaps because of the thought that encounters with a young woman such as she never went beyond compiling attributes to be listed in writing, estimated measurements (which couldn't even be realistic), conjectures as to the content of the words so hard to read at a distance from her stranger's lips, or just words such as pointed, pale, bare, which were neither level-headed nor informative. And then these 'data' were swallowed by an institution which was little more than an archive, so that he never saw them again. In other words, everything about this woman that grazed his five senses was prostituted to a bureaucracy ... and could end up filling entire filing cabinets; you'd have to search far and wide for such a selfless pimp.

Perhaps it was just a few sentences that had kept him from delivering the dossiers. He could have taken it if Feuerbach had learnt only that he found the Student 'rather pretty' and regarded her as 'rather intelligent' (which he couldn't prove) ... but then under the heading special behaviour patterns he had described how, despite the lingering warmth from the afternoon, she began to shiver in the garden as darkness fell. Standing in the light of a lantern hung from a tree, he'd written, she closed the black leather jacket over her white T-shirt, pulling up the zipper with a provocative-looking, resolute gesture, as though she sensed that she was being watched. Now her body seemed boyishly slender; she'd concealed her breasts, which stood out distinctly against the thin fabric of the T-shirt.—Oh no, that's practically a striptease! Some such exclamation would have been called for from the first lieutenant; W. had dozens of these quotes filed away. Oh dear, that'll have them drooling! We can't possibly inflict this on our venerable comrades up there, their pacemakers aren't the newest, they won't be able to take it.

From your prose style it's obvious you don't think much of Hemingway, Feuerbach commented on the reports in which W. hadn't remained completely level-headed. Now and then that sort of thing slipped through again . . . though by now he thought he had a handle on it; he'd written hundreds of reports (up until last April), and he knew how they had to look: dry and matter-of-fact!

Amid coughing fits, a cigarette in the corner of his mouth (like a screenwriter in a Hollywood movie), he pecked them straight into the typewriter, so absent-minded that he felt guilty when Feuerbach exclaimed admiringly: You're made for this work!—He typed so quickly and unthinkingly that the pages teemed with typos; Feuerbach described this as authentic grassroots work . . . for instance, in his haste he frequently wrote the word night instead of right, and the other way around; Feuerbach was enchanted by the phrases that resulted. He said W. sometimes dissolved language's semiotic character in a way that was practically analytical . . . you'd just have to watch out that the venerable comrades didn't have a heart attack at having so much darkness foisted on them, when he wrote that the Party is always night.—W. had noticed, however, that his case officer secretly changed back the switched letters.

Now that W. was focusing on Operation: Reader, this dissatisfaction persisted; his powers of observation were impaired by the Student's presence, his relapses into sentimental prose increased, and it was found unacceptable when his reports gave too free rein to his literary verdicts . . . A creative thinker doesn't theorize, he composes! said Feuerbach.

There were occasions, though, on which theory produced quite astounding effects, W. said to himself, and he had experienced these occasions himself.—When Frau Falbe managed, for instance, to entice him into her double bed (still banking on the wisdom of the formal 'you'), he had suddenly found it astoundingly easy to achieve arousal by imagining himself in a comparable situation with the Student rather than with his landlady. When, in other words, he felt theoretically embraced by the Student, while practically his landlady was clamping him tight in her bed . . . and Frau Falbe seemed quite inclined to see the advantages. She had even started a conversation with him on the subject, impressing him with her theoretical insights. As she often did, she had proceeded from her ex-husband . . . All he'd ever had on the brain, she said, was other women, and always several at once. Ever since then she could tell exactly when a man wasn't all there, when his mind was somewhere else. Who knows, she said, maybe I never really appealed to him that much.

How do you know all that, W. asked, did he tell you?

He practically pieced me together out of those other women, she said, and one time, yes, he told me. But it didn't bother me that much, I'd mostly figured it out already anyway. You ought to have the body of such-and-such a woman, and your head on top, and then the other way around, he said once, and I slapped him. But then I thought to myself, there's nothing you can do about it anyway . . . and then I was supposed to have a different bust, smaller, and then I was supposed to have a different waist, so-and-so's bust and so-and-so's waist, that's what he wanted. But your bottom, he said, is always just right . . . Her voice had that rough, slightly hoarse tone again which he knew by now and which goaded him. And of course he wanted to know what had happened after her husband told her this . . .

I know, she said, it's just the same thing with you . . . And after a while she turned on the light so he could see her . . . You're an intellectual, and you need fantasies, it was just the same thing with my husband.

How, just the same thing? asked W. There were plenty of men who couldn't perform with a woman, young men too, she said. Desire and capability were two different things. But these men weren't bad sorts. It was easy for women to talk, they didn't have to perform. She'd been married, after all, and a few times after that someone had tried to marry her, that didn't mean she was experienced, but she knew the ropes a bit. It had been just the same thing with her husband . . . Didn't I tell you he also worked for Security?

What's that supposed to mean, also worked for Security?

It's almost always like that with the guys from Security, yeah, that's probably why they go into Security in the first place.

And what does that have to do with me? asked W.

Well, she said, they're all intellectuals there at Security, my husband talked about that sometimes, he said, we're all at Security because we can't get anywhere with women. Because we can't get anywhere with people at all. All we can ever do is investigate people. Yes, I could really see that with my husband. Then he said: But I'm not like that, and I'm leaving Security now. Of course they wouldn't let him go . . .

And what did he do then, then he went West?

Yes, it was before August '61 still, we'd only been together two years . . . I didn't think about all that until later. I could tell he was like that after all, he always wanted to try everything out with his hands.

W. wanted to hear what her husband had tried out.

It seems like they do everything with their brains there, she said, and really letting go, that's also something they can only do with their brains. Foreplay, my husband once said to me, that's the real thing for me, that's just like my work. We only ever do foreplay there, that's much more exciting. Then he wanted me to kneel down in front of him, on all fours, he wanted to see everything, for example. He always wanted to see everything . . . Watching, he said, that's the thing . . . Or he wanted us to play with ourselves and watch each other.

Back down in his room, W.'s fantasies about the Student kept going through his mind . . . and it was as though Frau Falbe had given him the cues. Was this because of Frau Falbe's eternal formal 'you', with which she involuntarily created a distance between them?

(As in a conversation with that young woman from West Berlin, he thought. For C., the reserved manners she displayed placed her in a certain lofty class of human beings. The student had erected a virtually insurmountable barrier in front of the informal 'you'; could it be that she came from high society? At any rate from different, more sophisticated spheres, or so it seemed to him . . . C. had observed only one person who had surmounted the barrier to her informal 'you': the writer S. R., in his eternal pastoral black. All the other denizens of this primitive, vulgar territory, for which the oddly uptight term 'domestic' was used when trying to avoid long-winded explanations or politically conformist abbreviations, all the rest held to the formal 'you' and regarded her as rather fey. And of course that was exactly what made C. want to jump her bones . . .)

On the way to the tram, and during the three stops to the S-Bahn station, he thought about Thomas Mann, of whom he'd read in a magazine—a Western magazine; now that he was active in the Scene, such things came his way now and then—that he too had been a man of foreplay. And for this reason the writer of the essay described Thomas Mann as a true artist; Thomas Mann too had always been concerned with the interplay of approach and withdrawal. These thoughts had a comforting effect on W.; he owed them to his landlady.

But soon his anxiety seized him back: about to cross the station hall, he saw, in the crowd spilling from a just-arrived train, a figure who towered more than a head above all the others. He let the crowd wash him to the edge and the lanky guy pass him with the main flow, then followed him out onto the square in front of the station; he saw him lingering by the tram, evidently undecided whether to walk the three stops.— C. circled the longlegs and planted himself in front of him; it took a moment for the tall man to lower his eyes, his face showing neither surprise nor even a hint that he had recognized C., frozen in unchanging displeasure, or rather irreversible resignation.

So you don't even know me? asked C.; and when the other made no attempt to answer: Where do you think you're going, what do you think you're looking for here in Berlin? You wouldn't be heading to my landlady, by any chance, or who are you supposed to snoop after, you goddamn crooked question mark? Say something already!

Indeed the lanky guy was oddly hunched, but still said not a word, his resigned expression intensifying.

No doubt you're after a certain Harry Falbe! said C., unconsciously striking a tone Feuerbach sometimes used.

I said right from the start that we'd get caught here! The lanky guy finally found his voice.

What did you say, who did you say that to?

The boss, who else . . . it's the boss I said it to. In Berlin we're guaranteed to get caught some day . . .

So: Who is it you're looking for, now? C. repeated his question; they moved apparently unthinkingly towards a little park where a few benches stood under trees that still looked bare, their bursting buds just beginning to show.

I'm not looking for Harry, explained the lanky guy, we know we're not going to find him here . . . we can't find him at all, it's like in the movies, he just went to ground.

How can anyone go to ground here, said C., if you want to go to ground here in this country, you've got to burrow like a mole.

You'll laugh when I tell you. It was in that old industrial site out of town, you know the place. That's where he suddenly went to ground, simply vanished, we'd surrounded everything, a whole police unit, and the criminal investigation department, they worked with military precision, I can tell you, and suddenly, I didn't see it myself, but the boss was there . . . it was like he'd dissolved into thin air.

That can't be hard for Harry Falbe, said C.

The lanky guy was relieved to see that C. was taking it all in good humour.—Yeah, he said, that was one skinny son of a bitch, you could blow him through a window shutter, the boss always used to say, that's how airy-fairy he is . . . but not airy-fairy enough to blow through that cordon of cops . . .

And what's with you, don't you fit through the window shutter? asked C., How come you were looking for him, anyway?

We always suspected that he wanted to bail out. Anyway that's what the boss thought, Harry was always just about to flip. Then suddenly he was back again 100 per cent, with the wildest stories up his sleeve . . . he always had contacts in Berlin, you see. If you want I can even tap into the intelligence service over there, those were the kinds of big ideas he got. Or he wanted to join Sect. 20, he was always saying. But he just wasn't reliable, he wasn't consistent. The boss said, Sometimes you really do think all he wants is to go West, and for that he'll do anything. That's probably what got him down, constantly having to run around with the legend about wanting to defect, and then not being allowed to do it . . . and so then he overdid it, and people thought, hey, he really does want to bail out. No, he wasn't reliable, he had too many shady connections to people in custody, no surprise with him. You really couldn't always tell what side he was actually on . . .

The lanky guy had suddenly turned talkative; they were sitting side by side now on a bench under the trees on the station square, and they must have been a strange sight to see; the cool dusk came, but they seemed determined to talk on into the night.

You for example, the lanky guy went on, we knew everything about you from Harry, every word . . . only the most important thing, that we didn't know . . .

What was the most important thing? C. asked.

Well, that this kid wasn't even yours, we didn't know that, the lanky guy said with a touch of surprise in his voice. It was his kid instead, we didn't know that.

Since when does the Firm lack access to these sorts of documents?

His girlfriend put you down as the father, back when she was in prison . . .

What an honour! said C.

But then it came out, suddenly she claimed not to know any more, or she said she'd made a mistake.

And now . . . you really don't know why Harry was a wanted man?

Just say it already!

Because the kid has vanished . . . vanished without a trace.

All right, who vanished now, Harry Falbe or his kid? asked C. What kind of nonsense is this, anyway, how can anything vanish in this country, don't we have a Wall that's high enough, and isn't everything under control in this country, or what?

Both of them vanished! But the kid had already vanished back when we were still looking for Harry.

And now you're not looking for him any more?

We had to hand over the case . . .

For a moment C. had an uneasy feeling: Of course he knew nothing about this whole story . . . but maybe he should be careful not to let it on.—He had spread out his arms on the back of the bench and stretched his feet out in front of him, his face in shadow (Feuerbach sat on park benches in the same pose, but he was taller and thinner than C.); when he glanced slightly to the side he was looking at the weedy, dark-turtlenecked chest of the lanky guy from A.; it must have looked as though a grotesquely gangling child were nestled in his arm.

And now, the lanky guy went on in an innocent voice, now our idea is that he's in some embassy somewhere, some-where in the midst of those embassy occupiers . . . we don't have a lot of information down in our neck of the woods . . .

I thought you handed over the case, so why are you still interested? Do you think we wouldn't know that? said C., pondering how to unravel the snarl of interconnections; of course there were certain uncanny nuances to the whole affair, and he couldn't figure the lanky guy out . . . Suddenly he pulled in his legs and sat up straight on the bench: Now I know what you want from me, longlegs! You want me to tell you if you're finally rid of Harry Falbe. He's always been in your way, and now you want me to tell you if he might crop up again, the boss might prefer him to you! Harry simply had a lot more connections, am I right?

Quite astute, said the lanky guy, of course, no wonder . . .

So the boss didn't even send you here from A., you came on your own? You want me to tell you if your competitor's out of the way, and the whole story about the kid is pure bull-shit!—It was a foray which struck C. immediately afterwards

233

as rather haphazard . . . hadn't Feuerbach also been looking for Harry Falbe the whole time?

C. wasn't surprised that the other man disputed his theory: I didn't come on my own, no, the boss sent me all right. And he warned me, too: For God's sake, don't get yourself caught in Berlin . . .

What's that supposed to mean? asked C.

If you go get yourself caught, the boss said to me, if you run straight into the arms of the guys from Sect. 20, there's nothing I can do for you. But I don't want him to, I'm fine with them having me down as a probationer.

I get it, said C., you want to stay a goddamn grocery-store snoop.

You want to stay in the reserves, you don't want to be woken up, you want to sleep on in peace. Don't you know that those are the exact people who all get strung up sooner or later? Or dropped, you could say! The little guys always get hanged . . .

Of course I know that, the lanky guy grinned. But things can't be that bad yet. If it were that bad, Sect. 20 would know about it, and then we'd find it out too somehow, wouldn't we . . . the boss would hear it from you, for example, and I'd hear it from the boss, just like you'd know about it from your boss. And then my boss wouldn't have said: Steer clear of the guys from Sect. 20. Your old acquaintance the poet, for instance. Or I'll drop you like a hot potato, I'll be done with you. And I thought to myself, Done with me, that wouldn't be so bad . . . and now you've gone and caught me! You are Sect. 20, aren't you?

It had long turned dark and cool, C. had risen from the bench, standing as though paralysed, his hands buried in the pockets of his parka. The lanky grocery-store snoop crouched on the bench, bent forwards slightly, tilted face gazing up at him . . . Careful, thought C., the man's a snake!

How could he show the lanky guy he'd understood him? If C. so much as mentioned his visitor in a report, the boss in A. would be unable to ignore the fact that his 'UnCol Probationer' had deconspired . . . and that was just the opportunity this person saw, he wanted to be 'dropped'. But if C. didn't mention him in his reports, the same thing could happen to him: then he, C., could be seen as a deconspirative collaborator . . . no simple matter for him, since he was far past being a mere 'probationer' . . . for him it might even be treason.—He couldn't even let himself think the word, he'd walked into a neat trap!

All right! said C. You're going to head home now, for starters. And you won't snoop around my landlady again. You're going to leave now, right away, got it!

Sure I got it, said the grocery-store snoop.

We're both going to get on the next S-Bahn train, you'll sit in the front on the right, I'll sit in the back on the left. And you'll take it to the Central Station, I'll get out at Warschauer Strasse. And we won't have seen each other, you won't turn and look at me!

I won't turn and look at you.

And you'll take the very first train to Leipzig, from Leipzig on you can do as you like, got it?

I got the picture, said the grocery-store snoop.

And one of us will come soon and visit your boss . . . probably me, said C. And now we'll go our separate ways to the train. But first I want to know your code name!

Shorty, said the grocery-store snoop.

★★★

(He recalled the ride on the S-Bahn train and it seemed to him that at the time he had compared the dimly lit interior of the car with one of the vaulted basement tunnels he often roamed. That just as he now stared forward down this passage ... fixedly, for even in the basements the light bulbs sometimes flickered as though massive convulsions had been unleashed in the streets above ... he had stared down the car that catapulted through the night amid its own howling noise. At an ever-increasing velocity ... and as through nocturnal landscapes of ruins: he knew them from his childhood.

These were districts that for stretches looked utterly bombed out, broken by parks and allotment gardens, then by rows of new housing developments, black–yellow in a darkness thinned by the glow of the streets, sand-coloured sooty walls of porous concrete like diseased skin, then darkness again and forest-like parks ... to the left, now and then, the rows of floodlights on the Wall: the Antifascist Protective Barrier which shut out or in the neofascists and prevented their reunification. Allotment gardens and parks behind the Wall as well, now and then a complex of apartment towers flashed, walls of lacunae-filled light, like the inextricably complex consoles of illuminated control panels—the empire of signs in West Berlin. And at last the train crossed the Spree, the reflections of the car's windows dazzling on the broad, nearly black river.

Down here in the basement passages the howl of the train had slipped far into the distance; it had manifested itself—but only for him—in the nameless stone weight of the work of art that was Berlin, and had become as imaginarily substantial as the oxygen in the atmosphere, against which the jitter of a refrigerator sensed beyond the concrete wall at his back remained as unreal as glass breaking in the distance.—He had spent a long time down here reflecting, and remembering, interrupting himself many a time and climbing back up to the light again—did day still break up in Berlin?—and at last he had recalled those industrial ruins. It was possible indeed to vanish there . . .

When he had discovered the basement passages beneath the houses of Berlin and wandered through them for the first time, he unquestionably recalled that expanse at the edge of A.—A. had been the site of large munitions factories, separated from the city only by the railway line to Leipzig; on the town side there were even larger factory buildings that had once been part of the same complex, still intact and now used to produce consumer goods; but the bulk of those factories had been located outside town and had been destroyed by wartime air raids.—Even as a boy W. had roamed the ruins every day and knew them like the back of his hand; the expanse of ruins was the favourite playground of the children from the edge of town. And even as a child he had discovered beneath the bizarre building remnants—it was decades before the ruins could be cleared away—systems of underground passageways with a myriad of interconnections, evidently designed both as escape routes and cable tunnels connecting all the separate parts of production facilities that had been crucial to the war effort. There were actually still certain tunnels that extended under the railway line all the way to the basements of the factories in town . . . in the other direction they led out under the forest; walking through the forest, you might suddenly stumble in the underbrush upon mysterious, mushroom-shaped steel-plate caps a yard in diameter, hidden under deep layers of old leaves: this was where the air shafts descended to the tunnel system three or four yards below. And of course the children told the story that the underground tunnels led all the way to the shafts of the abandoned mines that arced around the city like a chain of sooty, battered fortresses.

And W. recalled his apprenticeship at the training work-shop, a bit uphill from the expanse of ruins. At that time he had already begun writing poems and short stories . . . and one day the workshop was investigated for written materials, he couldn't remember what exactly: books or texts copied out from books, magazines or journals, some sort of illicit printed matter was circulating, there were confiscations and searches. And he had tied his notebooks and papers in a bundle and hidden them in one of the underground corridors.

At the time it had seemed like a game to him; he was sim-ply uncomfortable at the thought of his secret writings spread out before the eyes of the training staff, and the passageways beneath the ruins were safe.—At a much later point in time he had divulged this hiding place to his drinking buddy Harry; it happened one night at a pub in A., when both of them—they were the only two left standing after a weekend on which they'd barely slept and outdid each other drinking—ended up sitting in a back room until long after midnight. There Harry had suddenly broken down crying, in part from alcohol-induced enervation, in part from genuine despair, saying some-thing about a series of cheque forgeries he'd been charged with—W. asked himself how such things were even possible—and that he already knew when he'd be arrested; tomorrow, Monday, a 'friend' from the police station had tipped him off, they'd be coming for him. But apparently the evidence was still shaky, they might have to let him go again, temporarily, if he could manage to hide something before then. Harry didn't say what he had to hide, he spoke of some sort of papers; W. offered to take them home with him. Harry refused; they'd been seen together . . . and he had to hide the things that very night . . . in a pinch he might even have to hide himself.—Why? W. asked, finding the whole thing implausible and incomprehensible.—His girlfriend Cindy was getting out of prison some day the coming week, he had to see her to clear up their future relationship . . .

And W. ended up telling his drinking buddy about the existence—at least the erstwhile existence—of tunnels on the edge of town . . . he'd only done it, he reproached himself later, so as to appear to Cindy in the right light . . . and Harry didn't seem to find this story at all improbable . . . Were the tunnels still there? he immediately wanted to know.

On Harry's urging they had headed there that very night; the terrain had long since been cleared and levelled, only on the edge of the forest, where they weren't in the way, had piles of rubble and a few remnants of walls remained, swallowed almost wholly by the outspreading underbrush, you could hardly see a thing in the damply breaking dawn, with the fog creeping from the forest.—Drunk as he was, Harry had suddenly slipped and slid down the grass and fallen leaves of a peculiar hollow, caught at the bottom by a bank of mud, gravel and shrubbery. He was lying next to one of the tunnel system's almost-buried exits. Only a narrow chink still indicated the opening in the vertical fragment of a wall overhung by a tangle of brambles . . .)

Brought to Light

When the train at Warschauer Strasse finally started moving, I was wide awake. 'Stand back' came the barely intelligible snarl, though there was no one on the platform; the bell shrilled and, as the red lights over the doors went out, a dull jolt travelled down the row of cars, the closed doors locking into place; first haltingly, then gaining speed, the train began to roll. I'd been asleep; despite my damp clothes, clammy on my skin, my sitting position (prenatal, I'd once called it) irresistibly induced sleep. It was a sleep that took practice: it kept my thoughts in full swing, or even seemed to increase their intensity, as they lacked all grounding in temporal relationships. I sat against the back wall of the empty car, squeezed into a corner, feet tucked up against the radiator under the seat, which sent up waves of warmth that seemed mingled with steam; I'd jammed my fists in my lap, and the back of my head, resting on the wall, picked up the trembling vibrations of the train's motion.

My thoughts shut out time, and so could not quite be called memories, veering without transition between spaces in time (you could no longer call them spaces of time) . . . I dispelled my fear that I'd see light in my flat from the street, and would have to go straight to the basement without changing my wet clothes, by reminding myself that I'd run into the Major on Alexanderplatz just a short time ago . . . of course he could have overtaken me, maybe he'd had a car parked nearby, I had no idea how long I'd slept in the train. As always when I came in from the rain, my watch had stopped, it couldn't cope with the damp which the radiator warmth released from the clothes I'd worn too long, nor, apparently, with the sweat I worked up on my way from the basement to the fifth floor; it could only cope when I rested, when my blood pressure dropped, it ran best in subterranean spaces, or lying atop my heating stove as it cooled off overnight . . . as though then reapproximating the temperature of its former owner: Harry Falbe's frosty girlfriend Cindy. With her knowledge it had been given to me at one time for safekeeping; when one of Cindy's prison stays ended, she had forgotten about the watch . . . it would have a certain role to play later on, a primitive men's watch of considerable size, the sort fashionable with a certain type of young woman several years before, that bellicose time when razorblades and carpet tacks had found their way into the jewellery shops.—One day—it was at the Whitsun holiday, presumably last year—a watch which readily stood my body's basement effluvia had been placed in my hands by the Firm . . . no, not in my hands; I'd found a note summoning me to Feuerbach's office; the Major wasn't there, the watch lay on his desk in a plastic case, next to it the certificate with the Firm's heraldic emblem, and next to that a note in Feuerbach's handwriting: Dear Cambert, this is for you, congratulations! Destroy the certificate immediately.

(W. had kept the certificate, folded over and over again and well hidden. Alongside other pre-printed, illegible signatures it had been signed by a Colonel Reuther, MSS Sect. 20, Berlin, the ?? of ??)

Upon leaving the office I had already forgotten the date; that was even safer than destroying the certificate . . . on the stairs I met Feuerbach, who slipped me an envelope with money.—We'll have to sign receipts again one of these days, he said, you haven't signed anything for quite a while. As if you had a problem with signatures . . . maybe tomorrow in the cafe, if that's OK with you.

When I signed receipts—always a whole stack at once, accumulated over the months . . . and I signed with my code name, which at first the Major didn't like at all . . . when he finally accepted it I asked him: What's my pseudonym now, I ought to have got a new one ages ago . . . on a regular basis I completely lost track of whether all the expenses I'd had and for which I wrote receipts had actually been reimbursed— sometimes there seemed to be too many, sometimes too few— and the signing in itself made me uncomfortable, I saw how it documented and immortalized me, archiving me, as it were, and making me manifest for the historical research of future morality paranoiacs.—Feuerbach took a very different view: You'll never be able to get any real accolades because you don't even crop up in our annals.

And I'll go empty-handed, too, because they'll tell me I just invented my comrade-in-arms.—He shuffled the receipts together: All right, he said in English . . . unfortunately that's how it has to be. With us it's like in a novel—at some point you have to figure out what the main character actually does for a living!

(But he planned not to use the new watch, a mid-priced Japanese model, until he was allowed to travel for the first time; it was much more suitable for another part of the city where time mattered. And he pictured himself arriving and pushing back his sleeve over the watch on his left lower arm to look at the hair-thin chrome-plated hands . . . that was important for his first report, which would have to begin thus: Border crossing ensued, date: . . . , place: Berlin Friedrichstrasse West, Wannsee-bound S-Bahn platform, time: 0.35 CET; cigarettes purchased at Intershop kiosk, one carton Lexington brand, target person lost in the crowd.

He'd dispense with the signature—maybe they'd give him a number. Feuerbach could countersign himself, if he liked, when the reports reached his office by post.

And perhaps one day he'd become M.W. again . . . it might take a long time—perhaps his lapsing attention would give the first sign of it: for several minutes he'd forgotten the target person completely in his effort to find his way around this train station.)

How childish were all these reports in their obsessive quest for linguistic precision; there was no form for them, since guidelines for their composition could not officially exist, at least not on paper; their form was left to the bureaucratic side of each individual employee . . . and how unimaginative these reports were—yet you could give free rein to your imagination once the border crossing had ensued . . . or so I pictured it.

Many a time I'd left Friedrichstrasse Station through the side exit and watched the lines of people outside the border checkpoint: there were more and more people each time—also more and more natives, too, and not just pensioners, either[10]— waiting outside the gateway . . . in fact, the line in front of the sign Departing Citizens of the German Democratic Republic was almost longer than the one for West Berlin day-trippers.— For me the only option was the so-called diplomatic checkpoint, since employees of the Firm could obtain a visa for official business, and so I went through in the middle, between the other two groups; for me there was no wait to speak of. Nowhere in this Republic were queues as patient as at the border checkpoint . . . and yet—you could virtually smell it— it was a forced patience, a patience of prudence, with feet of clay. And so I had to walk past the waiting people, quickly leaving behind the gigantic reptile which wound its way in disciplined rows of three all the way to the station square . . . I didn't want to know what went through these people's minds when they saw me. They didn't even look at me, but I sensed that in their eyes I was one of those they had to thank for their ordeal. Was there anger in them, was I already registered in their eyes . . . it was impossible to tell, their faces let nothing on.—My crossing went quickly, who knows which tiny symbol in my passport had this effect, which invisible mark, legible only to an X-ray machine or a computer, instructed the official to let me through at any cost, without any delay. Then the cubical caverns of the concrete labyrinth beneath the train station, through which hounded, enslaved people scrabbled their way, the bare catacombs meant for other things, several walls still faced with white-yellow tiles from a time completely banished from reality: the tiles of intact station underpasses . . . everywhere unlabelled steel doors, everywhere the double sentries of the border police . . . then, at an iron barrier, one more check, just a fleeting glance at the stamp in the document, then the ticket machines where people stood at a loss, lacking small change—they meant nothing to me, I'd heard I didn't need a ticket, as a citizen of the German Democratic Republic . . . then up the broad grey stone stairs to the platform, somewhere on the wall an advertising poster for the Berliner Ensemble, with admission times, with prices in DM, aimed at the visitors from West Berlin . . . at this time of night the crowds move up the stairs at a crawl; then the platform—this isn't West Berlin yet, but I'm out; the Intershop kiosk doesn't take Forum cheques now, just Western money.—The East German border guards (use this term from now on!) are still patrolling everywhere, and standing up on a scaffold beneath the glass roof of the station hall, armed with binoculars and submachine guns, and probably there are even more plainclothes men here, ensuring that order is kept . . . could they come and snatch you back even here? They could, certainly, but they'd avoid such a scene at all costs. Here they're nothing but a presence, the border troops, furnishings of the station's permanent state of emergency.—I must make sure to keep my eye on the target person, I must keep my eye on her in such a way that she doesn't catch sight of me, maybe she'd recognize me after all. But at this hour observation is easy, at this hour the platform is brimful with people whose day visas have just expired (lately, incidentally, one overnight stay is permitted)—they left the country half an hour before midnight, and half an hour after midnight they'll enter the country again, when the new day according to CET permits the next-day visa (lately for two days, for lovers), and the next payment of the fee and exchange of the minimum daily sum of currency.—You weren't really in West Berlin until Lehrter Stadtbahnhof, and you had to restrain yourself from getting out here, in this desolate part of the city . . . though maybe even here, by the Wall, there were still a few pubs open (in the front city of the Western world, with no bar curfew) . . . Bellevue and Tiergarten weren't it yet either: the goal was Zoo Station . . . meanwhile the target trundled on towards Charlottenburg or Grunewald. Actually, you weren't really and truly out until you were sitting in the Bistro at Zoo Station; even the Pressecafe, that much-frequented, multilingual halfway pub, didn't do the trick . . . to really be in the West . . . to really be no one but M.W.

Beneath the roof of Friedrichstrasse Station West, night-grey, extremely makeshift-seeming and soiled with all the filth of civilization, that would hardly be possible. Here I was still the one I'd been for so long now: the sober observer with no sense of time—time as nothing but a playfully deployable signifier on the left wrist—the person of perceptions, his mind trained to fit his observations into methodical-looking linguistic formulae . . . among the people on the platform, herded like cattle from one corral to the next, and in the far-too-weak glow of the station lighting, I was merely a nondescript member of a self-contained organization which could with equal justification be called a ruling tribe or a secret service, I was one of the last bleary-eyed refugees from the filthy movie theatres, someone for whom making the last night bus was the ultimate wish fulfilment . . . and dressed in washed-out grey to washed-out green, the universal colours of the underground, and probably at the point of turning transparent or invisible, as had Harry, whose name I could just as well have borne.—No, the border crossing hadn't made me M.W. again, not by a long shot, clearly that would take a long time, real time I'd have to spend in a completely different place . . .

But the border crossing could be a start, I thought. And then one day I could go to some West Berlin editorial office, or a literary agency, and introduce myself: I being identical with the poet M.W., known for a total of seventeen poems in magazines and anthologies, over half of them in so-called unofficial magazines; ranked, by the media that focused on such things, among those new young writers currently regarded as representing their country's unofficial literature . . .

At some point I'd slipped up and capitalized 'unofficial' in this context . . . a while later I'd suddenly found this form to be right and proper; I'd gone so far as to abbreviate 'Unofficial Literature' as UnLit in my reports.

Of course Unofficial Literature sounded rather like 'fictional literature', which referred not to fiction (Feuerbach used the English word), but to something that pretended to be literature.—I might introduce myself and meet with utter perplexity; logically enough, people in the literary profession (German Studies people, critics, etc.) dealt only with official literature; one couldn't rule out the possibility that they'd have no knowledge of UnLit whatsoever. Recently there had been an extensive anthology of this poetry, for whose slightly sentimental title I couldn't vouch: *Affection Is Just a Fringe* of Stasi language. The annotations in reference books on the Stasi sufficed for that. For me, the Stasi is an apparatus of diffusion; its practice was secret, indistinct, and to a large extent fictional (for the collaborators of the agency as well) [...] and that was exactly the climate I wished to dwell in while writing the work. It would have been virtually a hindrance for me to know very much.[6]

Judging by my research for this translation, however, Hilbig's vision of the Stasi's workings is remarkably accurate, and his riffs on Stasi language show a preoccupation with its specific culture. In fact, Hilbig's author's note indicates that he interviewed IMs as part of his research. According to his friend Lutz Nitzsche-Kornel, he also examined friends' Stasi files; he had explored Nazi language usage too (see Victor Klemperer's 1947 book Lingua Tertii Imperii) and spoke of the need to similarly analyse GDR-jargon. And he had first-hand knowledge of the language of the Stasi—from interrogations he underwent during two months in prison.[7]

Hilbig was himself one of the 'unofficial writers' who were spied on by the Stasi and its informers such as Anderson. In prison, he was subjected to recruitment attempts, which he withstood. Yet he was drawn to describe the experience of the perpetrator, not the victim. He declined to pass moral judgement on the IMs, often implying that in different circumstances he might have broken down and collaborated.[8]

The fact that Hilbig did have significant knowledge of the Stasi makes it all the clearer that his emphasis on imagination and intuition is an artistic statement, and a courageous one. By claiming the ability to imagine, from within his own psyche, the 'inner biography' of a Stasi informer, and indeed the Stasi system, he implicates himself. More explicitly, he implicates himself as a writer by comparing writing and informing.

Young: I'll be young again in my next life, said W.

Yeah, yeah, she said, that's what you're thinking about!

You're constantly thinking about your next life, that's no state for a young man to be in. You'd be better off thinking about the here and now ...

He woke up one morning at a time which struck him each day anew as profoundly ungodly, and saw light in his room (the blind was pulled down) ... his pyjamas were drenched with sweat, he'd covered himself only with a sheet, and as usual even it was tossed off, lying bunched up at his feet. As his initial rebellion against this forced awakening died down, he smelt coffee in the room and knew that Frau Falbe was somewhere in the immediate vicinity. The next moment he felt an urgent, almost painful pressure in his bladder (from

kept seeing it back, employing steam-powered wringers and
driers. Before these machines could be set to work at six in
that morning, this coal-fired boiler had to be pressurized

... what might you have been
thinking the whole time? You sat by the swing, staring out,
always thinking to yourself that this ... is the day better in West
Berlin, you may have asked yourself. Do you asked yourself

You only ever think of the goal, C. said to him.
And so it went, until one day I discovered by chance that
the writer S. R. had homoerotic proclivities ... or even a

For years, Hilbig travelled between Leipzig and his job in Meuselwitz. In the boiler room, he had the time and seclusion to write, producing poems and short prose pieces. The figure of the isolated stoker and the tension between the 'worker' and the 'writer' would pervade his work, which at that time remained unpublishable. In 1968, he placed an audacious 'personal ad' in the GDR's main literary journal, Neue Deutsche Literatur: 'Which German-language publisher would like to publish my poems? Serious offers only . . .'[20]

The answer came nearly 10 years later. In 1976, Faust moved to West Germany, and, at first without Hilbig's knowledge, had several of his poems published, drawing the attention of the prestigious S. Fischer Verlag. Fischer published Hilbig's first poetry collection, abwesenheit, in 1979, followed by further collections and novels. Hilbig's Western publications led to increased Stasi harassment. In 1978, he spent two months in prison on false charges of having burnt the GDR flag from the Meuselwitz town hall. There he was pressured to collaborate with the Stasi and provide information on his contacts; he refused.[21] In 1979, he was fined 2,000 DM for a 'currency offence' in connection with the West German publication of abwesenheit.[22]

In a bold speech from 1980, the eminent East German writer Franz Fühmann (1922–84) lauded Hilbig as an example of a whole generation of 'absent' writers silenced in their homeland.[23] Like Christa Wolf, Fühmann strove to criticize and reform the system from within, and he championed young nonconformists.[24] In Hilbig, Fühmann saw a kindred spirit: an heir to the Romantics and Rimbaud, a truth-teller, a rebel against socialist realism. Hilbig continued to rebel; in 1981, he wrote an open letter to the deputy minister of culture: 'I belong to a generation that will no longer let itself be censored.'[25] Under Fühmann's patronage, Hilbig published his first

'Forum cheques' at state banks; these cheques could be spent only at 'Intershops', state-run retail shops which offered Western goods. These measures ensured a flow of much-needed hard currency.

8 Walter Ulbricht (1893–1973): GDR leader from 1950 to 1973.

9 A common greeting in the Catholic regions of Southern Germany.

10 Pensioners were permitted to travel abroad.

11 Rührung ist nur eine Randerscheinung: Allusion to the anthology Berührung ist nur eine Randerscheinung (Connection Is Just a Fringe Phenomenon). See Afterword.

12 The official East German term for West Berlin, which the GDR did not recognize as part of West Germany.

13 Lavrentiy Beria (1899–1953): chief of the NKVD (Soviet secret police) under Stalin.

14 Yuri Andropov (1914–84): general secretary of the Communist Party of the Soviet Union from 1982 to 1984.

15 Samuel Beckett, How It Is (1961).

16 Giles Deleuze, 'How Do We Recognize Structuralism?' in Desert Islands and Other Texts, 1953–1974 (David Lapoujade ed., Mike Taormina, trans.) (Paris: Semiotext(e), 2004), p. 171.

17 On his visit to East Berlin in early October 1989 to mark the fortieth anniversary of the founding of the GDR, Soviet leader Mikhail Gorbachev warned GDR leader Erich Honecker to undertake reforms in response to the massive citizens' protests. Gorbachev is popularly quoted as saying: 'Life will punish those who come too late.'

18 Rosa Luxemburg's best-known saying: 'Freedom is always the freedom for dissenters.'

19 Hungary was a popular tourist destination for East Germans. In summer 1989, Hungary tolerated, then officially permitted travel across its border to Austria; hence, many East Germans used their Hungarian holidays to escape to the West.

past itself was meagre and disappointing enough. Now her whole appearance sent the message that those years were behind her . . . and this itself made W. suspect that she still harboured desires. And there were even signs of that, but she didn't seem conscious of them, or at any rate she compensated by venting her nurturing instinct upon her lodgers. And she did it so uninhibitedly, once you had acquiesced, that it exhausted her libidinous energy. Only now and then—at moments when there had been some expression of gratitude on W.'s part—had something flared up in her ever-insecure features, and her body tautened beneath the eternal bathrobe, which changed in colour once a week, her movements became quicker and more youthful, her gestures took on a look of unpractised grace and always went a touch too far, she thrust out her bosom, and a barely noticeable blush glimmered in her face.—W. had often wondered what she lived on, as it seemed impossible that she was already drawing a pension. She couldn't be especially well-off; whenever W. slipped the rent money into the cup through their letterbox, he was much obliged. W. asked her about her husband, whom she occasionally mentioned, but he had already died; she didn't know herself whether her husband (they weren't divorced) was still alive at all, he had at some point vanished in business in West Germany, and he hadn't been heard from to this day, over ten years later. Hadn't she ever tried to have him traced, W. asked. She'd forbidden her . . . , she said, as though she'd already revealed too much, she shook her head and started talking about the bedclothes again.

He recalled that one day he actually had brought a plastic bag full of bedclothes—for Frau Falbe and for himself—home from REWATEX. This was prohibited, but common practice; each of the forgotten pieces of linen was marked as rags with

Notes

1   The headquarters of the Ministry for State Security (or Stasi; here: MSS) occupied a complex in Berlin-Lichtenberg between Frankfurter Allee, Normannenstrasse and Magdalenenstrasse.

2   Also known as the Liebknecht-Luxemburg Demonstration, held each year on 15 January at the grave of leading German communists Karl Liebknecht and Rosa Luxemburg, murdered in 1919 by a right-wing militia. In the 1980s, increasing numbers of GDR citizens ultimately successfully applied for permission to leave; those whose applications were pending often could escape through their families, were marginalized and subjected to reprisals, merit by the authorities.

Alfred Kurella (1895 to 1975) one of the GDR's leading cultural functionaries.

In the summer of 1989, increasing numbers of GDR citizens sought asylum in embassies, notably the West German Embassy in Prague, or West Germany's Permanent Mission in East Berlin.

In 1976 the GDR expatriated dissident singer-songwriter Wolf Biermann, demonstrating a new hard-line and disillusioning broad circles of East German intellectuals, whose attempt to protest Biermann's expulsion was squelched. In the following years, increasing numbers of intellectuals left the country.

7   The East German state profited when GDR writers published work in the West, as the hard currency which they received flowed into the state coffers. Beginning in 1979, GDR citizens were required to convert any hard currency they owned into

We'd got high drunk that evening too, but I like to fall up, and became a Berlin, Leipzig, Rostock object health lower body, you don't ever faint or watch, Just as I remember, we visit lots glance, do we hope, we'll think of something ed away from the room to the wall; he heard a woman's low voice, his eyes fell shut again at once, and in the darkness that returned to his skull he tried to suppress a spasmodic twinge beneath the cranium. But Frau Falbe wouldn't let him go back to sleep, she seized him by the shoulder and hip and with gentle force—murmuring to herself ceaselessly—turned him onto his back again so he had to open his eyes; once again the aching organ on his lower body loomed into the light. Frau Falbe murmured something about her previous tenant Harry, in cases like this he'd been sensible enough to sleep upstairs at her place from the outset—otherwise there would have been even more of a drama on the days when he had to report . . . Finally W. put his feet on the floor. With the pain in his abdomen he had to sit doubled over; he stayed that way until the woman turned away for a few seconds to pour a cup of coffee, then went to the toilet outside in the stairwell.—The following mornings the coffee was already poured, and instead of turning away, Frau Falbe leant on the edge of the desk waiting for him to cross the room, and was still studying him unabashedly when he returned, relieved, from the toilet; then she sat sideways in her ankle-long bathrobe on the chair behind the desk, with the armchair pulled up for him to sit on. She'd poured two cups of coffee and set out a little jug of milk . . . Really I can't take coffee this early, she said, especially not in this heat! But on your own you might not drink any coffee at all . . .

You've got to wash your pyjamas, she said (of course he'd noticed her critical gaze fixed on the increasingly discoloured front of his pyjama pants). If you can't do it in the laundry, give me the pyjamas, I'll have them dry again by this evening.—

in the GDR found liberating. In a dogma-dominated society like that of the GDR, the eschewal of ideology could count as an ideological statement, the apolitical as political. Drawing upon Western poststructuralist thinkers, this literature focused on 'language as such': 'a response to [. . .] an increasingly mechanical public and official language of administration and declamation. This new tendency supersedes a more "content"-oriented literary culture created over the past decades by the generation of established [. . .] GDR writers [. . . such as] Christa Wolf.'[4]

Anderson gradually admitted his IM activities. His theoretical and psychological explanations for his behaviour were widely regarded as self-serving, even pathological obfuscation. 'Betrayal is the right word,' he told Stern magazine in 2001, '. . . It was also a betrayal of my own "I", an "I" that I still reject.'[5] Still active in the Berlin literary scene, Anderson remains a figure of morbid fascination. In 2002, Anderson published a lyrical recollection ('not an autobiography in the usual sense'): Sascha Anderson.

The story of Sascha Anderson, who was his own postmodern fictional creation, or the fictional creation of the Stasi, or the purveyor of fictions to the Stasi, or about the Stasi, or all of the above, clearly resonates with Hilbig's novel. However, 'I' is not 'Sascha Anderson', nor indeed any other specific IM. Appearing at the height of the scandals, uncannily prescient about the Stasi's modus operandi and the psychology of collaboration, 'I' was widely read as a roman-à-clef, but Hilbig felt misunderstood by this reading. He always emphasized that he had little knowledge of the inner workings of the Stasi (or, for that matter, of the Berlin Scene), and did not view his own Stasi files until after completing the manuscript.

Only in the final phase of my work on the novel 'I did I have to look up several so-called technical terms

23 Franz Fühmann, *Praxis und Dialekt der Abwesenheit* (Practice and Dialect of Absence) in *Franz Fühmann: Werke*, VOL. 6 (Rostock: Hinstorff, 1993), pp. 459–74.

24 A year later, Fühmann collaborated with Anderson on an anthology of young writers which was ultimately unable to appear in the GDR. It served as the basis for the later Berührung. See Klaus Michael, 'Eine verschollene Anthologie' (A Lost Anthology) in Peter Böthig and Klaus Michael (eds), *Machtspiele: Literatur und Staatssicherheit* (Power Games: Literature and National Security) (Leipzig: Reclam Leipzig, 1993), pp. 202–16.

25 Dahlke, Wolfgang Hilbig, p. 74

26 Ibid., p. 85.

27 *Hilbig: Eine Erinnerung* (Hilbig: A Reminder), documentary film, directed by Siegfried Ressel (a + r Films, 2011).

28 Dahlke, *Wolfgang Hilbig*, p. 71.

text this. would have been an especially valuable finding because ... opened up points of attack when I recalled the story with Harry Falb; they'd virtually tried to ... on him or perhaps because they thought they could use it. To blackmail him. What I'd heard about the matter had barely ... plausible ... asked myself how I could use my findings in the present paper for the time being at any rate I kept it from my superior. Probably the fact wouldn't interest him, it might not even have found its way into the pink file that had been set up for the Interop ... evidently it could only mean something to me. Lately the West Berlin editor's relationship with R. seemed to have improved, she came over more often ... had no idea how to evaluate that in this new light ... Did she even know about this? about sexual proclivities? I asked myself, she didn't speak to me, her dark eyes studied me from a distance, I seemed to detect a scornful interest in her gaze . . . As if I were the queer! I thought.

His organizing mind was not called for, in this chaos it became a machine ...

kept on the container in the yard, which the rag collectors emptied very irregularly, picked out a number of the best pieces, duvet covers and pillowcases and sheets, had them washed and ironed and took them with him. As he left the pub on Hannoversche Strasse, (across from the Permanent Mission of the BRD) with the plastic bag, a policeman stopped him and checked his papers. This proceeded in the usual fashion: the man in uniform demanded his ID, opened it and stared at it. — Tell me your name, citizen, time . . . address . . . birthdate . . . birthplace! — W. reeled off the information . . . into the tape recorder now storing his voice for the proof . . . of being a Stasi informer! And besides, it'll heighten the charm of the fresh start . . . so I'll have to adopt a new code name immediately: W. Do you have any suggestions? Washing . . . picked it up from the laundry. And why don't you use the laundry in your neighbourhood? — Because I work in the laundry here. — OK . . . move it, move now . . .

. . . that kind of thing happened only when you came directly from the Permanent Mission; on this particular day it looked as though something unusual were going on . . . they were sitting by the window in the café, on Frankfurter and gazing melancholically out onto the street, where torrents of vehicles raced past towards the centre of town, towards the West, washing a clogged mixture of fog and early dusk against the big pane; it was like explosions feebly ebbing. They sat in their dim light at their observation post by the window . . . We must look inseparable, thought the first Lieutenant, and in mere husk, finally, so that . . . somehow, that's just not our style . . .

It was autumn, and W. had already moved. And this didn't surprise him: ever since moving to the flat he'd lived in the writer S. R. had homoerotic proclivities . . . or even a

and only poetry collection in the GDR, stimme stimme, in 1983.

Hilbig's position in the GDR became increasingly untenable. At last, in 1985, he was allowed to travel to the West to take advantage of the increasing offers of literary prizes, fellowships and readings. But he was a stranger in the West, alienated by consumer society and cut off from his roots; his ever-present drinking problems assumed alarming proportions. He travelled back and forth, torn between East and West, a period of his life reflected in his last novel, Das Provisorium (2000).[26] In 1988, he settled in the town of Edenkoben with the writer Natascha Wodin; they were married from 1994 to 2002. Like all his intimate relationships, it was a difficult one. 'He didn't want to live, he only wanted to write. Life was a nuisance for him,' Wodin recalled.[27] For Hilbig, writing was a compulsion, always fraught with feelings of guilt: in writing, he abandoned others, especially his social peers—the 'workers'—and his friends and family. The inability to cope with intimacy was a recurring theme in his life; he had a distant relationship with his only child, Constanze, born during a 1979–82 Berlin sojourn with journalist Margret Franzlik.[28]

In 1994, he and Wodin moved to reunited Berlin, settling in still-bohemian Prenzlauer Berg. Here too, Hilbig never felt truly at home. While his work continued to explore the dark landscape of the GDR, his public statements on Western media society and the shortcomings of reunification were scathing. Hilbig commanded too much respect, however, to be written off as a mere provocateur. He addressed the conflicts of his East–Western existence with an integrity and intensity which made him one of Germany's most important writers. In 2002, Hilbig was awarded the Büchner Prize, Germany's most prestigious literary award, for his life's work. But his powers were already ebbing; his last major work, the story collection Der for that, he said to W., people feel that the grassroots groups are just using them. And if they don't yet, they will soon. And besides, the people in the Scene are much too intelligent for these night vigils on the street clutching candles.—In Feuerbach's view, it was impossible to find anyone in the Scene with a strategy to give resistance a manageable organization or even a unified line. On the one hand they simply lack a mastermind, that is, some guru who has the cheek to keep them on their toes, on the other hand none of them are dumb enough to fall for a charlatan like that... and that's what I love about them.—Feuerbach grinned and said, they were considering the possibility of providing just this mastermind ...Wouldn't you like to do it? he asked. You'd have to dye your hair green, or white, change your parka for a yellow leather jacket and paint a Chinese pictograph on the back. Or you'd have to go about all in black, pitch black all the time, that'd do the trick. And after a suitable gestation, we'd nab this master-mind and arrest him to boot, elegant.

What struck W. most about these circles, or this milieu—and what made both words seem righter to him than the expression 'Scene', though he used it constantly; it being the word that both the Scene and the State Security used in common (just as the term 'Firm' was used in common by the State Security and the Scene)—and what had also occupied Feuerbach for a time: the milieu had emerged unplanned, without preamble, as it were, and it continued its existence unplanned and divergent without anyone giving it a thought. Suddenly this Scene was there, in many places at once, in the urban neighbourhoods where renovation costs couldn't be covered, sprouting like weeds from the rubble whenever you'd looked away for a moment, characterized by the persistence of disorganization, in the equal credence given to opposing views, in the indifference towards all ideas; indeed, the sole

1 The headquarters of the Ministry for State Security (or Stasi; here: MfSS) occupied a complex in Berlin-Lichtenberg between Frankfurter Allee, Normannenstrasse and Magdalenenstrasse.

2 Also known as the Liebknecht-Luxemburg Demonstration, held each year on 15 January in the GDR. Leading German Communists Karl Liebknecht and Rosa Luxemburg were murdered in 1919 during the Spartacist uprising.

3 ... increasing suspicion on the GDR ... during the application process, applicants and their families were marginalized and subjected to reprisals and harassment by the authorities.

4 Alfred Kurella (1895–1975): one of the GDR's leading cultural functionaries.

5 In the summer of 1989, increasing numbers of GDR citizens sought asylum in embassies (notably the West German Embassy in Prague) or West Germany's Permanent Mission in East Berlin.

6 In 1976 the GDR expatriated dissident singer-songwriter Wolf Biermann, demonstrating a new hard line and disillusioning broad circles of East German intellectuals, whose attempt to protest Biermann's expulsion was squelched. In the following years, increasing numbers of intellectuals left the country.

7 The East German state profited when GDR writers published work in the West, as the hard currency which they received flowed into the state coffers. Beginning in 1979, GDR citizens were required to convert any hard currency they owned into

We're on night again. W. was reminded of the folks who had expressed... Berlin, Leipzig, Rostock... similar... the heat. Conversation, ... this... nature regularly... Just correlate with some others subjectively. W. was waiting for Feuerbach's response to his question as to whether it would be expedient to apply for a travel permit . . . Whether it was a convenient point in time, or perhaps too early, he'd asked to defuse the question from the outset.—What do you mean . . . now? the first lieutenant flung out and went on his way.—When such 'difficult questions' came up, Feuerbach generally gave the impression that he wasn't really listening, his replies came weeks later, and always as a surprise; in the meantime, presumably, he obtained (in higher places) his information guidelines.—It'd be possible in six months, he said, walking up one evening to the table in the cafe, where W. had been brooding for hours. W. looked uncertainly at his superior, who leant on one armrest (playing the role of a man pressed for time), bent down to W. and yelled: Now, listen, you asked me about it yourself . . . besides, that's all you ever think about, you've got it written all over you.— He'd delivered the second half of the speech more calmly, but it was too late—the waiter came up and reminded him that they weren't the only people in the cafe . . . Feuerbach waited until he'd gone away again, then he said: You arsehole!—W., familiar with such tantrums, held his tongue; Feuerbach continued his speech, still standing: Probably both of us are more than ready for it . . . I'm authorized to say that headquarters don't think half-badly of you . . . of course, they don't see you snoozing away at this table here. All joking aside, well, their view is that naturally it's no go unless there's a compelling reason. That means, for instance, that you'd have to have a contact in West Berlin. Now my question is, do you have a contact there?—Feuerbach fell silent and glanced around the taproom; if any interest had arisen at the other tables, it had died down

6   Wolfgang Hilbig, quoted in Birgit Dahlke, *Wolfgang Hilbig* (Hanover: Wehrhahn Verlag, 2011), p. 101.

7   Lutz Kornel-Nitsche, email to translator, 20 November 2013.

8   See Karim Saab's interview with Hilbig in Uwe Wittstock (ed.), *Wolfgang Hilbig: Materialien zu Leben und Werk* (Frankfurt: Fischer Taschenbuch Verlag), p. 222–8: 'They tried to recruit me, but I was not vulnerable to threats. In the boiler room, I could hardly sink any lower in the social hierarchy. [. . .] Emotionally, I fled to my colleagues and said: The Stasi is here and is trying to recruit me! The workers [. . .] gave me the security I needed' (p. 223). Once he had thus 'deconspired', the Stasi ceased its recruitment attempts.

9   Ibid., p. 224.

10 Kornel-Nitsche, email to translator, 3 December 2012.

11 Bärbel Heising, '*Briefe voller Zitate aus dem Vergessen*': Intertextualität im Werk Wolfgang Hilbigs (Frankfurt: Peter Lang, 1996), pp. 188–91.

12 Kornel-Nitsche, email to translator, 20 November 2012.

13 Dahlke, *Wolfgang Hilbig*, pp. 21–2.

14 Ibid., pp. 32–5; Kornel-Nitsche, personal conversations with translator.

15 Ibid., p. 35.

16 'Ich komme aus dem Wald', interview with Hilbig, Berliner Zeitung, 26 October 2002.

17 Dahlke, *Wolfgang Hilbig*, pp. 43–4

18 Cited in Dahlke, *Wolfgang Hilbig*, p. 51. For many East German intellectuals, the venerable Leipzig Book Fair was a rare chance to get their hands on Western literature, reading, copying or even filching books at the stands.

19 Ibid., p. 47.

20 Cited in ibid., p. 45.

21 Ibid., p. 68.

22 Ibid., p. 70.

He's blackmailing us! At least, he's trying to. He's been collecting material and hiding it for quite a while now . . . not just material signed with the code name Harry Falbe, he's got completely different things up his sleeve, signed with completely different code names . . . Not yours, of course, you didn't have it yet down there in A., but aside from that, I'm telling you . . . I said nothing, and he continued: I don't even know if I should be telling you this, you'll just forget it anyway, or you won't believe it. Haven't you ever heard the name Colonel Falbe . . . of course the old lady won't have told you anything. He worked abroad, in West Berlin, for one thing. And it's always said that Harry was born in prison, that's the only version he knows himself. But he was brought to East Berlin at the beginning of August '61, the colonel's son, and after that the colonel vanished without a trace . . . Feuerbach stopped for a moment to take a breather; by now his voice was slightly slurred.

We don't know if the old lady told him anything . . . maybe not, she's not the mother, after all! And we can't just bump her off . . . Feuerbach laughed rather artificially; it was supposed to be a joke.

Still, we're the ones with more staying power, I'm telling you, even if a whole bunch of people are already scared shitless. Yes, suddenly lots of people are scared shitless. And we don't know if he . . . if Harry told the old lady anything . . . The Major's story was starting to strike me as slightly incoherent.

And what are these documents Harry's sitting in the Permanent Mission with? I asked.

We may not learn that until it's too late, until you can read it in the newspapers over there, said Feuerbach. Because I'm telling you, we'll have to let all of them go, maybe even the ones in Prague and Budapest. Because they're down there too . . . can you picture what'll happen if that catches on? They'll have to stew a bit longer, and then batch by batch they'll all get to leave, what else can we do, we've lost that battle.

And I've lost my rank . . . for now! We'll let them all out and Harry with them. But we have an ace up our sleeves, believe me . . . or we'll have it soon!

I could only stare at him inquiringly; the barkeeper was back at our table.

Don't you know, Feuerbach whispered, that he's got his child's blood on his hands?

Evidently the Hong Kong flu had such a hold on me that I was no longer capable of horror; silent, I asked myself whether something resembling relief had passed through my numb interior.

He must have offed the kid, his son, or his girlfriend's son, the one who was born in jail . . . a veritable repetition compulsion, isn't it? At any rate the kid has vanished . . . without a trace. We don't have 100 per cent proof yet, we still haven't found the brat. But we hardly have any time left, we've got to find the evidence, or make it up, either way, because once Harry's over there, he'll cut and run. But not before he finds a taker for his material . . . he's not dumb, that little Harry . . .

Is that the same child I once . . . I asked.

Well, well, you're catching on . . . it's the same child. You signed the paternity form and never paid. The Fatherland footed the bill for you . . . oh, so you do have some residual powers of recall. And if you had evidence that Harry had gotten rid of the brat shortly after birth, you wouldn't even have to pay the burial costs.

But the child was a fabrication, I said, even back when it was supposedly my child . . . do you still believe in this lunacy?

You always left it pretty unclear back then . . . just like an artist, he added. I know, you've never seen the child . . . me neither. Still, you signed, and there are the documents from the prison, too. A child can't just up and vanish in this country. But that doesn't matter, if we can prove it on Harry Falbe that the child existed, or even better that he got rid of it, that'd be a windfall for us! Can you think how loud we'll yell, on TV, in the press: the West German Mission is covering for a murderer and smuggling him out! Because that's how far we have to take it! And as for you . . . go on writing your reports, keep at it . . . what's the Berlin Scene's latest kindergarten called, when's the next hip riot. But leave out words like riotous assembly, hostile activities, planned provocations . . . we've got to show our human face for a bit now . . .

The barkeeper came to the table and laid down a slip of paper with the tab; it was a pathetically small amount, with no charge for an extra beer . . . and then the barkeeper carried his tray around to the other tables and set filled glasses in front of the guests; it was a clear provocation. On his way back he shuffled up again and explicitly stated the sum on the slip of paper.—Excuse me, please . . . said Feuerbach, we'd like another round.—We've stopped serving, replied the barkeeper, and repeated the requested sum.—We both looked at our watches simultaneously, on mine it was three to twelve, on Feuerbach's five to twelve . . . the first lieutenant had told me quite a bit in the past three quarters of an hour.

All right, he said amicably, then we'll have another one up at the bar . . . And he placed the money on the table, two marks more than necessary.—Forget about it! said the barkeeper, and counted out exact change, down to the last pfennig. We've stopped serving.—Vexed, Feuerbach swept up the coins he'd meant for the tip, then said to me: Give me your watch—it's Harry's girlfriend's, right? I'm going to need it.

I refrained from asking where Harry's girlfriend was, unbuckled the watch from my wrist and handed it to him; he tucked it away in the inside pocket of his jacket. Then he emptied his beer in one draught and got to his feet; I left mine half-full as Feuerbach dragged me to the bar.—Two more beers, two schnapps . . . please! Feuerbach's voice had a slight quiver to it.

This ain't no glee club here, the barkeeper said broadly. For the last time, we've stopped serving . . . As he spoke he coolly tapped a fresh beer, wiped off the excess foam with care and handed it to an individual leaning on one of the stand-up tables by the bar a foot further down . . . These are all just friends and relatives of mine, explained the barkeeper, it's just family now.

I want another beer immediately! the first lieutenant forced out in that hiss I knew so well. And he made the mistake of slapping down his official ID on the tap fixture . . . There! So you know who you're dealing with. I can have your drinking hole shut down if I feel like it!—Without drying his hands, the barkeeper picked up the document gingerly and held it for an exceedingly long time before his bespectacled eyes, liquid dripping from his reddened hands. He laid it gently back down on the metal: You could be the Emperor of China for all I care! You caused a disturbance here, I'm banning you from my pub, effective immediately . . . And you too! Lightning-quick he turned his head towards me. He pointed to the door with two parallel outstretched index fingers: Leave my gastronomic facility at once! Icy silence filled the room, everyone was staring at us; I'd already taken our coats from the rack, and yanked at the Major's sleeve; outside I felt as though I'd saved his life.—All right, all right, he panted when I kept hanging onto him, I'm only going because of you, another minute and I would've strangled that swine!

And so we ended up on Frankfurter Allee after all . . . as we walked along the dark street that paralleled it, towards

Magdalenenstrasse, Feuerbach trembled all over (instead of putting on his coat, he'd slung it over his shoulder like a sack), not seeming to regain his strength until we turned down Magdalenenstrasse . . . as though sensing the great silence of the massive buildings on the right with their barred windows. He walked with a slight, newly confident sway, and the fragments of my report fell out of his trouser pocket; I walked along behind him gathering them up again.

The cafe was closed already, too, but Feuerbach gained us entry by drumming furiously at the door. We stepped inside the smoke-filled room where a few younger men, about our age, sat at the tables, usually by twos, in mutual silence (it was rarely this quiet here at this time of night, just an hour after closing, but that was consistent with the overall state of affairs). We took seats near the bar, where I'd never sat before, the Major ordered, and we fell silent, too . . . and now I realized that Feuerbach was completely and utterly drunk. Then he put his arm around my shoulders and begged: Come with me . . . let's go to my place . . . let's have another drink . . . but I'd rather go to my place, are you coming?—When I nodded, he said: This place makes me sick . . . I can't stand the sight . . . the way they all mope around here, the way they all snooze here . . . I just can't stand the sight any more . . .

I refused to believe that his suggestion had been serious; and by the time we'd reached the Frankfurter Allee Station he already seemed to have forgotten it. Without a parting word he got into a taxi and slammed the door. I was left behind on the pavement . . . See you tomorrow! I called; maybe he'd heard me, the sunken shape behind the back window. Then I took a second taxi to my flat . . . behind the fifth-floor windows the light was burning.

The city's depression seemed to spare no one, only I gradually stopped sacrificing to it, my head began to clear, even the weather seemed inclined to turn warmer.—Incidentally, depression was not a native Eastern term, it came from the Western part of the city, but there, too, it had found its way in by chance, its original manifestation had to stem from Western Germany, from sated regions; when I tried to pin down its source, I thought of autobahn-ringed Nuremberg. In East Berlin the term had been established by the Scene (it was a cultural asset), and we at the Firm, not wanting to lag too far behind the times, used it as well.

I had heard the word in a pointed voice from a tiny mouth that from time to time was painted blood-red, a dark-clothed boyish person's sole adornment; it hit me from the side, from two or three yards away: Soon she wouldn't be coming any more, depression was already raining down in this chaos here (meaning the polis of Berlin, Capital of the GDR).—Her addressee was silent, it was the writer S. R., and he left her standing there, having already geared up to go.

Feuerbach didn't show; bored (with the Hong Kong flu abating) I took up my aimless travels through the city again . . . yet again I hit upon the idea of travelling to A., and even tried it twice; in Leipzig the depression seized me (it was here, too, and maybe even worse) and I turned around again . . . then I hung out in the pubs, increasingly bored by the Scene's meet-ups; far too often I encountered the view that the readings by the writer S. R. (who had a code number for us, alongside the appellation IntelOp: Reader) used to be a big deal . . . it was true, I wouldn't have been surprised if you'd had to hunt for the IntelOp in the archive by now, a dead file . . .

It almost gave me another bout of depression . . . I thought back wistfully to the time when the entire Berlin underground had anticipated his readings, and I anticipated them as well (though not just because I wanted to hear him) . . . lots of female guests always came . . . he had an especially strong effect on women . . . and maliciously I thought that this was exactly what caused the neostructuralists' secret envy of totalitarian literary leadership cults, this eternal dark-varnished timbre of voice and clothing. Of course it wasn't like that, I just wanted to see it like that, Reader was a guy who had built up the image of a literary neurotic, who had managed to create the impression that he was compelled to flood the world with his work (I had got nearly all my ideas from him), while at the same time there was always a mysterious helplessness about him, something remote-controlled about his eyes behind the Isaac Babel glasses; he was always dapper, his outer shell consisting of a collarless black Russian-cut shirt with a slight glitter, it must have been some extremely expensive fissile fabric, and down below probably black trousers that draped over black shoes (usually I only saw him seated, hidden behind the audience); on the whole he was a perfect creation. And I was after the Student who always stuck by his side, with her contrasting lily-white face . . . by now, due to certain of Feuerbach's insinuations, I was more inclined to take her for a journalist. That side-line made the lady in the soft leather jacket (Feuerbach would have said lady in English) even more interesting. I was already happy when she wasn't unfriendly . . . I adopted nearly all Reader's quirks.

As his impact in the Scene waned (and my impact in the Firm along with it), I considered whether it was possible to find out or invent anything that could harm him (and benefit me)—the Scene offered no leads; I would have to penetrate his private sphere, and first I'd have to establish where he lived. Hadn't I practically been challenged to do so . . .? What do we need with this eternal lit crit? That was effectively such a challenge, if I wasn't mistaken. But suddenly a story involving the Permanent Mission struck me as too ticklish, maybe there were other things that would be awkward for us to know:

minor to middling money issues, currency offences, cheques
. . . things which none of us could avoid, but which, tackled
from the right angle, could be disruptive and neutralizing.
Disruption was what we doted on, we didn't even want to
think about court proceedings and other crudities . . .
Disruption, however contradictory it might sound, was the
true creativity.

It wasn't hard to find out where he lived; he wasn't from
Berlin, he had moved here, of course not quite legally, which
was why he occupied a flat in a rear wing—amid pre-
war buildings, which, in my experience, had an abundance of
basements—in a rather out-of-the-way area near Storkower
Strasse which I could almost have reached by foot, fit as I was.
Now I began to haunt this heavily industrialized district,
where the mud lay so deep on some streets that you thought
you were in the countryside.—One evening in his back courtyard I was lurking in an especially dark corner, behind the
garbage bins, worried that the location, in conjunction with
its temperature, would treat me to a relapse of the Hong Kong
flu. The object of my gaze was a lit third-floor window; I was
bent on seeing the Student again, who I believed had passed
the window an hour ago. I knew that she regularly used the
Friedrichstrasse border crossing (and very rarely spent the
night in the East . . . with Reader!); that was quite a long way,
she'd have to leave soon: I was wearing the Japanese quartz
watch, not because it made me feel honoured but because
Feuerbach had relieved me of my usual chronometer. She
came down at last, accompanied by Reader (who wore perfectly normal slippers); as they appeared in the door I wit-
nessed a rather heated altercation between them, of which
unfortunately I understood very little. She was the main insti-
gator of the argument, speaking in a muted hiss, while he,
almost whispering, merely admonished her to be quiet; she

accused him of elitist behaviour for refusing to sign a petition; he justified his refusal with the fact that the statement was to be published in the West. It was one of those standard conflicts we were already tired of . . . I thought of the whole series of petitions that had made the rounds lately, all of which I'd signed on my strolls through the Scene; just minutes later I couldn't remember which causes they had championed, probably I didn't even read them through (if I wasn't mistaken, there had even been a Letter to Gorbachev or Shevardnadze).

He wasn't a coward in her eyes, the altercation continued, but objectively speaking his elitist behaviour led to cowardice and opportunism . . . He said that he knew the score here better than she; apart from that I only saw him shake his head so that the lenses of his glasses flashed, giving the whole thing a vehement appearance. Finally she turned away, aggrieved, and headed across the yard towards the street; he made no attempt to hold her back, vanishing into the building so quickly that I thought he was glad to be rid of her. She walked right past me; I held my breath, and when I heard the front door slam shut, I followed her.

On the street, I looked around for her: it was astonishing, the confident stride with which she traversed this district's deserted, poorly lit streetscapes—she really didn't seem very fearful.—Maybe she felt worse things could happen to her in West Berlin . . . I walked a considerable distance behind her, as quietly as possible at first; when I thought she was about to turn around, I ducked into a doorway . . . but then I followed her more and more openly; finally, moving behind her at a constant pace, I resembled an automaton which she herself steered . . . I learnt very quickly to match her gait, and I didn't feel the need to hide from her, though I dimly sensed her listening to my steps . . .

★★★

In the dark streets swollen with filth and erosion the thought struck me that this was my mission for the immediate future: to shadow the woman I called the student!—The idea came to me in the peculiar situation of huddling in a doorway and gazing down the pavement until she had regained a sufficient lead . . . and at once I felt equal to the task. I had this feeling for perhaps the first time in my life . . .

(He'd first had the idea even before spring began, one evening when he'd left Feuerbach standing there on the S-Bahn platform at Alexanderplatz—an affront!—and rode back . . . it was possible that when the train stood too long at Warschauer Strasse—or Ostkreuz—he had got out and wandered through the streets . . . through the rain again, which let up only gradually. And each time he'd encountered a woman, he'd followed her cautiously for a stretch—until he knew it wasn't the Student. But he had felt the appeal, the obscene appeal of the self-destructive hubris that lay in taking up such a chase . . . and when he arrived at his house, drenched and filled with a base gratification, and saw light in his windows, his watch told him it was late at night . . .)

And even the appellation under which I filed her in my mind—and in at least one of my reports—was impeccable: she came over to pursue her studies, as a journalist, as an editor, more probably still at her own behest . . . from West Berlin at its dullest, perhaps the pampered hatchling of a wealthy family in ritzy Grunewald, her head full of left-wing manifestos and the notion that salvation lay, absurdly enough, in the East . . . and so she came, with a pack of 25 HB cigarettes in her handbag, and sometimes perhaps with a crumb of hashish, and a slew of ideological words in her head: immanent-elitist-authoritarian-antiauthoritarian-spontaneous-nonimmanent . . . and much more of that ilk, and she was hoodwinked by the so-called Scene and thought she could learn a bit about the GDR as alternative; she'd never stray into Wagner's. If she'd had the guts to get to know me, she might have been quite surprised—I didn't care if the country was an alternative or not, it was fine with me that our Republic existed the way it was, its footing among nations stronger from year to year, but I still wanted a travel visa for the West, albeit merely temporary, unlike S. R. I signed every petition unconcerned about the risks to my freedom or possessions, and I was game for every vigil, as long as I didn't have to stand there myself, but they had to be held, absolutely . . . Demonstrations, an excellent idea, I was all for getting together and spontaneously contemplating their concrete realization, I was always a fan of organization, noting every relevant date, though otherwise I was at odds with all time schemes.—Unfortunately she never showed any inclination to get involved with me, she clung to S. R.; now the two had had a falling-out, and I hoped it would last . . . it only seemed to bind her to him all the closer.

Feuerbach barely held me to my duties any longer; without a clear task I was left even more in limbo, his 'keep at it' was a weary phrase.—Thus I was able to track her; it had grown clearer and clearer to me that in the coming weeks, months . . . in the upcoming quarter I was to be her shadow. And wanted to be . . . and so she walked on ahead of me, never quickening her pace—my own private operation! And when I thought about it, I'd sought out Operation: Reader myself as well—Reader was a step ahead of me too, in literature . . .

And of course there was a sense of wonder at the 'value placed on literature' she'd discovered in the East. Weren't the lefties from the West all interested in these values in one way or another? Of course they were, for alternative reasons . . . in the West you heard about this high value all over the place— she'd had to discover it for herself, yes indeed, in East Berlin literature was valued more highly than a new, alternative shampoo . . . incredible! And the Party's ideologues tormented literature with all conceivable means, just to maintain its high value . . . in every respect the East was the alternative.—What would she have said if she'd met a literature lover like the boss in A., capable of sabotaging entire factories just to secure the existence of a few literati in his town, and not the best ones at that?

It was time I mastered a certain repertoire of speakable phrases about literature, as I still had the intention of talking to her one day . . . if we got into conversation, I'd have to demonstrate some opinion on literature, and not just hold my own against S. R., either. Ultimately literature's raison d'être (and, still more, its value) was a matter of utter indifference to me, except regarding my own texts. But I had no texts of my own . . . if they had existed, I would have needed paper and pen, nothing more. I wasn't even thinking of the experts, or publication opportunities . . . oh, I even had a typewriter, on permanent loan from the experts, but all that was not enough. I'd have to have more to show for the Student . . . the neostructuralists came to mind! I could reject them, but I had to know something about them!—I had time, though (I said these words just as slowly, with just as sunny a smile, as every Firm employee did at least once a week: We have time . . . we have lots of time!) . . . I had taken on the task of following her the whole prospective summer, and while completing these routes I could think about literature . . . until now I'd merely sat around, in what was perhaps a prenatal position; now I had awoken and could start to walk. I could have phrases at the ready if things got serious. One of them was: The effusions of the writer S. R. always had struck me as elitist. They presupposed knowledge of a whole slew of books that weren't even available in this country. He, for instance—M. W., author of seventeen poems published left and right of the Iron

Curtain—suffered greatly from his inability to engage with certain works . . .—Is that so? she'd have to reply, what books do you need?—And the contact would be forged.

At Storkower Strasse Station I had let her go her way. I'd recalled the downright sadistic route along the endless pedestrian bridge leading across the tracks to the platform. A pursuer in this dead straight glass-and-concrete tunnel, which smelt of dust and urine as though this were the smell of eternity, and where steps echoed as though in a horror film, was bound to give her a fright after all . . . and perhaps she would have run to seek help from the people at the rail station. I would have spoilt things for myself . . . it was just barely eleven, she was travelling towards Berlin's nocturnal tumult, she would have forgotten me by the time she changed at Ostkreuz. And I went in search of a bus stop to head out to Frau Falbe's.

Thinking back on that evening, I couldn't deny a certain uneasy feeling. The notion of pursuing a young woman through the night was a dubious one, to put it mildly . . . and dubious it remained, even if 'I' was the pursuer. I told myself I'd never known this side of me before . . . and I didn't know what it might have led to. No thought that I could have attacked her. No thought? There were moments on that path when I had pictured exactly that.

It was impossible not to think thoughts like that in the course of such an activity! It would have been a dead-certain means of losing my beloved job (even if they would have covered for me to avoid discrediting the entire Firm) . . . but there were certainly less troublesome options than that, and ones which didn't lead to a several-year 'training course'.— Nonetheless I had woken up the next day (to the finest spring weather, far remote from depression and the Hong Kong flu) with the memory of this idea . . . and I know the thought would remain. Nothing could happen to me as long as it was just the thought; you could think anything, in fact you had to . . . but what did I know of the capacity for escalation that lay in that 'I', that shadow on the Student's paths? I almost began to dread the next opportunity . . . fortunately it was not so soon to come; she stayed in West Berlin, the quarrel with Reader must have gone deep.

By the time I saw her again I had met with Feuerbach (he was and remained a ray of hope for me: in his presence I repeatedly managed to step back from thoughts that were plainly and simply impractical) . . . I tried to remind him of my travel schemes, which had crossed my mind again now that I could picture trailing the Student even in Grunewald. But Feuerbach was no help; he seemed to be in a strange state of shock, uncommunicative as never before, using barbaric expressions out of the blue, such as 'shitty literature', 'shitty underground', 'shitty GDR' . . . I concurred assiduously in the hopes of turning the conversation to West Berlin; he didn't say 'shitty West Berlin', but it was impossible to get a proper sentence out of him; I started to feel bored in his presence, which happened only rarely. I asked him whether he was aware that Reader was beginning to meet with a fair amount of resistance, people thought he was too out of touch, he'd probably even been dumped by his girlfriend, the Student, at any rate she hardly ever came over from West Berlin any more.—He shrugged his shoulders, a tiny bit too fast, was my impression: He didn't give a shit about that either . . . All at once he looked anxious: We aren't getting anywhere with the shit at the Permanent Mission!—Probably, he said, we're pretty much shit ourselves at this point . . .

That was my last conversation with the Major before the summer came . . . it left me feeling rather brutally dropped . . . left in the lurch, uprooted. His former cynical grin had often annoyed me, but it included me, I was in the know about the object of his disdain; in many cases I didn't share his disdain, but his scorn sought my approval; after I'd swallowed my irritation he even struck me as paternal . . . now I missed his grin.—Once again I thought of travelling to A. (I had time!)—was it two or even three years since I'd last seen my mother? I simply couldn't work it out, I couldn't even dwell on the thought— and I would have gone immediately if it hadn't been for the Student: every time I'd made up my mind, she suddenly appeared for the day . . . without the chase I wouldn't have been I.

There were one or two months that summer that reminded me of the time when I'd worked as a stoker in the REWATEX laundry—the Chausseestrasse branch, across from the Bertolt Brecht bookshop—only that I didn't stagger through the day so drugged by exhaustion now, only that I wasn't woken by Frau Falbe between three and four in the morning.—Berlin was overrun and paralysed by a similar series of heat waves, but I was able to take refuge in my basement passages. The heat seemed to take a special toll on art and literature, there was nothing going on in the Scene; what passed for events (a couple of exhibitions, readings, lots of talk interrupted by groans . . . Operation: Reader went into summer recess, and I sensed it was already on its way to the happy hunting ground), the arduously organized manifestations of Unofficial Culture were relocated to wild green gardens on the outskirts of Berlin, near bathing lakes, and the meet-ups resembled picnics or camping chaos. As I couldn't bring myself to embrace the bathing life, I lost touch somewhat . . . when I did join in I usually found that the Student was missing. Probably the locations were too far from the border crossing for her; when she did come, she had to head back late in the afternoon; I would have followed her half a minute later, at an hour when it would have drawn attention. I was careful and took my time, sporadically contriving to cross her path ... I wanted to see whether she would at least greet me; I couldn't figure out whether her gaze had ever lingered on me consciously.—By August the summer already seemed to have spent itself and proceeded to turn cool and rainy—and now I got back to business with full resolve.

During the sweltering weeks I'd had enough leisure, in the basement, to think about what I was actually doing. I already had the red armchair standing by the concrete wall beneath Normannenstrasse ... before the summer began I'd bought it from Frau Falbe for a token sum (in the end she'd wanted to give it to me for free), just in time before the worst of the heat; a little later and the monster's transport via S-Bahn would have turned into a debacle ... now I had a comfortable seat by the wall, in the cool basement smell I sat enthroned on the armchair like a broad-beamed deity (and like a Prince of Darkness, when the dense fumes of expired excretions wafted in from the city), arms outstretched on the armrests, head and back upright on the backrest, feet on the produce crate, and above me the phallic symbol on the wall behind which the cooling units purred—where a circumscribed parcel of Western affluence lay resplendent, installed by the Ministry in this earthly realm ... and beneath me I had the papers tucked between the cushions. Admittedly these were not possessions of a particularly delicate nature—at most the fact that I hadn't delivered them was delicate, but I was as reliable an archive as a file at the Firm, the stored findings for me being even more timeless—and yet the fact of them reminded me of Harry Falbe. He had fled to the Permanent Mission with a bundle of documents, resolved, according to Feuerbach, to extort his freedom from the godlike state. I wouldn't have thought him capable, but there was tenacity in his flimsy body, in his skull—the egg-shaped albino head with the red rabbit eyes, as Feuerbach had once described it—was initiative and guile; the other people at the embassy were pure and non-violent, as befitting the empty-handed, but Harry had broadened his knowledge at the Firm and taken along a bargaining chip which might earn him some spare change on his arrival in the West.

They'd been more careful with me; what code names did I know, anyway (I didn't even know the Major's real name) ... I'd had my Reader and a few other Intelligence Operations along those lines; my main task had consisted in making the mess in Sect. 20 even more hopeless ... sometimes I suffered from the fixed idea that I had been activated (I was blameless) as a poster boy for an office purge, and sometimes I had the impression that my duties consisted in penetrating Unofficial Literature in a missionary capacity, infiltrating it with my Firm's love of literature (wherever I cropped up, all my employers were blameless) ... and never had I had an inspired notion which provoked anything but laughter from my managers.—And I had no inspired notion how to make something out of the business which I had long since privately named IntelOp: Student.—My activities came straight from the cheapest training programme for bumbling new recruits: shadow a young West Berlin woman on her errands through East Berlin and write down, without her noticing, the addresses of the buildings she entered. It didn't have the makings of a career à la Harry Falbe ...

I told myself that the appeal for Cambert, the old pro, lay somewhere else entirely. With respect to the Major—if he came to me again with a job or proposal along these lines—I was inclined to continue acting as though I felt completely unqualified for such cases ... as though I were simply too hypersensitive for them. Observing men, perfectly OK, sniffing out the Scene's better halves, the Eastern ones, even more OK, there were even some women whose trust I enjoyed—but some hoity-toity little thing from Grunewald: impossible, I was bound to be shut down . . . or rather blown wide open, which wasn't necessarily the opposite. I decided to explain it to Feuerbach that way.

Without instructions, without the weight of expectation, it all worked out much better for me! And one day when I had enough material, I could plunk it down on his desk . . . not because I wanted a watch for a present; I was counting on the suggestion to keep pursuing the IntelOp in the West.— Besides, when I performed my work in peace and on my own initiative (judiciously, as they put it), I got a much better handle on the specific quality of such an activity.

The idea came to me that I must love the Student in some very singular way and that was why I was running after her . . . so far I hadn't written any reports about this—first I wanted some clarity in my mind regarding the theoretical situation. Otherwise there was a danger that my notes would spiral into psychological tracts. I could begin with the reports (perhaps this autumn?) when I was focusing on nothing but the woman . . . I had to fabricate a female character who fit the Firm's conception! The appeal for me was that it appeared I would literally have to invent or design her at my desk.—To make the Firm a person . . . and not one of our people, of whom there were millions we couldn't quite come to grips with . . . to produce a person for the Firm, that was the greatest service a collaborator could perform (and ultimately it was proof that we were unerringly right in all our exaggerated-sounding claims), to deliver into the hands of the Firm an exemplary person . . . I knew how the individual, especially when young, always seeks to conform to the image made of him or her . . .

The woman: that meant completely different thighs than the man's . . . they might appear weaker, but they were much harder to open than the man's, probably due to their more stable anchorage in the pelvis . . . completely different gluteal curves than mine, the scents arising from the hidden entries between these curves were completely different. Her difference was different by a further dimension, for it originated in the free West and had thrived in West Berlin, in an upscale area of Grunewald. And even her hands were completely different hands, her arms were different, her musculature made from a different, much finer stuff than anything I knew . . . her DNA was an absolutely Western DNA.—She didn't bear two breasts with palm-sized nipples flat against her torso, she had tiny pointed glands of some unknown material; she seemed somewhat plagued (in a very self-assured way) by these forms' lack of fullness, but this had been the intention of the nature god who had shaped her according to the somewhat eccentric idea that less fullness sinks the force of desire more durably in the body's depths. And below that came a belly which at its narrowest point tapered off beneath a patch of hair and vanished (the colour remained a riddle, the dyed hair of the head permitting no conclusions), and there beneath the hair (as beneath the hair of the head) everything dissolved into pure Spirit, timeless and thus untimely. And the intellect that perched upon this body was fluid and thus perhaps not describable as intellect; it had been endowed with freedom from the beginning (if all had gone with her as it should), for which reason it was able to soften the hardest logic.

When I followed her through the dark streets, a shadow in the night city's shadow-vaults, she seemed so carefree that all I wanted was to turn and leave her in peace, and had to summon up all I had learnt: when it came to fulfilling our duties, we took no prisoners.

As I saw her, this woman, she was a being as unapproachable as could be—and yet in the guilelessness laid bare at her temples she was much stronger than I. I couldn't help it, I had to surround the woman with an obscene thought if I was to gain hold of her.

With the thought of overtaking her one evening and laying her down on the cold stone in the murky half-light of the pedestrian bridge over the Storkower Strasse Station (when the station below was empty, giving me free rein), throwing her down into the Eastern dust of this concrete channel so that she lay at last in reality, and spreading her legs . . .

You can think everything, said the bosses in Security, you have to, in fact . . . Maybe they even said it was the writer's duty to think everything . . .

You see best when you look from the dark into the light, they said in Security.—That was true, and now it was time that I began: thinking about how my life would look over there in the Western world . . . as a literary man! Making contacts and thinking . . . it was here, from the haze, that you had to look upon that life . . . make provisions, take precautions.— The boss in A., I recalled, had weighed in on the subject, two years ago, if not three, and today it sounded as though he had long suspected that it was time for us to think about a life after we were gone. Even though no embassies had yet been occupied—at least nothing of that sort had filtered through, even in the purlieus of Security nothing was known of it, it was the sole remit of a small team of Special Forces—there were as yet no grassroots groups of hostile-negative forces, no coalition movements, hardly any perceptible upheaval yet in the Warsaw Pact.—I felt that he'd said you had to think about how to live in a changed world—and that he'd added just in case: You've got to be allowed to think everything.

What, for instance, is a writer on the other side? he'd asked. Let's take the writers in the West, what's an author there? A market-driven subcontractor of the media society! He's something like a hairdresser there, nothing more . . . a hair-dresser who attends to his clients' mental exercises and if nec-essary validates them. Of course you give the customers a proper dressing-down, but you don't harm a hair on their heads, the customers with their mental and verbal exercises. Well, here we can justifiably claim to wash a little deeper, a little deeper below the scalp! Yes, a hair salon, that's what the West is with its free literature, and especially the Federal Republic and the Independent Entity of West Berlin.[12] It never fails to astonish me, said the boss, that no one there has yet got a Nobel Prize for hairdressers! Am I exaggerating . . . maybe a bit. Whether or not you believe me, if I were you I'd be cautious about pinning my hopes on the free literature of the West.

I know people curse about censorship here . . . not just the nonofficial literature, everyone does. They all feel trapped by this cultural policy, by this censorship, by those idiots up there in the Ministry of Culture . . . that last bit's just a quote, by the way! And we especially, we're supposed to be to blame, when in fact we've got very definite thoughts of our own . . . and not just in the literary sphere. If you know someone who needs material for his new rain gutter . . . send him to us! We've got thoughts of our own . . . deviant thoughts, I tell you, we'd all have been deviationists for our Good Lord Beria,[13] who's long since burning in hell . . . and we'd have been deviationists still for Andropov.[14] And everything that looks oh-so stable right now, I wouldn't like to see it in ten years. What difference would it make for you to wait another ten years, or let's say three or four years? That's no time at all for literature! How can a writer think in such narrow temporal terms . . . for us, I tell you, such time scales don't even exist.

I ask you again, what is a writer over there—in that hustle and bustle, I know whereof I speak. They should all be called journalists over there, with all the journals to be serviced. But seriously, what would a writer be without us . . . after we're gone? After we're gone they'll all become journal subscribers, those literary gentlemen, so they can keep up to speed . . . yes indeed, they'll speed after the times. But you can subscribe to as much time as you like over there, you just won't get any, because time is on our side. Seriously, though, what is a writer after we're gone? And not just a writer, everyone else too . . . what is anyone after us?

Now it might sound like I think we're the inventors of some very special sort of people . . . and maybe we actually are. What'll they all do after us, when we've stopped oppressing and censoring them, I ask myself in despair. What do people do without their creator. Creator . . . if that's too high-flown for you, go ahead and say midwife . . . development worker— whatever you like.

I tell you, suddenly they'll all get the idea that they've become dispensable, the men and women of the writing trade—and not just them. Exactly, that's what we wanted to prevent! We made them all, and made them indispensable! You're absolutely right that by doing that, we ultimately made ourselves indispensable too . . . ha ha! (He laughed.) Just as indispensable as the poets! (It was one of the usual rants the boss had spilt out before him, two or three years ago, one of those futuristic lectures he'd just never known what to make of. Time had rushed forward since then, and suddenly these words began to preoccupy him again; they preoccupied C. that whole summer as he trailed the Student, and he felt as though his thoughts—the boss' thoughts—followed her even across the border, as though she were shadowed still further by his explanations, by his boss' explanations, in West Berlin territory. Later that year . . .

[Allow me to jump ahead; time presses, forcing me to anticipate the further course of events.]

. . . C. was abruptly cut short in this train of thought by a meeting with Major Feuerbach which lasted just minutes. Their reunion gave C. a proper scare; Feuerbach was sitting at the desk in C.'s flat, around noon, and typing something on the typewriter.—Don't stare at me like a fool, he said, I just dropped in and I've got to type up a few sentences.—He pecked out a few more lines in the greatest of haste, pulled the sheet from the machine, folded it up and vanished.

From an unnamed source C. learnt—that winter—what had transpired. The Major had sent a letter to Cindy, Harry Falbe's girlfriend, in A., since she'd gone into hiding somehow and couldn't be found at home. The letter was typed on C.'s typewriter and signed with his name, with M. W.'s name; it requested that the recipient meet M. W. at an appropriate location—the proposal was the restaurant at the A. train station— as he had a message for her from Harry Falbe. To prove the letter's authenticity, it contained the watch which Cindy had bequeathed to the sender and which Feuerbach had taken from him. She followed the request, went to the meeting place and was arrested.)

During my last encounter with Frau Falbe, one of the intimate ones—if some of the past encounters could be called that—the idea of the Student intruded once again; for a long while it thrust itself in front of the woman's body before me, only towards the end did the real sight prevail.—I had asked my landlady—it must have been towards the end of May—to sell me the red armchair that stood in my room, and she had agreed after some hesitation. I gave her the money, a purely symbolic sum she accepted after I'd refused to take the chair as a gift. I decided to spend the night in the room, so as to be on the spot the next day to transport it. It was too early to go to sleep, though; I decided to go into town again . . . And then you won't come any more! said Frau Falbe, standing at the door still as though she expected an explanation from me.—What gives you that idea? I asked in astonishment. I'll be back right this evening.—I was just thinking, she said, I was thinking, something's over when the armchair's gone . . .

Later I wandered around the city between the Dimitroffstrasse and Schönhauser Allee Stations . . . I had only strayed so far from Frau Falbe because I was waiting for fatigue to set in . . . ending up on side streets, and suddenly I spotted several people leaving a building where I'd often been before, and among them several of the Scene's most familiar faces; dusk was already falling, I crossed the street so as not to be noticed, expecting the Student at any moment . . . and there she came out, she said goodbye to some of the others and walked away. I followed her—at perhaps too short a distance. On Schönhauser Allee she walked down towards the Dimitroffstrasse Station. I kept behind her, matching the pace of her steps, maintaining a distance of fifty to eighty yards, which was probably too much now . . . Schönhauser Allee was quite busy still, the street lamps had blazed up, it was growing dark. Just before the station I was held up by a red light; she had already crossed the side street and was held up herself by the light which blocked the crosswalk to the station in the middle of the boulevard. My light turned green, I hesitated . . . suddenly she turned around and came down the zebra crossing towards me; for a moment we stood eye to eye, just a few yards apart. I felt a touch of dizziness, void; I turned to the right and walked quickly down the pavement of the cross-street . . . after a few moments I looked around and saw that she was following me, on the other side of the cross-street whose name I didn't know. I walked still faster, turning right again at the next opportunity, and again just after that, no longer sure of the direction, but at last I had escaped her . . .

After this incident I returned to my room at Frau Falbe's and tried to overcome my confusion.—There was no doubt about it, I'd fled from her. She had turned the tables and suddenly become my pursuer!

I was an intelligent person and I belonged to an intelligent institution . . . at least to think otherwise was absurd, indeed inadmissible—we were the hard core of intelligence, we were the sword and shield intelligence . . . how could I still take this little incident as an omen? An omen of what . . . I'd seen the sudden manifestation of a thing we didn't believe in! A little episode that could grow . . . that we couldn't believe in, refused to believe in, mustn't believe in, that, I made no mistake, was what had occurred that evening. And probably it had occurred because I believed in it. It was a sign that something in this country wasn't going our way, and that the constellations were no longer as unambiguous as they looked.

It was a long time before I slept that night, casting about for portents that my suspicions (which had surfaced in me before) were founded—the occupied embassies . . . the grassroots groups that kept springing up . . . more and more young people seeking refuge in the churches . . . the so-called punks and skins, louder and louder rows at sporting fields . . . a devastating, barely concealed greed for hard currency, the all-pervasive wheeling and dealing with it . . . the applications to emigrate, which had practically become a fad.—Despite it all we acted as though we'd come to terms with these circumstances, indeed as though we'd literally predicted them and were factoring them into everything we did . . . the chiefs seemed no more nervous than usual, they'd always spoken of the keenest vigilance which was called for now more than ever: and they'd been preaching this now more than ever from time immemorial with unchanging urgency . . . they'd preached it until this 'now more than ever' had become completely impossible to believe.—There were even things that gave the appearance of easing—the art and literature scene, always our special focus, seemed to have become veritably depoliticized. Feuerbach would get worked up about that, I could hear him still . . . They've all got so wimpy and blasé, he yelled, we might as well let them all into the Writers' Association! Or they could all go sit in the dive on Frankfurter, they'd fit right in there! They're simply ignoring us . . . they're almost like we are! They want to take our jobs away . . . one of these days we'll have to take to the streets ourselves . . . By the way, it's got to the point where we need to fill up their meetings with more and more of our people just to make them look dangerous. Hey, doesn't Sect. 20 look enough like a circus already? They want to get us shut down . . . Hey, Cambert, how do you feel about getting a job as an insurance agent?

Maybe not here, though, over there . . . I replied.

Keep your mouth shut, for Chrissake! Or do you have a pile of dough in the vaults of the Commerzbank already too?

(In the morning he woke in the dark airless room, the blind closed, and immediately sensed that Frau Falbe was in the room. Instead of raising the blind she turned the light on, she was wearing the robe she always kept on until afternoon; after a while—he was still drugged with sleep—she repeated last evening's lament: He wouldn't come any more now, once he'd taken the armchair away!—What does the armchair have to do with it? he asked.—Well, it had been her husband's chair, her last recollection, she didn't even have a picture of him.— Should I leave the chair here? he asked.—No, that's not it . . . I never would have given it away, but you . . . you can have it.—Straightening up, he said he still didn't understand her.— With you I'm not so afraid some other woman will sit in the chair. I wasn't afraid of that with my husband, either . . . at least not while he was still here. And you're just like my husband.

You know the sort he was . . . —C. had feared she'd say: You work for the same firm as my husband . . . And all at once he was wide awake. Then it struck him that that rough undertone he knew so well had crept into her voice again.—She came closer and sat on the edge of the cot beside him: He was a thinking man, my husband was . . . it was awful, what he was constantly thinking up. He always did his thinking in the armchair, and you do just the same . . . and then one time I caught him!—Thinking? he asked.—Can't you see what I mean? Of course he was . . . She hesitated: Of course he was jerking off!—She almost gasped out the words, as though they called up an image that made her shudder: I'd known he was doing it for a long time . . . I wanted to catch him in the act and confront him about it.—And what did he say?—It was awful! she replied. Awful for him, apparently . . . not for me.—C. looked at her questioningly, and she explained, her voice still rough: Or maybe it was dumb, what he said? This puts us in the opposition, he said, 'cause for us they're all jerkoffs, the people in the opposition. And then . . . then he wanted me to do it too.—And did you do it? asked C.—If I show you, you'll always remember me when you sit in the armchair . . .

She'd shed her clothes and sat in the armchair with her thighs draped over the armrests. With surprisingly adept, almost elegant movements she began to stroke herself between the legs, first moistening the fingertips of her right hand at her lips, her left hand behind her back, between her thrusting body and the back of the chair, as though attempting to facilitate the difficult jerky movements of her pelvis which strained towards the rubbing fingers of the other hand—as though these fingers were a touch too incompliant with the opened lap. Words escaped her, almost cries, held back in her breast with an effort: You'll remember . . . you'll always remember!—Unexpectedly, for the first time since C. had known her, she had switched to the informal 'you'.

And in the midst of her excited movements she suddenly clutched a piece of paper in the fingers of the hand behind her back; she had pulled it apparently unintentionally from the crack between the chair cushions, where still more were hid . . .)

She must have sensed that something prevented me from becoming fully or even very closely involved with her . . . and it wasn't just the shabby room that was uninhabitable in the winter. She'd got used to the fact that I had the other flat, but even in the warm months now I spent fewer and fewer nights at her place, I couldn't say myself exactly why.—I had failed at my plan: to use the room to work on my literary texts . . . and besides, I suddenly suspected her of searching my papers in my absence . . . probably she'd been wondering for some time who this student might be; fortunately I had always made sure that all incriminating passages (about my relationship to the Firm) disappeared from my desk when I left. The room was useless as a hiding place (of course Feuerbach could easily find it out) . . . no hiding place was any use to me, my talent for writing poems had gone so deep into hiding that I'd almost forgotten about it.—As I heaved the armchair onto a borrowed wheelbarrow, Frau Falbe watched with a look of such alarm and confusion that I promised to come back as soon as possible . . . Some time this week for sure! I said.—It was clear that she didn't believe me . . . You know you can have the room any time, she said.—I had no idea how soon I'd be forced to take her up on the offer.

Ever since that spring I'd been unable to shake the feeling that Feuerbach was trying to avoid running into me—I'd never felt quite at ease in his presence but now I felt still more unnerved.—What could I do . . . sit down and ponder vanishing entirely . . . or behaving still more suspiciously (which strictly speaking was the same thing . . . just as pursuer and pursued could switch roles abruptly, and without changing in their essence) . . . should I behave even more provocatively? Provoking the Scene and the Firm simultaneously—news of the little chase scene between me and the Student had to have got around . . . but no, it didn't happen, I was living in a simulation, in a land full of simulated logic.—Someone ought to have thrown me out after the incident with the Student, either the Scene or the Firm! Clearly I wasn't a proper UnCol, either for the Scene or for the Firm . . .

It was as though the very chairs I tried to sit on dodged me (my beautiful red armchair, for instance) . . . as though the void I moved in made all deliberation impossible, providing no more reference points I might have proceeded from. It was something like what a person suddenly released to West Germany had to feel: there was everything over there, and so there was nothing . . . nothing but politely smiling bureaucracies that expected nothing from you and failed to grasp that you expected something from them.—What should I do? . . . I compared myself to a spider suddenly lacking the ability to weave its web—and indeed I felt that all the strands of information and counter-information spun around me had torn. I was no longer informed about myself (no one informed me about myself any more!), and this was perhaps the most pathetic thing about my condition.—Information, I told myself, had been my home. Suddenly it unravelled like a spider's biotope . . . it unravelled and disappeared like a whole society, the one that sustained me.—And even my means of articulation were unravelling and atrophying; I had the impression that I'd spent an entire year using nothing but the sketchiest of auxiliary verbs: What is . . . what was . . . what will be . . . what did we have to be?

Sometimes I hoped to gain a sense of stability from those I'd once sought out, as a rule, 'on official business'; I was forced to realize that I was barely known as a writer any more. Again and again I'd had to reply in the negative when asked if I had new poems . . . I claimed to be collecting my thoughts, which evidently was too classic a phrase for them. I hardly ever got invitations any more; those hectographed sheets with the purple, barely legible, hand- or typewritten avant-garde monstrosities of syntax no longer turned up in my postbox . . . though I also thought it possible that someone was removing them. My visits to the Scene were hit or miss, often inopportune; once again I was the tiresome literary hanger-on I'd been before my seventeen poems were published . . . only that then living in the small town had prevented me from making unannounced visits, usually lasting half an hour, but sometimes one or two, during which I was silent or asked stupid questions: What's happening? What's going to happen? How's it going, who are you, who else have we got here?

The writer S. R. had altered the form of his readings (though not his external appearance); suddenly he sat in the centre of the conversation circle, making it possible to strike up a dialogue with him . . . not for me, though; I lacked the discursive capabilities for talking back and forth (I was utterly unarmed); and I had no desire to do so; and I almost feared I'd see the Student sitting in that circle and then be forced to start a conversation, I feared drawing the consequences from my wishes . . . fortunately she rarely showed up.—And when Reader held one of his now-rare readings, I wrote a report, unable to suppress my caustic comments: You could barely tell his texts apart any more; what he read today had the smack of reused dishwater . . .

And I left early, having lingered near the door for that purpose, murmuring that I felt a bit ill—not because of the reading, though!— and vanishing onto the street. There I jammed myself into a corner and waited for the Student; I wanted to see whether she would go off with him or head by herself towards the train station. Usually it was the latter, and I followed her doggedly at a constant distance (the role of the desperate lover was a stellar one which every self-respecting employee mastered perfectly!) . . . I had already adopted her stride, which was firm and sure, and the same degree of firmness and surety seemed to coalesce in me as well . . . and so we proceeded in lockstep until she ducked into a train station and abandoned me.—Target person released from observation at the Rosa-Luxemburg-Platz Station, I noted; I carried around a tiny pocket calendar already containing about twenty similar notes . . . usually mentioning the Friedrichstrasse Station checkpoint.

And then I'd prowl about the station square, fully aware that what I was doing was madness: unauthorized, I was chasing a young woman from West Berlin . . . I had utterly transformed myself into her shadow, and I'd lost my own shadow in the process . . . all in the flimsy hope that one day I'd receive permission to keep shadowing her over in the West. I understood that it was madness . . . it was foreplay without consequences, a pursuit without consequences, and the fact that I could tell myself this had no consequences either. And in my armchair in the basement I finished off the foreplay with my hand, thinking partly of her and partly of Frau Falbe . . . yet knowing I could remain nothing but a shadow, the Student's shadow-man, even if Frau Falbe had given me the chance to change this.

And I stared into the dark city's workings and heard it hum and murmur . . . a sound I couldn't forget, and perhaps no longer the hum of depression.—In my imagination I saw the Student waiting on the platform where the train to Wannsee departed, in the midst of the crowd beneath the grimy, grim station roof whose gable ends were covered in scaffolding—yet nothing was under construction; the scaffolding served as an observation post for the border guards . . . they'd stood there for a span of time I could no longer calculate, sleeping as they stood or as they paced up and down, and yet gazing down unwavering, unceasing, gazing on for all time to come.—Over and over I'd listened to the stories that began here in this station building: beneath the vault at the end where the trains pulled in and out hung a huge master clock, either stopped or utterly off. This clock had stopped counting long ago, perhaps ever since that 13 August 1961 . . . since the night following that Sunday it had run as it pleased, broken loose from CET, too fast, too slow, not at all, no use at all for human reckonings. The pigeons that lived in the station had taken possession of the clock, using it as a repository for their droppings, whose slowly growing encrustations began to encase the clock entirely; the corrosively seeping grey-white mass had paralysed the works and transformed time into a capricious, menacing authority. Below it this station resembled a theatre of war . . . it was the expiring Cold War's last theatre, overflowing with refugees and expellees, and the backward stronghold of a time turned impossible.

(And he himself had lived according to the time shown by this mad clock over this outpost of the Cold War. He had been at home in this ruined time. Since signing a paper covered with a tangled web of formulae, since setting his signature, spurred by exhaustion, renouncing the name his forbears had given him, to a contract of sale, he had become a traitor of human nature, whose essence it is to have bounds.—Think it over at your leisure before you sign, we've got time, we've got plenty of time! With these words the stranger had slid the paper over towards him, where declarations stood, declarations of assistance, declarations of support, declarations of paternity for the future generations of this state, he'd read all these words as veiled threats . . . driven by a sudden awful haste he signed, darkness descended on him, he began to live like a sleepwalker, in reporting periods, an existence that consisted in committing strangers' lifetimes to paper—for this his 'I' was uncalled for. It appeared only in the form of a figure by the name of M. W., fleetingly familiar, turning up by chance among others who fleetingly appeared and were later inserted into a reporting period that was often vague, and sometimes made up out of whole cloth when the game of intelligence demanded it. And at times he'd been forced to make up what this M. W. had said: trivial, vapid stuff which either riled up the others or placated them . . . whatever the game required.)

At the end of September—the summer had expired in downpours, and then turned sunny and warm again—a little note in my postbox summoned me to Feuerbach's office. The past several days I hadn't returned to the flat until late in the evening; it was such a tiny little note, newspaper-margin-sized!—they were already skimping on paper now when they sent me messages—that I hadn't seen it in the postbox: the meet-up was scheduled for 25 September, I'd discovered the snippet of paper on the afternoon of 29 September . . . in Feuerbach's office, not in the cafe; for the past half a year not much surprised me any more.—When I entered the room, for a moment I thought I'd blundered into the wrong place, another of the identical offices camouflaged as flats: at the desk sat a man I didn't know, an older vintage . . . only then did I see the Major, leaning against the wall by the door, looking pale and saying not a word in greeting. The man at the desk was broad-shouldered and evidently tall; though surely over sixty and slightly corpulent, he seemed athletic; beneath the short, curly grey hair a stolid face gazed out at me, now with a slightly strained and enervated look . . . I sensed immediately that one answered back to this skull at one's peril. Only his deep bass voice seemed familiar: Is this the young friend of ours we've been waiting a small eternity for?—The question was directed at Feuerbach, who merely nodded.—Good, said the bass, then I don't need you any more, Kesselstein. You can go now, explain the necessary modalities to him later.—The door clicked softly shut, Feuerbach was outside.

What he told me took little time, he didn't even offer me a seat: I was recalled ... herewith! A different field of operation, a different section! You know the town of A. from somewhere, don't you, must be in the Leipzig area, right? Have you been there before, my young friend? You'll proceed there as quickly as possible, immediately, your new managing cadres are awaiting you. Lieutenant Kesselstein has other duties, he's not your contact man any more. Have you got all that? Do you have any papers we need to take into safekeeping? No ... OK, we'll see about that! Make your arrangements as quickly as you can ...

With that he flipped open a file on his desk and hunted in the drawer for a writing utensil ... This place is a pigsty! he said; I no longer existed for him.

For several seconds I stood thunderstruck, not knowing if it was relief or panic I felt ... there was a faint hum or drone in the building, as from heavy machinery in the basement; perhaps it was just in my ears.—The man at the desk looked up from his file, his parted lips in barely perceptible motion as though tallying long columns of numbers ... What's on your mind, my young friend? he asked.—I excused myself and left the office.

Feuerbach was waiting for me in the stairwell, down at the next landing, and grabbed me by the sleeve: Well ... keen as a hound dog, isn't he, the old geezer? Come on, run on ahead, we'll see each other in the dive on Frankfurter!—Still speechless, I tried to free myself but he wouldn't let me: Have you been back to the flat? No . . . you've been out in your den again? Good, actually you're not allowed in the flat any more. Go over there today, get your personal things out by this evening, you don't have the flat any more! So, see you in the cafe.

For half an hour I sat waiting in the cafe, waiting to be served, the shadow-waiter didn't come, the barman stared past me . . . and Feuerbach didn't come.—Out on the boulevard what they called an Indian summer was in progress. The sunlight had lost its whiteness, tinged blue-gold in the nicotine weave of the curtains, a piercing mixture of sun glare and exhaust fumes, making blinding backlight come from all directions. Through the window thrust a flickeringly defined wall of brightness . . . not a wall, it was an irregular oblique pseudo-box filled with glare and dust and whirling smoke with a slumped cut-out of a shadow in its midst: the dark silhouette of my 'I' . . .

Then a male figure rose from one of the tables to the side, crossed the light-space to the bar and murmured together with the waiter, who had reappeared and fixed me with his gaze. The waiter moved towards my table and laid a slip of paper in front of me: We've had an unpaid bill of yours lying around here for a small eternity, enough is enough. The police will deliver you the bill. Leave the premises . . . right now, and for good!

This time, too, I left without a word, first glancing at the slip—it showed a sum of about forty marks with a question mark, and a date from last autumn.

Then I ransacked the flat for my so-called personal effects: a few pieces of clothing and a number of books, I thought I had them all; my complete possessions just half-filled the two duffel bags. For several days I'd gone to the flat just to sleep and hadn't paid any mind to the desk . . . now I found almost no written material left, which didn't surprise me. I searched all the drawers; there were neither notes nor letters, no other writing (my manuscripts, or what was left of them, were out at Frau Falbe's), even the wastebasket had been emptied, and my tear-off calendar was missing. All I found was an ancient Neues Deutschland and two sports papers; several borrowed West German literary magazines had vanished.

I tossed the key onto the floor of the long narrow corridor, picked up my two bags and left. After shutting the door behind me I removed my nameplate (bearing the name M. W.) and did the same downstairs with the postbox; then I headed out to Frau Falbe's.

In the train packed with sweaty people—I had a seat, though—I felt feverish; when the flickering snatches of evening sun shot between the trees from the West and struck my face, I felt as though I were being slapped about the head; I barely felt my own weight, perched on the seat as though on an air cushion ... How should I have answered the gentleman at Feuerbach's desk? I asked myself.—I don't care what you say or what you arrange for! I should have retorted. The Firm is my home, and I am my own informer. And I can wait, I've got time, I've got lots of time ...

From then on I lived in Frau Falbe's room, and it was peaceful there, when I left myself in peace; on into the winter I lived without any human contact, not counting my landlady ... until Feuerbach (or Kesselstein, as he had to be called now) reclaimed me—tried to reclaim me, a peculiar episode which thoroughly deranged my sense of time once again. But allow me to treat things in their proper order ...

Relations between me and Frau Falbe had become strangely cool, and I wondered what the reason was; apparently she'd adjusted quite well to my coming just once or twice a week, and now I was suddenly there all the time, without offering any explanation; she accepted it but stayed upstairs in her flat. I told myself that she could easily have read the papers hidden in the red armchair during my absence, back before the end of May, when the armchair was still here . . . maybe she'd got suspicious in the meantime, maybe she'd seen the light.—Various conflicts developed around my dealings with electrical appliances, on which she looked askance. Quite apart from the immersion heater, which she had always feared as the source of an imminent fire—and maybe she was also offended because I didn't take her up on her offer: Come to my place and make your coffee on the gas stove!—now I had an electric heater too, a so-called oil radiator I'd bought in the Intershop with the last of my Forum cheques at the end of October, when the cold crept into the room. Unfortunately the fuses, next to the basement stairs, did not hold up to prolonged use of this appliance . . . and Frau Falbe complained about escalating electricity bills; I tried to compensate by raising my rent payments, which rapidly diminished my bank account. Frau Falbe—she paid me back for the increased rent by inviting me to eat, occasions which she used to vent her complaints in concentrated form—quickly realized that I was in for financial difficulties and offered once again to find me a job.—I'd love to work, I replied (though I dreaded it), but I can't right now, I have to focus on my writing first . . . I had to finish a book, I was really a writer, she knew that.—Oh no, she said, that you most certainly aren't. I can imagine what you've got to write.

Back in my room, I laughed to myself—it was the first time in ages that someone had denied I was a 'writer' . . . and at that moment I felt a warm and long-familiar feeling: I was reminded of my time in A., when I'd sat constantly writing and thinking. No one knew me as a poet, I hid my poems even from my mother, a truly clandestine, oppositional writer taking a stand against his ignorant age.—When Frau Falbe said her angry words to me, I felt for the first time in ages that someone took me seriously. Now I actually recalled my project of presenting my poems to the Unofficial Literary Magazines, of which more and more were appearing, springing up like mushrooms from the humus of ignorance. Within two weeks I'd produced seven pieces . . . or at least ceased work on them once they struck me as readable. Now I needed a typewriter so that the manuscripts would look halfway professional . . .

I was thinking about that when Frau Falbe appeared, dressed in her robe . . . I realized that it was already nine in the morning.—She'd been surprised to see my light still on, she said, running her hands over my shoulders . . . I looked up, the room was a cave filled with thick smoke, the desk lamp's weak beam marked a yellow circle on the shambles of the desk, layered with paper, dirty cups and two smouldering ashtrays, while crumpled paper piled up in a semicircle around the desk . . . You'll smother here sooner than you'll finish a book, she said. And you haven't even slept!—Seeing my rumpled bed, she suddenly realized that there was nowhere for her to sit. She left off the stroking movements at the back of my neck and asked: Where did you put my husband's armchair, anyway?—I wondered whether I could tell her the truth: It's gone . . . —Gone? What's that supposed to mean?—I explained to her that the armchair had been stolen . . . and it wasn't a lie; soon after my abrupt departure from the downtown flat I'd meant to salvage the papers hidden in the crack between the cushions . . . the huge piece of furniture was gone, as though it had dissolved into thin air. Frau Falbe was deeply offended; she left and didn't show up for several days.—But she'd given me an idea: there was a typewriter in the downtown flat . . . I'd always referred to it as 'my typewriter'.

Now I planned to go and get it . . . to play naive and say: I just want to fetch my typewriter . . . Or: I'm supposed to fetch my typewriter!—Now I cursed myself for leaving the key there; just in case, I pocketed my collection of duplicate keys.—But when I rang the doorbell, I was in for a surprise. I had to ring a second time and finally heard soft steps coming down the narrow corridor . . . it was about fifteen steps to the front door, I remembered. The lock turned, the door opened and before me stood Reader. Dressed in black from head to toe as always, even the artificial leather slippers were black.— He gazed at me coolly through the round lenses of his glasses: How can I help you?

I beg your pardon, I mumbled; there was no sign that he recognized me in any way. I wanted to fetch my . . . typewriter . . .

Your typewriter! he said.

Yes, I said, I'd like my typewriter.

I don't understand . . .

It doesn't matter, I said, already turning on my heels.— Don't you have my red chair in the flat, too? I yelled up from the third floor; but the door had already fallen shut.

Out in my room I took the seven poems out of the drawer to draw them on paper in calligraphy, each separately, but I no longer had seven blank sheets of paper left. And the poems seemed a mistake to me, completely unacceptable.

When October was past I resolved once again to travel to A.; it had turned cold and even the oil radiator didn't manage to warm the room. And Frau Falbe treated me frostily as well; I already owed her a month's rent, with just enough money for a train trip to A.—One afternoon, already growing dark, I was tossing my possessions into the duffel bags when the door-bell rang . . . about half an hour later it rang again, several times, I gave in and went to the door. Frau Falbe was outside, ashen and distraught, she seemed to be trembling: Come on, there's someone upstairs for you!

Feuerbach sat at her kitchen table, grinning at me some-what sheepishly: Can I help it if you don't answer the door . . .

I wasn't sure if a tantrum would be called for, now that he was even denouncing me in front of my landlady . . . but I recalled that I had barely a pfennig to my name.

Come on, he said in his usual manner, say something, where can we go to talk . . . not at your place, we'd catch our deaths. So, don't snooze, get dressed and let's go!

In a neighbourhood pub—we tossed back a number of shots, and I seemed to feel a bit of warmth again for the first time in ages—he explained the following to me:

We knew perfectly well that you hadn't gone back to A., we knew that from the start. And that you'd holed up in your icebox again, to be honest, that's just what we expected. I'm telling you, we actually would have been disappointed if you'd acted any differently. If you'd passed up our assistance so quickly . . .

And then he, Kesselstein, as he was known of late, reeled off his sermon, one of those torrents of words I knew him for, and for which I'd known the boss from A., at whose end one was irresistibly sucked in:

Oh, God, I thought, what's he up to this time. He's sitting in his ice hole freezing his bones. What kind of foolishness is the poor loon up to now. I spent a long time thinking about what I could do for you. I don't always get ideas right away either, well, finally I do have an idea, Cambert! But first, please just sign these receipts. Don't worry, they're old receipts, I've had them in my pocket for three months now. Or longer, I'm a bit sloppy about these things, and the old geezer'll prob-ably fire me for it some day. How long has it been since we've seen each other, we've owed you money ever since . . . yes, that's the way it is, we're just a bureaucracy with a bunch of bureaucrats. And we don't pay in advance, you know that. Fine, maybe I could wangle an advance for you, too . . .

What have you been up to the whole time, anyway . . . You've been writing, I know, have you got any new work? A few pages of poems, for now . . . and where are you planning to place them? We'll talk about that, but first I have to tell you that that whole damn story with UnColSec Reader has been sorted out for you, they've come to terms with it, they've calmed down . . . by they I mean our demigods from Olympus. What else could they do, when you, Cambert, probably didn't suspect the full magnitude of the mess you created by running after that little editor. How on earth did you come up with 'student', the chick is quite a force to be reckoned with! We were staring at you transfixed, we had chills running down our spines. We thought, What on earth is he doing, he's got it bad, that Cambert, we just had to stop you. But it was already too late, you screwed up a pretty perfect story we had going . . . the kid just stayed away, and we were left high and dry!

We thought, that Cambert's going to bust it all up on us now . . . and I had to talk to the chiefs till I was blue in the face. I had to literally talk them out of sending you on a training course. I said, Forget the training course, the guy's much better on the street . . . and now he's just acting up, he's got a crush on the kid, that's all. No wonder, either . . . but did you really have no clue that she was Reader's contact person? She was supposed to get him a foothold in West Berlin, we had a perfect handle on the legend . . . we would have had him leave the country with tremendous difficulties, the eternally thwarted writer of stature . . . You were a lot of help with your constant critiques, even if they were starting to get on our nerves . . . See, you're the better writer after all. But with the little editor we would have had him doing business in West Berlin.

And suddenly you come and start stalking her! I thought, Now Cambert's lost it, this can't be happening. And she gets the jitters bigtime, she gets a persecution complex, she suspects everyone and his brother . . . she even suspects Reader, who used to be our totally safe bet, she accuses him of being an informer just because he won't sign some dumb petition. And then she stays away, stays in West Berlin—Can you imagine how furious we were?

I'm not saying you need to make up for it now, it's all forgotten already. You gave me an idea, you see . . . yep, somehow you always manage to get back on track. I thought to myself, By Jove, that Cambert always does manage to run his head through walls. To make a long story short, we're having problems with UnCol Reader . . . and you've got to sound him out. Whether or not you meant to, you uncovered a certain side of him . . . in a nutshell, he's suddenly started acting like you. Yep, it looks like he's fallen for his IntelOp too . . . I'm telling you, that happens more often than you'd think. That's what I've always said, and I've tried to explain it to the folks higher up. When you investigate and keep investigating, suddenly it happens: you only see the people from their human side . . . from their best side, you could say. And suddenly you've got qualms: What am I doing here, anyway? That's happened to every good man at some point, no one's immune to that . . . suddenly you ask yourself, Isn't my case officer a bigger swine than whoever I've got in my sights? I've shone a light on this person from all sides, I've practically X-rayed them, and suddenly I take a liking to the person . . . especially when it's a woman. And you don't know what side you're on any more . . . but our comrades the chiefs don't get that, or they don't want to. All they know is their slogans: You've got to know what side you're on, head and fist of the Party and so on. I've always told them that, whenever they asked me, this perpetual shadowing doesn't do any good . . . don't observe, obliterate, I said, you've just got to obliterate these people sooner.

So now we've got to keep an eye on Reader . . . put it however you like, you've got to spy on the spy now. There's no big difference there, instead of IntelOp: Reader, you have IntelOp: UnCol 'Reader' . . . I'm telling you, he's doing everything he can to get the kid back, writing letters, writing reports, even talking to her on the phone . . . but he's doing it without us! Yes indeed, he's a lot like you, my dear Cambert . . . He laughed (and when he laughed he was the same old Feuerbach).

Not outwardly, of course, you've got more meat on your bones, though you have lost weight. So, what's the story, will you take the job? We'll get you a proper flat in the meantime . . . come on. I'll give you the money once we get out of here.

You were right, by the way, the stuff he writes is nothing special, he said to me when we were outside. He handed me the envelope full of money: Count it . . . we'll deposit the next payment in your account, do you still have the same account number . . . ?

(With you it probably would have worked out much better, said Kesselstein. But you're too hypersensitive when it comes to female contacts, unfortunately, that's just the way you are, it has its advantages too, we have to take people as they come. That's another thing the bosses don't always get. But the writing part, you pull that off better than he does! He doesn't care about literature at all, that weird Reader guy, I think all he reads are comics . . . he always mixes up the temporal planes, and in the end he leaves time out entirely! He ought to read Thomas Pynchon some time, Gravity's Rainbow . . . You probably know it by heart, I only made it up to page seventy or eighty, unfortunately . . .

I've never even seen it, Cambert retorted.)

That put me back in the middle of my story. I sat in the cafe on Frankfurter Allee again as if nothing had happened, the waiter must have mistaken me for someone else, or Kesselstein had finally paid the overdue bill; I stuck with coffee and brandy, which imparted more inner warmth than champagne shandies—it was business as usual, I was on my way again. Only this way had grown somewhat longer, since I went on living at Frau Falbe's. I wasn't sure how it had ended up that way . . . I just didn't want to remind the first lieutenant about the flat. The fuse box in Frau Falbe's stairwell was suddenly replaced, I could leave the radiator on day and night . . . my landlady had her electricity bills paid punctually, almost too punctually, from some Berlin office, the same with my rent—the system worked, but she, Frau Falbe, had stopped speaking to me.

I could judge better than the first lieutenant what the texts of the writer S. R. (IntelOp and UnCol: Reader) were supposed to recall or what they drew upon. The title of the work of which I'd heard about twenty instalments derived from a Beckett novel: Brief Movements of the Lower Face . . . although the author citing him had long since proceeded to give the lie to the claim of brevity in his title.—If I wasn't mistaken, the phrase appeared on the very first page of a book by Beckett[15] . . . incidentally, what interested me about it was the sense that Beckett's characters had always reached their destination by the time the text began. They were already at the end, though they were constantly moving, or purporting to move, or waiting for movement or the end of movement: the end lay before the beginning of the text. A state, I thought, which Reader has learnt and grasped well. In Beckett he's found a far-fetched but apt analogy for the state of the agency that employs him.—It, too, was constantly in motion (was always on the way, which was the goal, as the first lieutenant was in the habit of putting it) . . . only here it was no literary phrase but the practical truth: when the agency began to move, it was already at the end. The agency was the end (the end in itself, the end and the goal), for the simple reason that it saw no way to leave an escape route for a figure turning circles inside it. The Firm was the end which must never be finished . . .

I thought these sorts of things as I wandered through the basements, almost warmer this winter than Frau Falbe's room had been back then. And sometimes in the basement I stopped at the wall which was the wall of Reader's study, if I thought of it as a perpendicular extension on up to the fifth or sixth floor. And when I gave free rein to my imagination, I could hear him typing . . . through the hum of the city which was indelible in all that was stone, which down here had turned into a silence, through the impenetrable silence which down here had turned into a hum . . . I could hear it, the keys of my typewriter (that Firm-owned machine I'd operated for a year or longer), I could hear them tick. Sometimes like an old-fashioned clock. And I could hear when he stopped again: he rarely kept the machine ticking for longer than an hour. I laid my ear to the damp bricks: there was the hum of the city, the hum of the city continued, and when in my ears stillness had settled over the hum, the typing and ticking filtered faint and clipped through the stone . . . he was typing! He was starting a new work! Still typing . . . now he'd stopped! And now I knew he had the beginning (and in it the end) on paper, I knew that in a few days his new reading would be held, I still had to find out the place, I knew the first lieutenant had per-suaded him to start all over again.—Would it be a wildfire again, eating its way through all the caverns of a Scene gone inert? Or something flowing, a flood! I thought. Once before, a venture of this sort had succeeded for nearly a year, but then the Scene had breathed easy again.

He'd been unwilling, in fact, the first lieutenant had told me, and they'd really had to put the screws on him. But in the end he'd been inspired by a phrase from one of the Western literary magazines they'd borrowed from me. Couldn't I remember the phrase . . .? You underlined it in the magazine and wrote next to it: Ghastly! It's a phrase from the Frenchman Gilles Deleuze . . .

I couldn't remember the phrase, only that I'd underlined something—something I couldn't make heads or tails of—in one of the magazines that had been removed from my former flat (now the flat of the author S. R.) . . . I'd only borrowed the magazines myself, I was sure to be asked for them the next time I showed my face in the Scene.

Does anyone know the title of the new reading series? I asked Kesselstein.—No idea, he said.

I titled the work 'Brief Movements of the Lower Face: Section II' . . . I never found out if that was correct, since I arrived late at the first reading. It was held in a flat on the sixth floor of a building in central Berlin, overheated and packed with people; on my way up I'd spent too long catching my breath at a window in the stairwell; I was admitted as he was just beginning, I'd missed the title and a brief introduction. As always, he was dressed all in black, the round lenses of his glasses aimed at me for a fraction of a second as I started to smoke . . . the first lieutenant had given me one of the cigars he puffed at sometimes so he could blow the stench of sulphur into the faces of people he didn't like . . . the lenses flashed at me like malevolent shards, Reader continued with a quote from Deleuze, which I noted down.

Since one does not recognize people, in a visible manner, except by the invisible and imperceptible things they themselves recognize in their own way.[16]

I thought: maybe the translation is just off?—I followed the quote with the word: Ghastly!—Then the cigar made me queasy and I left the room.

The second event, on the sixth floor of a different house, had about half the audience; only his most faithful followers, among whom I could now count myself, came to the third . . . and the Student stayed away the third time as well. In my report I noted in passing that the whole thing lacked fire, insipid and watered down, a sort of dishwater which had lost its cleansing effect.

And evidently he'd realized this himself—or the little West Berlin editor had told him—he'd announced a fourth reading, but it was cancelled.—In other words, the success of the venture (the success of Kesselstein's idea?) definitely had its limits.

Its limits! That meant that the writer S. R. had to go further now. He had to go further now! Further down the path . . . but what did going further look like? He had to cross the boundary, of course, the Western boundary, now he was ripe for the West. But how could someone—a type like him who used to turn down Western invitations by the dozen—suddenly get to appear in the West? That was where the Student came in, but she had to see a convincing reason too. She had to see that Reader (the author S. R.) was making no progress on his path in the East. He had to find himself in a position that could be described as no longer or just barely tolerable —for a type of Reader's constitution, that was the only convincing reason to go West. And how did you end up in this position: first you needed an informer! In the West they were allergic to informers, anyone who'd had an informer came to the West with a guarantee of a good reception. The trajectory of Western success had undergone this shift: if you wanted to be something there, you had to have had—proveably, if possible—an informer . . .

I had assumed this function, I was the proof that he'd had an informer . . . and I was there in reserve, there was proof I'd been after him, and after her, the editor, I'd created the proofs myself, I'd virtually constructed them, you could refer to me by name and address, and by proof of seventeen poems that established my actual existence.—And I didn't know, in fact, how long I'd already been performing this function . . .

In this function everything repeated for me, time and again I'd walked the compass of my paths, so many times now that I often felt subjected to the infinite series of a déjà vu . . . subjected on and on to this path, up the streets, down the streets, above them, below them, time and again . . . I'd seen every stone, I'd registered every name, heard every word that fell from these faces . . . it was desensitization work. Informing was ideological work, its essence was to investigate the same thing over and over until the appearance of deviation had receded into unreality. The work of the informer was a sort of promotion: it lavished its target objects over and over with the same attributes until the contrary attributes had receded into shadow . . . then the object was severed from its shadow—and the eternal life of this object was assured.

I now found it utterly impossible to sort in terms of temporal affiliations the constant repetitions of what I blundered upon . . . and it was no longer necessary, either, as we invented a retroactive time span for each episode we registered.

Here I increasingly had the sense of lagging years behind (sometimes just one year!) in everything I thought. Often I lived under the impression that the entire society over me, over me in the city's hum and drone, was lagging just as far behind. Behind whom or what . . . I didn't know. And this lagging behind (this coming too late in life[17] . . . I believed the expression came from Cervantes, referring to the great Don Quixote), this fear of being punished like a backward pupil

310

for coming too late in life was the reason for the depression I kept sensing in the city.

More and more often I had the feeling that everything that passed our lips was being said for the third, for the fifth time.—For instance, when I presented First Lieutenant Kesselstein with my plan to flood the non-official literary magazines with poems, with a whole raging torrent of poems (by this time the collection of my available texts had doubled, there were fourteen of them, and three were near completion) . . . And, I said, this time under the name Cambert . . . since that other name will soon be contaminated by the rumour . . . or the proof . . . of being a Stasi informer!—And besides, it'll heighten the charm of the fresh start . . . so I'll have to adopt a new code name immediately . . . Do you have any suggestions?—At that the Major swayed his head thoughtfully . . . A fresh start? he said. All you ever think of is the goal, my dear fellow, I believe you're aiming too high. When you'd do better to think of the way!

(And C. believed he'd been told the same thing yesterday, and he thought it possible that this yesterday had been a year ago: they were sitting by the window in the cafe on Frankfurter and gazing melancholically out onto the street, where torrents of vehicles raced burst by burst towards the centre of town, towards the West, washing a gaslogged mixture of fog and early dusk against the big pane; it was like explosions feebly ebbing. They sat in the 'dive' quite a lot again, peaceable at their observation post by the window . . . We must look inseparable, thought C.—The Major tried to convince him finally to order a champagne shandy—coffee and schnapps, somehow that's just not our style!

You only ever think of the goal, C. said to him.)

And so it went, until one day I discovered by chance that the writer S. R. had homoerotic proclivities . . . or even a homosexual orientation.—Reader is queer! In any other context this would have been an especially valuable finding because it opened up points of attack.—I recalled the story with Harry Falbe: they'd virtually tried to prove it on him or persuade him of it, perhaps because they thought they could use it to blackmail him. What I'd heard about the matter had barely seemed plausible . . . now I asked myself how I could use my findings in the present case; for the time being, at any rate, I kept it from my superior.—Probably the fact wouldn't interest him, it might not even have found its way into the pink file that had been set up for the IntelOp . . . evidently it could only mean something to me. Lately the West Berlin editor's relationship with Reader seemed to have improved, she came over more often now . . . I had no idea how to evaluate that in this new light.—Did she even know about his homosexual proclivities? I asked myself . . . she didn't speak to me, her dark eyes studied me from a distance, I seemed to detect a scornful interest in her gaze . . . As if I were the queer! I thought.

(And what does she know of me, what does she think about me? C. asked himself. I've been asking myself more or less the same thing for a year at least, it seems to me. And some day it'll devour me, this operation, it's probably devoured me already. I've been thinking since yesterday now about bailing out of this whole Reader affair . . . but haven't I been thinking that for the past year? Since a yesterday a year ago? Since then maybe all I've been after is what 'I' am in this story!—C. thought: 'I' am the one who believes nothing, except that all the characters in this story were made up at a writing desk . . . made up as characters who deify the State. But now we're forced to see that these characters won't play the game.— They're condemned to founder because they deify the State . . . and they founder, and the deified state along with them.

And in the end they want to get across the border to escape the deity . . . And 'I' too want to break things off, he thought.)

Simply stop . . . sometimes I stared at the whole story as though at an audio tape, unwinding faster and faster towards the end . . . but it refused to stop, it was a nightmare. And finally I hit on the idea of resorting to a minor disruptive measure. I typed . . . on the new electric typewriter I now had in my room, a Western model, which did a fine job of printing respectable, non-identifiable characters . . . a note which I smuggled into the editor's purse. It said that she shouldn't let herself be taken in, I could tell her many interesting things about the writer S. R. Just as a hint: I knew definitively that he had homosexual tendencies, which she might find significant regarding the ambiguities that surrounded him. But I could divulge even more. I suggested a date and time, and, as the meeting place, a pub on Hannoversche Strasse across from the Permanent Mission of the Federal Republic of Germany. —I dispensed with a signature, closing with: A very good friend.

Why I'd chosen the pub on Hannoversche Strasse of all places, I didn't know. It was evidently due to a sentimental recollection of the time in which, as far as my sexuality went, I was still living in satisfactory circumstances . . . in this pub I had sat and thought of Frau Falbe. Sometimes I was seized by the impression that it had been just yesterday; and I gasped for breath as though the city were buried by heat waves.

I had no idea how the student—I still called her that, in memory of my private IntelOp—might have received the message. Had she even read the note?—All I counted on was her curiosity.—In mid-December as I set out for this meet-up, Frau Falbe seemed to suspect that I was going to rendezvous with 'another woman'. I ran into her in the stairwell; a harmless question—she sensed my guilty conscience—

immediately sparked an argument with her. I quickly escaped and had to forget the scene just as quickly, since I was in a hurry . . . on the way to Hannoversche Strasse I was arrested.

★★★

I spent just a few weeks in the cell, in solitary confinement—there is little to say about that time, if I discount a few moments of fright. Towards the end I provided a second signature, once again without really reading what I signed. It was a commitment to observe secrecy on all I had seen or heard in the institution; the declaration was buttressed by the usual threats of punishment for any failure to comply with the commitment. The document was ultimately unnecessary, as I had seen and heard virtually nothing in that time; everything that had happened could have been engendered just as vividly by my imagination. After twice twenty-four hours had passed and the perfectly ordinary frenzy of panic was over—fear of beatings, fear of never getting out again, fear of madness—I led a tranquil, almost relaxing daily existence, at any rate a fairly regular one, and my face took on the pugnacious smile of a heavy who'd paid the hard way for the silence that surrounded him. All I saw was the man who brought me my grub twice a day and reacted to my questions like a deaf-mute, that is to say not at all. He struck the bunch of keys against the door, I stepped back to the far wall, as per regulations, then the hatch on which the dishes and coffee pot were placed rattled inward to a horizontal position; the hatch was left open until I replaced the empty dishes. I also saw him during the recreation period which I was allowed a week after my arrival; along with three other men who moved to cover all the entrances and exits with their hands on their shooting irons, he took me to a concrete quad in which I had to pace back and forth for twenty minutes; above me wire mesh spanned the walls, breaking the blue-grey ceiling of sky into tiny hexagonal segments. On the first Sunday—for a week I kept track of the days—the deaf-mute slapped a thick, greasy book down on the concrete floor of the cell: The Naked and the Dead by Norman Mailer. It was undoubtedly a friendly greeting from Kesselstein, who was a big fan of this writer.—He's the greatest, he used to exclaim, he's the only one who understands people like us. Unfortunately you have to get his books about the secret service smuggled in from the West, which is just typical of the idiots at the Ministry of Culture. Now that I know Mailer, I love the CIA . . . and not the KGB, that bunch of slobs. A secret service and glasnost, just picture it . . .

Feuerbach-Kesselstein visited my twice in my cell (and brought smokes, which was the main thing)—the second visit probably doesn't fall under the verbal secrecy agreement I signed right afterwards. He came in and immediately tossed a pack of cigarettes onto the table.—Man, he said, I could hear you coughing up there in the yard already, it's time you started smoking again! Oh, you've got something to read . . . I guess there's not much else you can do . . . what are you reading there? Ah, Mailer (he said the name with an exaggerated British accent, it sounded like the word Mylar) . . . as a matter of fact that's not allowed here, it looks to me like you've got privileges again.—I'm reading it for the second time already! I said. I demand a lawyer immediately!—You arsehole, he retorted, don't give me that icy glare, nothing's happened to you, anyway? If I get you that lawyer, then things'll get serious. I won't get you one until it's a question of putting you in a long intensive training course, but that'll be worked out at court, just like it should be. Yeah, I've been there too, it's no vacation, I'm telling you. If I were you, I'd rather go home instead. Do you want to? Tomorrow the cop will bring you some crap to sign, if you do, you'll be out directly. And then you'll proceed straight to A. and report to the boss there . . . no, don't worry, you're not getting dumped! Down there they've set up little shock troops now, public order groups, they call them . . . the Workers' Fist, you understand, you can join in with that. So you're going . . . OK? I'll come and get you soon enough when I get nostalgic for you, you were my buddy, after all! You've got to go, because we're banning you from Berlin for the time being anyway, you know the deal. How was your New Year's, by the way? Mine was quite pleasant, in the dive on Frankfurter . . . all I can say is: champagne shandy.

I hadn't realized that the year's last midnight was approaching until the muffled bursts of exploding New Year's firecrackers began to filter through. When the light in the cell went on late in the afternoon, I heard the first impacts . . . or so this warlike din sounded. My count had been off by a day, and at first I was alarmed, then relieved, without knowing why, not guessing at my departure from here.—Oddly, at first I associated the explosions with the Major's rage I'd experienced a few days before. It must have been around ten when the dogsbody came by, the deaf-mute, on duty again; he yelled through the spyhole the only words I would ever hear from him: Hello . . . I wish you life and three days, you crook! If you're not asleep in half an hour, there'll be hell to pay!—Hearing him yell these words only once, I gathered that I was the only inmate on the basement level. I lay on the cot with my eyes closed, only now and then squinting at the red light above the door, and hearing the distant in-rushing flicker of fireworks set off over Berlin, over all of Berlin. And down here my ears probably picked up only the very loudest reports, the rest swallowed by the walls; it must have been an infernal din out there. Sometimes there was a red or green flare in the square of glass bricks that formed my window up in the corner . . . one of

these bricks could be tipped to open up a little crack for air
. . . and when I closed my eyes again I saw people firing flares
at one another from both sides of the Antifascist Protective
Barrier, I saw the rockets' burnt ochre trails cross in the smoke-
heavy air above the Wall and the coloured canopies of their
light cascades unite . . . and coughing fits choked my laughter,
as though the sulphurous fumes of the New Year's night had
filtered into the cell to me.

(Sitting in the basement on his produce crate, at his back
the cool sense of security exuded by the massive concrete wall,
feet stretched out in front of him, to his left and right the
two packed duffle bags and above him the stylized phallus,
he recalled Kesselstein's first appearance in the cell. It was a
chilling memory; he hadn't wanted to tell it, he'd only meet
with incredulity . . .

[Cambert had always asked himself what point it could
have to set forth all these thoughts, these rants and memories,
perhaps he was wondering about the so-called addressee . . . I
was thinking of you, my distant relative M.W., he said to himself then, I thought of you as my addressee in all things decon-
spiration-related!—But after what I've heard about you, first
I'll appeal to you, Frau Falbe! You are the ear, and I've believed
every word you said.—In a land so lacking in consequences,
there is no choice but to prepare oneself for a state to follow
the existing one . . . But allow me to continue my story now:]

He was already drifting in the twilight that preceded sleep,
so it must have been between twelve and one. He lay rigid on
the mattress, on the upper bunk, less visible from the spyhole,
his usual evening stream of thought clouded over, the shapes
in his head reeled away; the sombre red light of the night lamp
over the door clung to his lower eyelids . . . suddenly, frantically,
the bolts were unlocked: Feuerbach came in, holding the
bunch of keys himself; just now, half-asleep, C. had heard a

loud altercation at the end of the cell block. He realized at once that the Major was appallingly drunk; the sour smell of vomit immediately filled the cell.—It stinks here, Feuerbach bellowed, and with the keys he smashed the light bulb over the door so that C. was showered with shards; in the pitch darkness C. felt a wet, cold, sticky form fall upon him. Why he hadn't called or cried out, he didn't know . . . You mustn't call for help against a drunken friend, he thought later, even if it's a matter of life and death. And there had been a touch of pity in him for this befuddled, foul-smelling form. Feuerbach shoved him against the wall in the darkness and pulled down his pants; he felt a hard cold thrust between his buttocks, iron, the barrel of Feuerbach's gun, its muzzle boring painfully inside him.—Should I do it, you dog . . . Feuerbach bellowed, it had a gurgling sound, barely intelligible. Should I do it, you bugger . . . should I shoot you up the hole, you queer bugger?—The Major burst into laughter and thrust the gun still harder . . . then his laughter changed to a strange sort of sobbing, interspersed with slurred unintelligible curses, the bed shook; C. had lain as though paralysed, now he tried to struggle, the Major left off with the gun and made him see reason with a few nasty moves, which despite his drunkenness he performed with ease. Then—once again using the gun to poke C. in the ribs—he crawled onto the bed and lay down beside him. He wrapped his arms around C., sheathed in the sodden, slimy suit jacket, and pressed his wet, cold face to the back of C.'s neck, enveloping him in the smell of alcohol and the bitter fumes of disgorged gastric acid. Feuerbach's whole body shook in a mixture of sobs and laughter . . . Never ask about Harry again, you bitch, he mumbled and drooled against C.'s neck, never ask about Harry again, do me a favour, will you . . . A few moments later Feuerbach had fallen asleep and began snoring loudly.

That night was so wild and implausible—it must have been around Christmas, incidentally—that C.'s recollection of it had grown indistinct. It was as though he had merely been haunted by one of the frequent nightmares he'd learnt to fear in prison, which usually featured Harry Falbe or his girlfriend Cindy.—For the rest of the night he'd slept on the wire mesh of the lower bunk, wrapped only in a blanket wrested from the grunting Major. In the morning Feuerbach had vanished and the cell was locked again. As though to prove that that night's scene had been reality, his anus hurt for a week after that every time he defecated. On his release he was charged for the smashed light bulb. There was no explanation for the incident . . . perhaps his case officer's second demotion.)

I couldn't remember asking anyone about Harry Falbe . . . I'd never gathered information on him, nor on his girlfriend . . . as far as I knew I hadn't gathered any information, Kesselstein had even reproached me for it on occasion. On the contrary, I had helped Harry, or at least I'd tried to . . .

Just once, one afternoon before Christmas, as I was about to head out for Hannoversche Strasse, I had asked Frau Falbe in the vestibule, rather rashly—just an awkward attempt at conversation, it seemed, since I had a strange mental block on the topic: By the way, do you have any idea whether Harry had a kid?

She was mopping the stairs and immediately straightened up from her work.—What . . . she yelled, you asked me that once before! How could he have had a kid, you people always claimed he was a queer. How could he have had a kid, then?—In her voice was a venomous screech I'd never heard from her before.

He could theoretically, I said, and besides, I never claimed that . . .

Oh yes, you did! she cried. You're one of them, too, you're all the same ilk, you screwed over my husband back then . . . The whole building, the whole street is full of your ilk. And now you want to screw over Harry . . . now he's supposed to have a kid, so you can blackmail him. I'll tell you something, you're going to have to move out of here, by the end of the month I want the room vacated. I don't want you people's money . . .

She was seething with rage; I was braced for a physical assault.—But you won't get Harry any more, he's in the West now, she scolded on. And soon the tables will be turned and Harry will report the lot of you . . . he'll report you all, he knows everything about you!

And then she worked herself up to a claim which I found monstrous.—Harry, she said, had evidence that the Security bigwigs were already setting up West German bank accounts.—Just in case, she said, they'd moved money over to West Germany, or to Swiss banks, Western money of course, hard currency . . . where they'd got it from? Maybe they took it off people, or they bought up the money. And Harry had it in writing and he'd collected documentation!—Yep, he knows everything about you, she repeated . . .

It's dangerous to make claims like that, I said to her. You're better off not talking about it, when people know things like that, they don't let them go running around scot-free . . .

But I only said it to you, she responded, shocked.

I hadn't heard anything about any of the so-called embassy refugees being shipped off already, maybe it had just escaped my notice. And I hadn't picked up any protest from our authorities about the Permanent Mission of the FRG ostensibly giving asylum to a child killer . . . it would have been all over the newspapers. So maybe Harry Falbe was still here . . . I knew too much, and it gave me the creeps.—On the S–Bahn train the anxiety stayed with me; I put it down to my landlady's unexpected outburst . . . I didn't stop thinking about it until I was arrested.

I was the only person, then—or almost the only one—with concrete knowledge of the child Cindy and Harry had brought into the world. I had even seen the child with my own eyes, I was the only person . . . if I discounted the pale, faceless girl Harry had dragged to his girlfriend's flat that night three years ago (or was it four years now?). Some authority or other had to know it, but their fastidious files were gathering dust in the archives . . . they ought to be glad if no claims were ever made on behalf of a child that had been registered. Or were the authorities already in their death throes?

Maybe in A. I could look for the girl who must also have seen the child . . . Yes, in the end I was going to A. to run after some random person again.—What Kesselstein—then Feuerbach still—had said about Harry and the child had immediately struck me as preposterous and completely implausible . . . and he had spoken as though he couldn't even trust himself. But the fabrication was like him, the avid reader of American novels: Harry Falbe was said to have killed his child, at any rate that child had vanished without a trace . . .

If anyone could know where it was, that person could only be me! It was I who had shown Harry the hiding place early one morning after a prolonged drinking bout. The child could vanish without a trace only in the underground tunnels in the tract of ruins by the forest of A., only there could a child, dead or alive, be hidden beyond finding. And a child in its infancy could hardly have survived even a few days in that system of caves.

I still recalled Cindy's words vividly: Making a baby in a state like this . . . that's something you can never put right!—

They couldn't have put it right, but they could have put an end to it.

The town must have felt like a cave to me back then, subterranean beneath the unbroken dark brown smoke cover of the night, I recalled; a stooped lanky snoop stood at the counter in the grocery swilling beer, and some elegantly dressed boss ran the town from the living room of his single-family home, and even then my desire had been to crawl underground, the subterranean passages outside town had fascinated me since my childhood . . . and clearly everyone in town shared these desires.—I had always wondered how the State, which struck me as comparatively harmless, could inspire the sort of hatred I'd seen in Cindy's face. What was so astonishing . . . so enigmatic about this state was none of the things that were constantly discussed there: it wasn't the advantages which its citizens, for all their dissention, managed to obtain themselves, the secret advantages and the public ones (the so-called social achievements); it wasn't its post-war situation either, to which it clung tenaciously; nor its servility, its lies, its vainglory, its vanity and foolishness . . . the enigma was the hatred which it had fostered, invisible, always hidden, buried, as it were, beneath this land's eroded air. And which no one noticed, because there seemed to be no compelling reason for it. The mere mention of the word hatred made people wince . . . it was an emotion which was ascribed implicitly only to the country's enemies. And yet it had germinated here in this soil, and under the dull, everyday surface it had prospered . . . this hatred expressed itself for now in infinite indifference, and blossomed beneath the depression. Indeed, as its official representatives proclaimed, this land was a blooming land . . . but the bloom was toxic, an ugly, tenacious, deep-rooted bloom of slime, and it was hidden to the eye. The reasons for this hatred were not the government's unsustainable or broken promises, not the blindness and sycophancy of its representatives, not the fraudulent elections, perhaps not even the Wall, the police, the Party bigwigs with their double standards and cowardice . . . the reason for this hatred was us (and I winced at the thought).—We, the blurry little low-down tireless shadows that clung to the people of this country—we were the sustenance of this hatred. We'd done no one any harm . . .

We'd done no one any harm, but we'd snooped into the human soul. We had divided them into fit and unfit souls . . . into ones we could use and ones we couldn't (the internment camps for the latter existed only on paper and only in case things got serious . . . but life in this country never got serious).

We'd done no one any harm, but our shadowy presence, our constant presence, like the ill-favoured, bad-smelling, badly suppressed semblance of each individual's soul, our covert existence was the trigger and the object of this hatred, we were the very hatred each person out there held. We were the shadow of life, we were death . . . we were the dark side of man turned flesh, turned shadowflesh, we were hatred isolated. 'I' was hatred . . .

We'd done no one any harm, but we had placed the people at a crossroads where we counted them off: all we could use were the informers . . .

We were the shadow of existence, we were the genitive of the person . . . we were the practice of the disruption measures to be implemented, we were the achieved results of the given intelligence operation, the stipulation of the life of the soul of the person, we were the hand and the head of the report of reports on reporting, we were the brief movements of the lower face.

Was I capable now of altering this condition?

No, I had to admit, in all probability I was no longer capable. I had made one attempt: I had wanted to unmask myself—presumably!—before the Student, myself and Operation: Reader . . . I now thought it possible that I had simultaneously been his operation . . . it had backfired on me, it had been taken out of my hands. Now all I could do was wait . . . for what? What all of them were waiting for, Kesselstein, Reader, the literati . . . like me they all gazed into some dark, tortuous labyrinth and awaited their expulsion from the darkness. The literati had resigned themselves in unprecedented fashion . . . and the powers that be had resigned themselves as well . . . and so they huddled peaceably, clutching one another's filthy paws . . . and waited.—The powers that be had disappointed the literati, and the literati had disappointed the powers that be; they had no cause to reproach each other. And Reader had disappointed and deceived Unofficial Literature as a whole . . . and thus me as well. And in the process had done me the great favour of allotting me to literature. He had indicated that I should wait like the others . . . I could sit where I was and wait.

Somewhere, suddenly, there'd been footsteps in the passages. It wasn't the first time I'd thought I heard them, several people's footsteps, for a year now I'd believed I was being frequented down here. I knew, not just from Kesselstein, that so-called public-order groups had emerged of late, goon squads, plain and simple, recruited among criminals who were promised reprieves as long as they functioned, cleaning things up if a coalition movement cropped up anywhere. I swallowed my last two tranquilizers and sank back into my prenatal posture on the produce crate . . . the steps kept coming closer. I unscrewed the forty-watt bulb from its socket and hurled it against the wall. Again I sat down in the dark and listened. It had been a mere dull crack, not enough to scare them, the steps grew more distinct. I picked up the two bags and groped my way towards the light I saw glimmering around the next bend, perhaps a hundred yards away.—The passageway must have branched off there at one point, it had been walled off, and a large piece had broken out of the barrier: from this opening—I had never dared to enter the hole—the densest darkness poured out at me, and a smell that filled me with dread. Sometimes I'd thought I saw a red gleam in this cave, I hit on the idea that the pieces of my red armchair had been hidden there, after being cut apart and searched. Now the hole was pitch black, and smelt of faeces and putrefaction, of putrefying flesh dissolving in a sludge of faeces. And it was from this hole I seemed to hear the steps . . . there was a ticking and dripping in there, a tapping like steps in the darkness, they came closer, and their shuffle set off echoes. Suddenly I had the vision that at any moment Harry Falbe's son would appear at the edge of the opening: four years old now, blind, white as chalk and covered with filth and scabs.—Thus he would re-emerge, a Kaspar Hauser of the new generation we had begotten.— The tranquilizers hadn't kicked in yet, I felt sick and took flight. The first basement door I tried to flee through was locked. I couldn't open it, I ran on. The next basement door—to the basement of the building I'd once lived in—was open . . . I had scrupulously left it open each evening until no one thought of locking it any longer. It was already dark out, cold and overcast, single snowflakes fell, the frost brought me back to my senses. Upstairs, where I once had lived, on the fifth or sixth floor, the light was burning.

★★★

With my bags, I travelled to A.; my time in Berlin began fading from my mind even in the train compartment. It was as though I were thinking back on a chain of events, soon confused and impossible to survey, which hadn't actually happened with my participation. And for that reason this chain thinned out, growing more and more fragmentary . . . I had merely stood nearby, invisible to others, shrouded in a diffuse sphere of shadows from which I gazed into a space of light: it swarmed with movement I failed to grasp . . . I was looking from outside into a lit room, I thought, whose closed windows conveyed to the outside not a word of the conversations held in there. And all the figures whom I'd met in Berlin, whom I'd followed, of whose endless speeches I had apprehended only the ecstatic movements of the mouth, all these people had been lost to me along with this time.—Suddenly I could think only in strangely old-fashioned and literary terms: the story of Cindy and Harry and their child . . . was it a tragedy? I would have been content if I could have answered in the affirmative. There was simply nothing you could do about tragedies . . . there was no point in posing yourself any questions of guilt. Not yet . . .

In any case I wanted to look for the pale young girl, whose name, I recalled now, was Herta. There was no doubt that this Herta, too, had seen the child at least once. I couldn't remember her face . . . when I tried to picture it, it merged, like the most natural thing in the world, with the Student's. This Herta was also dark-haired and slender, and her form had something similarly evanescent. Her face seemed just as white and small in my memory, it had the same strangely open expressionlessness for which the only word I could think of was naked. She could yet be shaped, I thought, she could yet be transformed into a semblance of the Student . . .

My mother was overwhelmed by my arrival in A., the extent of her surprise almost alarming; she had been convinced I'd been living for years in West Germany. At long but almost regular intervals she had received letters from various cities—Stuttgart, Mannheim, Frankfurt, most of them from

West Berlin—stamped with West German stamps and bearing the postmark of each city. At first she'd written back asking whether it would be possible to visit me, but I always claimed to have no time, and soon she gave up.—The letters she showed me, I saw at a glance, were typed on my typewriter, the last one, in fact, on an electric machine such as I had used in Frau Falbe's room. And the letters were signed by an expert who'd mastered my signature perfectly.—My mother was greatly aged, grown nervous, a bit frail; I thought it better not to undeceive her. I explained my unexpected return with the advantageous circumstances of a certain literary success ... but at some point, I told her, I'd have to leave again to continue my studies in West Berlin.

It was more than a week before I ventured out onto the streets of A., meagrely informed about the country's current affairs by newspapers, my mother's barely usable television and the radio. There was much talk of the fact that from 15 to 17 January unrest had erupted again in connection with the annual rallies honouring Rosa Luxemburg and Karl Liebknecht, not just in Berlin this time but also in Leipzig and other cities. Once again unauthorized banners had been unfurled, there had been chants demanding freedom for dissenters,[18] once again many of these so-called counterdemonstrators had been arrested. And the Western broadcasters kept bringing up the claim that embassy refugees were camping out in the Permanent Mission in East Berlin, and not only there, but also in the West German embassies in Prague, Warsaw, Budapest ... even at this time the situation in the embassies had to be described as precarious.—Even at this time! I thought. Just wait for the spring, when the East Germans feel the wanderlust.—The domestic media wrapped themselves in steadfast silence.

Nothing seemed to have changed in A. itself; in the evening the town was covered by the usual hermetic bell jar of industrial fumes, and fog clotted in the streets. Now even fewer lanterns were lit, to conserve energy, and at six in the evening the light in the shop windows was extinguished as well; the city seemed lifeless.

The boss, to whom I was supposed to have reported immediately, had been replaced (replaced, suspended, transferred—it was impossible to find out); he had a cultural-political assignment now, I heard; at some point I learnt he was heading the Railroad Workers' Literary Working Group in the district town.—His grocery-store snoop was nowhere to be seen, for all his six feet; then I heard he'd taken a trip to Hungary.[19]

The new boss now sitting in the old one's chair gave me an astonished but exceedingly friendly reception. He was a somewhat stolid man of medium height, about sixty, already with something of a stoop in his gait . . . or rather a crouch, with a hidden confidence in the ankles. His broad face radiated the certainty that he was approaching the goal of his career.

Be glad you're here with us now, he said to me jovially (I was silent, prepared for a rant); this was in the town hall, Room 17.

Don't let things get you down, he went on, don't think so much, take a little break first. Don't keep thinking about Berlin, you look shell-shocked, as if you were still half in Berlin. That's taken care of, now you'll have a little rest first, we've got time. Things are quiet here, we've got a few boys out there to keep the peace. They'll hold the others off when they get too loud. Always remember, history is on our side, we've got time . . .

Now standing at the double-winged window, he pushed the curtain a bit to the side and looked out at the street:

We're not right in the line of fire here, not like the folks up in the cities. Berlin, Leipzig, Rostock—the heat'll be on soon, you don't even want to watch. Just remember, we've got lots of time down here, we'll think of something . . .

Notes

1 The headquarters of the Ministry for State Security (or Stasi; here: MSS) occupied a complex in Berlin-Lichtenberg between Frankfurter Allee, Normannenstrasse and Magdalenenstrasse.

2 Also known as the Liebknecht-Luxemburg Demonstration, held each year on 15 January at the grave of leading German communists Karl Liebknecht and Rosa Luxemburg, murdered in 1919 by a rightwing militia.

3 In the 1980s, increasing numbers of GDR citizens—ultimately hundreds of thousands—successfully applied for permission to emigrate. During the long, difficult process, applicants and their families were marginalized and subjected to reprisals and harassment by the authorities.

4 Alfred Kurella (1895–1975): one of the GDR's leading cultural functionaries.

5 In the summer of 1989, increasing numbers of GDR citizens sought asylum in embassies (notably, the West German Embassy in Prague) or West Germany's Permanent Mission in East Berlin.

6 In 1976, the GDR expatriated dissident singer-songwriter Wolf Biermann, demonstrating a new hard line and disillusioning broad circles of East German intellectuals, whose attempt to protest Biermann's expulsion was squelched. In the following years, increasing numbers of intellectuals left the country.

7 The East German state profited when GDR writers published work in the West, as the hard currency which they received flowed into the state coffers. Beginning in 1979, GDR citizens were required to convert any hard currency they owned into

'Forum cheques' at state banks; these cheques could be spent only at 'Intershops', state-run retail shops which offered Western goods. These measures ensured a flow of much-needed hard currency.

8 Walter Ulbricht (1893–1973): GDR leader from 1950 to 1973.

9 A common greeting in the Catholic regions of Southern Germany.

10 Pensioners were permitted to travel abroad.

11 Rührung ist nur eine Randerscheinung: Allusion to the anthology Berührung ist nur eine Randerscheinung (Connection Is Just a Fringe Phenomenon). See Afterword.

12 The official East German term for West Berlin, which the GDR did not recognize as part of West Germany.

13 Lavrentiy Beria (1899–1953): chief of the NKVD (Soviet secret police) under Stalin.

14 Yuri Andropov (1914–84): general secretary of the Communist Party of the Soviet Union from 1982 to 1984.

15 Samuel Beckett, How It Is (1961).

16 Giles Deleuze, 'How Do We Recognize Structuralism?' in Desert Islands and Other Texts, 1953–1974 (David Lapoujade ed., Mike Taormina, trans.) (Paris: Semiotext(e), 2004), p. 171.

17 On his visit to East Berlin in early October 1989 to mark the fortieth anniversary of the founding of the GDR, Soviet leader Mikhail Gorbachev warned GDR leader Erich Honecker to undertake reforms in response to the massive citizens' protests. Gorbachev is popularly quoted as saying: 'Life will punish those who come too late.'

18 Rosa Luxemburg's best-known saying: 'Freedom is always the freedom for dissenters.'

19 Hungary was a popular tourist destination for East Germans. In summer 1989, Hungary tolerated, then officially permitted travel across its border to Austria; hence, many East Germans used their Hungarian holidays to escape to the West.

Afterword

ISABEL FARGO COLE

'*I*': Historical Background

The years following German reunification in 1990 were a wrenching time in the 'new German states'. The East German dissidents and civil rights activists who had brought down the Berlin Wall were overwhelmed by the rapid reunification, unable to navigate the new political system and assert their visions and concerns. Meanwhile, the opening of the Stasi files brought a long series of painful disclosures about some of East Germany's most respected political and cultural figures—most spectacularly in the literary scene.

When '*I*' first appeared in 1993, it was praised as the first serious literary exploration of the East German surveillance state and its demise—and its portrait of an underground writer turned informer caused a stir. That January, the playwright Heiner Müller and the novelist Christa Wolf had been exposed as 'Unofficial Collaborators' (Inoffizielle Mitarbeiter, IMs) for the Stasi.[1] The shock waves were immense: Müller and Wolf were internationally respected for their artistry and their critical stances.

Still, Müller and Wolf were establishment figures who identified with socialist ideals and chose to work within the system. More shocking were the revelations about the 'underground scene', long lionized as a hotbed of opposition. Its chief impresario was the charismatic poet Sascha Anderson (b. 1953) from Dresden. In the 1980s he dominated the Scene in Berlin–Prenzlauer Berg and beyond, organizing events and editing samizdat and officially sanctioned publications in East and West. He coedited a landmark anthology of young, 'unofficial' literature Berührung ist nur eine Randerscheinung. Neue Literatur der DDR (Connection Is Just a Fringe Phenomenon: New GDR Literature) published in West Germany in 1985. In 1986, Anderson moved to West Berlin but played an active role in the literary scenes on both sides of the Wall. [2]

In 1991, singer-songwriter Wolf Biermann accused Anderson ('Sascha Arsehole') of having worked for the Stasi. It emerged that Anderson had worked as an IM since 1975, sent to Berlin for the express purpose of gaining control of the Scene:

> By 1984 he had reached his goal [. . .] he pulled all the strings [. . .]. His verdicts held sway in East and West alike [. . .]. Anderson's main task was to depoliticize the Prenzlauer Berg Scene. That meant that he committed the younger poets and painters in his circle to an aesthetic master plan and systematically marginalized and vilified the older, politically engaged or active authors . . .[3]

Anderson was not the only writer to straddle the line between the 'unofficial literary scene' and 'unofficial collaboration', but his central role made his betrayal truly devastating. Among his peers, anger mingled with defensiveness, with some critics going so far as to call the entire Scene a 'simulation' of the Stasi.

Simulation, a favourite term of Jean Baudrillard, points to the sort of hip postmodern attitudes which Hilbig takes to task, and which Anderson embodied. Anderson propagated an experimental, ironically anti–political literature which many in the GDR found liberating. In a dogma–dominated society like that of the GDR, the eschewal of ideology could count as an ideological statement, the apolitical as political. Drawing upon Western poststructuralist thinkers, this literature focused on 'language as such': 'a response to [. . .] an increasingly mechanical public and official language of administration and declamation. This new tendency supersedes a more "content"–oriented literary culture created over the past decades by the generation of established [. . .] GDR writers [. . . such as] Christa Wolf.'[4]

Anderson gradually admitted his IM activities. His theoretical and psychological explanations for his behaviour were widely regarded as self-serving, even pathological obfuscation. 'Betrayal is the right word,' he told Stern magazine in 2001, '. . . It was also a betrayal of my own "I", an "I" that I still reject.'[5] Still active in the Berlin literary scene, Anderson remains a figure of morbid fascination. In 2002, Anderson published a lyrical recollection ('not an autobiography in the usual sense'): Sascha Anderson.

The story of Sascha Anderson, who was his own postmodern fictional creation, or the fictional creation of the Stasi, or the purveyor of fictions to the Stasi, or about the Stasi, or all of the above, clearly resonates with Hilbig's novel. However, 'I' is not 'Sascha Anderson', nor indeed any other specific IM. Appearing at the height of the scandals, uncannily prescient about the Stasi's modus operandi and the psychology of collaboration, 'I' was widely read as a roman-à-clef, but Hilbig felt misunderstood by this reading. He always emphasized that he had little knowledge of the inner workings of the Stasi (or, for that matter, of the Berlin Scene), and did not view his own Stasi files until after completing the manuscript.

Only in the final phase of my work on the novel 'I did I have to look up several so-called technical terms of Stasi language. The annotations in reference books on the Stasi sufficed for that. For me, the Stasi is an apparatus of diffusion; its practice was secret, indistinct, and to a large extent fictional (for the collaborators of the agency as well) [...] and that was exactly the climate I wished to dwell in while writing the work. It would have been virtually a hindrance for me to know very much.[6]

Judging by my research for this translation, however, Hilbig's vision of the Stasi's workings is remarkably accurate, and his riffs on Stasi language show a preoccupation with its specific culture. In fact, Hilbig's author's note indicates that he interviewed IMs as part of his research. According to his friend Lutz Nitzsche-Kornel, he also examined friends' Stasi files; he had explored Nazi language usage too (see Victor Klemperer's 1947 book Lingua Tertii Imperii) and spoke of the need to similarly analyse GDR-jargon. And he had first-hand knowledge of the language of the Stasi—from interrogations he underwent during two months in prison.[7]

Hilbig was himself one of the 'unofficial writers' who were spied on by the Stasi and its informers such as Anderson. In prison, he was subjected to recruitment attempts, which he withstood. Yet he was drawn to describe the experience of the perpetrator, not the victim. He declined to pass moral judgement on the IMs, often implying that in different circumstances he might have broken down and collaborated.[8]

The fact that Hilbig did have significant knowledge of the Stasi makes it all the clearer that his emphasis on imagination and intuition is an artistic statement, and a courageous one. By claiming the ability to imagine, from within his own psyche, the 'inner biography' of a Stasi informer, and indeed the Stasi system, he implicates himself. More explicitly, he implicates himself as a writer by comparing writing and informing.

'Not equating, comparing. [. . .] Both, the informer and the writer, create a fiction of reality and a fiction of characters whom they ponder, sound out, observe.'[9]

For Hilbig, the 'writer as informer' is not a paradox or a postmodern peculiarity of Prenzlauer Berg, but an intrinsic human problem. Hilbig transcends a specific historical irony in part by seeking its roots in the individual psyche, in part by setting it seamlessly in a broader literary tradition. Kornel-Nitsche named Edgar Allan Poe's 'The Narrative of Arthur Gordon Pym' as the primary inspiration for 'I' in its rhythm, syntax and narrative logic.[10] The unreliable narrator of Poe's novella, spiralling further and further away from reality, also seems echoed here. In Hilbig's two epigraphs, the modish experimentalism of the Scene is set against Ludwig Tieck's Romantic fairy story 'Der Runenberg', in which a hunter is lured into an underground realm. Other Romantic motifs, such as the doppelgänger, pervade the book as well. 'Feuerbach' harks back not only to the philosopher Ludwig Feuerbach, who influenced Karl Marx, but also to his father Paul Johann Anselm Ritter von Feuerbach, benefactor of the foundling Kaspar Hauser, another figure who haunts these pages.[11] Though the novel is most clearly marked by the tension between Romanticism and postmodernism, there is an abundance of other literary references, as to Samuel Beckett (a strong influence on Hilbig) and Bertolt Brecht ('you see best from the dark into the light' plays on the final verse of 'Mack the Knife'). Most telling, perhaps, is the implicit allusion to Hilbig's idol, Arthur Rimbaud: 'I is another.'[12]

With its richness and scope, since its first publication, Hilbig's 'I' has only gained resonance as a universal parable of state power and paranoia, the structures of surveillance and secrecy in the individual psyche and society as a whole.

Wolfang Hilbig: Biography

Wolfgang Hilbig was born in 1941 in Meuselwitz near Leipzig. The town's tunnel-ridden forest, open-cast mines and decrepit factories would haunt his work. His father was lost in the Battle of Stalingrad; he was raised by his mother and grandparents. As a young man (nicknamed 'Kaschi' after his Polish-born grandfather Kaszimier, a key father figure),[13] Hilbig was known mainly as a boxer and gymnast. But early on, he began reading his way through the well-stocked town library, fascinated by Poe and the German Romantics, writing and sharing stories at a young age.[14] This made him 'an outsider in his own family', especially for his illiterate grandfather. He invested his first pay cheque, as an apprentice lathe operator, in the works of E. T. A. Hoffmann. During his military service, his scathing letters home first attracted the attention of the Stasi.[15]

Back in Meuselwitz, Hilbig worked in the factories, notably as a stoker. Superficially, he exemplified the type of the 'worker-writer' which the GDR sought to foster. In 1964, his factory delegated him to the local Railroad Workers' Literary Working Group satirized in 'I', but his work was rejected as too negative and wilfully obscure and he was ultimately expelled. Besides, as he later claimed, he was the only real writer and real worker in the group.[16] He had better luck in Leipzig's budding alternative scene, where he met like-minded young writers such as Siegmar Faust and Gert Neumann.[17] Faust was astounded by Hilbig's knowledge of Western literature; 'the riddle was solved when Hilbig took work leave to attend the next Leipzig Book Fair, spending days hanging around the West German stands and copying poems out of books.'[18] Western music, such as Jimi Hendrix and Bob Dylan, was another shared enthusiasm.[19]

For years, Hilbig travelled between Leipzig and his job in Meuselwitz. In the boiler room, he had the time and seclusion to write, producing poems and short prose pieces. The figure of the isolated stoker and the tension between the 'worker' and the 'writer' would pervade his work, which at that time remained unpublishable. In 1968, he placed an audacious 'personal ad' in the GDR's main literary journal, Neue Deutsche Literatur: 'Which German-language publisher would like to publish my poems? Serious offers only . . .'[20]

The answer came nearly 10 years later. In 1976, Faust moved to West Germany, and, at first without Hilbig's knowledge, had several of his poems published, drawing the attention of the prestigious S. Fischer Verlag. Fischer published Hilbig's first poetry collection, abwesenheit, in 1979, followed by further collections and novels. Hilbig's Western publications led to increased Stasi harassment. In 1978, he spent two months in prison on false charges of having burnt the GDR flag from the Meuselwitz town hall. There he was pressured to collaborate with the Stasi and provide information on his contacts; he refused.[21] In 1979, he was fined 2,000 DM for a 'currency offence' in connection with the West German publication of abwesenheit.[22]

In a bold speech from 1980, the eminent East German writer Franz Fühmann (1922–84) lauded Hilbig as an example of a whole generation of 'absent' writers silenced in their homeland.[23] Like Christa Wolf, Fühmann strove to criticize and reform the system from within, and he championed young nonconformists.[24] In Hilbig, Fühmann saw a kindred spirit: an heir to the Romantics and Rimbaud, a truth-teller, a rebel against socialist realism. Hilbig continued to rebel; in 1981, he wrote an open letter to the deputy minister of culture: 'I belong to a generation that will no longer let itself be censored.'[25] Under Fühmann's patronage, Hilbig published his first and only poetry collection in the GDR, stimme stimme, in 1983.

Hilbig's position in the GDR became increasingly untenable. At last, in 1985, he was allowed to travel to the West to take advantage of the increasing offers of literary prizes, fellowships and readings. But he was a stranger in the West, alienated by consumer society and cut off from his roots; his ever-present drinking problems assumed alarming proportions. He travelled back and forth, torn between East and West, a period of his life reflected in his last novel, Das Provisorium (2000).[26] In 1988, he settled in the town of Edenkoben with the writer Natascha Wodin; they were married from 1994 to 2002. Like all his intimate relationships, it was a difficult one. 'He didn't want to live, he only wanted to write. Life was a nuisance for him,' Wodin recalled.[27] For Hilbig, writing was a compulsion, always fraught with feelings of guilt: in writing, he abandoned others, especially his social peers—the 'workers'—and his friends and family. The inability to cope with intimacy was a recurring theme in his life; he had a distant relationship with his only child, Constanze, born during a 1979–82 Berlin sojourn with journalist Margret Franzlik.[28]

In 1994, he and Wodin moved to reunited Berlin, settling in still-bohemian Prenzlauer Berg. Here too, Hilbig never felt truly at home. While his work continued to explore the dark landscape of the GDR, his public statements on Western media society and the shortcomings of reunification were scathing. Hilbig commanded too much respect, however, to be written off as a mere provocateur. He addressed the conflicts of his East–Western existence with an integrity and intensity which made him one of Germany's most important writers. In 2002, Hilbig was awarded the Büchner Prize, Germany's most prestigious literary award, for his life's work. But his powers were already ebbing; his last major work, the story collection Der

Schlaf der Gerechten (The Sleep of the Righteous) appeared that same year. He died after a long struggle with cancer in 2007. Since his death, the radical outsider has become canonized, with Fischer Verlag releasing a definitive edition of his works, and his papers archived at the Berlin Academy of the Arts.

★★★

I met Hilbig several times at readings in Berlin. He was a visibly awkward reader. Once he played the provocateur at a podium discussion, interrupting a highly theoretical discussion with the passionately stammered interjection: 'But the main thing is imagination!' He had a warm, avuncular aura, a kindly smile on his battered face, no trace of standoffishness—and yet was infinitely unapproachable. Later I met some of his old friends; each said, at some point, exactly what I had felt as his tongue-tied translator, trying to chat with him at the bar: No one could really know Hilbig.

Note on the Translation

'I', like all Hilbig's prose, is characterized by swirling, labyrinthine, often stuttering syntax. Here it echoes the labyrinths wandered by the narrator—up above and down below—and the increasing dissolution of his 'I'. More than any of his other works, 'I' mixes disparate language registers: the formal and the vernacular, the dark lyricism of the descriptive passages, the postmodern verbiage of the Scene, the soulless banalities of Stasi jargon and syntax, Feuerbach's slightly skewed attempts at colloquialism. I have done my best to preserve its complexities and strangeness, rendering it readably without smoothing away rough edges. Above all, I have tried to convey the rhythms that carry the reader through even the most difficult passages.

Lutz Kornel-Nitsche described to me Hilbig's own attempts at translating the lyrics of 'Maggie's Farm' by Bob Dylan. Hilbig spoke no English, but he would listen over and over again to the recordings to capture the sound of the original. For him, translating was 'listening behind the wall'—an image strikingly echoed in '*I*'—a wall he would also describe as a curtain of rain, a rushing; white noise.

Notes

1 Christa Wolf was listed as an IM for the years 1959–61. The Stasi complained of her lack of cooperation, and she was dropped from the rolls and subjected to nearly three decades of surveillance herself. Heiner Müller, who had suffered official reprisals due to his critical work in the 1960s, was accused of a decade-long Stasi connection beginning in the 1970s. See 'Die ängstliche Margarethe', *Der Spiegel* 4, 25 January 1993 (available at: http://www.spiegel.de/spiegel/-print/d-13680284.html [last accessed on 1 April 2015]); 'Krieg der Köpfe', Die Zeit 4, 22 January 1993 (available at: http://www.zeit.-de/1993/04/krieg-der-koepfe [last accessed on 1 April 2015]).

2 Joachim Walther, *Sicherungsbereich Literatur. Schriftsteller und Staatssicherheit in der Deutschen Demokratischen Republik* (Security Sector Literature: Writers and State Security in the GDR) (Berlin: Ch. Links Verlag, 1996), p. 640.

3 Ibid., pp. 640–1.

4 Elke Erb and Sascha Anderson, Preface to *Berührung ist nur eine Randerscheinung. Neue Literatur der DDR* (Cologne: Kiepenheuer und Witsch, 1986) (available at: http://www.planetlyrik.de/saschaanderson-elke-erb-hrsg-beruhrung-ist-nur-eine-randerscheinung-/2010/06/ [last accessed on 4 September 2014]).

5 Sascha Anderson, interview in Stern (15 June 2001).

6   Wolfgang Hilbig, quoted in Birgit Dahlke, *Wolfgang Hilbig* (Hanover: Wehrhahn Verlag, 2011), p. 101.

7   Lutz Kornel-Nitsche, email to translator, 20 November 2013.

8   See Karim Saab's interview with Hilbig in Uwe Wittstock (ed.), *Wolfgang Hilbig: Materialien zu Leben und Werk* (Frankfurt: Fischer Taschenbuch Verlag), p. 222–8: 'They tried to recruit me, but I was not vulnerable to threats. In the boiler room, I could hardly sink any lower in the social hierarchy. [. . .] Emotionally, I fled to my colleagues and said: The Stasi is here and is trying to recruit me! The workers [. . .] gave me the security I needed' (p. 223). Once he had thus 'deconspired', the Stasi ceased its recruitment attempts.

9   Ibid., p. 224.

10   Kornel-Nitsche, email to translator, 3 December 2012.

11   Bärbel Heising, '*Briefe voller Zitate aus dem Vergessen*': Intertextualität im Werk Wolfgang Hilbigs (Frankfurt: Peter Lang, 1996), pp. 188–91.

12   Kornel-Nitsche, email to translator, 20 November 2012.

13   Dahlke, *Wolfgang Hilbig*, pp. 21–2.

14   Ibid., pp. 32–5; Kornel-Nitsche, personal conversations with translator.

15   Ibid., p. 35.

16   'Ich komme aus dem Wald', interview with Hilbig, *Berliner Zeitung*, 26 October 2002.

17   Dahlke, *Wolfgang Hilbig*, pp. 43–4

18   Cited in Dahlke, *Wolfgang Hilbig*, p. 51. For many East German intellectuals, the venerable Leipzig Book Fair was a rare chance to get their hands on Western literature, reading, copying or even filching books at the stands.

19   Ibid., p. 47.

20   Cited in ibid., p. 45.

21   Ibid., p. 68.

22   Ibid., p. 70.

23 Franz Fühmann, *Praxis und Dialekt der Abwesenheit* (Practice and Dialect of Absence) in *Franz Fühmann: Werke*, VOL. 6 (Rostock: Hinstorff, 1993), pp. 459–74.

24 A year later, Fühmann collaborated with Anderson on an anthology of young writers which was ultimately unable to appear in the GDR. It served as the basis for the later Berührung. See Klaus Michael, 'Eine verschollene Anthologie' (A Lost Anthology) in Peter Böthig and Klaus Michael (eds), *Machtspiele: Literatur und Staatssicherheit* (Power Games: Literature and National Security) (Leipzig: Reclam Leipzig, 1993), pp. 202–16.

25 Dahlke, Wolfgang Hilbig, p. 74

26 Ibid., p. 85.

27 *Hilbig: Eine Erinnerung* (Hilbig: A Reminder), documentary film, directed by Siegfried Ressel (a + r Films, 2011).

28 Dahlke, *Wolfgang Hilbig*, p. 71.